DANGEROUS
LOVE

DANGEROUS
LOVE

BEN OKRI

Q P D
Quality Paperbacks Direct
London

This edition published 1996
by QPD by arrangement with
Phoenix House, The Orion Publishing Group
CN 1667

First published in Great Britain in 1996
by Phoenix House
Orion House,
5 Upper St Martin's Lane
London WC2H 9EA

Typeset by Deltatype Ltd, Ellesmere Port, Cheshire

Printed in Great Britain by Clays Ltd, St Ives plc

To the staff of Orion, and in particular
Maggie McKernan, for all their support.

And to R. C.

Shouldn't these ancient sufferings of ours
finally start to bear fruit?

Rainer Maria Rilke

I was walking through a dark forest when it happened. The trees turned into mist. And when I looked back I saw the dead girl. She walked steadily towards me. She didn't have a nose or a mouth. Only a bright pair of eyes. She followed me everywhere I went. I saw a light at the end of the forest and I made for it. I didn't get there.

BOOK ONE

ONE

Omovo was emerging from a long dry season. When he looked at his face in the mirror, and saw that his hair needed cutting, he didn't know that he was emerging from a long dry season. The barber's shed was next door and when he went there an apprentice told him that the master had gone home to Abeokuta for a few days. Omovo asked whether he could still have his hair cut and the apprentice replied enthusiastically:

'What kind of a question is dat? I have cut about five heads today. I cut them well.'

Omovo dozed off during the haircut. When he woke up he found himself looking like a newly recruited policeman. He told the apprentice to cut his hair shorter. And as his hair got progressively shorter he thought he looked progressively worse. Exasperated, he told the apprentice to shave off the whole damn thing. When the barber had finished, his head looked bony and angular in the large mirror. At first he was terrified. Then gradually the freshness of the experience grew on him. After paying the apprentice he gathered up the dark masses of his hair that were scattered on the floor, tied them in a cellophane wrapping, and went home amid taunts of 'Afaricorodo, shine-shine head' from the children around.

The next morning he went for one of his walks through the ghetto of Alaba. He had only gone a few hundred yards from home when an unexpected fine shower of rain started to fall. The flesh of his head tingled. He resolved not to run for cover and went on walking. He passed a building that had been burnt down in a fire the night before. Not far from the building some men were cutting down branches of a withered tree to use for firewood. Near the tree poorly dressed children

5

were hitting a goat with sticks. He stopped and stared at the children and at the same time felt a shiver, which started from his head, run through his being. Something froze and then flashed within him. Something shimmered in the sky. He suddenly shouted: 'Leave the goat alone!'

The children stopped. They stared at his bony angular head. The goat they had been hitting trotted slowly towards the tree. The men looked at one another: one of them threw down a branch with dead leaves and the other one shouted: 'What's wrong?'

Omovo felt awkward. He couldn't explain. 'Sorry,' he muttered.

Then he rushed home, brought out his drawing sheets, and began to sketch furiously. He worked and re-worked the lines, curves, and shadings a hundred times. And then he hit upon the idea of using charcoal. He felt he was capturing something more strange and real than the actual event, and he was joyful.

When he finished the drawing, he put down the charcoal and went down the corridor to the backyard. As he walked past the twin strips of bungalows that made up the compound, the airless trapped heat, the stuffy smells and the bustling noises crowded his senses. The cement ground was grey, dirty and full of potholes. Above, the sky could be seen through the corrugated eaves.

In the backyard the compound men were having an argument about something in the newspapers. Their nostrils flared angrily, arms were flung about, voices clashed. When Omovo went past one of the men detached himself from the argument and called to him.

'Hey, painter boy . . .'

Omovo replied irritably. 'I beg, don't call me "painter boy".'

'Okay, Omovo . . .'

'Yes?'

'I see you have begun to draw again.'

Omovo's face brightened. 'Yes,' he said. 'Yes.'

The man nodded and stared at his shining head. Omovo went into the communal bathroom. The stench was overpowering. While he urinated he gazed at the scum that had collected around the drain. As soon as he had finished he hurried out.

On his way back he again passed the men who were arguing. The argument had become more intense, as if it had been whipped up by something other than the heat. He knew what they were arguing about. It had been in all the headlines. He didn't want to get directly involved. He had to keep his emotions intact.

A few people had gathered in front of the balcony where he had been working. They stared at the drawing and whispered among themselves. Omovo paused. As he stood there, uncertain, one of the compound men walked past, stopped, came back, and tapped him on the shoulder. It was Tuwo. He was very black, robust, on the squat side, and good-looking in a fortyish way. He spoke with an affected English accent. It was something he had worked on for God knows how long. It gave him distinction and, added to the other things he was infamous for, confirmed his notoriety.

'It's good to see you arting again. Honestly. That's a strange piece, honestly. Reminds me of the war.' He paused. 'Good work,' he continued and then added, 'but be careful about the girls. Especially the married ones.'

He smiled and his hairy nostrils flared. As Omovo watched Tuwo's nostrils, a flicker in one of the windows caught his eye. He guessed it was his father's wife. Tuwo shifted his gaze to the parted curtains and his face almost imperceptibly brightened. Without seeming to be aware of it, he stuck a hand deep into his pocket, scratched discreetly, and went outside to the front of the compound to chat with some of the young girls who had come to buy water. As he went, the curtains dropped and the folds resumed their old stillness.

Omovo stood before the drawing. He drew back step by step, slowly, to view it from a changing distance. Then he stumbled over a stool. When he regained his balance he squinted at the figures he had painstakingly worked on. It was a drawing of children playing around a tree. The tree was thick-bodied, permanent. Its branches had been unnaturally amputated close to the trunk. The children were naked, curved, and had protuberant stomachs. Their legs were wiry. The sky above the tree and rooftops was defined by clouds of charcoal shadings that resembled a bundle of dead bodies. The drawing was stark and basic. It had in it something quiveringly, inherently, cruel.

He thought to himself: 'Yes. Yes. Strange.'

He reached up and touched his head, feeling again the surprising clamminess of his palm. He spoke quietly to the drawing: 'I have never seen you before. But it is wonderful that you are here.'

And then he became aware of the argument his work had been generating.

'Omovo, what's that you draw?' asked one of the compound boys.

'It's a tree,' said another.

'It's not a tree.'

'Then what is it?'

'It's like a big mushroom.'

'It's not like a big mushroom.'

When Omovo looked around at the many sweaty, intent faces, a certain panic rose inside him. 'Look,' he said loudly. 'Why don't you people just go away and leave me alone!'

There was a hush, but no response. The faces still hung around. Then an unfamiliar voice in the crowd asked Omovo whether he wanted to sell the drawing. The boy said he knew some 'Europeans' who would pay as much as twenty Naira for some works if they were properly framed. Omovo studied the boy's ravaged face. It was lean and prematurely wrinkled. The eyes glittered like freshly minted coins. He had seen those eyes around a lot, but these seemed just fresh on the path to independence.

'Say sometin' now,' the boy said irritably. He was taller than Omovo, dark, slim and cocky. He had on faded jeans and a white crew-neck shirt with a Yamaha sign printed in red.

Omovo shook his head. 'There's nothing to say.'

There was a silent tension as the boy glared at Omovo with such bleary ferocity that a fight seemed imminent. But then he grinned absurdly, shrugged and said: 'I'm jus playing.'

The next moment he turned round, made his way through the crowd, and disappeared. Omovo picked up a pencil. He signed his name at the bottom of the drawing and then wrote: 'Related losses'.

He drew back. He felt wonderfully clear inside. He knew it would not last. He went into the apartment, taking the drawing with him. He barely noticed his father, who sat expectantly at the dining table.

His room oppressed him. There was a phantom presence on the bed and a shadow hung over the table as if it were writing a secret poem in a hurry. His two brothers. The shadow made a fluttering gesture and the phantom raised its head.

'Hi brothers.'

He put on the light. There was a slight depression on the bed and an open notebook on the table. Everything was just as he had left it. His mind had been filling out the spaces. The room had once been too small for all three of them, and now that they had gone it was still occasionally crowded.

He carefully, almost reverently, placed the drawing board amid the clutter on the table. And then he made the board stand against the wall. He stood thinking to himself: 'I can't stay in this room now. There are too many things here.'

8

The dark spaces and half substances re-defined themselves when he put out the lights. He left the room. His father was now eating yam and stew at the table. Blackie, who sat opposite, watched him and made intimate comments and laughed at his replies. The sight of them in such apparent rapport deepened Omovo's detachment. He walked through the sitting room as fast as he could.

He sat on the wall in front of their apartment and watched the men arguing. The sight fascinated him. The assistant chief bachelor of the compound said something about a massive bag of worms. Tuwo in his affected accent said something about corruption being the new morality. And one of the men Omovo could not see shouted: 'They are pissing on our heads. We are like gutters.'

They teased and chaffed one another and made theatrical gestures. They were comic and at the same time they were serious. Then they dispersed, bit by bit, till one of the men suggested that the rest all come to his room and get drunk. There was applause and they crowded to the man's room, being comic and serious as they went.

As the men crowded away Omovo experienced a feeling of impermanence. In the backyard the children played and ran errands. The women plaited one another's hair, or washed clothes near the well. At the compound front little girls made imitation soup in empty tomato cans, over mock fires. Two men went past balancing buckets of water on their heads. Omovo's feeling of impermanence passed into an awareness that familiar things were becoming new images within him.

The joy which he had felt was now dissipated. He jumped down from the wall and went to the compound front and set out on another of his walks.

This walk would subtly change his life.

TWO

Dusk fell. It was evening, but the sun beat down on his shaven head. He could feel it simmer. He made for the Badagry Express road. Slum dwellings stretched out all around him. He was irritated by the airless heat. Sweat dribbled down his skin like little maggots and the smells around merged in his nostrils. From behind him there came the noise of a car horn. It was a battered Volkswagen and it bleated like a goat. He jumped aside, and crashed into a corpulent woman, and was sent staggering across the street. She was barely shaken. In an irritated voice she said: 'Foolish egg-head boy! Can't you look where you're going?'

Omovo picked himself up. 'Madam, you are like a lorry!' he shouted back at her. She ignored him and shuffled past the shops that lined the sides of the road. Women with lean faces sat beside their stalls. They sold provisions blanched by the sun. Omovo avoided a puddle and fled when a motorcyclist rode past with both legs lifted and spattered mud about the street.

Omovo turned a corner. His eyes passed over a mechanic's workshop. Fanciful designs of clothes had been painted on the walls of the tailor's shed. He passed shops and kiosks and his eyes grew tired. When he got to Dr Okocha's workshed he was confronted by a life-size painting propped up against an electric pole. Something happened to the tiredness of his eyes. It was a painting of a well-known Nigerian wrestler. The painting was in black and white. The ability of the artist was apparent in the immense physical presence and the defiance that were conveyed.

The artist's workshed stood on a corner of the street. The large wooden door was open. Omovo went into the shed, wondering if the old painter was around. He hadn't seen Dr Okocha for some time. The shed was stuffy, oppressive and untidy. The place smelt of turpentine, kerosene, oil paints and freshly cut wood. An earthy mustiness hung densely in the air. Unfinished carvings and hand-made boards were scattered all over the unkempt bed. Signboards of different shapes and sizes leant on the walls, and some were on the floor. There were a lot of paintings on the table. Beneath the table there were stacks of old books and a collection of dust-covered correspondence courses on art. They looked as if they had not been read for a long time – like things bought cheaply in a frantic self-education campaign.

Omovo became aware of the low roof with its long dark rafters. There was a large bulb swinging in the centre of the room which gave off a curious dry heat. The dull light barely illuminated the thick shield of cobwebs high up amongst the rafters. When Omovo turned round, with the intention of leaving, the light changed in the shed. A man stood in the doorway.

'Yes? What do you want, eh?' The voice was deep and the Igbo accent was thick.

'Dr Okocha, I saw your painting outside.'

'Ah, Omovo. It's you. It's been a long time. Where did you go, or have you been avoiding me?'

'No. It was the rainy season. All these roads were flooded. I take the other side to the office now.'

'Sit down. Find somewhere to sit. Throw some carvings to one corner, yes, good. So how are you, eh?'

'I'm fine.'

Dr Okocha, as he was called, was thickset, like a wrestler. His face was strong and sweaty, and his forehead was massive. His small nose repeated the curves of his rather large, friendly lips. He had piercing eyes and thick bushy eyebrows. His hair was thinning. A brown agbada covered his thickset frame and made him seem shorter than he really was.

'You know, I did not recognise you at first.'

'Yes. My head.'

'Hope nothing happened. Nothing bad?'

'No,' Omovo said, without conviction.

There was a fine strand of silence. Dr Okocha made a movement with his feet.

'Ah yes, let me give you some palm wine, eh?'

'No, don't worry. I won't drink anything.'

'Not even a Coke?'

'No. But thank you.'

The cobwebs high on the rafters reappeared each time the bulb did a complete swing. The musty smell deepened the general clutter. Shadows leapt about the walls. Two flies did a waltz across the room and a lizard scurried from under the table and ran behind the signboards.

'How is the work going?'

'Fine, my friend, fine. Did you see the painting outside?'

'Yes. It's good. It's just like him standing there. Has he seen it yet?'

'Yes. I took it to him and he said he will buy it for fifty Naira. It took me one month to finish. You like it, eh?'

'Yes. It's very good.'

Dr Okocha became radiant. His finely wrinkled face took on a paternal shine. His eyes narrowed with pleasure. Rolling back the sleeve of his agbada, he pointed at some paintings.

'I am working on those two for the exhibition coming up.'

He got up and then, without finishing the motion, he sat down again. His excitement bubbled. Omovo nodded and stared at them. He hadn't seen them when he came in. For some reason he didn't like them. They seemed forced, lacked passion, were like bad photographs, and had obviously been done without models. But they were sincere.

One was a painting of an old man. He had a vacant expression in his eyes. His chest was bared and bony, and his cracked face was an image of grey-brown desolation. In his thin arms, he cradled something indefinably alive.

'The old man is holding a baby, Omovo. They are both babies.'

The other painting was larger. It was of a group of sharply depicted young men. They looked fierce, determined, and ruthless in their denim shorts. The fierceness was more in the cast of their faces. Their eyes were quite blank.

Dr Okocha softly sang an Igbo song. He watched Omovo.

'They are good. They are good. I like them.'

'You know, you are the first person to see them. It's a good sign.'

The shadows suddenly moved on the walls. The waltzing flies had chased one another to a corner of the room and buzzed beneath the cobwebs. The bulb went on swinging.

'Did you pass the tailor's shed when you were coming?'

'Yes.'

'I did those designs on the wall.'

'Ah. Good. So do you have many signwriting jobs now?'

12

'Yes, they are pouring in. I've got more than I can handle at the moment.'

Another silence.

'Did you hear about the exhibition?' the old painter asked.

'I remember reading something about a private showing but for some reason I didn't take it seriously.'

'Ah, they are having a big exhibition at the Ebony galleries in the first week of October. Many people are coming: critics, rich people, students and even a big man from the army. I don't know if all the tickets have been given out and without the tickets you can't exhibit your work. But it's a good thing I saw you now because I am going to town during the coming week and I could find out about tickets for you. So how is your work coming on?'

Omovo smiled. 'Fine. I have just finished a drawing. I called it "Related Losses" – I don't know why I called it that. I was happy.' He paused and then went on: 'I have been going round and round that pool of green scum near our house.'

'Why?'

Omovo turned to the old painter. 'I don't know. To look at it, I suppose. I look at it a lot.'

There was silence. The flies had stopped buzzing. The cobwebs had become sinister, and shadows jumped about the walls. The musty smell, rising from the earth, pervaded the shed. Omovo looked up and saw, on the awning near the door, a dangling white sack. It was a juju. Omovo had not seen it there before. Suddenly he wanted to leave. The shadows had become real.

'Dr Okocha, thanks for the information about the private showing. I've got to be going now. Hope you don't mind?'

'No. I understand. The call of duty, yes?'

Omovo smiled and nodded.

'Anyway, try and see me in the week. Or I might just come and see you. With any luck I could get you a ticket.'

'Thank you. I didn't know when I was coming that I would run into this.'

'It's okay. Just get on with the work. And I hope your hair grows fast. You look strange.'

Omovo smiled again, his eyes vague. They shook hands. The old painter threw the sleeves of his agbada over his shoulders and then wiped the sweat off his face.

'See you in the week.'

Omovo went out of the shed. The sounds, the sights, and the smells of the ghetto crowded back to him. Things were clear all round.

And then lightning flashed in the sky. An uncertain rain drizzled. The sky was in a bad mood. He walked faster. He felt his head spinning gently, the sensation like a sudden rush of blood to the brain. He felt good and he felt strange. Night fell like soot from the clouds. Kerosene lamps appeared on the stalls. Their flames were blown thin by the wind.

When he got home, the rain had stopped. Children played hop and skip games in boxed areas on the sand at the compound front. Two of the compound women plaited the hair of two others near the chemist's shop. Some people had come to buy water from the grey aluminium tank.

Then he saw her. And when he saw her, weakness and longing flooded him in waves. Blood flushed his ears and his face felt hot. She stood at the entrance of the compound. When she saw him she bent over and whispered something to a little boy with a long face. Her hair was plaited in thin knitted bundles. She looked melancholy and pretty and contained. When she stared at him a wonderful and dangerous emotion happened inside him. Her face underwent a sad–happy darkening. He did not slow down. He desperately wanted to do something, to reach her in some way. But he did not stop.

He had barely reached the low cement wall in front of their apartment when her husband emerged from Tuwo's room. He was short and menacing. His name was Takpo. Omovo felt something else waken in him: an unsuspected pang of loneliness. Sensing the imminence of an assault, Omovo shrank into himself.

Takpo slowed down, glared at him, smiled, and then said in a loud voice: 'Ah, painter boy, how are you, eh?'

Omovo couldn't find his voice and experienced a moment of inner panic. He felt naked. He felt as if all his stifled desires could be read on his face and were visible on his head.

'Ah, painter boy, why you cut your head, now? You were handsome before-o. Now you are a . . .'

Someone laughed roughly from the room behind him. Someone else shouted: 'Moro-moro.'

Omovo turned into the enclosed space in front of their apartment. The laughter rippled and then passed away. He thought: 'I mustn't let them do this to me. I must be strong.'

Ifeyiwa's husband passed from sight. The boy he had seen her whispering to came towards him and went right into the room. Omovo went after him. The boy hid behind the door.

'She say I should give this to you.'

It was a note. Omovo tapped the boy on the head, brought out a coin, and gave it to him: 'Thank you, eh.' The boy nodded and ran out of the room into the unsuspecting compound.

The note was from Ifeyiwa. It read:

I miss you. I haven't seen you for a week. What's happening? Hope you are all right. I saw the drawing you were doing. Have you finished it now? Omovo, can we meet tomorrow, Sunday, at the Badagry road? I want to see you very badly. Tomorrow at this time or earlier. I will be waiting. Love, Ifi.

Omovo did not read the letter a second time. He crumpled it, got a box of matches, and burnt it. He watched as the paper was consumed, as if in pain, by the moving areas of flame. He felt within him a joyous disquiet. The room seemed too small. His frenzies filled everywhere. Outside the compound bustled with moving figures. It was noisy. His head throbbed. Darkness had fallen and all the corridor lights were on. The pale bulbs swung balefully. Mosquitoes came and assailed his relative peace and bit him all over.

And then from the sitting room behind him there came a sustained peal of feminine laughter. The curtain swished and out came his father. He was with Blackie. A fine perfume swam over him and suffused the air with a delicate and mocking presence. His father was well dressed. He had on a clean white shirt over a resplendent wrapper. And he wore a fancy felt hat which Omovo had not seen before. There was a feather in its grey band. He waved a fan of peacock feathers.

Blackie was also prettily dressed. She had on the same kind of expensive wrapper, a white blouse, a high, colourful head-dress, bright bangles and earrings, and an imitation gold necklace. They made a lovely pair.

Omovo shrank into a corner. But he had no need to. His father spontaneously began to dance at the mouth of the door. He danced with an engrossed smile on his face. He didn't notice Omovo.

When the brief show was over, he became businesslike. He took his wife by the hand, walked briskly down the corridor, and acknowledged greetings as he went out into the street. The compound people stared at them, some even cheered. Children trailed behind them excitedly. Then they were gone. To a party, to a meeting, or something. It was not often the man went out like that. He was something of a natural showman, but ever since Omovo's mother died and his business began to fall to pieces and his two sons were turned out of the house, there had been no occasion for being a showman. This was a departure. He seemed to be celebrating life again with his new wife. But Omovo knew otherwise; he saw beneath the dignity, the fine clothes, and the feathered hat to the bright crack within and a threatening void.

Omovo, feeling abandoned, tried not to think of anything. His mind whirled lightly. The bulb swung gently. The wind whistled through the compound. Mosquitoes attacked in squads. And the children howled. Omovo felt very far away from the life about him. A keen, ill-defined revolt simmered and died away within him. The perfume still hung in the air. The compound throbbed with its characteristic jangling noises.

He did not put on the lights in his room when he went in. He tried hard to sleep. The room changed shape and the darkness pressed on his mind like an incubus. The old decrepit fan whirling on the table blew back the stale sweaty smells in the room. And the whirling fan blades became disconnected sounds and images of unrest in his mind. And then, as if from a great distance, he heard the disconnected sounds stop. The noises of the compound which filtered into the room suddenly died away. And he was glad because nothing, not even the darkness, could claim him. As he dropped farther and farther away into the bright void, he had the curious sensation that he was dying and that everything was dying with him.

THREE

They both walked in silence. They had been silent ever since she came up to him where he stood beside the mechanic's workshop, touched him lightly on the shoulder, and said: 'Omovo, I'm here. Let's go.'

The Badagry Road stretched like a mirage before them. It was well tarred. It was also full of treacherous potholes. Cars of various makes and in various stages of decay drove past noisily, and left sickening fumes in the air.

They were silent when they crossed the road. Cars whistled past close to them. Omovo brushed his hand against hers. She half turned towards him, her mouth opened as if to speak. But she decided against it and slipped her fingers into his hand. The two hands were linked for a moment and when he pretended to scratch an itch on his head, they disengaged lightly.

The sky was clear and clean; a spaceless blue dome. The air was fickle. One moment it was light-tipped, fresh, and the next it was full of smoke and gasoline fumes. Birds swooped past twittering, and he felt their presence keenly. And then they were black specks scattered in the canvas of the sky. He was suddenly touched with a sense of things that were irrevocably lost, of places that cannot be reached.

'I had a dream, Omovo.'

Her voice came as a surprise. It was there, had gone, and wasn't there any more. Her face had shadowed over. He held his breath, his heart beating a little faster, as he waited for her to speak.

'Ifeyiwa, you were saying . . . ?'

'I'm not even sure whether I was dreaming,' she said.

'Well, say it then. I am listening.'

There was silence. And then even that was destroyed. Cars went past. A helicopter flew overhead and motorcyclists roared down the sun-drenched road. She began to speak.

'I was in a hall. The hall changed into a coffin. Then rats began to chew at me in the coffin. I fought my way out and found myself in a forest. The trees were ugly. And as I tried to find my way out of the forest everything changed back into the hall. This time there was nothing except the sound of something scratching and chewing. I wasn't afraid. When I woke up I found that the trap under the bed had caught a big rat.'

Omovo looked at her and, when she instinctively looked up at him, he turned his eyes away.

'Then I began to clean up the whole house. I swept away the cobwebs, cleaned the corners, broke down the insects' nests on our ceiling, and drove out all the wall geckoes and lizards. He came into the house and saw me cleaning and was angry that I did not go to the shop when he came home to eat. And he beat me again. Omovo, what does it all mean? Did I do wrong?'

Her voice rose and dropped as she spoke. When she had finished she brought her hands up to her face. The gesture reminded Omovo of how his mother used to raise her hands in defence when his father was beating her. The dream Ifeyiwa described assumed a thousand shapes in his mind, and the whole experience somehow became his. He shook his head.

'I don't know, Ifeyiwa.'

'I'm not afraid of anything.'

'Have you told him about it?'

'Omovo, you know I can't tell him anything.'

'Yes. I know.' He looked at her. 'I got your note, Ifi. It was very nice.'

'I had to buy the boy sweets before he agreed to take it to you.'

'I gave him some money.'

Ifeyiwa smiled and swung her arms. Her mood had brightened and the shadows had lifted from her face. She was radiant in her plain white blouse. A glimmering gold-painted chain dangled from her neck. It rested in the valley between her lightly moving breasts. He knew she did not have on a brassiere. The thought started a stab of passion inside him.

'You know, he came in yesterday and was saying how strange your drawing was.'

'When he walked past me and suddenly said something about my head I thought he was going to pounce on me.'

There was a light descent of silence. Something happened in the sky. The air darkened. The sky had now acquired sprinklings of yellow, ash-grey, and a wistful fading blue. Everything around was faintly touched with that darkening quality of twilight. It happened imperceptibly.

'Omovo?'

'Yes.'

'I've been wanting to ask you why you shaved your head.'

He reached up and touched his head. Flesh touched flesh. It felt bare as a calabash.

'Oh, it was a barber that did it. An apprentice. I decided on impulse. Like that. I don't know.'

'It makes you look as if you were mourning someone.'

'Aren't there many things to mourn?'

'Do you think of your mother often?'

'Yes. Always. One way or another. She's always there.'

'Sorry I asked.'

'There's nothing to be sorry about. It's good of you to have asked. It gets lonely when nobody asks you these things.'

'Yes. It does.'

'Do you think of your family too? I mean, often?'

'No. I hate them for what they did to me. And I love them. I worry about mother, though. It is hard.'

'Yes. It is.'

'You know, when I first saw you with your head like this I could not recognise you.'

'I don't recognise myself.'

'Why don't you paint a new self-portrait?'

'That's a good idea. I might.'

'What about the painting you said you would do of me washing clothes in the backyard?'

'I will do it soon.'

'Will it be as good as the Mona Lisa?'

'Do you have anything to smile enigmatically about?'

'Yes. You,' she said.

They passed the rusted junk of a car by the roadside. There was a patch of dust-covered bushes just after it. Palm trees stood tall in a depression. Next to the trees was an expansive clearing where a building was being erected. In the distance a tailback was forming. A sudden wind blew and Omovo's shirt lapels flapped. Ifeyiwa's blouse billowed. In a moment the wind was gone, and there followed a tiny stillness.

'I will do the painting, I promise.'

'Okay. You know, it's a long time since you did some real work.'

'Yes.'

'The rainy season is nearly over now. Things will get better for you.'

'I'm happy about my drawing.'

'I'm happy for you. You have your art. I don't have anything. Except, maybe, you.'

'Tuwo warned me yesterday. I don't know why. He said I should be careful, especially of married girls.'

'He's jealous.'

'Does he know we see each other?'

'I don't know. He went after my girlfriend, Julie, the one I went to evening class with. Then he wrote me a note that he wants to see me. He has been secretly after me for a long time. He's jealous, that's all.'

'What's his problem anyway?'

'He is my husband's friend. They sometimes drink together and talk of women and gossip about other things. Let's not talk about them.'

'Yes.'

'You know, I saw him . . . no, I shouldn't tell you.'

'Why not? Tell me.'

'Well . . . I saw him with your father's wife, Blackie. They were walking together one night at Amukoko.'

'My father's wife used to know Tuwo. They lived in the same street before.'

'Let's not talk about them.'

'Yes.'

'Omovo?'

'Yes?'

There was a silence in which she stopped suddenly and held his hands. Her eyes were ardent in their liquid brightness. Omovo thought: 'Can I find my way out of those eyes?'

'I don't belong here,' she said. A certain anguish had come over her face. Omovo touched her cheeks.

'Ever since I was taken from home I don't belong anywhere any more. I hate my husband and I hate this life my family forced me into.'

'Don't talk like that.' Omovo's voice was husky. He looked at her. Her face was lean, pretty, a clear coffee-brown. Her eyebrows were neat black lines. She had small firm lips and a fine nose. But it was her eyes that moved things in him. There were intelligent and hopeful. They had mysterious depths to them. He looked into her eyes and he again felt that wonderful and dangerous something rise within him.

An army lorry drove slowly past. There were many soldiers on the back. They all carried weapons. They shouted and sang raucously. Their presence introduced something violent into the atmosphere. The tailback had built up, and the army lorry came to a stop. When Omovo and Ifeyiwa went past one of the soldiers made a comment and pointed at them. The others stared and then laughed. Ifeyiwa felt for Omovo's hand and drew closer to him.

'Ifeyiwa.'

'Yes?'

'Nothing. Don't worry.'

The sky was clear and melancholy. The evening light was gay on the dusty green leaves of the bushes. A soft moaning wind that whispered of rain came and then went. The tailback eased and the army lorry drove on. The noise of the soldiers faded into the distance. There were heavy diesel fumes in the air.

'Let's go back home,' Omovo said finally. They turned around and walked back in silence. When they got near the mechanic's workshop where she had met him, she said quietly:

'I'll go first. You take another route.'

He nodded, and stared into her eyes.

'I am happy.'

'You'd better be going. He must be waiting angrily for you.'

'I am happy,' she said again.

Omovo smiled. 'So am I. Really. I'm just worried about other things.'

'Will I see the drawing afterwards?'

'Yes. I'll show it to you. I have always done that.'

She smiled sweetly. She looked her seventeen years. But her eyes were sharp. He kissed her gently on the lips and then held her close to him.

'I am happy you came. I'm happy I could tell you about my dream.'

'I'm happy too.'

She turned and half ran, half skipped, in that fashion of hers, down the path. When he looked again she had vanished behind the new buildings that were being erected in the area.

He turned and walked slowly down the Badagry Road. He stared but noted nothing. He tried to think of the drawing he had done. But he knew he was really thinking of Ifeyiwa and her husband and of many other silent things.

FOUR

The first thing he became aware of was that his drawing was missing. He had come into the room with a new desire to look at it. He wanted to show it to Ifeyiwa, who would be coming round to the backyard later. He found it refreshing to see his work through her eyes.

He looked on the table where he had last put it and then he looked underneath, thinking that it had fallen down. It wasn't there. He soon worked himself into a frenzy: he ransacked the things on the table, turned over his mattress, looked under the faded linoleum, leafed through his sketchbooks, and went through his pockets. But he still couldn't find it. He sat back on the bed and took a deep breath. He tried to remember. He began to sweat.

He remembered finishing the drawing. He remembered that he went to the toilet, came back, put the drawing on the table and then rested it against the wall. That was all. His forehead throbbed. He got up and searched again beneath the table where he kept his drawings and the discarded jujus, the tortoise shells, the broken combs and the other curious objects with which he practised. And then he looked under the bed, where he kept some of his paintings in a large polythene covering. He opened the drawer and scattered the things in it. He came across his mass of hair which he had kept in a cellophane wrapping. He stared at it for a long time, his mind twisting it into all kinds of shapes. Then he put it back. Confused and fatigued, his head throbbed again. He had been searching for thirty minutes.

And then he remembered the young man with the hungry eyes who has asked him if he would sell the drawing. He remembered the prematurely wrinkled face, and the unspoken menace. Omovo was flooded with a numbing sense of loss. Many years later he would walk into a bookshop and come upon a bestselling book written by an Englishman on the African condition. His long-lost drawing would stare back at him, transfigured by time, from the cover. The name of the artist was – Anonymous.

After a while of sitting in his sorrow he got up and went to the living room. The old pictures stared down at him from the drab walls. There was nobody around. It occurred to him to ask his father if he had seen the drawing. The idea died naturally. He knew he couldn't even ask. He thought: 'Maybe someone sneaked into the house and stole it. That hungry young man, perhaps.' But still it didn't make sense. He considered many other maybes and came around to thinking that his father might have taken it to look at in private. After all, when Omovo was much younger it was his father who had kindled his interest in art, and he liked going over his work alone. But Omovo knew all that belonged to the faraway place called childhood. The emotions in the scattered family had become too complicated for such sentimental gestures.

But as Omovo sat there, in the stiff-backed chair, in the spare and musty sitting room, a sentimental doubt festered.

His father's yellow-painted door with its peeling skins of paint was slightly ajar. He wanted to knock when he heard sounds from within. He stopped and looked.

On the bed his father, naked and hairy and lean, made love to Blackie. There was a certain violence about his thrusting motions and Blackie moaned and responded beneath him. Omovo, stunned, knew that he had seen something he should not have seen. It had all happened so unexpectedly. Then he heard his father give a long, pathetic wail and Omovo fancied that he heard his dead mother's name in that wail. Omovo gave a short, strangled gasp. The moaning stopped, the motions stopped, the other sounds stopped somewhere in space.

Omovo tiptoed nervously back to his room. He sat on the bed and stared at the wall. A deep surf of loneliness swept over him and he recalled something else he had innocently witnessed. He was nine. He was ill at the time. His father had asked him to come and sleep in his room. At night he woke up and found that his father was not beside him. The adjacent door leading to his mother's room was open. His father was making love to his mother. It was strange to see them doing it, and they seemed to him like people he didn't know, but somehow he could understand. He did not feel deserted. He did not feel he had done wrong. He turned away and fell asleep. They lived in Yaba then and things were different. But what he had accidentally witnessed now was disturbing. His mother's name, which he thought he had heard, swam around in his head like a crazed goldfish.

He heard heavy footsteps. Someone cursed and grumbled. The door to his father's room was slammed shut. The key was fumblingly turned. And then there was a long silence.

He stared at the soot-spirals on the ceiling. Blankly. It was many moments later before he realised that the electricity board had again, quite arbitrarily, cut off the lights. He felt the trapped heat rising under his skin. The darkness of the high corners pressed on him. Mosquitoes decended on his head as if they each had a private grudge. He found release in an uncomfortable sleep. Omovo had just emerged from a long dry season, and his first real fruit had already been violated.

He woke up deep in the night, irritated by the mosquitoes. He was aware of an unnatural silence. As he stared towards the window the shapes in the room emerged from the amorphous, crowding darkness. They resolved themselves into the white ceiling, the clothes rack, the large snail shells hanging from corners of the room, the exotic shapes of broken calabashes, and favourite paintings.

And as he got used to that ringing quality of silence other things composed themselves in his mind. He didn't want them to become definite. An expanded sense of loss filtered through his inner silence.

Then there was a noise from the sitting room. Separate noises. The scraping of a chair. Footfalls. Pacing. A sudden indistinct soliloquy. A deep drag on a cigarette. A soft sibilant exhalation. Then another silence. Omovo turned over on the bed. The light was on in the sitting room. Omovo knew: the man was having another bout of insomnia.

Omovo got out of bed, put on his khaki overalls, and went to the sitting room. His father was now at the dining table. His head was bent over a pile of documents. He wore a singlet over the large white bedsheet he had wrapped round his waist. The light fell on one side of his face. The other side was in darkness. His forehead was creased in cracks and wrinkles. The eye that was visible was red-veined and sunken. He looked desolate sitting like that in the semi-darkness. He turned his head slightly when Omovo came out of his room.

'Are you okay, Dad?'

'Yes. I can't sleep. It's nothing. It often happens to big men.'

24

Omovo lingered. He hoped that his father would warm to his presence. Omovo remembered how his father used to talk gently to him, how they would both be awake at night when everyone else was asleep, and how he sometimes told stories of what happened in the 'olden days'. But his father stayed silent. Then he took a drag on his cigarette, and turned back to the documents on the table.

Omovo went outside. The compound was quiet. There were one or two lights on in the verandah. A strong wind blew through the compound that made him aware of his shorn head and flapped the clothes that were hanging on washing-lines in front of the rooms. As he went to the backyard his footsteps ricocheted through the compound and magnified in his brain. The communal bathroom was dark, smelly, sinister. In the oppressive space of the slimy walls, with their cracks and shadows, he experienced something familiar. He looked upwards and again confronted the terrifying mass of cobwebs. The roof was hardly visible. When he had urinated he went to the front of the compound. He opened the wrought-iron gate. Its hinges cranked and groaned in the night.

He stood in front of the building and let the cool wind run through him. It had been so hot in the room. Now it was so cool. He stared at the sky. It was a dark blue coverlet full of holes. The ghetto was quiet. One or two characters stumbled down the deserted street. A few front lights, candle-dull, shone from the silent bungalows. Stalls stood in front of various houses. The usually noisy hotel was shut and drenched in darkness. Omovo scanned the corrugated zinc roofs of the buildings and then he looked towards Ifeyiwa's house. The front light was dull but Omovo could make out a figure sitting on the door ledge. He wondered if it was Ifeyiwa. He felt the blood rise to his face, and a tremor pass through him. Between him and that human being was the dark and filthy street. The darkness between them was almost tactile. It was a fluid presence, separate from and yet a part of everything. Omovo stood still for the long moment during which the figure slapped its thigh, stood up, paced the cement platform and then sat down again. The figure raised its hands skywards and then brought them down.

Soon afterwards the main door opened and a man wearing a wrapper came out. He too shouted something that was lost in the wind. Then he dragged the figure into the house.

Omovo stared at the door for a long time. The night became cold and the dark coverlet of the sky pressed in on his skull. The pool of scum gave off a bad smell. The wrought-iron gate cranked and groaned. His footsteps ricocheted through the compound and through his skull.

Back in his room he got out his paintboxes, palette, and easel. He tried not to think of his lost drawing. He began to paint. The room was stuffy and hot. And the mosquitoes whined and stung him in vulnerable places. He worked with unswerving determination. He caressed the white canvas with brush strokes of a deep muddy green. Then he punctuated the green tide with browns, greys, and reds. Out of all this he painted a snot-coloured scumpool full of portentous shapes and heads with glittering, dislocated eyes. He knew what he wanted to do. And he was happy.

He worked at the painting, cleaned off a bit, retouched an edge, washed off some aspect, started a fresh canvas, and decided that the first one was appropriate. As he continued he thought he heard his father's footsteps near the door. He stopped working to listen. The silence was broken now and again by the whining insinuation of a mosquito. Omovo tried to imagine what his father was doing or thinking outside his door. A moment later he heard footsteps move towards the sitting room. An incoherent emotion swept over him.

He returned to his painting. He worked intently, unaware of the passing time. He was surprised when on looking towards the window he saw the shy fingers of light prising through the yellow curtains. Then he felt suddenly tired and old. His eyes burned with fatigue. His body smarted and itched where the mosquitoes had stung him. He was drenched in his own stale sweat.

When he had finished with the night's labours he took up a pencil and wrote 'Drift' on the bottom part of the canvas. He signed his name (even though well aware that he would still have to re-work it) and turned the painting to face the wall. He cleared up the room and cleaned away the familiar stains of paint. The paint had got everywhere.

When he made for the backyard he saw his father asleep on the cushion chair. His legs were sprawled and his head was slumped forward. Omovo stood there at the doorway, and he felt sorry for his father. Then he remembered many other things and he did not feel quite so sorry any more. At the backyard he washed his paint-stained hands with kerosene and turpentine and then had a light shower. When he came back to his room he drew aside the curtains. He felt trapped by his own emotions and felt very empty and dried up. Having nothing better to do, he searched around for his missing drawing. He gave it up. Then he rubbed some Vaseline on his parched hands and got back into bed.

He was studying a mass of accumulating cobwebs, which had

26

festooned a high corner of the room, when sleep closed in gently upon him like the silent immensity of the sky.

The following week he worked furiously to complete the painting. When he finished it, however, he was uncertain and a little unsure of what he had created. It seemed to him strange and at the same time familiar. He knew, wordlessly, what he had attempted. He had walked round the large green scumpool a thousand times. He had smelt its warm, nauseous stench and had stared at it as if hidden in its green surface lay the answer to a perennial riddle. He was also a little afraid of the uncharted things that had happened within him: the obscure, the foul correlatives which had been released on the canvas – snot-coloured, viscous, unsettling.

On Tuesday evening, Omovo went to Dr Okocha's workshed. It was shut. Freshly painted signboards leaned against the door. There was a large faded painting on the door. It was of a brooding green eye, with a black pupil and a gathering red teardrop. It stared all-seeingly at the teeming streets and back into its own darkness.

The week passed tortuously for Omovo. Evening after evening, when going out to 'take fresh air' he would lock his room door. The other loss still rankled. On Thursday evening he stood at the house-front playing with the children when the chief assistant deputy bachelor sidled up to him. That was what they called him because he was the oldest bachelor in the compound. He was a gaunt, dry-chested, hatchet-faced Igbo man in his early forties, who owned a small shop in the city centre where he sold all kinds of provisions.

'Painter boy, how now?'

Omovo was swinging around a scruffy little child and when he saw the chief assistant deputy bachelor he dropped the boy, touched him on the head and told him to go and play with the other kids.

'My name is not painter boy, you know.'

'Okay now, okay. Anyway, how your body?'

'Fine. What about you?'

'Managing. What else can a man do?'

Omovo saw him jerk the wrapper round his waist and rearrange it.

'See-o, see-o,' he whispered, nudging Omovo. 'Those two girls near the tank think they can see my prick when I arrenge my wrapper jus now!' He laughed and then shouted: 'Hey, what are you lookin' at, eh?'

The two girls self-consciously turned their heads away, picked up their buckets of water, and staggered into the street. Omovo wanted to be left alone. He yawned. The yawn accomplished nothing.

'Why are you yawning? Tired, eh? You young people. What is it that can make a young man just starting life tired? What's making you tired? Is it work, is it too much fuck, is it woman palaver, or what? When I was your age I did all these things from morning till night and I was never tired.'

Omovo grunted. Two women from the compound chatted past, carrying stools, and paused near the chemist's shop. They were going to have their hair plaited. One of the kids ran behind Omovo, and another chased after him. They scurried behind the old bachelor, pulling at his wrapper, hiding underneath it, and then they ran off again. The old bachelor seethed mockingly.

'These children sef. They want to pull off my prick, eh!'

Both of them laughed. Another compound man came outside and, seeing the chief assistant deputy bachelor, went towards him. They both became involved in a never-ending argument.

Omovo moved away, relieved. A light wind blew over the scumpool. His head tingled. The sky was strewn with clouds. The light about Alaba darkened. A few grown-up boys rode bicycles round and round the street, and jingled their bells, and chased after pariah dogs. Little girls made mock food over mock fires. They had baby dolls tied to their backs. Someone waved. Omovo straightened. It was a stocky man draped in an agbada. It was Dr Okocha. He had some signboards under his arm. Omovo went to meet him.

'I have got you a ticket.'

'Thank you, Dr Okocha. Thanks a lot.'

'It's okay. I told them that you were a good artist and people might be interested in your work.'

'Thanks again . . .'

'Anyway, the manager of the gallery wants to see your painting. So take it to him, say, tomorrow. If he doesn't find a place on the first day maybe he will later when other works have been bought or something. Anyway, I am in a hurry. I've got many signboards to paint. I will see your new work at the showing, eh?'

Omovo felt the keen edge of a thrill. A joyful feeling deepened within him, then began to fill up and to expand. He felt wonderful. It was the same lightness he felt when he saw Ifi. He walked down the thronged street with the old painter. He could hear the older man's breathing and the rustle of the threadbare agbada and the footsteps and a thousand other sounds. But they all seemed out there. He could hear other sounds within him: keen, fine, soundless sounds.

The older man began to speak. His voice quivered slightly. Omovo thought he sensed now the reason for the older man's anxiety.

'My son is not well. I just took him to the hospital.'

'Sorry-o. What's the matter with him?'

'I don't know. His body was like fire yesterday night. The boy is very lean, his eyes . . . you know . . . deep. So deep.'

They went on. Nothing was said for a long moment. Life bustled about them. They passed the hotel where Dr Okocha had painted the frolicsome murals.

'So how is the wife?'

'Well, she is fine. You know, she is pregnant and is worried about Obioco. She's a good wife.'

The older man's face darkened. The wrinkles deepened on his forehead. The skin of his face seemed to shrink and the flesh bulged under it. He looked strange. The evening darkened as if regulated by his sadness. Omovo felt that the dome of the sky repeated and oppressed the dome of his own head.

'I hope Obioco will be well soon.'

'Amen.'

Not long afterwards Omovo told the old painter that he was going back. The old painter nodded and trudged on toward his workshed. Omovo turned and picked his way back home through the debris, the thronging passers-by, and through the falling darkness.

Omovo walked away from the house, towards the fetid-green scumpool. He had felt good in his room. The room had been in a mess. He hoped nobody would steal his painting and toyed with the idea of insuring it. He thought: 'There is nothing like having an idea and seeing it through to its manifestation.' He was filled with the simple wonder that he had created something on the canvas that wasn't there before. The shock and surprise still enthralled him. He thought: 'If your own work can surprise you then you have started something worthwhile.' He wondered if he would remember to write this down in his notebook. He doubted it. He wondered also if in completing the painting he hadn't disturbed or dislocated something else. He had read about the dangers of this somewhere. When he couldn't expand the thought he abandoned it.

He had passed the scumpool when a group of wild-looking men

marched towards him as if they were going to pounce on him. He waited, tense. He could see himself being flung into the filthy water. But nothing happened. The men marched fiercely past as if they had a constant mission of terror to accomplish.

He recalled what Ifeyiwa had said in the backyard, near the well, when he told her that his drawing had been lost, stolen. She stared at a bird that flew past overhead, and said: 'Omovo, something has been stolen from all of us.'

Omovo felt that she had uttered something unintentionally profound.

'You know, I didn't understand the drawing,' she said after a while.

'It was simple. But neither did I.' Then Omovo said: 'Were you the person who sat outside . . . ?'

'Yes. I knew it was you. It was dark, and he came out to get me.'

He remembered, and then he tried to forget. Then he remembered something else. She had gasped when he had shown her the new painting. She then stared at him, and said nothing.

When he left the room he had searched the painting for a portent, an intimation of the future. He tried to read life through it. But his mind could not get beyond the images, the sickly, vibrant colours.

But through Ifeyiwa's silence he had intuited a form, a morass, a corruption, something flowing outwards viscously, changing and being changed. He sensed then, vaguely, that the future was contained somewhere in his mind.

He stopped in his wanderings, and suddenly decided to go back home.

FIVE

He obtained permission from his office manager on Friday morning to present his painting at the gallery. The Ebony Gallery was situated in Yaba. The roads there were well tarred, and the tarmac tinselled with illusions in the early afternoon heat. Palm trees, swaying, lined the road. Their shadows stretched across to houses opposite. Women retailing wares sat under these shadows. When any person went past they roused themselves and chanted their wares.

The Ebony Gallery had a large signboard with a painting of a Benin sculpture as its emblem. The building was two-storeyed, American-style, with a porch. It was painted black. The windowpanes were white and some of the windows were frosted. At the reception desk an excessively bleached young girl told Omovo to wait while she talked to the gallery manager. She spoke with a sickly English accent. A few moments later he was told to go in.

The gallery manager was a tall man. He swayed as he got up to shake hands with Omovo. His hand was bony, his arms hairy, and his neck was rather long. He had on a pair of black trousers, and a black silk shirt. A gold cross hung round his neck. His face was obscured by his neatly cropped black beard. He wore dark glasses and Omovo could only make out the dull obliqueness of his eyes. He sweated relentlessly and dabbed himself with a saturated white handkerchief, in spite of the fact that an air conditioner groaned sonorously in the pine-smelling office. His movements were nervous, but he was very alert. He spoke with painful slowness, as if every word was wrenched from him like a bad tooth.

'Okocha told my assistant about you.'

Omovo nodded, and then looked around. A wall gecko vanished behind the sculpture of a Yoruba chief. Then it fled up the wall and ducked behind a flapping poster of an African Arts festival. Omovo thought: 'This is a zoo.'

'Is that your work?'

Omovo nodded again. Outside, through the window, Omovo saw a woman selling roasted ground-nuts. Somebody stopped her and bought some. Omovo's mouth watered.

'Can I see it, please?'

Omovo nodded again. He was for a moment aware that he was playing an obscure part in a silent drama. A wall gecko, smaller than the one he had just seen, did a cross-country across the black wall. Then it stopped. Its stillness was perilous: a fly hovered in the air. A tongue shot out. And missed. Another stillness. The fly jetted across the ceiling. The wall gecko somersaulted and hit the ground. Then it scurried out of sight. It turned out to be a serrated lizard.

He carried the painting over to the gallery manager, who pushed back his chair, balanced the painting straight up on the mahogany table, and studied it.

For a moment nothing happened. Omovo listened to the manager's laboured breathing. A telephone jangled somewhere in the building. The air conditioner groaned, changed gear, purred, then groaned even louder. Omovo's heart seemed to stop beating. He shut his eyes. Darkness fell over him. And he thought: 'An inner darkness is darker than an outer darkness.' He took a deep breath and slowly exhaled, the way he had learnt long ago when he practised yoga.

The manager went: 'Emmmmmm. Interesting.'

Omovo's heart beat erratically.

The manager paused, looked out of the window, and again went: 'Emmmmmm. Very interesting.'

For the first time Omovo became aware of the photographs of terracotta images, and the sculpted heads of African children: negritude in ebony. They all seemed to glare down reproachfully at him from the walls. He looked at the crowding presences and the question skimmed his mind: 'Are you all dead?'

'Yes. It is decidedly . . . yes, interesting. A vanishing scumscape . . .' said the manager, studying Omovo over the painting. Omovo felt uncomfortable.

'Is this a . . . a . . . ?'

Omovo felt he should help him. The drawn-out words stretched his nerves.

'Yes. It is a painting.'

32

The manager knifed him with a glare. 'Yes. A painting. I knew that. Are you a . . . a . . . ?'

'Well, eh, I work at . . .'

'Yes, of course. I know. Yes.'

Omovo felt dislocated. The whole turn of the dialogue had a mind-prising aspect. He wondered if the manager was an artist himself or if he was a university man. He looked quite learned.

'What . . . eh . . . I mean . . . what . . . eh, made you paint . . . it?'

If the very air had turned into a giant serrated lizard and proceeded to grab him by the collar, Omovo couldn't have been more surprised.

'I just painted it. That's all.'

'Well! Will you let me be with . . . it a . . . whole day? I need to absorb its . . . its . . . qua . . . lities. The best . . . li . . . li . . . ghting and po . . . po-sition.'

'Sure. Okay. You mean you would like to . . . ?'

'Yes.' It came out like a repressed sneeze.

They both sat there opposite one another. Between them was the table on which were bits of paper, black ballpens, a copy of Ousmane's *God's Bits of Wood*, the serviette of a palm-wine restaurant, and a large diary. And there was this silence. Omovo wondered what had happened to all the sounds. He decided it was time to go back to the office.

The manager began to inhale some snuff. And then he sneezed again.

'Yes. When some of the works have been bought we will display yours. It is a good work. And yes, emmmmmm. Let me also tell you that a celebrity from the army will be present to grace the occasion. Well. That's that, then.' Where was all the stammering and the nervously drawn-out words?

'Artists always have that effect on me. I stammer when I see their works. So.'

Omovo scented an anti-climax. He had been right. It had been a silent drama, and the manager had been acting all along.

He said goodbye. The manager grinned, then sneezed as if he meant it, and then asked: 'Shaving your head, was that a . . . a . . . ?'

Omovo let him finish.

'. . . a . . . gimmick, an artist's trick for getting attention?'

Omovo turned and walked out of the office. He heard a quiet, self-satisfied rumble behind him. As he left, the last spectacle he witnessed was a lizard doing a futile cross-country across the poster of a sculpture of an old African chief.

The anaemic receptionist smiled secretly when he fled past. Out in the street, in the colourless glare of sunlight, he looked back. He discerned a black curtain drop. He wondered why things seemed to be repeating themselves.

He made his way through the dappled shadows of tall, gently dissenting palm trees and ignored the throng of tired eager women who exhorted him to buy their wonderful wares. He returned to the office, to the chores, to the scheming hanging ghosts, and to the pressures of self-imposing customers.

When he went to the showing on Saturday the bleached receptionist wasn't at her desk. The whole place reverberated with a ceaseless stream of murmurs, shouted conversations, steamed speeches, clinking glasses, throaty monologues, and octaves of borrowed accents. Walton's 'Belshazzar's Feast' raged in the background.

He felt lost in the dense crowd. A child screamed somewhere in the centre of the collective clamour. He pushed his way through fat women, spitting women, pretty women, tall bearded men, nondescript men, stammering men, through stinging sweat smells, fresh perfumes, jaded aftershaves, mingled odours. Drinks were spilt, conversations went round the same groove, text-book theories on the derivations and healthiness of modern African art were flung about like mind traps. And the child in the dead centre screamed even louder.

On the black walls there were paintings, small framed canvases, large etchings, gouaches, pastiches, cloth-bead works, cartoons. There were caricatures of the white man's first arrivals. Some of the images were the usual ones of the white missionary armed with Bible, mirror and gun. Others were grotesque, surreal representations. There were paintings affirming national unity; various tribespeople drinking palm wine together and smiling broadly. Paintings depicting traditional scenes: women eating mangoes, women with children on their backs, women pounding yams, children playing, men wrestling, men eating. Omovo saw Dr Okocha's two paintings and he felt that they had lost a certain desperate quality by being stuck side by side, unimaginatively, with the others.

Art theories stung Omovo's ears. The many mouths talking sprayed their saliva at his face. Words assaulted him till he screamed implosively. He passed Dr Okocha's painting of the wrestler. It looked forlorn, gross and robbed of vitality. Omovo fled from it by dipping into the crowd. He sweated viciously. He raised a hand to wipe the beads of sweat from his forehead and in the process dragged up a woman's skirt. The woman shrieked: 'Hey! someone is raping me-o!' The crowd rumbled with laughter.

Someone shouted: 'Picasso's forefinger.'

Someone else shouted: 'Joyce Cary's mischievous painter!'

Omovo mumbled. His finger felt sticky. The child still howled in the centre of the showing.

And then something caught his interest. It was a riotous painting of two red skeletons. Their faces were hollow. They had deep white blotches for eyes. A mirror of a river forked many ways behind them. A white bird circled over them. There was a golden sky all around. The work fascinated him. It was entitled: 'Hommes vides'. Omovo looked at the credentials of the painter: 'A. G. Agafor. Exhibited internationally. Studied in Nigeria, London, Paris, New York, India.'

A clean-shaven man came up to him. 'Do you like the work? It explodes in the brain with visual impacts of predominant red. I think Mr Agafor is something of a pioneer in giving visual lacerations to apocalyptic motifs . . .'

Omovo, irritated, murmured: 'Artists long before the first illustrations of Dante have been doing it.'

'But the first Nigerian . . . Not really, but . . .'

Another man, with dark blue glasses, jostled them. 'I say . . .'

Omovo ducked. Words bashed his ears. Confused, he wondered where his painting was. Walton's 'Belshazzar's Feast' raged in the background as if someone had maliciously increased the volume of the invisible stereo. When Omovo saw his work he gasped. He saw his own painting, for the first time, with the eyes of a stranger. It was right beside another painting of an agbada-draped Yoruba man. The snot-coloured scumpool looked as if it had been done by scouring the canvas on the slimy walls of the bathroom at home. It seemed obscene and badly executed. His first impulse was to fling away the blasted people who were analysing it, and rip the shameful work to shreds. He stood there glaring, and he hated the work as much as he momentarily hated himself. Contractile waves of nausea swept through him, the child screamed inside his head, and he shouted: 'It's fucking useless . . .'

Then the screaming stopped. Distorted faces and old eyes stared at him close up. The crowd pressed on him and breathed on his face. He sensed menace.

Someone laughed and shouted: 'Gimsey's broken tonsils.'

A woman whose face he vaguely recognised said: 'Van Gogh's roasted ears.'

Omovo broke down and cried. Something felt wrong inside him. Conversations were resumed, people went back to the circularity of their arguments, and he felt he was going to suffocate from the sheer density of mingled smells in the hall. And then someone came out from the crowd, touched him on the shoulder, and said:

'Hey, Omovo. What's the matter?'

Omovo looked up. Through a swollen teardrop the face was like something seen in a drunken stupor. Tears broke loose and raced down his face. Omovo turned away and quickly wiped them off. It was many minutes before he could find his voice.

'Hi, Keme. It's good to see you,' he said, eventually. He glanced at the painting. 'Keme, look, let's leave this sector.'

'Okay. But are you all right?'

'Yes.'

'I saw your painting. It's strange and well done. Really.'

The crowd had moved away.

'It's very good. And a bloody good commentary on our society!'

Keme was a journalist with the *Everyday Times*. He was a good friend. Slim, good-looking, intelligent, he was about the same height as Omovo. He had a small face, twinkling eyes and a large nose. He had a way of smiling which radiantly transformed the whole of his face. He was a self-conscious physical weakling, with a sense of inferiority that made him eager to prove himself. He was also something of a loner.

'What have you been doing with your life? Someone told me you had shaved your head. I didn't believe it. God, you look strange.'

Omovo emerged gradually from his wretchedness. The emotion that had gripped him receded. The gallery was still packed full of people. A group of women near him were dressed in matching wrappers and lace blouses. The murmurs rose and fell like a giant's snoring. In the centre of the crowd the child had stopped screaming. He saw the gallery manager, his dark glasses on, as he swayed and laughed with a couple of women. The bleached receptionist tried to sell some black booklets to a group of young men.

'Keme, I saw your coverage of the old man who was thrown out of his house by the authorities. It was very good. I understand you received many letters of support condemning the action.'

'Yes. It was hard but worth it. The man is still sleeping outside. They haven't given him back his room.'

'Just because he didn't pay a month's rent?'

'Yes. People even sent in cheques covering the amount. It's nice to know some people have a sense of justice.'

'Yeah. It must have been good for your ego.'

'It was good for my heart.'

They said nothing for a while. Both of them stared at the strange animal of the crowd. Drinks were passed. A voice mentioned T. S. Eliot very loudly. Another voice went on and on about terracotta. A woman's shrill and authoritative voice took over and declaimed about Mbari.

Omovo said: 'Words words words. Voices. A damn zoo.'

Keme smiled. 'Hey, Omovo, what is that painting really?'

'Keme, a scumpool. What do you think?'

'It is disturbing. It's a commentary on our damned society, isn't it? We are all on a drift, a scummy drift, isn't that what you are suggesting?'

'Keme, you can read what you like into it . . . Have you seen Dr Okocha?'

'Yeah. That way,' he said pointing. 'Two people have bought the paintings he exhibited. He's happy and talking a lot.'

'I liked the paintings when I saw them in the workshed. Here they look somehow out of place.'

'Omovo, why did you paint that scumpool with those disorientated eyes?'

'You know, I'd done a lot of drawings of that scumpool near our house. One evening our compound men were having an argument about that issue of dismissed corrupt officials . . .'

'. . . When that ex-commissioner said: "Everybody is corrupt . . . it is all a massive bag of worms . . ." Man, it was a friend who did that report . . .'

'Yes. Yes. So anyway, while they argued and then suddenly went in for a drink, something struck me. I had a sudden sense of . . . you know . . . something coming together . . . You won't believe this, but I hate that painting now. Anyone who buys it is a bloody fool.'

Keme laughed. Sensing how unreal he must sound, Omovo laughed as well. Beside them a woman loudly expounded her ideas on contemporary African art to a cowed and sweating man who passionately smoked a cigarette. Omovo recognised her as the woman who had mocked him when he broke down a moment before. He vaguely knew she was a feature writer for a newspaper. She was not attractive. She had on too much red lipstick and beads weighed down her hair. Her voice was hoarse. She was saying:

'. . . we have no Van Goghs, no Picassos, no Monets, no Goyas, no

Salvador Dalis, no Sisleys. Our real lives and confusions have not been painted enough. You cannot describe a place, or setting, or character, by any reference to an African painter – because there are truly none! We have no visual references. You cannot say that a palm-wine bar is straight out of a painting by . . . dash, dash, dash, you cannot say a traditional meeting reminds one of a painting by . . . dash and dash. There are no quintessentials. It's all arid. Why?'

There was a white woman with them. She wore a black suit and also sweated. She looked anguished and kept saying: 'But no, but no, but Negritude . . .'

Soon afterwards Dr Okocha came over. He wore a tight-fitting nylon-mixture French suit. He too sweated and he talked fast. He was excited. His cheeks hollowed into the shape of scallops whenever he smiled. Laughing loudly and semi-drunkenly, he moved on to talk with some students who were interested in his work.

Then Omovo began to notice a dangerous silence in the area of his painting. A man in plain clothes, obviously a soldier, obviously powerful, stood glaring. His gestures were imperious. He was sur-rounded by his aides. Suddenly, something happened in a blur. A flurry. Silence spread in ripples of dying murmurs. 'Belshazzar's Feast' ranted absurdly. The gallery manager pushed to the centre of the hall and, encompassed by 'Belshazzar's Feast', announced:

'Will Mr Omovo please come over this way immediately! Will Mr Omovo come this way immediately!'

The music went off. Keme started to protest. For a long moment Omovo was transfixed. Disconnected thoughts skeltered through his mind. Then came sadness. Then a sense of terror. The terror of individual reality. A vast shadow. He and Keme went towards the manager, who led them to a corner. There was a blanket silence, snuffing all sound. Faces stared at them. Peopled nudged one another. The plain-clothes man said something about mocking national progress, about corrupting national integrity. A photographer's camera flashed twice.

'You can wait behind,' a very black man said to Keme.

'I am a journalist with the *Everyday Times*,' Keme said, producing his press card.

'So what? Wait behind!'

Omovo said: 'It's okay. Take care of your end.'

There were a few black-painted chairs in the room. Omovo was made to stand with his back against the wall. The manager was nowhere around. Only unfamiliar faces.

'Why did you do that painting?'

'I just did it.'

'You are a reactionary.'

'I painted what I had to paint.'

'You want to ridicule us, eh?'

'I read a newspaper report. I heard an argument. I had an idea. I had to do it, so I did it.'

'You are a reactionary.'

'It is you who are reading hidden meanings into it.'

'You mock our independence.'

'I am not a reactionary. I am an ordinary man, a human being, I struggle to catch a bus, I get shoved, I go to work, I cross the filthy creek at Ajegunle every day.'

'You mock our great progress.'

'My mother died. My brothers were thrown out of the house, I am not happy. Nothing is what it could be.'

'We are a great nation.'

'I am a human being.'

'You are not allowed to mock us.'

'I had to paint it, so I did.'

'You are a rebel. Why did you shave your head?'

'I had this impulse. So I shaved it. That's freedom, isn't it? Does it offend the national progress?'

'Your name? What's your name?'

'Omovo.'

'Your full name?'

'Om . . . ovo . . .'

'We are going to seize this painting.'

'Why?'

'This is a dynamic country.'

'Why is my work being seized?'

'We are not in some stupid drift, in a bad artist's imagination, you hear?'

'It is not illegal to paint, is it?'

'The work will be returned to you at the appropriate time. If at all. You can go, but be warned. Worse can happen to you.'

'Is it illegal to paint? I want to know.'

'For your own good ask no more questions.'

'Is it illegal?'
'NOW YOU MAY GO!'

Omovo walked slowly out of the room. There was a curious half-smile on his face. Dr Okocha and Keme rushed to meet him. Before they could say anything Omovo raised his hands.

'They just tried to frighten me with accusing questions. I had nothing to be afraid of. I can't help it if people see things.'

The painting had been photographed before it was taken down from the showing. The arts editor of a newspaper whom Omovo had been listening to, later wrote a clever article about the state of the modern Nigerian psyche. She used the fate and her interpretation of the painting as a peg. Omovo's name was not mentioned. The next day a two-column report appeared in the *Everyday Times*. The report was badly printed. Omovo's name was mis-spelt, and the photograph of the painting was dark and indistinct.

Omovo left the gallery immediately after the sinister event. He walked down the dark road. The branches of the palm trees swished and swayed. Women chanted their wares. Cars did dangerous turns. His thoughts stretched darkly before him. Keme came up behind him, pushing his Yamaha motorcycle. After a long moment's walking in silence, Keme said:

'Take it easy, Omovo. If anything the whole ugly business vindicates you. Come on, let's go to Ikoyi Hotel and then later you can go and meditate at the Ikoyi park if you want.'

Omovo climbed on the back seat. Keme kick-started the bike, and sped off into the bowels of the disturbed evening.

SIX

The evening turned out worse than they could have imagined.

At Ikoyi Hotel, Keme met a former classmate, the son of a wealthy businessman. At school he used to hire boys to wash his clothes and run errands for him. He failed his School Certificate and afterwards it was heard that he was a 'big man' in his father's company. Keme waved at him. The classmate nodded, and looked away. Keme thought he had not been properly remembered. Omovo saw Keme walk over and traced the words that formed on his mouth. Then the former class-mate shouted:

'So what? I have no money or jobs for anybody, you hear?'

Keme stormed out of the hotel foyer. Omovo followed him. Outside, Keme's face was swollen with indignation. He was from a poor family and there was not a day that passed in which he was allowed to forget it. The difficulty of surviving the miasma of Lagos life made him especially sensitive to financial insults and social humiliations. As if to deny the treadmill of his life, he jumped on his motorbike and started it furiously. The bike jerked forward. He grabbed the brakes. Omovo stood and watched his friend's anger define itself against the machine. Keme sat still and took a deep breath.

'Let's go to the park.'

Keme's face was still heavily scored with anger. 'I don't know who he bloody well thinks he is! Me beg him for money? Me go and ask him for a job, eh? What does he fucking think he is?'

'Keme, let me ride the bike.'

Neither of them uttered a word as they rode to the park. The wind was cold. Omovo felt his face flushed. The air became something immensely tangible. The city lights gleamed. Cars hooted and shot past

41

them. Motorcyclists sped challengingly, their shirts flapping behind them as if thrashed by an insane spirit. The rush of air to the face and head, the sheer physical speed, the sensation of things racing past and receding, filled Omovo with euphoria. The machine purred under his grip. With his head and shoulders pressed forward he had the appearance of one going through a defiant ritual. Swaying the motorcycle from side to side, rising and dipping rhythmically, he snaked across the wide road. Then a car, speeding towards them, flashed its lights in the distance. Keme gripped him. Omovo gripped the brake and slowed down. The moment passed. He felt very alive. His being sang. His universe contracted into a vision of frictionless motion through strange places. Keme shivered with fear behind him. He was not sure if Omovo could handle the motorcycle at that epiphanic level.

People were leaving the park when they arrived. The evening had darkened over. The sky above the trees had a sombre ash-grey light. The clouds, dimly illuminated from within, cast a ghostly silvery sheen on the treetops.

They walked between the trees and talked about life. Keme talked about his poor mother who worked hard and believed in him, and about his kid sister who had been missing for three years. They had given up the girl for dead. Thoughts of her haunted Keme. He felt responsible for her loss. That fateful day he had sent her on an errand to buy bread and had told her not to come back without any. He had meant it jokingly. There was a serious bread shortage at the time. She went, and never returned. Adverts were placed in the papers. They got the police to investigate her disappearance. They hired native doctors. They searched endlessly. No avail. She was never found.

As they walked down the park twigs cracked and broke underfoot. Leaves crunched. Empty cans, accidentally kicked, rattled in the night. Keme climbed a tree and swung from a branch. Omovo sat on the ground near a snake-thin stream of water. There were narrow wooden bridges not far from where he sat. He watched the play of light and darkness on the glinting metallic surface of the streamlet. As he watched he noticed the distorted shapes of trees, clouds, birds, and people. He pondered the surrealism of distorted reflections, and how unique the perceived world became if familiar images were re-ordered into freshly juxtaposed fragments by a disinterested vision.

As he sat there, touched by serenity, the pain of losing his second painting receded. It had all happened somewhere in time, in space. A fine breath of vitality coursed through his nerves. He breathed deeply and concentrated on the top of his head. He tried to create mental images of himself painting, living, and struggling. The joy momentarily actualised itself in his being.

Keme said they should go to the beach on the other side of the park. They went. The grass was dark. The muscular roots of trees were exposed above the ground like brown snakes. Branches weaved everywhere. Leaves descended, gyrating. Omovo heard an owl hoot. The trees were dignified, like guardians of terrible mysteries. The whole place had the haze, and the silence, of things experienced in forgotten dreams.

The murmurs of the ocean beckoned them. The sands gleamed. The foreshore was white under the moon. There were still a few people around. Keme sat on the shore and tried to catch crabs. Omovo lay down and watched the waves tumble, gather themselves, and then rage forward like an immense fluid piston, an interminable passion. Then the waves smashed the shore, and shards of water were flung everywhere. When the motion was complete, the waves rolled back on themselves and Omovo felt the vibrations travel through the earth and up his stomach. The extended hiss of the sea took on a primeval quality.

The night seemed to Omovo a calm mistress, suffering the passions of the ocean. Keme sat there, slept and dreamt. Omovo felt cleansed. His whole universe rolled itself into a single crystalline moment. Time vanished. Sea, night, sky hazed over and became one.

Then the heightened moments were intruded upon. Mosquitoes came in malicious squads. The cold became bone-chilling. The murmurs of the ocean became monotonous. The haze of the sky dulled the mind. Sounds became sharp and extended. The quality of the night imperceptibly changed. Keme rose and ran up and down the beach.

'Hey, Omovo, let's get going. It looks like we are the only ones around.'

His voice was shrill and it merged into the whispers of the night. Omovo got up, dusted the wet sand off his trousers, and tried a few kung-fu kicks.

'I didn't know you did karate.'

'I used to. My legs are damn stiff. It's a long time since I practised.'

'Let's be going.'

Omovo could not see Keme's face. 'God! It's dark already!'

'Didn't you realise?'

'No. I've been wandering inside myself.'

They walked, trying to trace their way back to the entrance. The night was suddenly much darker. The realisation fell alarmingly.

'Omovo! We are lost.'

Keme's voice, strangled in the night, sounded like a joke. They went back to the shore and tried to find the way they originally got there. It was hopeless. Somewhere in the darkness an owl hooted, three times. Jangling bells rang in the distance. The sound of breakers deepened their fear.

'We can't be lost. There is an exit somewhere.'

Omovo didn't recognise his own voice. But he recognised the terror in its dry timbre. The night, a protoplasmic mass, engulfed everything. The darkness was alive. Visibility was reduced. Omovo's mind, unable to leap, made out a figure standing near them. It seemed to move. The darkness conferred on it a sinister presence.

'Keme, there is someone there!'

'Who?'

'How would I know?'

They were still. They waited. Time stretched out their nerves. Keme breathed heavily, as if quickened by a mounting fear.

'It's not a person.'

'How do you know?'

'It's a stick or a tree.'

'Go and touch it then.'

'I'm not going.'

'Coward!'

'Eh, I'm a coward.'

They went round trees, crossed bridges, and came to an open area of grass and flowers. Perfume scented the air.

'What are we going to do, eh?'

'Why don't we shout?'

'No. That won't help.'

An owl hooted repeatedly over them. They fell still. The disembodied sound floated on the air like an omen. Keme cried out. Omovo felt his entrails go cold. The chill ran through him. Omovo thought desperately: 'This is a silent drama. It will soon be over.'

Keme gripped him. 'There is a light near those houses.'

'It is a false light.'

'How do you know? It is a hope.'

They went towards the light. They stumbled. They kicked things. They stepped into little streams and got their shoes wet. They clambered over wooden bridges, and were frightened by the reverberations of their footsteps. It turned out to be a dead end. The light was from an uncompleted building. It was separated from the parkland by water and barbed wire.

'Let's wade through.'

'Yes, and get your tail bitten off by a guard dog, eh?'

They turned back and picked their way aimlessly through the obstacles in the dark.

'This is a bloody anti-climax.'

'No, man, the night is balancing itself, claiming what it gives.'

'Then the night is bloody selfish.'

Omovo thought: 'God, the silent drama is becoming dangerous.' The night had assumed the aspect of ritual: a thing enacted by the dark-cast trees.

'God, Omovo, this is not a joke any more. My mother is waiting at home. This is how my sister . . .'

'Shut up, Keme! You are making it worse.'

'Omovo, you are pretending! You are as afraid as I am.'

'Even more.'

The trees were brooding, watchful figures. The shrubbery took on different shapes. The wind howled like a thing possessed and the raging surf orchestrated the separate terrors. Then, mercifully, the moon unfolded its soft radiance. But when the anaemic fingers of moonlight passed under a massive cloud, the parkland darkened again.

'God is playing games with us.'

'We are in a zoo.'

Leaves crunched. Twigs cracked and broke underfoot. Empty cans twanged. Footsteps thudded away from them. Keme kicked something and stumbled heavily. Omovo growled: 'You damn oaf. Get up and let's get out of here while the moon amuses herself!'

His voice was forced. Then Keme shrieked. It was a lone sound. Omovo's heart missed a thousand beats and the chill held his vitals in a relentless grip. Keme screamed again. And this time Omovo knew that the nightmare had materialised.

'Omovo, Omovo, come and see . . .'

Omovo dashed behind the scrub. His friend was kneeling besides a body.

'Omovo . . .'

'Stop calling my name!'

'Sorry. I think . . . it's . . .'

45

'Dead?'

'Yes . . .'

'Have you a match?'

They lit a match and covered the flame with two cupped hands. It was the body of a girl. Her head had been roughly shaved. The eyes were half open. Her mouth was abnormally pouted. Her teeth gleamed. There was a bronze cross round her neck. It dangled towards the earth. Her flowered cotton dress had been torn and was bloodstained. A white foul-smelling cloth had been used to cover her lower parts. She was barefoot. She couldn't have been more than ten years old. And she was pretty. There was a blank, pale expression on her face. Omovo gave a low, helpless cry. Then the matchlight flickered. Shadows leapt and the light died out. The night was silent.

The shock exploded in their minds. Omovo was seized with a strange bitter feeling. And then he experienced a sensation of 'déjà vu'.

'It's a ritual murder.'

For Keme the night had tipped over the electrified edge of nightmare. It brought sharply back to him the horror of losing both his father and his sister. A blurred aspect of evil conjured itself before him.

'We've got to do something.'

'Yes. We have.'

Omovo looked at Keme. The emergent moonlight touched his face with sheen. Something had happened to Keme's face. It had transformed itself into a rock-hard abstraction. Omovo felt a coldness on his skull, as if a pair of invisible icy hands had been placed on his head. He shivered. Then the implications of the fear and the terror became lucid.

'We can't take her out or report directly.'

'Yes. We would be the first suspects. God, this is meaningless . . .'

'Senseless . . .'

'God, I'm going to follow this up to the end. It's stupid . . .'

'Let's go to Dele's place and ring the police. Anonymously.'

'Yes. First problem is how to get out.'

'I wonder if your bike is still safe.'

'We will cross that bridge later. It's all . . .'

'You are no longer afraid.'

'No. I'm angry. This fucking night . . .'

'Come on. Let's go. I have a feeling . . .'

They trudged on and searched for another ten minutes before they eventually found the entrance. It was as if the night had released them from its terrible enchantment. The moon too was released from the obscurity of clouds. Keme's motorcycle was still where he had hidden it behind a bush. They climbed on.

'That was a bloody nightmare.'

'It might not be over.'

They made it to Dele's place in silence. Dele's father opened the door when they rang. He was short and good-looking. He had tribal scarifications as big as fingers on his face. He shouted: 'Dele, awon ore wa ibiyi-o. Your friends are here.'

Dele came down. He had been watching TV in his room. They called him aside and told him their mission and summed up what they had experienced. Keme rang the police anonymously. An uninterested sleepy voice at the other end took notes grumpily and promised to investigate the matter.

Dele told Omovo that one of his girlfriends was pregnant by him. He had tried to get the girl to have an abortion but she refused. Omovo wasn't listening. He made suitable noises and soon said he was going. On the way out Dele said: 'See how Africa kills her young ones . . .' Then he added: 'Africa is no place for me. That's why I'm going to the States . . .'

They were silent on the ride back home. Keme dropped Omovo off at the Badagry road. It was very dark. Everything was clear in his mind. The experience was still close: close, and terrible.

SEVEN

As he made his way home he was unaware of the vibrant night life about him. The orange-seller raised her voice when he tramped past her. The akara and dodo woman called out to him. When he went past without so much as looking up, she muttered: 'Moro-moro! You dey carry dis world on your head?'

Omovo quickened his steps. The hotel was loud with discordant tunes. Garish prostitutes drunkenly pottered about the street. Omovo went past without looking at the murals Dr Okocha had done which brightened the otherwise dreary-looking hotel.

His mind quickened somewhat to attention, however, when he got to the bushes near his home. They were massed shadows in the darkness. Babies had been discarded in that patch, women had been raped there, and inexplicable sounds issued from the bushes as if they had acquired an infernal life.

Omovo's heart beat faster when he heard the familiar voice of his father's wife. In that harsh but soft tone of hers, she was talking and laughing with a man in a wrapper. Nothing was clear. Omovo was confused. He didn't know whether to go on or turn back. His legs carried him on. He went so far to the side of the road that his shirt brushed against the branches and dried leaves.

His father was angry with him when he walked into the house. Caught in the middle of a pace, his father turned round and spluttered at Omovo. His anger was incoherent. He muttered words from which Omovo could only make out forgotten grudges and arguments. There was something about the witchcraft of Omovo's mother, and how she was responsible for his present condition. And there was something else about debts. As he talked the wrinkles on his face and the red raw veins in his eyes defined themselves sharply. His face was shrivelled and his mouth was compressed in a delirious passion. One moment Omovo felt warm and loving. The next moment left him with a soft-hued indifference.

'Where is Blackie, Dad?'

'It's not your business. Leave her out of this. I sent her to buy me some milk.'

Omovo fell silent. He watched his father pace round and round the dining table. And then he remembered many things: his mother dying while his father ran after other women, his brothers thrown out when they questioned him about the aimlessness of their lives. His father stopped pacing and brought up a fresh complaint about how useless all his children were and how unmerciful God had been to him in this respect. He said it with a sad passionate conviction. And over every one of his actions was that impression of acting out a feverish mania.

The white documents were still on the table. They were in the same position as when Omovo last saw them. Their presence conjured up in Omovo's mind overdrafts that had been stretched beyond their limits, court cases, teeming debtors, office notices to quit, unrealised import deals.

His father raised an ogogoro bottle to his mouth. Omovo sped on to his room as his father put down the ogogoro bottle with a certain dignity and resumed his raillery to the gloom-etched sitting room.

In his room the events of the day eddied in his mind. He got out his notebook and wrote:

Ideas take form and haunt me. My drawing was stolen. Today my painting was seized by government officials. Things happening in vicious circles. The portent has acted itself out: a silent drama of losses. This evening I walked through a landscape of nightmares. The night moved from peace to terror. Keme was very hurt: I have never seen him like that before. Dele is to be an unwilling father; he made a remark about Africa killing her young ones. Poor mutilated girl – why did they do this to you? Sacrifice to an African night? What can I or anybody do? Hide? Be anonymous? It's lousy.

He paused. Then went on:

When we were younger our parents often frightened us with the darkness. 'No go there-o. O-juju dey for there,' they would say. As we grew older the fear was lost on us. We found we could walk through the alleys without the darkness banging us on the head. The day is bright. Everything seems present.

49

We lost our fear of the darkness. But we never lost our fear of what it possibly contained, its frightful mystery. The 'O-juju' takes different shapes in the mind and in the land. Now the 'O-juju' has claimed a soul. The earth claims what is left. The water washes the hands . . .

He stopped. The act of writing seemed futile. Waves of nausea poured through him and he flung the notebook towards the ceiling in climactic disgust. Constructing a parabola in the air, it hit the wall and brought down some of the snail shells that were dangling there. The shells hit the ground and shattered. The shattering echoed in his mind. When it all stopped, he thought: 'Good. Something unnecessary has been displaced.'

He got into bed and went to sleep.

That night he had a dream. He woke up sweating. He reached for his notebook and wrote down the dream as he remembered it. And throughout the rest of the night he could not sleep, or so he thought. But sleep came. Mercifully.

I was walking through a dark forest when it happened. The trees turned into mist. And when I looked back I saw the dead girl. She walked steadily towards me. She didn't have a nose or a mouth. Only a bright pair of eyes. She followed me everywhere I went. I saw a light at the end of the forest and I made for it. I didn't get there.

BOOK TWO

ONE

Omovo couldn't escape from the dead girl. She followed him in his dreams and haunted his memory. She reminded him of an event he had witnessed when he was in Ughelli, his home town, during the civil war. He was nine years old. That night he had been sent on an errand by his father to go and buy some herbs. Omovo had walked in search of the herbalist's house and was soon lost. He came to a mighty iroko tree. He stood under it and began crying. There was no-one around. He had wandered into curfew time.

As he stood under the tree crying, he saw a crowd of wild people coming down the street. They had sticks and cudgels. They chanted and in their songs called for the killing of Igbo people. Then they went towards a hut that wasn't far from his position. They sang around the hut, broke down the door, and charged in. Then he saw them drag out an old man and a girl. They beat the man into a bloodied, whimpering mess. And they carried the girl away. He didn't understand what was happening. Then he saw the crowd run towards the hut with a big piece of timber. They banged the hut several times. The walls suddenly gave way and the roof caved in. The crowd broke into a riot of cheering. And from within the hut came muffled cries that inexplicably reminded him of beetles being crushed with a bottle.

When he got home his elder brothers beat him for staying away so long. But he didn't cry because he knew that he had seen something terrible. He had never been able to come to terms with the forbidden sight, the serious stain of that night. Whenever he witnessed an act of terror, he always became that little boy who watched helplessly. And he could never escape the fact that he too was stained in some way.

★

That week there was a one-column article in the newspaper about the dead girl. The article only ventured to say that it was probably a ritual killing and an anonymous policeman was quoted as saying that such murders were almost impossible to investigate. Omovo didn't see Keme throughout the week, but he couldn't forget the rock hardness that came over Keme's face that night.

On Saturday morning he was in his room when someone knocked. Omovo opened the door. It was his father. 'A letter from Okur,' he said, flinging it on the table. Then he left. Omovo felt that a phantom finger had suddenly touched him. He had got on well with his elder brothers, in spite of the fact that they beat him a lot when he was much younger. As the years passed they all seemed to grow away from one another. They grew into themselves, each wrestled with private torments. He knew very little about his brothers. When he was growing up, they were away at boarding-school. When he went to boarding-school, they had finished. Whenever he came on holidays he saw them lying about the house, depressed, ragged, unfriendly. And they often fought between themselves. It was only after their father had turned them out of the house that Omovo sensed how hard it had been for them all those years. Especially when mother died.

Omovo sat at the dining table and read the letter. It was brief. It wasn't dated and bore no address. The handwriting was scratchy. The envelope was filthy. And there was a poem contained within. Okur often wrote poetry when he was depressed, or when he was stoned. Nobody took his poetry seriously. But Omovo often found lines from them echoing in the gloom-cramped chambers within him.

The letter read:

Hi little brother,
I just had to write. I'm working my way on a ship. It's hard. I think often of you and of home and I feel like crying, but I don't. I think of Dad too and I try to understand him and to forgive him, but I can't. You, however, must try to understand him and to love him the way you always have. Try to forgive him too. He is weak and tired. I have no home and no destination and every day as I drink I see the dangerous things happening to me. And I fight a lot. Umeh says hello. He is ill. Injured. And by the way, do you still paint? I enclose a poem

I wrote yesterday. Omovo, we have all badly lost something. I know you are growing strong.

Your loving brothers, Okur & Umeh.

Take care.

Omovo read the letter several times, hoping to perceive the light he had failed to reach in his dream, hoping to see a portent of life that Umeh had hinted at on the day they were leaving. But Omovo only saw self-destruction. When he put down the letter he knew that his brothers' lives out there would always be hidden from him, and what he perceived as their degradation would always haunt him. But when he read his brother's poem Omovo felt something else: a quickening intelligence of possibilities.

> When I was a little boy
> Down the expansive beach I used to roam
> Searching for strange corals
> And bright pebbles
> But I found sketches on the sand
> While voices in the wind
> Chanted the code of secret ways
> Through the boundless seas.

The poem spoke to Omovo: and he spoke to the poem. Reaching back in memory in an attempt to connect the scattered threads of their lives and to weave a pattern, he thought: 'Life has no pattern and no threads. Is it futile trying to weave something through this maze?'

Unable to answer the question he got up, and went to the kitchen and dug out his food that had been placed indifferently on the top shelf of the filthy cupboard. He moved as if in a daze. He ate his breakfast absent-mindedly. His food was eba, and it was rather too heavy for the morning. It was full of lumps which crumbled into grains of unsoaked garri when he took a handful. The soup was cold and the oil had congealed. The breakfast was tasteless but it was manageable. He swallowed the eba with difficulty.

As he ate without pleasure, he thought about his last dream. He remembered it only as dislodged images and as words he had written in his notebook. His mind turned round on its hazy axis and soon he felt the throb of an impending headache.

He brought his mind reluctantly to the immediate realities of his life. He looked down and saw the cracks on the eba plate. The white coating of the soup bowl had peeled off and its metal was rusted. Omovo picked up the only piece of meat in the soup and threw it into his mouth. It could easily have been a hard piece of rubber. He looked round the sitting room. It served also as a dining room and was partitioned by a little bookshelf. His mother had bought it a long time ago when they were in Yaba, and now it was the only piece of furniture in the room which had any distinction.

The sitting room was scantily furnished. There were four cushion chairs. Their bodywork was multi-coloured with age and use. They creaked like barely suppressed farts whenever anyone sat down. The coverings of the cushions were a faded red. They were washed every fortnight by Blackie. Omovo made out a couple of holes on one of the cushions. The holes, dark green, revealed the colour of the original cloth beneath the faded covering.

Between the two sets of chairs was an over-large centre table. The one that used to be there was broken the day Umeh and Okur left home. Omovo wasn't sure if it was Umeh who had stumbled backwards and fallen on the table when his father whipped him. But Omovo remembered the day his father brought home the new over-large centrepiece. There was an 'I-have-managed-and-I-can-damn-well-manage-alone' expression on his face. When he placed the centre table between the chairs it shrank the available space. It was hilariously large. The expression on his face changed. He shrugged his shoulders and said, in a manner of adjustment: 'Well, it's big . . . Good. We need some big things in this house. Yes.'

Omovo later found out that his father had acquired it second-hand from a carpenter near the Alaba market. The surface had now acquired multiple scratches, burns, and stains; the brunt of indifferent usage. One of the legs was now shorter than the others. It was broken during one of his father's parties when a drunken visitor stumbled upon it. But the carpenter, rather crooked in his measurement, fitted a shorter leg and requested more money if the right size was needed. He was a huge, vociferous man. Omovo's father, unable to stand up to him, took the table home, weighed down with his pretended dignity.

The walls were originally a marine blue. Now they had fingerprints and smudges stamped beyond arms' reach. Omovo could not figure out how those stains had got there. Suddenly he was assaulted with a vision of stains and of filth. He couldn't breathe. And it was only when he imagined himself painting the walls a fresh colour and cleaning out the house that there was a miraculous change in ambiance. But then a lizard scurried across the wall, shattered his fantasy, and wrenched him back to a world of disconnected sounds. His eyes fell on the linoleum. It was the most obvious symbol of the state of the house. It was faded. The red-painted floor showed through its holes.

There was a stale smell in the dining room. It was the odour of a kitchen badly in need of a thorough cleaning.

Omovo thought about his father, whom he loved in his silent kind of way. But Omovo also felt sorry, and at the same time not at all sorry, for the man. He saw his father as a failure. But he admired him a little for making a bold show of maintaining whatever dignity he could: to fail was not a crime. Omovo thought about his father's impulsive acts. Then he tried not to think of them. The various thoughts mingled, fed on one another, and shuffled out of his mind. Then his sense of loss came back to him in the form of a light, stomach-seizing nausea. Then it left. And he realised that every day he had to do something with his ability: and that if he didn't he would be doomed to the same destructive impulses that preyed on his family.

He gave his mind over to thoughts of the painting: and he confronted another kind of emptiness. There was nothing within but bare images, phantoms, shadows. At that moment he also realised that he would have to make something out of the dream. He thought: 'It's going to be difficult. A kind of pilgrim's progress through the mind.'

He sighed, shook his head, washed his hands in the kitchen sink, and went to his room.

Omovo began some tentative sketches. The efforts were irritating. He needed to define the outlines in his mind before he embarked on the painting. His method of creation was usually spontaneous. But this work was different. It had to be coaxed, attuned to, grasped, released. Before he could paint it he had to live it, and be possessed by it, he had to expand the cracks within, to deepen, to go through terrains of dark soul-suffering, to include all that was miserable and sweet, and to grow inwardly. But the sketches looked foolish. In a burst of anger he ripped up the paper. He was in this state when a banging on the door assaulted him. His voice rang out full of anger:

'Who is bangin' on my door like that?'

'Omovo! Omovo! . . . won't you come and clear the place where you ate? Who is your slave dat you left the plate for, eh? I don't want trouble-o!' Blackie's voice rang back. It was loud and calculated to attract attention.

'What plate, what plate?'

'You ask me what plate? You chop food that I cook and now you ask me what plate, eh?'

'What food? The soup that tasted like gutter water, or the meat that was like hard rubber?'

'Omovo, I have said my own-o! I have said my own-o!'

Omovo's mood lightened: he sensed a provocation that needed only the slightest excuse for an open confrontation. Blackie was an expert at confrontation. Omovo had seen her verbally tear down some of the compound women. He had also witnessed her destroy a man who had come to Omovo's father about a long-standing debt. He fled before she was finished with him. And he never returned for his money.

'Okay, it's all right. It's all right,' Omovo purred as he came out of the room. He recognised the signs in her amber-black face. She was small, waspish, and cunning. She had clean white teeth, small marks on her cheeks, a well-shaped body, ample hips and a cantankerous disposition. She would flare up for seemingly trivial reasons: an allusion to her childlessness could dangerously turn the tone of a conversation; and anyone who used her bucket to fetch water and who didn't put it back in the right place, could be lacerated by the sharpness of her tongue. She was an irrepressible gossip and often let out 'home secrets' to other women – which were just as often used against her in subsequent quarrels.

When she first came to the house, she was warm, understanding, and self-sacrificing. Omovo's brothers treated her with mild condescension. She tried hard to please them and sometimes made a fool of herself in the process. Then gradually she revealed herself. She was good at dissembling. She listened at keyholes to significant conversations. And when the two elder sons left she saw a whole vacant terrain before her. With Omovo's detachment from the course of events in the house, she wormed her way into his father's heart. The man came to depend upon her for those little necessary comforts. And they even did business deals together that Omovo knew nothing about. His father saw in her something that wasn't in Omovo's mother: a readiness to submit and agree to everything he said, a desire to worship him silently. Not very long after she entered the house, she became pregnant.

But then she lost the baby: she miscarried. She nearly died of humiliation. She fell ill and dried up. She developed a cruel streak. She took part in clandestine activities, made strange trips, was seen in strange dark places. Omovo's father confronted her, and she confessed that she had been going to see a herbalist to find out what had made her lose her baby. Relationships in the house became lop-sided: she was loyal to Omovo's father, made him the choicest dishes, but was indifferent to

Omovo. They once had a ferocious argument about food and afterwards Omovo, fearing she might take to poisoning him, started eating outside. Bits of these hanging tensions came together now and then – and ignited into a quarrel. Omovo sensed that this was one of those occasions.

'Blackie, it's all right,' he said again loudly, rising to her level. 'You have told me already, so why go on shouting? Why make noise over such a small thing?'

Omovo's voice was deliberately gentle. There was a mocking gleam in his eyes. He looked down at her. She was serious. His forehead gleamed and his shaven head was like the ridge of some longish squat yam. He knew he looked comic. Normally she would have laughed, like the day he shaved his head. But her face, in inverse proportion, was serious. She seemed intent on dragging him into a quarrel. She didn't look at him but at the floor, tense and ready.

When she looked up Omovo was shocked. He saw hatred in her eyes. This wasn't the first time he had seen it. He remembered seeing her look at him with such venom the first time they met. Her marriage to Omovo's father was done traditionally. It was only on the morning before the event that the man told Omovo and his brothers what was happening. It was barely a year since their mother had died and it came as a shock.

None of the sons attended the ceremony. Okur and Umeh stayed in friends' places getting stoned and drunk. Two weeks passed before they returned home. Omovo stayed away only for the ceremony. When he came in late at night he confronted the solitary sight of his father and Blackie in the sitting room. There had been a power failure, the light had been seized and the flickering candle on the over-large centre table played havoc with their faces and their shadows. The man looked up at his son. And Omovo saw years and years of suffering, hiding, and defeat in those eyes. This was supposed to be a new life, his first real victory for some time, and none of his sons had been there to share it with him. After a long harrowing silence he asked Blackie to kneel down and greet Omovo traditionally. A long moment passed before she finally knelt. And there was that venomous look in her eyes when she greeted him and stood up hurriedly. He smiled at her: she glanced at him fiercely. Afterwards Omovo went outside and walked round the whole of the ghetto trying to defuse the emotions that threatened to choke him. From that day Omovo sensed that the house would not contain them both.

Her voice brought him back to the present. She said something and proceeded to tie her wrapper with exaggerated gestures, in a manner that always suggested trouble.

'Eh, you say I am making noise? You are abusing me not so? Am I your age? It's your mother who is making nonsense noise wherever she is!'

Omovo's anger rose. Any reference to his mother that was in the slightest way abusive enraged him. The statement was calculated to achieve exactly this: and he knew it. His fists clenched involuntarily.

'Who are you setting your fists for? You can't do anything, you hear me, you can't do nothing. You want to fight me not so, you want to fight me, eh?'

She worked herself up and then she reached out and grabbed him by his shirt front. Her bared teeth flashed and her breath angrily fanned his cheek.

'I think you want to fight me. Beat me now! Beat me, let me see you! Beat me-o-o-o!'

She made a movement with her hands, as if making for his eyes. He was not sure. But pushing her away was all he could do to save himself. His hands quite unintentionally squashed her breasts. He felt confused; and suddenly the memory of his father making love to her came back to him. He felt strange, as if he were a spectator to his own actions. He must have pushed her with more force than he intended for she staggered backwards, fell, and screamed piercingly:

'Omovo wants to kill me-O-O-O! . . . Omovo want to break my back-O-O!'

The noise brought Omovo's father rushing from his room. His wrapper hung loosely on his thin waist and his upper body was bare. The lines on his face, deeply drawn, showed he had been woken up from sleep. Age, drink, and hardship had taken their toll on his face. He was unshaven and his mouth reeked of beer and an overnight staleness. He was alarmed by Blackie's scream.

'Blackie, what's happening . . . ? Omovo . . . !'

His alarm turned to genuine concern when he saw her on the floor. She rolled her eyes in a peculiar fashion and gasped and moaned.

'Your son beat me up. Omovo beat me and punched me on the breast!!'

'That's not true, Dad. She's acting. All I did was . . .'

'Omovo, shut up!' his father shouted, his reddish eyes flashing. Then he went on to ask her: 'Why did he do that?'

For a moment she cried tearlessly, then said: 'Just because I told him to clear the table where he ate. Am I his slave that I should do that?'

Omovo's father looked up and saw the plates still on the table. 'Why didn't you just clear the table when you ate? Why? Why can't you let a man sleep, eh, after doing a whole day's work so that all of you can eat eba, why can't I rest when I come home? What is all this? Omovo, don't let me get angry with you, you hear?'

Omovo said nothing. He just stood there watching his father with an even and composed gleam in his eyes, as if he were beyond the reach of his father's passions.

'Omovo, there are things I am not going to tolerate from you, you hear? Now get out, get out of my sight, useless boy like you . . .'

Omovo looked at his father. Through the corner of his eye he thought he saw a triumphant smile hover on Blackie's face.

'Yes, Dad. I remember you said that before. That's why they went. I am not fighting for you with her . . .'

'Omovo, shut up. Are you mad talking to me like that? Something is wrong with your head . . .' His father rose to his full height.

'It's enough, dear, it's enough.' Blackie put in quite gracefully.

Omovo walked out of the house. As he slammed the door behind him, he heard his father abusing him and saying something about behaving like his elder brothers.

It was warm outside. But momentarily something turned cold within him.

TWO

When his brothers were thrown out of the house, Omovo had felt the same hardening within. His brothers had become alienated from their father. The alienation had existed as gestures, unspoken words, looks. They always took their mother's side when she was being beaten and badly treated by their father. Their detachment grew into something secretly frightening to Omovo. He often heard them say that they would get together and beat their father. They never did.

Their bitterness grew when their father refused to sponsor them through university. They were both bright and had both done well in their A-levels. They got admissions to a university, but their father said he couldn't afford their education. Scholarships were rare and were largely based on an informal system of corruption and nepotism. Whenever the subject of their education came up their father was always ready with pep-talks like: 'Fight for yourselves. That's what I did. If you can't go to university, become an apprentice. Do you think I would have become the person I am today if I kept on waiting for someone to fight for me? No! I did not even go to university myself.'

As they couldn't take up their places at the university, because the fees couldn't be paid, and as they couldn't get a job either, because the jobs were simply not available, they became restless and embittered. The gulf between father and sons widened in the house. They hardened. They withdrew into themselves. They became their own weird way of punishing their father.

When their mother died the mood of the house intensified. For hours, for days, stamping up and down, they accused their father of being responsible for their mother's death. They left home and did not show up till the day of the funeral. Afterwards their rebellion became bolder. They wore their hair rough. They smoked marijuana. They brought strange, wild friends to the house. They drank a lot. They fought. And they stayed out late. They hung around in the sitting room and became an unbearable presence of menace. They seldom spoke to their father, and when they did it was with an unmistakable air of insolence. Then they came up with a new passion. They wanted to go to America, where they hoped to work and attend university at the same time. It was every young person's passion, fed by Hollywood films and album covers of popular disco musicians. But for Omovo's brothers it was, really, an escape. They schemed about it defiantly. They talked about the money they would make, the people they would meet, and the new life they would begin. Omovo knew that their fantasies were a reaction to the shock of their mother's death.

Things took a turn for the worse when their father announced that he was taking a new wife. The next day she was led into the house. Omovo and his brothers learnt that her dowry had been quite expensive. They learnt also that their father held a lavish marriage party in her parents' house. After she arrived they felt shut out of their father's life. They felt like strangers. The house became too small for everyone. Tempers were taut. Omovo's brothers would brush past their father, almost shouldering him, and not a word would pass between them. It became almost impossible to breathe in the house.

Strangely, Omovo was able to reach his father in this welter of raw emotions. Any act of his which was less angry than his brothers' defined itself as something positive. The truth is that Omovo could not take sides: he knew his father's difficulties and understood the anger of his brothers. And although he knew how bad the relationships in the house were, he was not prepared for the exposure of raw nerves, the definitive parting of ways, which happened that Saturday morning.

Omovo was woken up by noises of a quarrel. He went to the sitting room and saw his father standing near the outside door. He held a blood-stained belt in his hand. He trembled with barely controllable rage. Umeh stood by the bookshelf, his head lowered. He had a thick welt on his neck. Okur was at the other end of the room, near the dining table. He stood tall, and there was something strategic in his bearing. He sweated. At the kitchen door Blackie pretended to be winnowing husks from rice on a tray. She watched the events with sideways glances.

Umeh lifted his head. Tears streamed down his face. Omovo knew that he was not crying. The tears were involuntary. In front of him the centre table lay on its side. One leg had been wrenched out of shape. On the floor, beside him, there was a stuffed travelling bag. Then it struck Omovo, for the first time, that Umeh was leaving home.

The compound people gathered to watch the events through the window and through the open door. There were children and strangers amongst them. They stared gravely, impassively. Omovo could imagine them whispering the public history of the family. He felt sad. He was part of it all, and there seemed to be nothing he could do.

Then his father began shouting. His anger was directed at Umeh, but what he said seemed more general.

'I want you out of my house now. Get out of the house! This place can no longer contain the two of us. You are a man, go out into the world and fend for yourself as I have done. And let's see if you can do any better. So, okay, I have not been a good father, eh? Go out and find yourself another one . . . Go on . . .'

Omovo had never seen his father so angry before. Not even during the terrifying quarrels with his mother. He seemed to have inflated. His neck, trembling, was held straight. His anger shook the place.

'I cannot tolerate you in this house any more. The time has come for you to go your own way and I to go mine. You say I have been a bad father, eh, that I have not done anything for you, that I refused to sponsor you to university, that I have failed you as a father . . . and you have the guts to wake me up to tell me all this. You have no shame, you do not respect me. I am your father and yet you do not fight my battles with me. If I died today you would not care, you would not even know the hardships I have been suffering, the debts I have been trying to clear. You do not know my difficulties. You do not know my enemies. In spite of all the suffering I endured to provide for you when you were a child, all the money I spent educating you, your only gratitude is in accusing me. You are a man now and yet you are still living with me. Your comrades are all married. They have settled down, they have children, and they are progressing. But you roam about, smoking marijuana, fighting, and coming home whenever you want. You are here doing nothing. Useless, that's what you are. Useless . . . Get out of my house and go where you like, do what you like, I don't care. What business is it of yours if I marry a new wife? What's your business with it, eh?'

He paused in his rhetoric, exhausted, and breathed in deeply. He had worn himself out. It was too much for Omovo. He seemed to be in a terrible dream. He felt he had to act, to make a movement.

'What's all this, Dad?' he said, stepping forward. But his father turned to him and lashed out with the belt. It caught Omovo on the back. Omovo twisted, the pain searing through him.

'Get away, you small fool! Or do you want to follow your brothers as well?'

Mist formed in Omovo's eyes. And through the mist everything seemed to be gyrating. Omovo blinked and the mist cleared. Umeh looked at Omovo with brooding and vacant eyes. Okur stood still, his bearing as strategic as ever. Blackie continued to blow the husks from the rice. The compound people were still at the window and at the door. They seemed excited by the latest scene in the family drama.

Omovo shut his eyes and said a silent prayer. He prayed that it was all a dream, and that harmony would be restored. If a word existed, potent like mystic syllables, that he could utter to save the disintegration of the family, he would have given anything to know it and to be able to voice it. When he opened his eyes, he was scorched by the indifference of reality.

He heard Umeh say: 'I'm going, old man. I hope you will find happiness with yourself when I am gone.'

Then Umeh picked up the travelling bag and pushed past his father. At the doorway he screamed obscenities at the people gathered round the window. Then his heavy footsteps were heard leaving the compound.

'You can go,' Omovo heard his father say.

Before he could do anything, Okur suddenly pulled out his own bag, which had been hidden under the dining table. He picked up the bag and moved towards his father. Omovo felt himself swaying in the sheer inexorable force of events.

'If Umeh goes, I go,' Okur said, towering over his father.

Tension hung over the room like a shroud of immense gloom. Nobody moved. Then their father took a deep breath. His neck stiffened. His chest expanded. Then he looked around, as if everyone present were crucial to the next thing he was going to say. Okur moved towards the door. Their father grimaced. Omovo could imagine him saying in a drinking session, much later: 'I don't take nonsense from anybody. I turned them out. Just like that.' Then, with heaviness and exhaustion in his voice, he said:

'If you want to follow your brother into madness, then you can follow him. You two have been bad children to me. It's all a waste.'

Then he went, unsteadily, towards the sprawled chair. He stood it up straight, slumped onto it, and took a long drink directly from the bottle of ogogoro.

Omovo looked up and saw the old framed photographs on the wall. In one of them his father, bearing a fan, his expression dignified, stared proudly down at the sitting room. Something passed through Omovo. He shuddered at its irrevocability. He felt hollow with the shared guilt, the disembodied sorrow. Okur came over to him and, with a hand on his shoulder, said:

'Take it easy, little brother. What happened had to happen. We shall seek the true meaning of our lives. This is a dream we might wake up from one day.'

A moment later, Omovo was alone. The hand had left his shoulder. It had happened. It had happened.

The compound people, having witnessed the end of the drama, went back to their various duties. The strangers left. The children ran up and down the corridor, playing. Omovo's father drank his ogogoro. His eyes were bloodshot and dazed. Blackie disappeared into the kitchen. Only the faint rattle of shuffled rice grains could be heard. Omovo went to the door and looked outside. The corridor was deserted. It was difficult to believe that a moment before their door front had been crowded. The damage had been done and life had resumed its altered course. Nothing seemed to be real.

He went to the house front. The area bustled. Pulsating noises sounded from everywhere. The scumpool was green and covered with filth. People streamed past. Children played. Girls came to buy water. A hawker of roasted groundnuts, dressed in tattered clothes, went past, calling 'Ele ekpa re-o!' in a sweet high-pitched voice. He could not see his brothers anywhere in the commotion. He ran towards the garage. He still could not find them. He came back home, stood on the cement platform, his back against the wall, and shut his eyes. When he opened them he looked up at the tranquil expanse of sky. He thought: 'It's a dream from which we might wake up one day.' He hoped that they would not wake up too late, when the nightmare had gone too far, when nothing could be done any more.

After that day his father took to drinking heavily. Omovo fell deeper into painting. It was once a childhood hobby. After his mother's death it became a world full of his bizarre feelings. With the departure of his brothers it became a passion. It became a way to explore the hidden meanings of his life and to come to terms with the miasmic landscapes about him. Painting became a part of his response to life: a personal and public prism.

THREE

Omovo took in the sounds and activities of the compound. Children in varying stages of nakedness ran up and down the corridor. Their shrill voices filled the air. They liked him because he was generous to them. He liked the children as well. But as they ran up and down they ignored him, as if they sensed the mood of his dark thoughts which they could not share.

Omovo felt far away from the bustle around him. He looked up through the gap left by the eaves of the zinc roofs. Against the unobtrusive sky, his thoughts formed themselves. Something warmed within him. He smiled. His face began to glow. The children playing around must have sensed this brightening, for some of them soon gathered around him.

'Brother Omovo, give us money. We wan buy groundnut,' they said, as if they had rehearsed the request.

He smiled at them. It pleased him to hear them call him 'Brother Omovo' in chorus.

'Brother Omovo, give us five kobo, you hear?'

His hand moved to his breast pocket. He felt in a playful mood. He drew back his hand and looked at them in pretended severity. The children fell silent. Omovo crossed his eyes. The children laughed. Then he bent down and said:

'I go give una money if una fit do arithmetics.'

The children nodded. Omovo found himself staring at the protruding stomach of a little girl. She had a yellow-brown complexion. A boy with a head like a pear broke the silence.

'Oya now. Give us the arithmetic.'

Omovo turned to the boy. 'Okay, you, wetin be three times seven?'

The boy counted with his dirty fingers, racking his brain. 'I don get am!' he soon announced. 'Na twenty one! Oya where di money?'

Omovo gave the children twenty-one kobo. They cheered, as if with one voice, and ran out of the compound to buy items of their fancy. As they went one of the children shouted: 'Shine-shine head' at him. He could not tell which one it was and he smiled after them forbearingly.

He turned his gaze upwards at the sky. With his eyes wide open he tried to imagine objects. He tried to imagine darkness. He couldn't. Then, shutting his eyes, he tried to imagine trees. He could sense the remembered shapes of trees, but he could not see them in all their solidity. He found that, as alwayas, he had to create the image within him, he had to bring it into being as if he were painting it internally. When he opened his eyes he felt serene.

With his serenity he tried thinking about the painting he had resolved to do. But the idea was too abstract, and he felt he was deceiving himself in some way. He was aware that there was something he wasn't facing. He wasn't sure what it was. He began to think about the concrete basis of all ideas, and about the long silent phases it had taken him to trap the scumscape on canvas, when his mind clouded.

Life outside began to intrude. A baby cried, a husband and wife quarrelled publicly, and there was the hiss of food being fried. A radiogram blared traditional music. A woman demanded to know, in a loud voice, whose baby had excreted on her doorstep. A man with a wide mouth and kola-nut-stained teeth called to his children with merciless repetition. And there were the constant noises of passers-by. The cacophony was a vibrant assault on his senses.

His mind wandered amidst the babel. Then he came up with the notion of trying not to hear the noises. He concentrated on a television aerial on the roof. For a moment he heard nothing. When he bent his mind to affirm whether he was really hearing nothing, he began to hear the tumultuous sounds of the world. He smiled. He began to concentrate on space, on the gap between the roof and the sky. He was shifting the focus of his eyes when the clarity of her voice penetrated his consciousness.

'What's the matter with you?'

It was Ifeyiwa.

'Omovo, why are you staring like that?'

Her voice was soft. He tried to hold her voice in his mind. But it had been there, and it was gone. She looked at him quizzically.

'Omovo, did you hear me?'

'Yes, yes.'

He became suddenly aware that she was close to him. She held a bucket full of water in her hand. He felt the heat from her exerted body. A warm and earthy smell came from her, filling him with remembered passion. Her eyes, clear, and white-brown, were widened as though in wonder. She had a blue scarf about her head, framing her face. The expression on her face excited him. He swarmed with uneasiness. He became conscious that the compound people were staring.

Imitating the stance of older women, Ifeyiwa said: 'What does a young man like you have to think about? You have no wife, no children, so why do you have to keep staring at the sky?'

She smiled. Omovo, smiling back, said: 'It's good to hear you teasing me.'

She drew closer to him. Her breasts heaved with sensuous dignity, rising and falling, as if she had difficulty in breathing. They carved provocative shapes on her simple blouse. Omovo's eyes could not avoid being drawn to them.

'I was just thinking about my brothers. I had a letter from Okur this morning.'

Ifeyiwa did not know Omovo's brothers. What she had come to know had been picked up, sifted from gossip and from what he had told her. Some time ago, in the backyard, he had shown her photographs of them. Since then he spoke about them to her as if she had met them in the flesh.

They were both silent. The cocoon they had woven about themselves did not protect them from the compound. People jostled past, quarrelling, shouting, cursing. Music blared through open windows. Children cried. Some of the compound men glanced somewhat enviously at the two of them. The men winked when they caught Omovo's eye. The air was shot through with curiosity and conspiracy.

Ifeyiwa's eyes swept round the compound. Her posture became defiant. Her eyes hardened. She stared at a spot of paint in the hollow of Omovo's neck. He became uneasy. He felt the eyes of the compound boring into them. He could feel himself and Ifeyiwa becoming a theme of the next gossip session.

'Have you had trouble with Blackie again?'

He looked at her, thinking: 'How is she able to sense these things so accurately?'

'Just a little misunderstanding,' he said.

There was silence. He continued: 'Don't you think you should be going with the water now? He might be waiting for you.'

Her face underwent a transformation. It changed from brightness into hardness, became a mask. Omovo, agitated, said: 'No . . . I . . . I didn't mean . . .'

'It's all right,' she said, her voice cool. Her face was expressionless. Then her lips began to tremble. In that moment he glimpsed her dilemmas and her terrors. As he watched her he remembered her dream. The images passed through his mind and mingled with elements of his own dreams. He thought: 'What a love of life she has! What a gift!'

'Omovo,' she said, gently.

He nodded. Her face lightened. He smiled. He knew.

'Yes,' he said. 'Yes, let's meet afterwards. You have something to tell me.'

Her eyes lit up. He went on. 'And thank you for washing my clothes. It's really lovely of you.'

'I like doing it.'

'But you are spoiling me.'

'I don't mind.'

'I'm so lazy. I'm ashamed that I keep leaving the clothes to soak in the backyard.'

'I'd like to do more for you.'

'But you wash them so clean.'

'They could be cleaner.' After a short silence, she said: 'So we will meet later in the evening.'

He nodded.

'How did you know that's what I wanted to ask?'

'I wonder,' he said, not without an air of mystery. He was in a fine mood. There wasn't a cloud within him. He fairly trembled with the promise of the moment. He felt that he had unexpectedly touched a pulse of sweet and vibrant life.

'So where shall we meet?' she asked, bending down to pick up the bucket.

'Don't worry. I will be outside. When you see me just start walking. I will follow.'

She lifted the aluminium bucket. Her eyes shone. 'Take it easy, Omovo. You make me worry when you look at the sky that way.'

She started to move. Then she came back. With her eyes fixed on his, she said: 'That was exactly what my elder brother used to do before he killed himself.'

73

Then she left the compound. She strained with the bucket. Water spilt over and left splashes in her trail. He watched her as she went through the gate, and round the water tanks that gleamed outside. He noticed the sweat on her neck. Her blouse stuck to her back. Still full of the sadness in the last thing she had said, he felt a little guilty that he had been watching the shape of her gently moving backside.

When she disappeared from sight he noticed that Tuwo had been staring at him. When their eyes met, Tuwo waved. Omovo nodded. Tuwo always seemed to be following him. Whenever he was with Ifeywa in the backyard Tuwo would keep turning up for one reason or another. He would talk to Ifeyiwa, he would ask after her husband, and was generally irritating.

Tuwo had an infamous reputation with the women of the compound. He was always involved with someone's wife, or daughter, or sister. The compound men were wary of him in this respect. He had been married once. But the woman, stronger than he was, very nearly ruined him, nearly 'scraped his head', as they say.

Omovo noticed that the men were beginning their fortnightly cleaning of the compound. They made clanging noises with buckets and shovels. They waved ropes about and brandished cutlasses. They sang traditional work songs and performed impromptu barefoot dances. They stopped outside Tuwo's room and shouted at him to come and join in the cleaning. They sang his numerous nicknames. His face darkened. He got up, went inside, and came out wearing a long pair of dirty khaki shorts, which greatly amused the men.

'Hey!' one of them exclaimed. 'Were you a headmaster in the olden days?'

The other men laughed. One of them pulled at the long flaring shorts.

'Where did you get dis colonial short man's trouser?' said the chief assistant deputy bachelor.

'His grandfather gave it to him.'

The men laughed again.

'I bought it at a jumbo sale in England,' Tuwo replied with unassailable dignity.

'He doesn't even know where the airport is,' someone said, and the men fell about in robust laughter, slapping their thighs, tears rolling down their faces.

Soon the laughter died down and they turned to the serious business of cleaning. The cleaning day had a story of its own. It began when the women revolted against having to do all the dirty jobs in the compound, sweeping the corridor and the backyard, unblocking the bathroom drainholes, cleaning out the toilets. They had a meeting and decided to ask the men either to contribute to the work or to pay them for their labours. But the men laughed at the idea. It was simply inconceivable. The next Saturday, however, the women refused to do any cleaning. The bathroom began to stink. The water that couldn't flow from the bathroom into the gutter soon flowed through the compound and gave off an infernal smell. The toilet became unusable. The men were furious. They too held a meeting and came up with the decision to prove that they could do the jobs without grumbling or asking to be paid. They did, and it became a compound tradition. It also became a social event. Every second Saturday, while they cleaned up, they told one another outrageous jokes and improbable stories, they made a lot of noise, they chattered and laughed and sorted out the little quarrels of the week. And after the cleaning was over one of the men would invite the others to his room for an evening's session of drinking and mantalk.

Omovo watched the men and knew that they would be coming to rouse his father next. They just might draft him too, if the mood took them. He came down from the wall and ducked into the sitting room. He heard one of the men say: 'Hey painter, are you running away?'

Omovo fled into his room and locked the door behind him. He heard the noises of the men as they clanged the cutlasses against the buckets, and called his father, who was the 'captain' of the compound, to come out and join them. Blackie went outside and they teased her with insinuations:

'So it's you who doesn't allow our captain to come out, eh?' said one.

'You and your husband can do the thing at night, habah!'

Blackie laughed and said she would go and get her husband. Soon he joined them and they carried their noises with them to the backyard.

Omovo felt relatively peaceful. He sat down on the only chair in the room and began to contemplate his life. Where was he going? Where was this mixed-up road leading him? His life seemed aimless. He had nothing to show for his existence. He had done well at school. But just when he was about to sit for his school certificate his father fell on hard times and couldn't pay the school fees. What made it worse was that he kept deceiving Omovo's mother. He said there were no problems, that he had seen to everything. The principal of Omovo's school was a bald, severe Igbo man. He prevented Omovo from sitting six papers in the finals, because the fees hadn't been paid. The principal had long

75

concluded that all the students of the school, without exception, were rotten, and that Omovo must have 'squashed' his fees on a spending spree, or lost them gambling. Omovo's result was incomplete. The final grade was failure. All he needed was a chance. But the chance never came. With his mother's death his whole life turned into a maze of insecurities.

The only thing that sustained him was the vague, mystical certainty that he would gain unique heights, paint works that might last, and that he would live an unusual life. It helped that his brothers believed in his potential as an artist. He treasured the fact that his mother was quietly proud of the beadworks, wood sculptings and paintings he had done as a child. It also helped that his father encouraged his interest in art from when he was six years old. His father used to go over his work painstakingly. He made Omovo enter for a competition which he won when he was twelve years old. And he used to read aloud from books on great artists which he had bought for his son.

Omovo did a quiet stocktaking. He had lost his mother. His brothers had gone out into the world and were destroying themselves. He loved Ifeyiwa, but she was married. He was alienated from his father. He had a bad school certificate result. He had a mindless job in a hostile office. He thought: 'Aha. There we are.'

His head throbbed. The room was dark. The curtains had not been drawn. A solitary mosquito whined above him. He felt empty. He remained in that state, motionless, for a long time. He thought of the painting he had to do. He felt a moment's excitement. In doing the painting he felt he might begin to feel his way towards some sort of orientation, of meaning. The impulse swept softly through him. He thought about the mutilated girl in the park. He wondered what Keme had done so far. He wondered if the police, notoriously slow in their duties, had begun to investigate the horrible crime. As he thought about the girl, he felt guilty. He felt he should be doing something about it. But he was powerless. He felt in curious need of redemption. He felt that his powerlessness, and the powerlessness of all the people without voices, needed to be redeemed, to be transformed. With this feeling his urge to do the painting reached fever pitch.

He remembered a drawing he had done when he was thirteen years old. It was composed of jagged lines that suggested the obscure shapes of pyramids, rock-faces with the eyes of birds, mountain ranges inseparable from sea and sky. The ends of the lines were lost in the maze of entanglements. His father saw the drawing and praised it. His teacher pondered it and pinned it to his office wall. Their interest had baffled Omovo: he had simply taken up a pencil and made movements on paper. When his teacher saw the drawing he said:

'Omovo, do you know what you have done?'

'No,' Omovo had said.

'Well, this is life. But you are too small to understand. One day, if you are lucky, you will understand. Give this drawing to your father. When you are older he will give it to you. Then you will see the things you did in innocence.'

Later, Omovo drew other lines, which were lost in themselves, in their formation of obscure shapes. But his father shook his head gravely and stayed silent. And his teacher smiled indulgently and also shook his head. Omovo understood wordlessly that he had done it once and could not do it again till he really knew how. And as if life were leaving him no option, the drawings got lost when they were moving from one house to another.

Omovo, sitting in the darkness of his room, wasn't sure why he remembered those incidents. He felt his deeper mind was trying to tell him something. He didn't know what.

Then he remembered that he was going to meet Ifeyiwa later in the evening. It made him feel happy. He got up, drew the curtain, and reached for his sketchbook and pencil. He drew lines that became the obscure shapes of crowds at the markets, mother and child on the edge of a precipice, clouds full of faces. He drew the lines without trying to interpret the emerging shapes, nor to will their destinations. And the ends of the lines were always lost in themselves. When he got tired he stopped. He had done ten different drawings. He wrote 'Lifelines' boldly on the top of the first sheet. Then suddenly, as he looked through them, he thought: 'Nonsense.' He ripped the pages from the sketchbook, and tore them into shreds.

His head throbbed. The noises from the compound became strangely muted. He knew that the lights had been seized. He got into bed and tried to sleep off his confusion.

FOUR

As Ifeyiwa passed the wooden window of their apartment she saw her husband sitting on the bed. His legs were sprawled carelessly apart. His mouth formed the beginnings of a yawn. She hurried on with the bucket of water.

'Ifeyiwa!' he called loudly. 'What have you been doing, eh? Why did you take so long?'

When she heard his rasping voice her legs weakened with fear. Her heart beat faster. Quickening her steps, she went past the apartment without answering his queries. She went through the scurvy backyard and into the stinking bathroom. She dropped the bucket on one of the stones people stood on while having a bath. Then she shut the door. The bathroom, for that moment, was her only refuge. The zinc roof was low and the compartment was small. The cracks on the walls widened at night and looked snake-like in the day. Slats of grey light filtered into the murky darkness. Slimy substances clung to the walls. The floor was covered in a stagnant pool of slimy water. As she stood there she was suddenly startled by the noise of something thrashing around in the water. It was a rat. She opened the door and watched the rat as it kicked and swam in the bathroom scum. When it scurried out through the drain-hole, she withdrew to the kitchen and sat on a stool.

The compound was quiet. A fowl strolled through the backyard. A woman came out of one of the rooms, hurried past the kitchen, and rushed into the toilet. Ifeyiwa heard sounds. Then after a while the rusted zinc door of the toilet creaked open and the woman went leisurely back to her room.

Ifeyiwa looked round the backyard. In spite of all her honesty, her energy, her dreams, this was where she had wound up. This was where life had washed her up. Her mother had named her Ifeyiwa. It meant 'there's nothing like a child'. This was where that child had ended. With rats. With a man she hated. With someone she loved but could not reach. Ifeyiwa cried.

She cried often. It was all she could do when she rememberd her brief school days. Then she would sit in the field in the evenings with her friends and dream about life. Or she would tiptoe to a friend's bed at night because she couldn't sleep and they would sit up talking about their futures, the men they would marry, the children they would have, the careers they would embark on. But her life was wrenched out of the shape it could have taken, as if by a sinister design. First there came a terrible piece of news. Her father had gone hunting one evening with his dane gun. He was alone. He saw an antelope. He followed it deep into the forest and lost sight of it. Not long afterwards he saw the animal moving in a thicket. He aimed at its head and pressed the trigger. He couldn't believe his eyes when he saw the dying animal turn into a little girl with a gaping bloodied head. He seemed to be hallucinating. He screamed. People rushed to him and saw the girl that he had shot. This was his story. Afterwards he became quite mad. Ifeyiwa knew little about what followed except that the two neighbouring villages began fighting one another over a boundary dispute which had been given a violent new dimension.

Her father grew lean, haggard, lost in spirit, unable to sleep. His eyes began to stare at nothing. He wandered aimlessly. Harrassed and obsessed, he complained of seeing ghosts. He kept mumbling: 'I killed a girl. Me, I killed a girl.'

One morning the village was rocked with another shot. They buried her father on a hill miles away from the village.

Ifeyiwa was withdrawn from school. Her fees could no longer be paid. She came home and helped the rest of the family on the farm. Blight had entered their lives.

Around that time Takpo went home to his village to find himself a wife. He wanted to marry a young girl who would take care of him in his old age. Family friends had told him of a beautiful girl who had attended secondary school. He made his approach to the elders of Ifeyiwa's family. The dowry was paid and almost all other arrangements had been finalised before Ifeyiwa knew what was happening. Without any choice in the matter the marriage was forced on her.

She ran away from home, but she was caught and brought back before she reached the village boundary. She made attempts at poisoning herself, but gave up each time at the last moment.

During the period in which her marriage negotiations dragged on, another blow fell on her. Nobody knew why it happened. It was her brother. Some people said that his mind became tormented, that he stared vacantly at the sky, that he had detached himself from the life about him. He began to go around like a madman. He talked of seeing spacecrafts land on the farm. He talked of a young mermaid who had a hole in her head, and who kept calling him to the river. He ranted about an old man who kept calling his name deep in the forests. Then he began tramping the bushpaths, following a madwoman around like a demented lover. He shouted that he was going to travel far into the world, into life, and that he would withhold his secret discoveries. When he began to talk incoherently of dead bodies tilling the farms in the dead of night, of ghosts eating the crops before their harvest, it became clear that he needed extreme treatment. The next day his body was found on the swollen river.

His death made up Ifeyiwa's mind for her. She had to escape that ravaged, neglected landscape. Her mind teemed with visions of demons, of dead people dancing on the hills, and the voices of young girls singing from the bottom of the river at dawn. Then she began to be haunted by dreams in which she was drowning. In the dreams she drowned slowly, over a period of time. She always woke up with a feeling of unbearable suffocation.

The marriage ceremony went off without a hitch. Her mother had urged her on, saying that life would take care of its own. Ifeyiwa had only one consolation: that her dowry might be of use to her mother. Ifeyiwa was the only daughter and one of her secret dreams was to be able to take care of her mother as she grew old. Her mother didn't even cry when Ifeyiwa left for Lagos with her husband. She had made her compromise to the terrors that hung over her family and the village. Ifeyiwa had succumbed to the marriage with Takpo in the hope that the elder women of the village were right. They had said that with time she would learn to live with him, and might even grow to love him.

She had no sooner arrived in Lagos than she realised that her act of compromise had forever caged her buoyant spirit. A feeling of isolation and a sense of having left too much behind crowded the first few months of her arrival. She had taken the step. And every step after that became another foot forward into a landscape of losses.

Ifeyiwa found her husband revolting. He had a small head, severe eyes, a large elastic mouth, and browned teeth. He was quite tall, and stooped, and he had long arms. His habits appalled her. All morning he masticated his chewing stick and spat the mangled fibres all over the house. He had no style. He was incredibly hairy. And he treated her like a slave: this was the part to which she found it hardest to adjust. After a hard day cooking the food, cleaning the room, washing his dirty clothes and his old-fashioned khaki underpants, fetching water three times a day for his baths, splitting firewood, sweeping the corridor, going to the market, she was barely able to snatch time to eat. Often, as she ate her food in a corner, he would calmly fart. She would hear the sound and soon afterwards the smell, which she had grown used to anticipating, would overpower her. She would immediately lose her appetite. But she wouldn't be able to get up and leave the room for fear that this might annoy him.

His temper was unpredictable. And he was a very jealous man. There once used to be a photographer in the compound who was friendly to Ifeyiwa. Absolutely nothing passed between them. But one day Ifeyiwa's husband paid two men to beat up the photographer. He lost two of his front teeth and had a swollen eye. His shop windows were broken. One night he packed and moved away from the compound and the area. Ifeyiwa's husband took to keeping a machete in his shop and another one in the room. He said the machetes were for any person 'foolish' enough to linger about with her.

For over a month she totally resisted being touched by him. He talked sweetly to her. He begged her. He even tried bribing her with offers of money and gifts. But her revulsion was uncontrollable. He grew angry. He beat her. He punished her. He starved her. It became an absurd war of his will against her absence of desire. Sometimes, at night, he went around naked and forced her to look at his erection. She never forgot the first time she saw him naked. The size of him terrified her. It reminded her of a long, curved plantain. She ran, screaming, out of the room. One day, before she could escape, he caught her, pinned her down, struggled over her, and suddenly slumped over her, cursing and spent. The stuff from him was smeared over her stomach and on her torn dress. She rolled out from under him, tied on a wrapper, and went and threw up in the backyard. She bathed three times that evening.

Then on another day he came home from the shop in good spirits, smiling, bearing gifts for her. He seemed happy. He seemed harmless. Then he began to talk about himself. He spoke of his struggles in 'this hell-hole they call Lagos'. He seemed capable of humour. He laughed.

He spoke of his ambitious plans for the future. She warmed a bit to him as he talked. He was unusually attentive to her. She even smiled at one or two of the funny things he said. She stirred. She began to feel that he wasn't as bad as she had thought. Then he sent her to buy some drinks. She went in good spirits. When she returned, and had her back to him, he dropped two Madras tablets into her coke. Afterwards she felt groggy. Drowsiness overcame her. And she could not summon the energy or will to resist him when he took off her pants and climbed on her. She tried to fight him off, but her limbs were heavy and she moved as if she were submerged beneath oil. She felt the blurred form of her husband struggling over her. In a curious way she felt that it was all happening to someone other than her, to someone she didn't know. Then she felt him as he penetrated her, plunging, ripping her open. She felt her blood drip down her. She started to cry. But he stopped. She held her breath. He got off her, opened a bottle of Vaseline, came back, and spread open her legs. After applying the vaseline he struggled over her again, and penetrated roughly. She felt the tear of her flesh, and she cried out. She bled profusely. She cried all through the crudity of his movements. He didn't enjoy the act. When he got off her, and got dressed, he stunned her with a slap on her face.

She never forgot, nor forgave, the state she found herself in. The next morning her mind cleared. She spent most of the day on the bed pondering her rape. She cried. She slept. She woke up and called helplessly for her mother. She washed herself obsessively. She refused to eat for days. She kept talking about wanting to die. She was listless, her eyes became dull, her movements sluggish. She sat and stared out of the window. She walked oddly for weeks.

Her compromise had betrayed her. For the first time she realised how alone she was in Lagos. With no one to turn to, nowhere to run, she learned her first lesson. She gave the appearance of being subdued. With this pretence a strange quietness insinuated itself over her. But within her there was a seething fermention which fed on the morass of her life. She learned to be patient. She learned to wait.

It was around this time that something unusual entered her life.

Ifeyiwa and her husband had moved house from Ajegunle to Alaba, from one ghetto to another. Their former room in Ajegunle had been continuously flooded during the rainy season. Their new compound was directly opposite Omovo's. Ifeyiwa fetched water from Omovo's compound because both houses were owned by the same landlord. There wasn't a well in Ifeyiwa's compound. She had been fetching water from the house opposite for some time without being aware of Omovo's existence. She first noticed him one day when he was painting in front of his room. She stopped to watch what he was painting. She had a bucket of well water on her head. He turned, saw her, then looked away. After a moment he looked at her again, longer. She felt her heart beat unusually fast. He went on staring at her. Then, to her astonishment, he smiled. And to calm her beating heart, and to prevent herself from dropping the bucket because of the sheer force of her unexpected confusion, she said: 'Do you paint?'

He looked at the canvas. He had almost finished an acrylic study of a woman plaiting the hair of a younger woman. The woman whose hair was being plaited had a child playing at her feet. All around them was the vibrant decrepitude of the compound. There was a green bird perched on the wall near them. The bird seemed to be staring at the child.

'Yes,' Omovo said finally. 'Yes, I paint.'

With a touch of wonder in her voice, Ifeyiwa said: 'Your painting is like a magic mirror.'

After a while Omovo said: 'I have been noticing you for a while. Are you new in the compound?'

'Yes. But I live across the road, in the house opposite.'

Then they were silent. Omovo stared at her with an intense scrutiny. Then, with his head turning in slow degrees, he returned to his painting. She waited for a bit, not knowing why. Then she said: 'Goodbye.'

And she left.

The next time she saw him he was sitting in front of his room reading a novel she had just finished. It was Ngugi's *Weep Not Child*. He didn't look up when she paused and stared at him. For the first time she noticed the softness of his features and the sharpness of his eyes. It was only when she came back with the bucket of water, and spilt some in front of him, that he looked up. He smiled. After that, she noticed that whenever he looked at her there was the flame of a secret interest in his eyes. Then their coincidental encounters in the backyard became more deliberate. One day she was washing clothes at the backyard. He came to do some washing as well and they fell into a discussion of Ngugi's novel.

'I cried when I finished it,' she said.

'I didn't like the idea of the hero wanting to commit suicide.'

'The world should not make people want to do that.'

'He was young, and too much of a visionary, and people of the world are trapped in social roles.'

'I like the title.'

'It's from Walt Whitman.'

'Weep not, child.'

'Let none of us weep.'

Omovo paused. His eyes narrowed. He continued.

'Weeping doesn't really do anything. It only cleanses us and prepares us for more weeping. Meanwhile the mad world goes on. Wicked things go on happening. The world has forgotten how to love. The gods don't respond to weeping any more.'

'Do you know the gods, Omovo?'

'They are here. Somewhere.'

'What book are you reading now?'

'A collection of short stories by a Russian writer called Chekhov.'

'Are you enjoying them?'

'Yes. They are strange. At first they seem ordinary. But the writer notices everything and he makes no judgements. He makes his characters so real that I see them here in Alaba. But I got a bit tired of "A boring tale". Maybe it's the title. Maybe I didn't understand it.'

And so their innocent conversation turned into an exploration. There was no strain. Each time they met they always had something to talk about. The swell of their feelings always provided some excuse or another for meeting in the backyard. And whatever grew between them grew in the midst of the grime, the overcrowding, and the wretched sanitation of the compound. Ifeyiwa began to go to his compound more than she needed. She washed clothes there more often than she had done. She fetched more water than they could use. And every errand she made had to involve a call at Omovo's compound. It became necessary for her to see him, and to know that he existed.

He became her contact with what was loveable. Her feelings for him grew into a yearning that dominated her days. She sometimes had dreams in which she made love to him. For her he became a spiritual husband, one that she could only embrace in her dreams and fantasies. It got to a point that when her husband forced her into having sex she could only survive the experience by imagining that it was really Omovo who was on top of her. But when she saw Omovo afterwards she felt ashamed of her imaginings. And then she bore the ordeals with her husband by thinking about death till he was finished. She would then make sure that she avoided Omovo for a day or two. And when she did see him it was with a deep unhappiness, and a deep joy. She began to see him as an escape from reality.

She sensed in his eyes the possibilities of the love that had been denied her. She was fascinated by the despair and the brightness of his paintings. She liked the way he stared into the distance, the way he seemed to enter another realm, when an idea possessed him. She liked the way his face lit up in moments of fervour. It could be said that her love grew also from the innocence of the private images she had of him. One such image was of Omovo standing in front of his canvas, a brush in one hand, his clothes mottled with paint, his eyes staring into another dimension of reality. Another one was of Omovo returning wearily from work, his face pale with dust, sweat, and exhaustion. When she saw him like that she had the desire to bathe the tiredness from his limbs. But when he went to his room, had a bath, slept, and reappeared in the compound she never failed to be quickened by his look of a wise child, and by the radiance of his sleepy charm. He reminded her of a child that is lost but not frightened. He sometimes also reminded her of her brother who had drowned.

Their affection grew in an atmosphere of risk. It was probably the risk that made it sweeter. They began to extend their meetings from the backyard to the streets. They would arrange to meet at an appointed place. Sometimes when she was returning from an errand she would find him coming towards her. They began to take long walks together. They walked down bushpaths, dirt tracks, streets without names. They passed huts devastated by the rains. Children, with their heads covered in sand, played and cried on the roads. And even the dirt littering the streets, the rotting fruits and vegetables, and the carcasses of dead animals at the roadsides, became part of the enchantment of their walks. Ifeyiwa thought often of those moments they spent together. They walked through scenes of unbearable poverty, their faces lit up by the sun. She would tell him about some of her fears. He would tell her stories, he would talk about his ideas, his visions, his torments. They talked mostly about unhappy things. And yet Ifeyiwa mostly remembered the joy of those days, with every moment vibrant and golden.

She also couldn't forget a particular night when her husband went on shouting at her and beat her up. When he went out she was filled with uncontrollable anger and bitterness. She contemplated killing herself. Then she decided that she was going to walk the three hundred miles home to her village. She left the house, having packed her things, with this insane intention. But at the bus-stop she ran into Omovo and after she had cried on his shoulder and told him of her anguish, he persuaded her to stay and to think more carefully about her chosen act. They went on a long walk. He carried her bag. Then afterwards she went home. She was grateful to him for having saved her from herself. She liked to think he had also saved her for himself. The secret and dangerous love for him grew more careless. Her mind was trapped in a maze of desires, of pain, of compromises, and of love. But she felt she could find happiness and could feel more complete.

In between these heightened moments, however, were hours and hours of a dreary life. In the mornings she cleaned the bathroom, fetched water for her husband to bath with, made his food, swept the room, washed the plates. When her husband had gone to town she bathed, ate, went to the market, and stayed at the shop selling his provisions. When she could find the time she read a novel, or a magazine, or she obligingly plaited the hair of one of the compound women.

She was revolted by the decay of life about her. The women around seemed to age so quickly. They bore many children and struggled to feed and clothe them. They quarrelled endlessly about all manner of small things. They became embroiled in petty compound intrigues. The hot afternoons poured through their lives and made them look much older than they actually were. They became flabby-breasted, weary, absent-minded, servile. She didn't want to be like them. She didn't want to have poorly dressed miserable children crying at her feet. She was quietly proud of her education and took pains to maintain herself, to keep herself youthful against the merciless passing of time. Her pride isolated her, and made her an outsider.

Seeing that her life was drifting away, and that she had no girls of her age to talk to, she managed to persuade her husband to allow her to take up evening classes. She knew that getting a job was completely out of the question. He finally agreed, mainly because she nagged him about it, and he interpreted this as a warming of her spirit towards him, but also because it would give him an edge over his mates. (At a drinking session later he boasted, saying 'Ah-ah, my wife attends evening classes, you know. Can your wife even read a newspaper sef?') She enrolled for a secretarial course which included typing, accountancy, and shorthand. But when, after a week's trial, she began to return later than he expected, he began to worry. One night, as he sat in the room, brooding, waiting for her, he found himself imagining all sorts of things. He imagined her getting up to funny things with the teachers. Driven by an excess of insecurity he got dressed and went to the school to spy on her. The school consisted of a small, uncompleted wooden hut. It was incredibly stuffy inside. There were no fans. The electricity had been seized, and classes were conducted by the light of hurricane lamps. He was confronted with a multitude of ghetto people, young men and women, who were being adroitly cheated in their intense hunger for knowledge, for some meagre skill, for certificates with which they could get jobs. They were crammed in classes that were short of just about everything – desks, chairs, blackboards, teachers, typewriters, and books. And what he saw convinced him. He found Ifeyiwa laughing with a group of boys and girls. Her face shone with sweat. Her eyes were animated. She was possessed of a brightness and a sociability that he had never seen before. His heart was lacerated by the fact that she seemed more natural with her age group than with him. More than that there was the feeling that once she left his company she became another person, she changed into something inaccessible to him. Overcome with a fit of jealousy he stormed into the midst of the chattering young men and women, seized Ifeyiwa by the arm, and dragged her home. He forbade her to return to the evening classes again.

Desperation filled her daily. Her patience and her quietness began to turn sour. Her mind began to work strangely. She started to have fantasies of murdering her husband. Her fantasies became so intense and detailed that her mind began to frighten her. Then she began to have dreams in which her husband turned into a hairy monster who shut her away in a cave. In one such dream she got hold of a knife and managed to kill him, and she laughed till darkness came over her. Then she woke up and found that her husband had been shaking her. He looked at her with strange eyes and asked why she had been laughing in her sleep. The contrast horrified her. But she mumbled something, turned over on her side, and pretended that she had fallen back into sleep. After that night she took to sleeping on the floor. A few days later her husband fell ill and she convinced herself that she had somehow poisoned the man by a deviousness of which she wasn't conscious. She developed a morbid suspicious of decay, and of punishment and of visitations. She was plagued with dreams of rats and suffocating forests. She began to see herself as a purveyor of sadness.

FIVE

I feyiwa began kindling a fire on which to cook a fresh pot of soup. Her hands went through the practised motions. But her mind was in a crepuscular and dimly remembered landscape. She thought about an item she had read in the newspapers. Her village was still in a state of aggression with the neighbouring village of Ugbofia. The item read: 'Farms have been ravaged and there have been killings. Stout adults are believed to be standing armed at the village perimeters, guarding it.' A delegation had been sent to effect a truce. The report concluded by saying that 'the peace seemed an uneasy one'.

The two villages were about a mile from one another. The stream that flowed past both villages connected them in many ways. In the past they had intermarried. Then a boundary dispute grew and acquired serious dimensions. They now regarded one another with deep mutual suspicion. The things that connected them also provided elements for discord. Histories were dredged up. One village called the other the descendants of slaves. The other village replied in words just as strong. The forest that separated them, the stream that connected them, the air that they both breathed, became permeated with violence. Ifeyiwa wondered bitterly why there should be any fighting at all.

Compound women came into the kitchen and tinkered around. Outside, children screamed. A fowl strayed into the kitchen and began clucking. She chased it out. The embers of the fire crackled and she fed it some more twigs. She was woken from her thoughts by her husband's voice.

'Ifeyiwa, is my water ready?'

The voice made her shudder. She stiffened.

He stood outside the kitchen. When he got no response he stuck his head round the zinc door. Then he came in. She was crouched in a corner, fanning the embers into a flame. She looked up at him, her eyes red with tears. He had a wrapper round his waist and a towel round his neck. He was hairy-chested.

'Ifeyiwa! You are here in the kitchen. So why don't you answer me?' he said with all of his mouth, believing that the louder he talked the more commanding he appeared, and the more people listened.

But Ifeyiwa stayed silent. She blew furiously at the embers till the kitchen became suffused with thick grey smoke. He chuckled, shook his head, and went out towards the bathroom.

Ifeyiwa went on fanning the fire. The firewood was wet. Smoke rose into her face. She coughed and tears poured down her face. Her husband came back and said: 'Ifi! Ifi! There is another rat in the trap, you hear? When you've finished go and remove it before it starts to smell. After that I want you to go to the shop and take care of things till I arrive, you hear?'

She remained silent. Then she coughed.

'If you are coughing why don't you leave the kitchen, eh?'

Silence.

'Foolish girl. Choke as much as you like, hah!'

Silence.

Exasperated, he slammed the zinc door and went into the slime-ridden bathroom.

When he had gone the fire sprang up. The yellow flames lit up her sweating tear-mingled face. Then she got up, opened the door, and went outside to get some fresh air. She sat on a stool and listened to her husband bathing. She looked over the soggy backyard. The place was a clutter of unwashed plates, rusted buckets, and babies' potties. The wall had jagged edges of broken glass on its top as a deterrent to thieves. It was only when she remembered she was ·meeting Omovo later in the evening that she smiled. Something kindled within her.

But later that afternoon Tuwo paid a significant visit to Ifeyiwa's husband. He knocked on the door and waited. A loud voice from within called:

'Come in if you are good-looking!'

Tuwo entered. Takpo was sitting on the edge of the bed. Before him, on the small centre table, was a plate of steaming eba and a bowl of vegetable soup. He barely looked up when Tuwo came in.

'Welcome, my townsman. Come and join me in my poor man's

food,' Takpo said, as he swallowed a handful of eba that could easily have choked a lesser man.

'Thank you, but I have eaten already,' replied Tuwo, who had some difficulty preventing his saliva from interfering with the dignity of his refusal. The gusto with which Takpo ate tickled his throat and made him hungry.

'So how is the wife?' Tuwo asked after a moment's silence, suitably toning down the affectation of his speech.

'Emm, she's fine, she dey.'

There was another silence. Takpo was not one to talk while eating. He had an excellent appetite and he gulped the food with shameless, concentrated relish. Tuwo took the opportunity to look round the room, even though he was quite well acquainted with it. The room was fairly large. There were three cheap cushion chairs, a centre table, a large bed, an ancient radiogram which looked as if it had not played a sound in many years, and a reading table on which were some of Ifeyiwa's books and magazines. In a corner of the room there was a full-length mirror which gave distorted reflections. On the walls there were almanacs of their home-town dignitaries and photographs of Takpo and Ifeyiwa. In one of the photographs she sat in a rather stiff pose, unsmiling. Takpo stood beside her, dominant and proud, and he wore a traditional wrapper and a white shirt. There were other photographs of Takpo standing, legs apart, in front of his provision store, and of him reading a newspaper. There were mildewed posters of white women drinking Coca-Cola, and faded postcards of various cities in the world.

When Takpo finished eating he washed his hands, wiped his mouth, and took a long gulp from his glass of stout. He went and sat in a cushion chair. With his fingernails he picked at fibres of meat that had lodged between his teeth.

'So, Tuwo, how are you? Are you still running after all the girls in the area, eh?' Takpo said eventually, his eyes dilating. Then he chuckled. His face crumpled in mirth.

Tuwo smiled somewhat chillingly. He might have been contemplating the fact that he had just about survived being married to a tough and slightly bearded woman. He had developed a passionate lust for her and married her in spite of all the warnings from his father that 'she is the kind of man-woman that will scrape your head-o. Before you know it you will be bald.' On their first night together she 'humped' him till it was said that he had a temporary stoop and had to walk around with a walking stick for an entire week. When she pounded yam it was with the

90

same uncontrollable energy, the same symbolic drive, and she wore out three mortars and two beds in their first month. He soon realised his mistake. She was fearfully possessive and domineering. He found himself living under her relentless control. She began to change every aspect of his routines. She went with him everywhere. She was loud, lusty, and picked arguments indiscriminately, in the backyard or even at a party. She criticised him mercilessly. They fought for days without end. Her passion for quarrelling was matched only by her passion for sex. In three months every valuable thing he owned was destroyed in the fights. Harassed, maddened, and on the perpetual brink of losing his job, Tuwo couldn't take it any more. One morning, in the midst of a new quarrel, Tuwo seized a machete and chased her round the room. He lashed at her with the machete twice and missed both times. Murder raged in his blood. He pursued her out into the compound and chased her down the streets. He was like a madman that day. He didn't catch her, but he stormed back home and threw her possessions out into the street. That night she came and packed her things in a van. She was heard to utter the ominous curse that one day someone would chase him around with a machete as he had chased her. Then she left his life forever.

When the storm of that tempestuous passion blew over, Tuwo found a new diversion: he discovered young women. He was always suspected of having had secret affairs with women in the compound, but his preference now was for the younger ones. That may well be the reason why he was always stumbling upon Omovo and Ifeyiwa as they chatted in the backyard. It may also be the reason why he seemed always to be watching Omovo. It had crossed his mind that Omovo was having an affair with the lissom and desirable Ifeyiwa. And he was somewhat envious. He began to have designs on Ifeyiwa the first day he saw her. But she always ignored him, always seemed to shrink from his contact. He felt that her husband didn't deserve her because he was too coarse. And Omovo was too young to enjoy her. Besides, Omovo had to be put in his proper place. Since Tuwo had received an early pension from the ministry, and had been planning to go into business, he had nothing better to do with his time.

His smile grew less chilling and became ironic, as if he were amused at a secret joke. 'Yes,' he replied at last.' The girls are fine. They grow riper every day.'

Takpo laughed out loud. 'So, what would you like to drink?'

'Ogogoro would be okay.'

Takpo fetched some, and two glasses, and they drank in silence for a while.

'My friend,' Tuwo began, a little uncertain. 'I came to warn you about your wife . . .'

Takpo sat up straight. His eyes became alert. 'It's that boy, isn't it?'

Tuwo didn't say anything.

'I heard two women saying that he is having something with Ifeyiwa and that they are always talking in the backyard.' Takpo paused. 'I like the boy. He is quiet. Do you think . . . ?'

Tuwo shrugged. Takpo fell back in the chair and shut his eyes.

'I asked Ifeyiwa about it. She said they just talk about books, that's all. But she didn't look at me as she said it. She has been strange from the day I married her. But now . . .' Takpo looked old and tired. Blue shadows appeared under his eyes. 'The boy has started painting again.'

'Yes. I saw him.'

'The other day I wanted to ask him to paint me and Ifeyiwa. But when I saw his bald head again I couldn't ask him. He is a nice boy, a strange boy. But he would not dare to touch my wife.'

Tuwo smiled a little pityingly and said: 'In the morning, before we began cleaning the compound, I saw them talking. You need to have seen them. The whole compound watched them, you know. You need to see the way her eyes shone on him. She didn't even hear me when I greeted her.'

Takpo fidgeted. He emptied his glass of ogogoro. Then he poured himself some more. 'I have to see them with my own two eyes first before I will do anything.'

'True.'

'Maybe he has not heard what I did to dat foolish photographer.'

'What did you do?'

He gave Tuwo a strange and terrible look. 'I sent two hefty men to beat him up one night. They beat sense into him and he ran away from the compound.'

'You are a hard man-o.'

'Didn't you know? Well, now you know. But I have to see them with my two eyes first.'

A moment afterwards Ifeyiwa came into the room. She looked beautiful in her violet blouse and her single wrapper which stopped just under her knees. Her eyes were still inflamed from all the smoke in the kitchen. There was a bruised innocence on the simple charm of her face. She greeted Tuwo traditionally and asked her husband if he had finished eating. He said nothing. She began clearing the table. With her hand she swept the bones on the table into the soup bowl. Then she wiped the table with a rag. She put the two plates and the tumbler on a tray. Then she said to her husband: 'Would you like some more water?'

He still said nothing. Then she became aware of the silence in the room. She sensed that her entry had interrupted something. She sensed that they must have been talking about her. She drew herself together, intact, against the awkwardness she felt. In a calm voice she asked again if he wanted more water. There was a longer silence. Takpo's eyes were narrowed and distant.

Tuwo leaned forward. 'Look, Takpo,' he said. 'Answer your wife.'

Takpo stared at him, then at Ifeyiwa. His voice quivered with barely contained anger when he said. 'Pick up the tray and go. Go! Can't you see that we were talking? You dese foolish girls of nowadays, hah! You see two men talking and you ask me nonsense question about water. Get out before I begin to beat you!'

Takpo got carried away, then he shouted, stood up, and pushed Ifeyiwa. She went crashing at the door. Tuwo rushed to help her.

'Takpo, did you have to do that?'

Ifeyiwa got up and picked up the fallen objects. The two plates had broken into bits. Bones had scattered everywhere. The tumbler alone survived the fall. She picked up the broken plate shards and the bones and put them on the tray. She got the broom and the dustpan next to the cupboard and swept the jagged plate pieces. She did all this methodically, patiently. Her face was blank and her eyes were as hard as crystals. When she finished she left the room as she had come in: detached, intact, and calm. She walked out, the tray in her hands, with a sinister air of dignity.

When she shut the door behind her Tuwo let out a deep breath. He got up and sat down again. He started to speak, but he stopped. Then he looked round the room and at Takpo, as if he was seeing everything for the first time. He understood what had always been wrong about the atmosphere of the room. The unreality of the marriage became clear to him. In the past Takpo had endlessly boasted to him about his beautiful wife, about how obedient and respectful she was, and about how much love there was between them. He boasted that he was paying for her education and that when she qualified as a secretary he would leave the running of the shop to her and open another business. He even said that they watched Indian films together and danced at parties on weekends. Tuwo knew then that it was all a lie, and this confused him.

'You didn't have to do that,' he said. 'She is still young. She will learn. If I knew you would treat her like that I would have kept my mouth shut.'

Takpo stared stonily at the door. After a long uneasy silence he said: 'No wonder your wife used to beat you up. Dis is how to train a woman to become a husband-fearing wife. You are too soft with women. Dat's why your wife could fit to misbehave and quarrel with you and do what she like.'

'Is that so?'

'Yes.'

Tuwo fidgeted. Then he got up. 'My townsman,' he said. 'I have to go.'

'Thank you.'

'For what?'

'For telling me all these things.'

'Don't thank me.'

'Don't worry, I know how to treat women.'

Tuwo went to the door. Takpo gave him that strange and terrible stare. Then he said: 'I thank you anyway. But I still have to see them with my own two eyes – first.'

His voice was unemotional. His eyes became blank. Tuwo opened the door and gently shut it behind him. Takpo remained in his chair, in the drab room, brooding.

SIX

Omovo did not sleep for very long. When he woke up he was sweating. He got up and dried himself with a towel. When he went to the sitting room he startled his father who sat alone on a cushion chair reading a letter. There was an envelope and some photographs on the centre table. The handwriting on the envelope looked like Okur's, but Omovo wasn't sure. When his father saw Omovo he acted strangely. He quickly gathered the letter, the envelope, and the photographs and hurried into his room. He looked older and more defeated than Omovo had ever seen him.

Omovo waited in the sitting room with the hope that his father would come out again. Then after a while he heard his father talking to himself. It was as if he were explaining something to an imaginary creditor. Omovo gave up waiting and went outside.

The sky was bright. The sun was like a flattened, fiery orange. Everything around was clearly defined. The road was dusty. He could see far into the distance. He could see the houses, the sheds, the children playing, the men dancing in front of record stores, and the blue outlines of the forest. He even fancied that he could see how the heat haze slightly distorted the shapes of objects.

As he went along he tried to avoid kicking empty milk tins, stepping onto patches of mud, or stumbling over pariah dogs with flies buzzing around their sore ears. He was also wary of treading on knurls of dehydrated faeces that lurked on the road. It depressed him that he had to keep a careful eye on the ground to avoid the unclean aspects of his society. 'The problem is with me,' he thought. 'I see these things too much. I wonder if it is good.'

He had been walking along, thinking, when he felt a shadow over him.

'Hello, Omovo. How are you?'

For a moment he was startled. It was Dr Okocha, the old painter. He wore a paint-stained blue shirt and khaki trousers. There were stains on his hair and face. He looked tired. Omovo smiled.

'Were you surprised to see me?'

Omovo nodded, thinking: 'Another problem with me. I live too much inside my head. Maybe it is bad.' Then, aloud, he said: 'Yes, you surprised me.'

'So how are you?'

'Fine, I suppose.'

'I haven't seen you since the exhibition.'

'Yes.'

'Did you know that two of my paintings were bought?'

'Yes, I'm pleased for you.'

'Thank you. I was quite drunk that night and later I heard that they seized your painting.'

'I've almost forgotten it.'

'I don't believe you, but I am sorry. No one has the right to seize an artist's work.'

Omovo was silent.

'I didn't even get a good chance to look at it. What reason did they give?'

Omovo shrugged. 'They said I was mocking our country's progress.'

'And so they mock our freedom.'

'I wasn't mocking anything.'

'I know. But what can we do? If you tell the truth you are in trouble. But if you see the truth and you keep quiet your spirit begins to die. The position of the artist is a terrible one.'

Omovo said nothing.

'Have you tried getting it back?'

'No. I've lost interest in it. Besides, where would I start?'

Dr Okocha stared hard at Omovo. Then he said: 'Well, I hope they give it back to you. If this sort of thing gets worse we are all in trouble.'

'We are in trouble anyway.'

There was a short silence. Omovo tried to change the subject. 'So how's the work?'

'Which one?'

'Not the signwriting. Your real work.'

96

The old painter looked even more tired than before. He grimaced. His eyes became dull. He looked at if he were staring some sort of defeat in the face.

'I haven't done a single painting since you came to the shed.'

He stopped, looked around, and continued. 'The signwriting, work for bread and butter, is stealing all my time.' It was the old painter's turn to change the subject. 'So where are you going?'

'To see Okoro, and then maybe to see Keme.'

'Your journalist friend?'

'Yes. We were at the exhibition together.'

'I saw him.'

'But something happened afterwards.'

'After they seized your work?'

'Yes.'

'Hope nothing bad?'

'Yes, bad,' Omovo said, but he didn't continue.

'Are you still painting? Have you done something new?'

'I am trying. It's difficult. After the exhibition I and Keme saw something terrible. I dreamt about it twice. It keeps haunting me. It wouldn't let me go. And I've been trying to paint it, to leave some sort of record that I witnessed it.'

'Have you begun it?'

'Yes. But I tore up what I had done.'

'Why?'

'I'm not sure. The subject is very difficult. And it takes me a long time to understand what I have seen. And there are some things I am afraid of painting.'

'Why?'

'I don't know. Maybe I am still afraid of the original experience.'

Dr Okocha thought about it, and then asked: 'Like what, for instance?'

Omovo looked at him. 'Like something I saw during the Civil War.'

The old painter's eyes became intense. His wrinkles deepened into hieroglyphs of private torment. Omovo hesitated. He did not often talk about these things. But the intensity of the old painter's eyes made it necessary for him to continue.

'There was a curfew then, and I had gone walking through the streets of Ughelli. They had warned us not to go far from home. But something in the air, something in the mood of the town, made me restless. Planes were flying past overhead, circling the town. I heard guns firing far away. I heard people screaming. I had this desire to see things. I had this wanderlust. I was a child and war did not make sense to me. I thought that war was only a game that children played. On the main road, near the police station, I saw the corpse of a dead man.'

'An Igbo man.'

'Yes, an Igbo man. Anyway I stood there and stared at the dead man. His body had begun to swell. His stomach was a mess of flesh and green blood. He stank. The flies were thick all over him. I didn't move. I went on staring at him.'

Omovo paused. There were deep shadows on the old painter's face. Omovo cursed himself.

'Then a vulture swooped past my face. The flies rose and scattered. Then I saw the dead man's eyes. One of them was hooded and big. The other was normal. Then I became aware that the dead man was staring at me, fixing me. It seemed as if he were watching me. I was transfixed. It was only when someone knocked me on the head that I became aware of myself. I opened my mouth, but no sound came out. I looked up and saw the man who had knocked me. His eyes were crossed and his face was terrible. "Get away," he said. "What's wrong with you? Why are you looking at a dead body?" I began crying. Then I became aware of the confusion all around. People were running, as if out of a fire. Women screamed with their children on their backs. The men were running all over the place. The world was like a nightmare. "Whose son are you?" the man asked. Then for the first time I realised that he was a soldier. I pointed at the dead man's eyes. "Why are they open?" I think I said. But before he could say anything a crowd ran between us. I felt myself kicked everywhere by the mighty feet of adults. Someone tripped and fell on the dead body. I found myself at the other end of the road, in a corner. I got up and wandered through the confusion of the town. Then my father saw me, rushed to me, lifted me high and ran home with me.'

Omovo paused again. The old painter's face was drawn.

'I dreamt about the dead man's eyes for two weeks. Because of them I couldn't sleep. When the lights went out I saw the eyes on the wall, on the ceiling, watching me, fixing me. Then I began to see them everywhere. Suddenly while playing I would begin to scream. I was ten years old but I think those eyes began to make me go mad. It got so worrying that Dad had to take me to a herbalist in the village to cure me of seeing the eyes. I stopped seeing them, but the herbalist didn't really cure me because I have never forgotten them. I can't remember exactly how they look, and I will never paint them, but those eyes will never leave me.'

When Omovo finished he felt empty and exhausted. He felt that he had spoken too much, that he had talked himself into a kind of unreality. He heard the wind howl gently. He imagined he could hear the sunlight as it poured on the ground. The old painter's face clouded over. Eventually, in a hollow voice, he said:

'I feel the same way. I have not told my experiences in the war to anybody, except my wife. And I haven't painted anything about it either. I remember so much that I can't really remember anything. That is one of the problems of the artist.'

Then Dr Okocha fell silent. After a while he said: 'The original experience must be the guide. But what you make of it, what you bring back from it, the vision, call it what you will, is the most important thing. What you forget returns in a hundred other shapes. It becomes the true material of invention. To learn how to remember creatively is to learn how to feel. But to paint that dream of yours will mean a long descent into yourself. It will also mean learning how to think differently. I am happy for you, for you are young and you are on a threshold.'

He fell silent again. While they had been talking some boys in the area had started up a game of football on the street. The old painter watched them, his eyes far away. Omovo watched them as well. The boys began shouting. A goal could have been scored but the goalkeeper's foot knocked the ball over into the scum of green water. They fetched it out with a stick, resumed their game, and unluckily one of the boys kicked the ball and it went and hit an old man on the head. He had been riding through the game on his equally ancient bicycle. The boys rolled over laughing. The old man got off his bicycle and chased the boys. They scattered in many directions. He couldn't catch any of them so he chased the ball instead.

'The young boys of nowadays don't respect old people,' he muttered as he seized the ball, which had rolled near Dr Okocha and Omovo. The old man thumped the ball, but it jumped out of his hands. He caught it and, removing the pin holding his trouser fly together, pierced a hole in the ball. He flashed a wizened smile at Dr Okocha, who nodded, then he got on his bicycle and rode away, chuckling to himself. The boys abused him. The game ended. Dr Okocha and Omovo walked on.

'Yes, I'm happy for you,' the old painter continued. 'This is one painting that will change you. Craft is important. The greater the idea, the greater the craft you need. But in finding the right colours, the right

99

shapes, to capture that dream you will begin to discover unsuspected dimensions within you.'

They passed the scumpool with its green water. Omovo stared at its surface. He stared at the rubbish that had been poured into the stagnant pool. He noticed a mattress in it on which had grown bright red mushrooms. He shivered. Then be began to see why Ifeyiwa had been silent when he showed her his painting of the scumscape.

'We don't look at ugly things enough,' he said.

'Ugliness is the face we always turn away from,' the old painter said. 'When things are bad people don't want to face the truth. I don't know why the old painters always made Truth a beautiful woman. Truth is an ugly woman. But her ugliness exists only in the eyes. I would choose the face of the Medusa as a good image of Truth. She is actually a profoundly beautiful woman and we can only face her with the help of a mirror. That mirror is art.'

'In ugliness,' Omovo said, 'we see ourselves as we never want to.'

'And so ugliness festers while the people cry for images of beauty, for illusions.'

'But how can we be happy if there is so much ugliness around and if we paint the ugly truth?'

'How can we be happy if we lie to ourselves?'

'We can't.'

'Things have got to improve. But first we have to see ourselves clearly, as we are.'

'But you don't really paint ugliness,' Omovo said.

The old painter smiled. 'I used to. That's all I used to paint. I would draw the bad roads, paint the women in their filthy backyards. And I did it so much that my life became filled with misery. You reproduce your work in your life. And I am poor. My life became unbearable. So I started to paint bright things, happy subjects, the smile of the child on the edge of a sea, the proud hunger of the truck-pusher, the defiance of the motor tout. My life opened up a little. Now I try to do both, to have the ugliness as well as the dreams.'

'I can't seem to do anything. Often I am overwhelmed by unhappiness.'

The old painter stopped and looked at him affectionately. Then he put a hand on Omovo's shoulder and said: 'You are young. Everything you feel and see now will be your reservoir later. But you feel things too much. Art is a poor substitute for real life. I like you. But live! Live fully.

Act whenever you feel the necessity. Don't live only in your head. You are in the world.'

Dr Okocha went on walking. Omovo stayed still. He experienced a rush of being. Then he touched his head and felt the fresh bristles and his sweating skin. He could not see beyond the distance of run-down houses and dust-covered bushes. People went past him as he stood. He didn't notice them. After a moment he hurried and caught up with the old painter, who said:

'I will be out of town for two weeks on a commission. When I come back I will look you up and see how you are doing. We have a duty to make manifest the good dreams, the visions, that we are given. An Indian poet once wrote that "In dreams begin responsiblities." I prefer the word "vision" to "dreams" in this context.'

He stopped again. And this time Omovo knew that he was in a hurry and had to go. Omovo, grateful for the older man's interest, could not find anything to say. The old painter smiled. His eyes brightened. In a dramatic flourish, waving his hand as if throwing confetti in the air, he said:

'We cast our nets out into the darkness and draw in ourselves. Sometimes, if we are fortunate, we also bring back . . .'

'Bright corals.'

'Bright things.'

'With light and wonder.'

'I will see you when I return.'

Dr Okocha turned somewhat abruptly and began striding towards his workshed. Omovo watched him stride away. He felt a great wave of affection for the older man. As he began walking to Okoro's place, he pondered on the things the old painter had said. He became so lost in his thoughts that he walked right into a crowd of young men. They were arguing about money. They did not notice him in their midst. He left their midst and stood away from them, resting his back on the wall of a house. He watched them. The more he looked at them the more he noticed the individuals within the crowd. They were all different from one another. The only thing they had in common was their frantic hunger to make money. He listened to them as they talked about deals, contracts, loans. He imagined that they dreamt of deals. He had seen others like them, victims of poverty. When they returned from work late in the evening they talked incoherently to themselves, they made calculations with their fingers, blind to the world which someday they might rule. Premature wrinkles ravaged their faces. As Omovo carried on walking to his friend's place he felt, suddenly, that he didn't understand the world. In the face of its manifestation, its realities, he seemed to have only bewilderment and morbid fascination.

SEVEN

W hen he got to the wooden bridge, a short cut which spanned the marsh separating Alaba from Ajegunle, the woman in the tall shack wouldn't let him cross over because she had no change. He had to wait for a few people to pass. The woman had drooping lips and large eyes. She sat behind the counter, eating beans from a plate with her fingers, and eyeing Omovo disdainfully. When she had got enough change Omovo paid his five kobo.

'Go gently,' the woman said, as he began the crossing.

The bridge wobbled. There were no railings on either side. As Omovo crossed over, he felt vulnerable, he felt that a false step could send him falling into the marsh. Birds thrilled all around. Weeds grew luxuriantly from the marsh, which had long become a dumping ground for communal rubbish. The air was permeated with a damp, sulphurous stench. The marsh was surrounded by a haze of forest.

Omovo felt someone step on the other side of the bridge. It wobbled dangerously. He waited. The person who had stepped on the bridge was a woman in high-heeled shoes. She wore a bright yellow dress and she swayed her hips as she walked. Apart from Omovo there was no one else around to appreciate the sensuality of her movements. The bridge shook. Omovo said:

'Take it easy. Don't make yanga on this bridge-o.'

But she carried on swaying. She brushed past him with such violent nonchalance that it was only the good fortune of having stepped aside which saved him from falling into the marsh. He went on. He was nearing the other side when he heard her heel scrape a dislodged plank. He heard her scream. Then he heard the dreaded splash. He ran over and managed to drag her out. Mud oozed from her brassiere. Her yellow dress was covered in green and black slime. She was extremely miserable and bad-tempered. She kept abusing Omovo, as if it had been his fault. One of her high-heeled shoes had completely vanished in the marsh. Omovo led her to the woman at the toll shed, who gave her some water with which to wash her feet. Then Omovo watched her leave. She didn't thank him. She was still bad-tempered and she walked gingerly down the street, holding up the bottom of her slime-covered dress.

His friend, Okoro, was seeing off his new girlfriend when Omovo arrived.

'Hey! Hi man! Long time no see,' shouted Okoro in his incorrigible American accent.

Okoro was of medium height and good-looking. His prematurely wrinkled forehead shone with perspiration. He had high cheekbones, and shadows under his eyes, and the vaguest terrain of a moustache. He was wearing a blue jacket, with sweat widening under the armpits, a pair of white trousers and black high-heeled shoes. He was brimming with enthusiasm. His new girlfriend was pimpled and pretty. She had wise eyes. She was wearing a white blouse over a red skirt. Okoro, putting his arm round her promising hips, said: 'Where are you coming from, man?'

'Home.'

'How have you been?'

'Fine. How are you?'

'Okay. Great.'

'Good.'

'I saw Keme.'

'What happened?'

'I'll tell you when I get back.'

'Are you going to introduce me?'

'Oh, don't you know her?'

'No.'

'Meet my girl, July, flavour of all months. July, meet Omovo, painter of all seasons.'

They shook hands.

'She's at the College of Technology.'

They stood regarding one another for a moment. Then Okoro said: 'Let me see her to the bus-stop, or do you want to come with us?'

'I'll wait. Is your door open?'

'Yeah. Everyone's out. I'll be back in a moment.'

Omovo watched them go. They had gone a short distance up the untarred street when Okoro, placing his arm possessively round her shoulders, turned around and winked. Omovo smiled, and went into Okoro's compound. His friend's room was small and stuffy. The windows had to be kept permanently shut because of the sewer smells that came in from the backyard. In spite of it being daylight all the curtains were shut, the room was quite dark, and the blue light was on. The blue lightbulb had been intended to give the room a romantic atmosphere. Omovo noticed the sex-smells and opened the windows. Light and vague sewer smells came in. Omovo, with nothing to do, looked round his friend's room with a stranger's eyes. It was something he had been practising. It was connected to his belief that he had to learn how to see more clearly, look more carefully, without strain, without prejudice. He had to learn how not to let his eyes be bewildered by manifestations, and thereby learn to treat appearances as signs and codes of the interior.

On the blue walls of his friend's room there was a poster of Fela Anikulapo Kuti, hand raised in a revolutionary gesture. Next to the poster was an Airways calendar with bright pictures of London, New York, Paris, and Amsterdam. The calendar was two years out of date. A large bed occupied most of the living space. There was a small round table next to the bed. There were two chairs. On the floor were scattered pairs of shoes and slippers. At the foot of the bed was a clothes rack, weighed down with the latest fashions. Omovo sat at the only big table in the room, on which an impressive stereo stood. The rest of the space on the table was taken up with application forms, cassettes, keys, address books, brochures of American universities, and correspondence course booklets. Okoro was studying for his Ordinary levels for the third time.

Omovo was exhausted by the scrutiny of his friend's room.

Usually when he came to visit the room would be rocking with loud music. The silence and the heat made him drowsy. He laid his head on the table and was beginning to doze when Okoro came back in and slapped him excitedly on the shoulder.

'What do you think of that broad, eh?' he asked. But without waiting for a reply he put on a record. Then he turned up the volume.

'Just what do you think, eh? Isn't she heavy, eh?' he said, shouting above the music.

Omovo made a vague gesture. Then he said: 'I expected you last Friday.'

'I went to a party with Dele.'

'Did he tell you we went to his place?'

'Yeah. The party was swell. That was where I met July. So what do you think of her, eh?'

'Lower the music.'

'What?'

'Lower the music.'

Okoro lowered the volume.

'I thought girls in higher education scared you.'

'Yeah, they do. They are too proud. But she's all right. You never can tell with these girls, man.'

'Sure.'

'Don't sound so bitter.'

'Me?'

'Yeah. Just because you had a girlfriend who left you as soon as she got an admission to the university.'

'What's that got to with it?'

'Frankly speaking, a girl like that never loved you in the first place.'

'Sure.'

Okoro stared at him. The music reached the point where he usually got carried away. He increased the volume, and made sinuous movements, his eyes rolling in disco-hall ecstacy. Okoro sang along with the lyrics which spoke of yearning and love. When the song ended Okoro shut the window and stood near the table. With a positively lecherous gleam in his eyes, he said:

'I met my girl at a party. Before I met her I was lonely, man. I saw her sitting with two other girls. She looked special, man. I don't know what came over me but I went over and said: "Would you mind dancing with me?" I was wearing my new jacket, not this one, another one. It cost a bomb. I also had on new shoes. Anyway, she looked at me with cool eyes and said "No". You won't believe it, man, but for a moment I stood there dumbfounded. I didn't know how I was going to walk back across the room. I thought she had said "No", that she wouldn't dance with me.'

'She did say "No".'

'Sure. But then she stood up and looked at me as if I was supposed to do something. Then I realised that she had said "Yes". Man, the English language confuses you sometimes. Anyway, we danced. She's a good dancer. You should feel her body, man. I don't want you to feel it, if you know what I mean.'

'Sure.'

'So anyway, I wrapped my arms round her. We danced close up. I asked about her. It took three records to get her talking. I put on my best accent and told her about myself, lying where necessary, you know.'

Okoro winked. Omovo smiled.

'Then I took her away from her friends. They didn't look too pleased about it, but who cares. A man only gets one chance. And before the party ended I was doing things to her that I couldn't have dreamt of. I was so happy, man. I can't tell you how happy I was. I felt powerful. I felt like I could move the world, and do all the things I hope to do. I felt lucky.'

Omovo began to feel uneasy, restless. He wasn't terribly interested in all the details that Okoro sounded as if he were going to launch into. Omovo picked up one of the booklets on government and put it back down again.

'Omovo, you know how hard it is. We all want love, man. It makes me feel lonely walking down the street and seeing everybody else holding a woman.'

Omovo said nothing. He sensed desperation in his friend's voice. They stayed silent. Okoro looked a little embarrassed.

'How are your studies?' Omovo asked, then wished he hadn't.

Okoro looked away. He increased the volume of the music till the room fairly rocked. Then staggering a little, as if he were exhausted, as if he had woken from a dream, he went to the bed, and sat. He stared ahead of him with a sad and vacant stillness. Then he stretched out on the bed, his shoes still on, and shut his eyes. The wrinkles deepened on his forehead.

Omovo watched him, saddened by the expression of pain on his face. The war had scarred Okoro forever, and in ways that were not always visible. When Omovo first met him, he had just finished secondary school and he used to talk obsessively about the war. He was driven then. Okoro had fought in the war, first as a boy cub attached to an officer. He used to sneak into villages near the fighting and steal food. He was a look-out who would climb up trees and watch out for invading soldiers and communicate what he saw by a system of signs. He survived three bombings, without the help of bunkers. He saw his village destroyed by air raids. He carried the wounded across minefields. He went on regular reconnaissances at night, deep in the forests, through fetid swamps, scouting out the whereabouts of troops. On one such reconnaissance he saw three of his friends killed by booby-traps. He was given a crash course in soldiery and conscripted into the main army. He wasn't yet seventeen. He used to talk about the war and how it interrupted his schooling, and about the horrible things he had witnessed, like a woman who was shot through the breast, or the baby that sat screaming in the midst of an air raid, or a soldier who was fifteen years old and who ran through the forests with a leg that had been pulped by bullets. He talked about the long nights in the swamp, with no blankets, while it poured down with rain, and while villages burned about him, while the bombs fell, and lightning became indistinguishable from relentless shelling, and thunder inseparable from the bombs. He talked about friends who had deserted and who were caught by their comrades and shot point-blank. He talked about how lucky he had been to escape injury and death, about how his father had died on the battlefield and was buried in a mass grave. When the war ended he resumed his education. And when Omovo first met him he burned with vitality and fire, with despair and hope. He burned with the feral determination to reconstruct something from his life, to make up for the lost years. Omovo saw him as a hero, as one who bore the ineradicable memory of violence, as one who had come of age in the midst of ambushes and shelling, as one who had seen death, seeing the dying with the eyes of youth. But the years came and went. Okoro got various jobs and gradually his fire died away. Working in offices for so long and so aimlessly, living a life of mindless routines and grey regularity, had sapped his feral drive. He stopped talking about the war and began to sink into moods of unrelieved bitterness. But he had a happy spirit and when he felt bad he would plunge into parties and discos, he would chat up women, he would laugh loudly, while the wrinkles tightened on his face. Omovo knew that his friend lived with more terrors than he could ever understand.

The record stopped playing. The room was silent. Omovo thought about how his own childhood had alternated so sharply between laughter and loneliness. Growing up had been irredeemably spoiled by the difficult discovery that people have to struggle grossly for what amounts to a miserable compromise. It seemed to him a wonder that his people could bear their hard lives without going insane.

Okoro moved on the bed. His eyes were wide open and his face had hardened. 'You can't beat the establishment,' he said. 'Play me some music.'

Omovo turned the record to the other side and lowered the volume.

'You ask about my studies? My studies are there. One gets fed up of reading for examinations,' Okoro said.

'Make this your last one.'

'Sure.'

They fell silent. Okoro sat up on the bed and held his head between his palms.

'My mother wrote. She is not well. She has been ill for a long time. I keep sending money home. It's a terrible life. Everything is struggle. There is no rest. I feel like an old man. I feel tired.'

Omovo said nothing for a while. Then by way of changing the subject he said: 'Have you seen Keme?'

'Yeah. I don't know what has come over him.'

'Why do you say that?'

'I went to his place yesterday. He was angry. The police had detained him for a day. He didn't tell me why because of his anger. He said something about his editor refusing to publish his story. He is threatening to resign. Do you know why he is so furious?'

'We went to the park some days ago and we found the body of a dead girl.'

'What?'

'We saw a dead girl's body. It was mutilated. They had shaved her hair.'

'Really?'

'Yeah. We went to Dele's place and phoned the police. Maybe something has developed. I knew Keme would follow up the story.'

They were silent again. Okoro stood up and walked around the cramped space of the room. He kept waving his hands without saying anything. He seemed agitated. He sat down again. Then suddenly his face contorted and he laughed. Then, quieting down, he said:

'But why is he so worried about a dead body? I mean, I saw many of them stinking along the streets during the war. I mean . . .'

'But we are not at war.'

'Who said so? Our society is a battlefield. Poverty, corruption and hunger are the bullets. Bad governments are the bombs. And we still have soldiers ruling us.'

'Okay. Okay. I don't want to argue.'

They were silent again.

'Okay. So it affected you. But you are too sensitive for our society. If you worry too much about these things you will go mad. Or you will commit suicide. You have to learn to forget, to shut them out, and to concentrate on yourself.'

'I don't agree, but I don't want to argue.'

'So what can you do about it? Can you bring the girl back to life? Can you catch the people who killed her? Is there one day in which you don't see a dead body in the street? And what can you do about a drunken soldier who shoots someone just like that? What can you do about armed robbery?'

'I don't want to argue.'

'Why not? Tell me: what can you do? You either keep quiet or you do something.' Okoro laughed. 'Or are you going to paint her dead body? What will that do, eh?'

Okoro was getting more agitated. He made violent gestures. Omovo began to think of leaving. Okoro came over to him, touched him roughly on the shoulder, and was about to launch into a new set of questions when knocks sounded on the door. Okoro shouted: 'Come in if you're good-looking.'

Dele came in, grinning. 'Of course I'm good-looking, you fool,' he said.

Okoro laughed, and eased the tension in the room.

'Hey, Dele, how are you?'

'Great!'

'Man, guess what?'

'What?'

'I've just got myself a new girl.'

'That's great, man!'

'Hi, Dele,' Omovo said.

'Hey, Omovo, is that you?'

'Of course.'

'We never see you at all. How are you?'

'I'm fine. Thanks about that night. I hope we didn't disturb your father.'

'It was okay. You know, when I saw you that night I didn't recognise you at first. Your shaven hair makes you look like a stranger. You should get a hat.'

Omovo smiled. Okoro said: 'Have my hat, man. It's an expensive hat.'

'I'm all right.'

'Have it, man. Protect your brains from the sun.'

Okoro got up and fetched the hat, which had been hanging on a nail behind the clothes rack. He dusted the hat and put it on Omovo's head.

'Wow! You look like an artistic gangster.'

Okoro brought him a mirror. Omovo looked at himself. He looked even more of a stranger. 'It's good for disguise,' he said.

'Disguise your baldness, my friend,' Dele said. 'Or the whole world will treat it like a drum.'

Okoro laughed. Omovo took the hat off and put it on the table. 'I'll take it,' he said.

'Great,' said Okoro. Then turning to Dele he said: 'Let me tell you my news, man.'

Dele hovered by the door, smiling in anticipation. He was tall, handsome, and he had an even complexion. He wore a pair of sunshades, which he kept on in the relative darkness of the room, and which made him look like a minor film star. His father was a wealthy and illiterate businessman. Dele was one of those people who aspire to a life of great ease and luxury. He despised the wretchedness around him. His single greatest ambition was to go and study in America. He believed that life would begin for him out there. But in his own country he felt that he was living in a state of suspended animation. He worked in one of his father's firms as an assistant manager.

'Tell me your good news,' he said, sitting down on the bed.

Okoro talked excitedly, as if he were telling the story of how he 'captured' July for the first time. His face was animated with pleasure. He went into some intimate details and Dele laughed, slapping his thighs. When Okoro finished, Dele launched into stories of his own recent exploits. While they talked Omovo listened, smiling when they turned to him to include him in their stories. And while he listened he couldn't be sure what his friends enjoyed the most: the actual experiences or the telling of them. When the narratives had been exhausted, Okoro got up to play another record. Dele turned to Omovo and said:

'Hey man, how is that business with the dead girl?'

'I don't know. I haven't seen Keme since.'

'What really happened that night anyway? Tell me from the beginning.'

Omovo told him briefly about the exhibition, the park, and the body. When he finished they were both silent. Dele became serious.

'So they seized your painting, eh?'

'Yes.'

Okoro lowered the music. 'But why?'

'They said it insults our nation's progress.'

Dele laughed sarcastically. Okoro said: 'I must admit it is strange. What can a painting do to anyone, eh? A painting can't hit you, can't shoot you, can't make you faint, can't drive you mad. And yet they seized your painting. Very strange.'

'What really annoyed me,' said Omovo, 'was that the officer said I was a bad artist. He's probably right.'

Dele laughed again. 'Why would he bother to seize it if it is so bad, eh? And besides, what do soldiers know about art? They seized your painting because they did not understand it.'

'I disagree,' said Okoro. 'They seized it because they understood it.'

'Neither of you has seen the painting anyway,' said Omovo.

'It doesn't matter,' replied Dele. 'They seized it because it was probably truthful. People in power don't like the people's truth. I mean . . .' and here Dele connected with his favourite subject, 'I mean, in America they wouldn't do a thing like that. Why are we so trivial? That's why I want to get out of this place. One should live as fully and as freely as possible. I bet that girl was a victim of a secret society, you know, one of those frightening secret societies. Our own people. We just destroy our young ones, like that . . . without thinking . . .'

Dele trailed off into silence, momentarily trapped by his inability to articulate what he meant. He sat on the edge of the bed. He took off his sunshades and stared ahead of him. Then, as if he were caught in a strange passion, he began to fidget. He leaned forward. His features darkened. He made helpless gestures with his hands. He continued:

'There are too many unnecessary struggles in our lives. It's a struggle to wake up in the morning, to bath, a struggle to catch a bus, go to work, and make a decent living. It's a struggle to come back from work, to relax, to have electricity and running water, to get a good woman, and to keep her. It feels like a lifetime of struggling. That's why I want to leave. I want to go where people are building new, exciting things every day.' He fell silent for a moment. But the silence only served to increase his passion.

'Man, can't you see me getting on the plane, breathing good air, having a conversation and exchanging addresses with some beautiful woman? Can't you imagine me arriving in God's own country, looking around, walking like a real important guy? I can feel the freedom already. I can see me shaking hands with black Americans and I can hear my American accent improving rapidly. I will be dressed in style, man. I wouldn't wear rubbish. I'll have the best clothes in town. And I'll send you guys pictures of myself. I'll take pictures with chicks, in nightclubs, in parks, and my photo album will be heavy. You won't catch me with any useless women, man. Only the best. Heavy white women, black women, Spanish women. I'll have real fun and I'll buy myself a sports car. You won't catch me doing all those stupid jobs Nigerians do when they go to America, man. No waiters' jobs or cleaners' jobs for me. No! I'll study hard, I'll learn all their tricks, and I'll come back and make a contribution to our society, man. But when I'm there I'll visit the Empire State Building, the White House, Disneyland, the Wild West – and maybe I'll even get myself some famous actress, man.'

Okoro laughed nervously.

'Don't laugh, man. Of course I might get a famous actress, you never know, man, and she might take real care of me. I must go out there! And when I come back,' he said, slapping Okoro on the shoulder, 'you guys won't recognise me. I will have changed. You guys can stay here and enjoy the insane struggles. But me, in the name of God, I must leave this place!'

Dele had spoken excitedly and wholly without embarrassment. The room became silent. Omovo stared at the posters on the walls. Okoro's face bore the despair of one continually left behind. He looked sad. It was obvious that Dele had touched on his own desires. Dele had done this with such authority, such certainty, that he had unknowingly deepened Okoro's sense of helplessness.

Omovo opened the curtain. He stared out through the only window in the room, out into the muddy street. He had a smile on his face. The fantasies Dele had expressed meant nothing to him. 'We are a new lost generation,' he thought. He got up and played Fela Anikulapo Kuti's mocking 'Follow Follow'. Then he went and lay on the bed.

For a while everyone was silent. Omovo felt the need to breathe deeply, but the air was too dense. Then Dele went on and on about how life was really being lived out there in 'God's own country'. Omovo felt exhausted. His head spun. He felt restless. He wanted to do something. Okoro began to dance away his despair. Dele went on about the beautiful life that was really only in his mind. Then Okoro said he was going to get some drinks. Dele didn't· want to go with him. When Okoro left, Dele said, in a low voice: 'Omovo, I'm in trouble.'

'What's wrong?'

'Do you remember that girl I told you about?'

'The one that's pregnant by you?'

'That's right.'

'What about her?'

'She doesn't want to get rid of it.'

'So?'

'Look, I'm going to the States in a few days' time.'

'You didn't tell me.'

'Things have just broken through.'

'I'm glad for you.'

'But I don't know what to do about the girl.'

'What do you mean?'

'I can't marry her. I don't want the baby. What do you suggest?' Omovo stammered.

'Well?'

'I . . . I . . . I mean . . .'

'What's wrong, man?'

'Nothing. It's just that I, eh, I don't know what to say. I mean it depends on you.'

'Sure.'

'I'm sorry.'

'About what?'

'That you're in trouble.'

'Sure. Anyway, do you know what I did?'

'No.'

'I tricked her to a friend's place and both of us threatened her and made her drink some tablets. Later she began to complain about stomach troubles. The doctor said she would be all right. What does that mean? Is she going to have the baby or isn't she, eh?'

'I don't know.'

'Man, I don't want any complications in my life. The whole thing frightens me.'

'What does your father think?'

'At first he was furious. Then he began to like the idea of having a grandchild. To make matters worse her father is a family friend and I think they have decided to get us married. He even offered to take care of the girl till I returned. Then later he said he doesn't want me to go to the States. I'm scared, man. I'm scared.'

'Why?'

'I don't know.'

They were both silent. Then Dele said, in a voice so low that Omovo could barely hear him: 'He has threatened to disown me.'

'What for?'

'If I disobey his orders.'

'What are you going to do?'

'I'm going to disobey them. Either I remain here and become stunted. Or I leave, discover the world, and find freedom. But I'm scared.'

Omovo said nothing. His mind was blank. Dele stayed silent, deep in

114

thought. The record had stopped. Then Dele got up and said: 'I'm going for a walk.'

He went out with his head bowed.

When Dele left, Omovo stared at the door till his thoughts became indistinct. Then he reminded himself that he needed some oil paints and water colours. He thought about the folding easel he had seen at the art shop and decided to spend most of his next salary buying it. There's nothing like painting from nature, he thought as he imagined himself at the seaside or at a village. He felt good thinking about the future things he would paint. He resolved to keep his mind open and clear. Overcome with the possibilities of perception, things to see, things to express in art, he felt that life was calling to him with the voice of the ghetto, the voice of his experience.   .

Omovo lay on the bed and waited. He felt the sudden wash of euphoria. He let himself be carried on its crest of melancholy and joy. He breathed in deeply and as he exhaled Okoro stormed back into the room, bearing drinks.

'Time for boozing!' he announced.

Omovo stirred.

'Wake up! It's boozing time!'

Omovo had a sudden urge to paint.

'Where's Dele?'

'He went for a walk.'

Okoro put the bottles down on the table, got out some glasses, and put on a record. Dele came back in, his sunshades on, sweat glistening on his brow. Omovo got off the bed, seized a pencil and sheets of paper. He began to draw Dele as he sat at the table listening to Stevie Wonder with his eyes shut.

'Take off your sunshades, Dele.'

Dele took them off and began nodding to the music. Omovo did a drawing of Dele's face, introducing a sad delusion over the accuracy of his features. Dele looked at the drawing and remarked that Omovo was 'a devil'.

Okoro said: 'You are there in that drawing. You look like a child.'

Dele turned to Omovo. 'Am I a child?'

'Ignore Okoro.'

Okoro, smiling, said: 'Do what the soldier did. Seize it.'

Dele laughed. Omovo stayed serious.

'I was only joking,' Okoro said.

'Sure.'

They were all silent. Then after a while Omovo said he was going. Okoro tried to persuade him to stay and have something to drink, but Omovo was obdurate. He picked up the blue hat and put it on. His two friends saw him out into the street.

'When are you leaving for the States?' Omovo asked Dele.

'Okoro will tell you. It's not definite. I'll be having a small party. I would have come round to visit you, but the roads in your area are so bad.'

'Well, if I don't see you before you leave, take care and don't get carried away.'

'You bet.'

'Write to us.'

'I will. And you take care too. Don't let anything get to you.'

'Sure.'

'That hat suits you,' Okoro said.

'Yeah. Thanks. I'll see you at Waterside on Monday. Watch yourself.'

Omovo nodded and left. The street was clear. Everything was clear. He took off the hat. The bridge wobbled when he got on it. The woman at the toll shed collected her money without looking at him. He felt lonely again. The sun faded from the horizon and the sky had a bright orange glow with streaks of poignant blue. The wind blew litter across at him. Boys chased tyres and hoops along the street. Everything was bright in Omovo's mind. Things were coming together within him. When he got home he had a bath. He changed into clean clothes. Then he went outside and waited for Ifeyiwa to show up.

EIGHT

While he waited, the ash-grey evening fell, and the day
darkened.

The compound men were sitting outside. They had
gathered in front of the shop. Sitting on stools, with little tables before
them, they drank and gossiped. Most of their wives formed an outer
circle around them. The children played at the house front and on the
road.

Omovo could hear the loud voices of the men. He watched Tuwo
talking about and demonstrating a wrestling contest he had won in his
village when he was a young man. The others didn't seem to believe
he had ever won a contest in his life, and laughed at his comic
exaggerations. Another man interrupted and talked about a family in the
compound – whom none of the others really liked, and who did not
participate in the events of the compound – who had not washed their
plates for many days.

Omovo's father came out and joined the men. They got him a chair
and filled his glass with ogogoro. He listened to their conversation with
an expression of detached and elderly amusement on his face.

As the men got more drunk their conversation got more bawdy. The
assistant deputy bachelor began to talk about how he had stumbled into a
huge wet pair of underpants that had been drying on the line. It was at
night, he said, and at first he thought he had been slapped. Upon
investigating he found it to be a woman's undergarment.

'It was as large as a sack,' he said, unable to restrain his laughter. 'The
thing so big, eh, that the woman's buttocks must be bigger than a barrel!'

The others burst out laughing. They rolled over and slapped one another on the back. 'Dat's the kind of woman Tuwo likes,' said one of the men.

'Na lie!' said Tuwo, who began to describe, with drunken geometry, the shape of his ideal woman.

'She must be slim,' he began.

'And someone's wife,' said another.

'And she must have good breasts, proud breasts, pointed . . .'

The men shouted in delight. The women wrinkled their faces. Omovo's father smiled.

'Where must they point?' asked one.

'In my direction,' said Tuwo.

'Both of them?'

'Everything.'

'What about the nyash?'

'You mean the buttocks, the posterior, of course,' said Tuwo, passing a glance over the women.

The men laughed again. The assistant deputy bachelor, ever serviceable, filled everyone's glass and shouted for more ogogoro to be brought. Tuwo took a precious sip before continuing with his elaborations.

'The posterior is for the hands and the eyes. A man needs to get a good grip on them or he's lost.'

'So you like them big, eh?'

'Not too big. Not like that of an elephant.'

'Don't mind Tuwo,' the assistant deputy bachelor said. 'Na only by the nyash nai he deh take recognise woman. One day . . .'

And he told the story of how he had seen Tuwo in the market. Tuwo wasn't buying anything, he said. Tuwo was confused at the sight of so many massive buttocks, so many large-breasted market women. The men laughed again, slapping their thighs, throwing themselves backwards on their stools. One of the men, carried away by laughter, fell over. The men got riotous with amusement. The women helped him up.

Darkness fell. The stalls were weakly illuminated by kerosene lamps. The sky was clear. There were no stars, no clouds. The sky was a mysterious expanse of blackness.

Omovo listened as the assistant deputy bachelor, whose voice was the loudest and most drunken of all, began to narrate another of his experiences in the compound. He said that one night when he had gone to urinate he had witnessed something. The others quietened to hear what that something was. He said he had heard noises in the bathroom and upon further investigation had found that there were a man and a woman in there.

'What were they doing?' someone asked.

'What kind of question is dat? What do you think they were doing, eh?'

'You mean they were doing it?'

'Seriously. You should have heard the woman.'

'You mean they were doing it in that stinking place?'

'You should have heard the man.'

'Is that so?'

The men laughed a bit, but not as wildly as they had before. The wind blew suddenly. Omovo shivered. The men were silent for a moment. The day darkened in their midst.

'Who were they?'

'Nooo! My mouth gum for that one-o!' said the assistant deputy bachelor, as he refilled Tuwo's glass.

'But did you see them?'

The assistant deputy bachelor refused to be specific. He kept drunkenly evading the questions, till the men started to doubt him.

'Don't mind our permanent bachelor,' said Tuwo. 'He's never had a woman and he's beginning to imagine things.'

'How are you sure it's not you who caught yourself, eh?' said one of the men to the assistant bachelor.

'To tell you the truth,' he said, 'I didn't see them. But if I hear them doing it again I will push open that door.'

'But what if it's a husband and wife?'

'Then they should do it in their rooms. We have one bathroom for all of us in the compound. The door is old and the nail that holds it is weak. If they don't want to be caught they should do it on their beds.'

Everyone was silent. Everyone was uncomfortable.

'I have a big bed,' said Tuwo.

The men laughed nervously. 'But do you use it?'

'You want me to show you how weak the springs have become?'

The men began to regain their old form.

'That former wife of yours,' said the assistant deputy bachelor, 'must be . . .'

'I will give you her address if you want,' interrupted Tuwo.

'Thank you, but I have to concentrate on business.'

'Let's give this bachelor a new name,' suggested Tuwo. 'Let's call him Business-Without-Pleasure.'

But the men preferred the former name, which had evolved by communal accretion. They had begun by calling him the chief bachelor and everyone had added gradations of their own.

'Let's call Tuwo Pleasure-Without-Business,' said the assistant bachelor.

But the men didn't support that either. And after a while, attacked by gnawing suspicions, the men fell quiet. Only the noises of the children, and the sounds of the ghetto, could be heard.

The wind blew over from the scumpool, mingling freshness with stench. Omovo felt strangely happy because there was not yet a black-out.

'But what sort of man,' said one of the men suddenly, 'would do it with his wife in that bathroom?'

'A strange man.'

'Maybe it wasn't man and wife,' said the assistant bachelor.

Everyone was silent again.

'This is serious, you know,' said one of the men, looking around as if, suddenly, he was not sure of the company. The men began to look at one another slightly suspiciously.

'More ogogoro!' cried the assistant bachelor. Then he said, getting up and sitting down again: 'If that happened to my wife I will kill her.'

'They will just lock you up for a long time,' said Omovo's father, with unassailable dignity. The 'Captain' of the compound had spoken. The other men agreed.

'Yes,' said. 'They will just lock you up.'

'For murder,' said another.

'Manslaughter,' said the assistant deputy bachelor.

'They might even execute you at the bar beach, you know,' said Tuwo.

'They don't execute for murder, only armed robbery and failing to succeed in a coup,' said Omovo's father. 'But if you have a good lawyer,' he continued, 'and I know a few, then you might get off for what they call . . .'

The men listened intently.

'. . . Crime of passion.'

'I know that one,' said Tuwo. 'When I was in Britain . . .'

The men shouted him down. The assistant deputy bachelor took over.

'Maybe I won't kill her then.'

Tuwo got up. Waving his hands, slashing out as if with a big and clumsy instrument, he said: 'I will kill him. If I caught them I will kill him. I will cut off his prick!'

The men fell about laughing at his exaggerated passion. He began to laugh as well. He laughed as he dramatised how he would chase the man, pursue him through the compound, and slash him down.

'And,' he said loudly, 'the police won't be able to do anything to me.'

'Why not? Are you God?' said someone.

'God doesn't fuck people's wives,' said another.

'Because,' said Tuwo triumphantly, 'it's a crime of passion. Didn't you hear what our Captain said?'

'I have thought about it,' said the assistant deputy bachelor. 'Being a man of God, I won't do anything to either my wife or the man.'

'You can say that because you don't have a wife.'

'His wife is business.'

'So if someone wants to steal your business, won't you defend it?' asked Tuwo.

'My business is not my wife.'

'I agree with the assistant bachelor,' said Omovo's father. 'One must learn forgiveness.'

'Don't let your wife hear you,' someone said.

'What sort of forgiveness is dat? You mean if you catch them you will forgive them like dat? No, I don't believe you,' said one of the men, made bold by drink.

'Look, my friend,' said Omovo's father, turning to the man, 'I will be angry, but there's no need to kill anyone and spend the rest of your life in prison. There are plenty other women in the world.'

'You can't get a woman in prison,' said the deputy bachelor.

Omovo's father continued: 'I won't take her back, and she will never step foot in my house again, but I won't kill anybody. Only fools and criminals do that sort of thing.'

'It's true,' someone said.

The men nodded drunkenly.

'But it's enough to drive a man mad though,' said the assistant bachelor, waving his empty glass. 'I know of a man who caught his wife in bed with another man. He didn't do anything. They ran out of the room. Later his wife came back with relatives and elders to beg him. But he didn't say anything. The wife left and didn't come back. To this day that man doesn't talk.'

'It's enough to drive a man mad.'

One of the younger married men of the compound said: 'I have heard that there is a medicine that can be applied to a woman . . .'

'To make them do it better?'

'No. When you use this medicine, if another man does it to your wife they will stick together, unable to separate . . .'

'Like two dogs.'

'. . . Until the husband releases them. I even know a native doctor who makes this medicine.'

'I don't like it,' Tuwo said loudly. 'I could not bear it. Why would a man want to catch his wife and another man naked, eh? I would prefer not to know. It's too much for me.'

'What's the address of this native doctor?' asked the assistant bachelor jokingly.

The men laughed again. The women teased and mocked him.

'Don't laugh,' he said. 'As for me, if I use the medicine and caught them I tell you – I will tie both of them up and throw them in the nearest river.'

Omovo grew restless and uneasy. His sense of guilt made him melancholy. The children came to play with him. But he was not really with them and they sensed it. They soon ran back into the compound and crowded outside the window of a neighbour's room to watch television. Omovo's melancholy only increased his desire to see Ifeyiwa.

Tuwo, louder than ever, was still speaking:

'In England, though, they don't mind these things. They have something called wife-swapping. They have these clubs where married people share their wives and husbands.'

'Is that so?' someone said.

'How do you know, eh, Tuwo?' came the assistant bachelor. 'Did you join them?'

'Of course not. But I know. I have even heard of some Englishmen who like to watch another man doing it to their wives.'

'NOOO!'

'Yes.'

The disbelief spread. The discussion widened. The men drank solidly, laughing into the ghetto night. The women, no longer content to stand listening in the outer circle, began to tease the men. Then they developed their own punishments for husbands caught being unfaithful.

Omovo, feeling restless and desolate, moved away from the compound front. He went past Ifeyiwa's husband's shop twice. She was not there. He saw Takpo counting his money and arguing with an old man about change. Omovo went back home. Most of the men and women had gone in. Only the younger ones were left. They carried on the arguments and discussions. Standing a good distance from them, Omovo watched Ifeyiwa's house. The mosquitoes came at him. The darkness mellowed.

What is happening to me, he thought. He had never felt like this before, never felt so crossed, so much a victim of his own perverse love. He thought he knew the limits: that she was Takpo's wife. But still he could not understand what was happening inside him, what was pulling him, crushing him with unbearable anticipation.

He began to convince himself that she wouldn't show up, and that it was all for the better, when a figure waved in the distance. He shivered. A light flashed through him. His senses came alive. The figure waved again. It was her. It was her all right. He looked around. No one was watching. He began walking, slowly. He felt wonderful. He felt nothing could touch him, or alter the destiny of his desire. He thought: 'I can see the distance clearly. The night is so beautiful. I will do some painting when I get back. The air is so sweet.'

NINE

As soon as he set out after her the wind blew hard. Sand and dust were whipped up in the air. Dead leaves circled the street. The wind blew him backwards and he lowered his head, for the sand was blinding him. He pushed against the wind. Leaves rose to his face, roused by the gale. The pages of newspapers, turning, were propelled towards him. An open page of lurid news-stories stuck to his head. When he tore it off and let it be blown behind him, he became aware that people streamed all around him. The street was full of people going in all directions, rushing past him. He pushed through the women on their way to the night-market. He pushed through hawkers and street-traders, children and herbalists, night-workers and the sellers of charms.

The roadsides were crowded with the people of the area, men and women outside their over-populated compounds, children playing and fighting. A group of young men pursued a little girl round a stall. The evening was lit here and there by the orange of kerosene lamps. Some of the street-traders dozed on their wares. Others dispiritedly called the world to come and buy their goods. Omovo passed the zinc-roofed huts, the unpainted bungalows, the uncompleted tenements with aluminium water-tanks standing outside on blocks of crumbling cement.

Ifeyiwa walked at a speed calculated to be just ahead of him. He could barely make out her yellow outline in the shadowy crowd. He hastened, fighting past the crowds, to keep her in sight. He got to the intersection when a ramshackle lorry, weighed down with bags of cement, nearly knocked him over. Omovo ran back and the driver shouted at him. The lorry drove on into the street, blasting its infernal horn and sending up fountains of dust and cement. When Omovo started to cross, the lorry suddenly began to reverse. Omovo had to run back again. The lorry kept reversing and going forward, for no reason that was comprehensible to Omovo, effectively blocking the street. Its wheels, clogging in the sand, raised dust in Omovo's face, blinding him. Clouds of cement settled on his head. Some men screamed abuse at the driver's family, while others shouted at him to reverse this way and to cut the steering wheel that way. The lorry eventually got stuck and had to be pushed. Omovo, freed from the obstacle, ran past. He looked for Ifeyiwa in the crowd and couldn't find her. The fear that he had lost her plunged him into a frenzy. He looked everywhere for her till his head began to whirl. His agitation exhausted him. He became confused by all the motions on the street. His eyes began to hurt. Then he stopped looking and stood still and breathed gently. A star pulsed in the sky. He stood apart and let the agitation flow from him. As people brushed past him, crisscrossing his vision, he felt amazed at the simplicity of his feelings. All he wanted at that moment was to be with her, to be in her presence.

The simplicity of his desire, and his stillness, were rewarded. From the shadows, under the eaves of a deserted blue shed, a voice called out to him. The blood pounded in his ears. The sudden realisation that she might have been watching his agitation confused him and made him stumble as he went towards the voice. He found her leaning against the rough wooden frame of the shed, a miracle of the ghetto night.

She was wearing a yellow dress, with a white belt round her waist, and white shoes. Her hair had been tied back with a red ribbon. She had a white head-tie round her shoulders, like a miniature shawl. She looked as if she had stepped out of a bright magazine. She looked both beautiful and a little awkward, as if she had borrowed someone else's clothes.

When he saw her he was astonished at her transformation. Her presence disturbed the air. All his doubts, all the guilt awakened by the men's talk, were dispelled by her presence. On her face was the brightest and the saddest smile he had ever seen. Her perfume was new to him. She looked happy. He didn't know what to do with himself, what to say. She disturbed him. If she had not dressed the way she did, had not embodied her own transformation, he would never have been able to see that she could look so beautiful, and in her beauty so alien, so untouchable, so mysterious. He followed her silently. She led him into the ghetto night.

They went up the street and came to another intersection. He stopped. She went on and stopped further up when she became aware of his absence. She turned and looked at him quizzically, as if she had been gently awoken from a dream. He ran up to her. For a moment they stood close together. Then he drew up to her till her breasts were touching his chest. The confused motions of people milling about made him feel as if the world were closing in on them. She was very still, except for the gentle heaving of her breasts, and there was something sensual and coiled about her immobility. He felt her presence so intensely that his legs began to quiver. He wanted to kiss her, but he couldn't summon the courage. He didn't know why.

'Let's walk on,' he said, his voice thick. 'It's cold here.'

But when he moved he felt as if his legs wouldn't bear him.

'You're like a dream,' he said, his voice weak. 'You're so beautiful.'

She stayed silent. She didn't even smile. As they came to the hotel, the silence grew between them. The hotel was noisy with hi-life music and the shouting clientele, and prostitutes strutting about. A powerful smell of stale beer, of stale sex, and of sweat, came out of the open hotel door. As they passed the hotel, prostitutes with strangely distended stomachs called out to potential customers. One of them said loudly to Omovo: 'Shine-shine head, leave your woman and come with me.'

The other prostitutes laughed.

'Sweet time with me,' she said again.

Omovo was embarrassed. Ifeyiwa, walking fast, leaving him behind, hurried on ahead. Omovo tried to keep up with her, but she half ran, and the laughter of the prostitutes rang out harshly behind them. When Omovo caught up with her she had taken the head-tie off her shoulders and was tying it into a knot. He touched her arm and she shook away his hand. He slowed down. As he walked behind her, his eyes fixed on the movements of her hips, they passed men sitting on hard stools outside their houses, drinking ogogoro and laughing. The men were silent as Ifeyiwa went past. They watched her. Then one of them blew a wolfwhistle. Another said:

'Woman, don't run from me, marry me or I die!'

Ifeyiwa rushed passed them. Omovo ran and caught up with her and put his arm round her shoulders. She rested her head slightly on him as they passed children who screamed at the roadside as if they were utterly lost. Their sullen fathers smoked cigarettes while their harrassed mothers, who sold cheap provisions, attended wearily to customers. Omovo smelt the burning wick of their kerosene lamps on the night air.

Ifeyiwa turned suddenly down a street without a name. It was a dark street and the houses had no electricity. The air was filled with the sounds of night insects. Ifeyiwa slapped her arm. They walked on in

126

silence and Ifeyiwa kept turning into nameless streets, areas that were alien to Omovo, places where the houses were squat and unpainted, where the electric cables sagged on the wooden poles. Omovo began to feel lost. He felt as if he had been led into another dimension, a foreign country. He knew the desolation of the Amukoko ghetto, but he had never known that there were places as desolate, as garbage-ridden as the streets Ifeyiwa led him into. Deeper and deeper into the ghetto they went. It frightened Omovo that desolation could seem to have no end, no boundaries.

'Do you know where we are going?' he asked her.

'No,' she said.

They passed a rough graveyard that shaded over into a wasteland where garbage was piled high. Crude gravestones, cheap wooden mementoes of the dead, cement crosses with one arm crumbling, jutted out of the earth. The forest, breathing the potencies of nocturnal vegetation, was dark around them, noisy with insects. They passed a blue mosque, with its fading paint, as a cracked voice intoned the evening prayer over a loudspeaker. Through the open door Omovo saw the Moslems on their mats, beads between their fingers, their mouths working in prayer. Omovo stared at them and at the curiously beautiful Arabic lettering on the mosque's signboard.

Further on they passed a wooden Aladura church with the poor still praying and singing fervently, while their minister preached over a crackling loudspeaker. Then music struck up in the church and the worshippers, all in white smocks, began to dance and sing their alleluyas. The music was heavy with drums and the worshippers danced themselves into trances.

Ifeyiwa led him down an incline in the land. It was quiet except for the sound of a child howling in the distance. They climbed up again. Omovo felt lost in the silence. He could make out the blue shadows of bushes. He saw a wooden bridge which led over a marsh. The bridge seemed to lead to, and end in, darkness. The silhouettes of the palm trees and the iroko trees against the sky made him feel lost and stretched out.

'Omovo, do you believe in God?'

Her voice startled him. It was only a few moments later that he understood what she had said.

'I'm not sure. I believe in something. Does one have a choice?'

'Maybe not.'

'Do you?'

'Sometimes. I suppose so.'

They walked on through another stretch of silence. Then Omovo said, suddenly: 'It's impossible to express how happy I am sometimes.'

'Me too.'

'But sometimes life is very hard.'

'Yes.'

'Sometimes I feel it so much it's as if my soul would crack.'

'I feel,' she said, 'as if everything is pressing me down, trying to make me disappear.'

'You will never disappear,' said Omovo passionately.

She held his hand. Then she let go of it. Omovo, sensing the way she held herself tightly, knew instantly that something had happened to her. He wanted to say something but she got there first.

'You said your brothers wrote to you. What did they say? Are they well?'

'No,' he said.

He told her about the letter and the poem. He said: 'You know, we are all on different journeys.'

She nodded.

'I fear for my brothers,' he continued. 'When they left I had the feeling I would never see them again.'

'When I was leaving my village I felt I would not see my mother again.'

'Don't say things like that.'

'Okay, I promise.'

They were silent. Ifeyiwa, smiling brightly, tugged his arm and said: 'Go on. Tell me about your brothers.'

Omovo stayed silent for a while before he said: 'Sometimes I try to remember them and I can't. They keep receding. I have almost totally forgotten the details of their faces.'

Ifeyiwa held him tighter. They passed a palm tree. The road narrowed and became a bushpath. Mosquitoes whined in their ears. They went down the path and emerged in another street. Ifeyiwa kicked an empty Bournvita tin and it rattled. Then she told Omovo that her husband had been asking questions about him that day.

Omovo stopped. 'Why? What happened?'

She told him about Tuwo's visit.

'Afterwards he started to beat me, but I ran out of the room. He hasn't stopped threatening me since.'

Omovo started to say something, but she interrupted him.

'I can stand anything,' she said, 'so long as I can be with you.'

'We are playing with fire, you know.'

'Yes.'

They walked in silence. Ifeyiwa caught Omovo's hand. They linked their fingers. Omovo looked at her and noticed that she had loosened her hair. A doomed smile played on her lips.

'Let's go to the beach one day.'

Omovo said nothing.

'I dreamt that we did.'

'Don't dream like that, please. Dreams can betray life. It's hard.'

'It's all right. I'm scared of water anyway.'

'Can't you swim?'

'I can, but I'm afraid of the sea.'

For a moment silence fell with the wind. Omovo stopped and turned to her. She looked childlike in the half-darkness. The lights from a nearby house touched her face. He noticed, for the first time, that she was wearing eye-shadow and mascara and that she had on the gentlest trace of lipstick. She moved on, beyond the lights, and he followed. He touched her and she stopped, her face a mystery, hidden in a soft darkness.

He stood before her, tense and restrained. A man wearing a wrapper came down the street towards them. Omovo had a sudden vision of Ifeyiwa's husband. As the man drew closer Omovo saw that he held a machete in his hand. But as Omovo turned and began to walk away Ifeyiwa caught his hands and pulled him to her. Omovo stayed still, watching the man over Ifeyiwa's head. The man slowed down and stared at them as he passed. When he disappeared into the darkness Omovo sighed. Ifeyiwa threw her arms round his neck and kissed him full on the mouth. Her lips were very warm. With great sensual deliberation, Omovo enclosed her in his arms. He felt her warm body and the softness of her breasts against him. The wind blew round them. Omovo held her tightly to him, his lips lost in the language of her desire. Then suddenly Ifeyiwa pulled away from him and came back and rested her head on his shoulder, sobbing gently. Omovo stared at the trees silhouetted against the night sky and he felt a curious kind of happiness rise in him. Then the wind blew on them. Omovo felt cold. Ifeyiwa shuddered.

'Someone has walked over my grave,' she said.

'It's just the wind.'

Ifeyiwa pulled him by the arm. They moved on. Ifeyiwa walked jauntily; her face was bright with a hard kind of joy. She threw her arms in the air.

'I have never been so happy before,' she said.

'I am happy too.'

'I can feel sadness coming.'

'I am afraid.'

Ifeyiwa laughed. Her laughter transformed the night. She was a yellow radiance and every step he took behind her was slowed down by incomprehension. He felt as if he were walking into a golden childhood, into a past which never existed. He felt as if he had walked into a dream. The darkness glowed. He heard snatches of curious melodies within him. He heard sweet voices on the air. When he looked around he realised that they were near the stagnant stream. The wind blew hard and seemed to make the darkness wavy. Then suddenly, as if it were meant to be underlined forever as a witnessed moment, Omovo saw two birds on the bank of the stream. He heard the water flowing, as if the wind had dislodged the obstacles of rubbish. The two birds, startled by his presence, flew over the stream, bathed in the sussurations of the wind on water. When the birds disappeared, Omovo felt calm. Everything was wonderfully clear in his mind. He could see beyond the bungalows, the haze of candlelight in isolated huts, and the dark silent trees. The sky was like a wash of dark-blue ink. Two stars pulsed. Ifeyiwa spoke suddenly, as if the words were forcing themselves to be uttered.

'I dreamt that I cut my husband's throat with a sharp knife.'

Her voice sounded miserable. The desolation, the misery, of her voice seemed to come from so deep in her that it frightened him.

'The strange thing was that he didn't bleed.'

Omovo held her close.

'I am afraid of the things I might do,' she said, relaxing into Omovo's embrace.

He caressed her face with his palms. Her body heaved. He kissed her forehead. Then she began to sing softly to herself. He smiled. Her eyes stared beyond him. He couldn't understand her, couldn't grasp her. To please her he began to dance. When she smiled, he stopped. Then he said:

'You were right.'

'Why?'

'None of us belong here,' Omovo said. 'Firstly this is Lagos. We are victims here, we are strangers, refugees from the poverty of the interior. And even if we were in our villages we would still be strangers. It is odd that in our own country we don't have a home. Maybe that's why my brothers left.'

Further on along the street they saw the stall of a woman who sold Akara, fried fish, and fried plantain. They smelt the oil smoke on the air. The stall, with the woman's large frying pan over the grill of blazing firewood, was the only point of illumination in the street. Beyond, in the darkness, they heard the strains of traditional music. They came to the stall. The woman sat behind a table on which was her tray of fried food. Her daughter was at the fire, dropping dollops of ground beans into the sizzling oil. The girl's face poured with sweat. Her clothes were greasy and in tatters. Ifeyiwa asked Omovo if he wanted something to eat. He nodded. They bought some food. Ifeyiwa insisted on paying. They ate from the same wrapping. When they finished eating they went into a shop and bought soft drinks and had to finish them there because the shop-owner didn't allow bottles to be taken away.

They went on. The road sloped downwards. Ifeyiwa ran down, her yellow dress fluttering stiffly. Omovo ran after her. When they got to the bottom they were both panting. They climbed up the road. Ifeyiwa's eyes shone. Her breasts heaved. They were silent and they kept looking at each other. Traditional music sounded all around them.

They turned a corner and found to their amazement that the entire street had been taken up by an open-air party. In the middle of the street there were wooden folding chairs round tables. And behind the chairs, poles had been stuck in the ground. Red light bulbs and blue fluorescent tubes were attached to the poles. There was a standby generator. The party was crowded. Tables were loaded with basins of beans, jollof rice, basins of fried chicken, moin moin, and fried fish, and countless bottles of drink. The guests were lavishly dressed, with families in clothes of identical pattern and colour. There was a live band on a wooden platform. They performed a popular Apala tune which sang the praises of the celebrants. People dressed in bright agbadas danced around the tables.

'Let's go and join them,' Ifeyiwa said.

'Okay.'

Holding hands, they wandered into the midst of the party. The musicians played another song. The loudspeakers kept squeaking. Near the stand an argument broke out. Two men in voluminous and expensive agbadas began shouting. Suddenly they became entangled in a fight. Their hands blurred. Voices were raised. They fell on one another, and it became impossible to distinguish them. They seemed to have become woven out of the same cloth. The fight widened. The musicians sang of peace and unlimited wealth. The fight quietened, and vigorous dancing took the place of its passion.

Omovo and Ifeyiwa found vacant seats. Everywhere Omovo looked he saw people dressed traditionally. The crowd grew, passers-by joined in, and soon Omovo felt overpowered by the smells of Arabian perfume and sweat.

'We are not properly dressed,' Omovo said.

Ifeyiwa laughed and said: 'Let's dance.'

As Omovo got up, the wind blew hard into the party and overturned paper plates with food on them. Omovo watched as a whirlwind raised the litter in the street. The whirlwind approached the party.

'What are you looking at?' Ifeyiwa said, tugging him.

'The wind.'

They pushed into the centre of the party. Omovo felt awkward. Ifeyiwa began dancing, her face brightened with the yellow of her dress and the light from the blue fluorescent tubes. She danced sinuously to the Yoruba music. Omovo was struck by how well she danced, how fluently she shaped her body to the music, and how at home she was in the air of ghetto celebration. He, however, felt less at home with the music.

'Where did you learn to dance to this music?'

'By watching,' she said, and danced round him.

Staring at her, dancing stiffly, he was struck by how odd it was that he felt more familiar with disco music than with traditional movements. Ifeyiwa seemed at home with both. She dazzled with vitality. She danced so beautifully, with such ease and grace, that she began to attract the attention of the men around. They danced round her. One of the men, richly attired in lace and beads, a fan of blue feathers in one hand, came forward and pasted a twenty Naira note on her forehead. The crowd cheered. Ifeyiwa was obliged to dance with more vigour, to surpass herself. She did, and more men came forward, and dancing suggestively round her, pasted Naira notes on her sweating face. Omovo watched her with a mixture of amazement and uneasiness. She had begun to attract too much attention. The musicians on the stand sang to her, describing her curves, her movements, and the fantasy of her body. The wind rose. Omovo drew closer to her and said:

'Let's go.'

'Why?'

'I don't know.'

She giggled joyfully. She held his arms and twirled and he caught her. He held her in his arms and felt her heat and the palpitations of her heart. They stayed still. People danced round them. Omovo looked up and said: 'Let's get something to drink.'

'Okay.'

But as they turned towards their table, Omovo caught sight of a familiar face in the crowd near the stand.

'Oh no!'

'What?'

'I think Tuwo's here. Let's go.'

At that moment Tuwo looked in their direction. He wore a red agbada and a blue hat. Omovo, not sure if Tuwo had seen them, ducked. They crouched low, mingled with the crowd, and left the party. As they went they kept in the shadows. A cat with glowing eyes followed them.

They walked for a long while without speaking. They passed a bungalow with all the lights off and from one of the rooms they heard a woman scream ecstatically. They came to a huge tree. Birds rustled in the branches. They stopped under the shadows. Omovo turned and caught Ifeyiwa's neck and pulled her to him. They kissed passionately as if, at any moment, the world was going to tear them apart. Omovo tasted her lipstick and the sweetness of her mouth. When they stopped, Ifeyiwa uttered a curious sound and said, almost wretchedly: 'I have never been in love before.'

Omovo buried his face in her hair. Ifeyiwa pushed him away gently. He misunderstood the gesture. He went a short way up, came back, and leant on the tree. He breathed in the scent of bark and leaves. Ifeyiwa struggled with her pocket and brought out a ring. She gave it to Omovo. He received it in his palm, went into the light, and looked at the silver-painted ring. He came back to her with his palm still open.

'It's for you,' she said.

Omovo was silent. He stared into the distance. Nothing was clear any more.

'My mother gave it to me when I was leaving home.'

He felt mists rise to his eyes. He tried to be hard. 'I don't want it,' he said.

'Why not?'

'I don't know.'

'It's a good-luck ring and I'm giving it to you.'

He looked into the distance again. All he could see was the sky over the ghetto, oppressive and beautiful. He felt a lump in his throat.

'Thank you, Ifi, but I lose things.'

Ifeyiwa made her curious sound. It wrung his heart. He took the ring from his palm. He tried it on a finger. It fitted. He removed it, put it in his side pocket, then took it out again. When he put on the ring she said:

'How is your painting coming on?'

'It's not coming at all,' he said.

Then he told her about his dream of the girl. With barely controlled passion, waving his hand despairingly in the air, he told Ifeyiwa that he knew he had no choice but to do the painting. He said he had no idea what it should be like, he had no visual images. All he had was the mood, the spirit of the painting floating about inside him on waves that wouldn't go away.

'But what will it be about?' she asked.

'I'll have to tell you a story first. Do you remember the last painting I showed you?'

'Yes. It frightened me.'

'Well, the government seized it.'

'What?'

'The government seized it. They said I was mocking our country.'

Ifeyiwa was silent for a while. Then coming closer to him, till he was almost leaning against the rough bark of the tree, she said: 'They, too, were frightened.'

Then Omovo told her about how he and Keme went to the park afterwards and how they stumbled on the mutilated body of the girl.

'Something happened inside me,' he said. 'It was something beyond fear. I don't know what it was.'

Ifeyiwa drew back from him.

'Then afterwards I dreamt about this dead girl. In my dream she didn't have a face. She only had eyes.'

Ifeyiwa let out a sharp breath. The wind rose and blew and rustled the leaves of the tree. Omovo shivered. For a moment he felt as if he had been talking in his sleep. Ifeyiwa drew further away from him. She walked a short way up. He heard her coming back. Only her yellow dress was visible in the darkness. The yellow dress and her eyes.

'But why would anyone want to kill a girl?' she said. 'Why?'

'I don't know.'

'But why? Why did they mutilate her?'

'I don't know. For sacrifice, maybe.' Then after a short silence, he said: 'When I think about it, even in broad daylight, the whole thing scares me.'

'But why?' she kept saying, almost as if Omovo should know, as if he were in some way responsible.

They fell silent. Ifeyiwa moved towards him. She stopped. She threw her arms in the air. Then she made that strange noise of hers. Then, in a low voice, almost as if she didn't want the wind to hear it, she said: 'This world is so wicked.'

She said it with great bitterness. Omovo searched for her face in the darkness and found it had taken on the hardness of rock. She was strangely immobile. The wind blew, rustling the stiffness of her dress. The leaves on the tree were in a frenzy. Omovo looked up. Then he looked around. In the distance, from the forest round the marsh, he heard cries and cultic chants. He heard the irregular beating of drums. He heard animal cries that could have been human. It was very dark. He heard the wind in the leaves and he heard the tree breathing near them. He breathed in the darkness and the ghetto smells. He seemed to be seeing his surroundings for the first time. As he turned to Ifeyiwa a yellow light flashed in his eyes. He caught a glimpse of Ifeyiwa, half-enclosed in darkness. For a moment he saw the dead girl's face in Ifeyiwa's features. The wind made him shiver. He shook his head.

'Omovo, what's wrong?'

'Nothing. Nothing at all.'

Then he reached out, took her hands, and pulled her to him. He held her as if he didn't want her ever to go away. He held her for a long time. It was his way of dispelling his sense of terror. Omovo held her so tightly she had difficulty breathing. He soaked in the full reality of her being, breathed in the lightness of her perfume and the earthy aroma of her body. He felt her hair and touched her face and her arms as if he had never touched her before. It seemed the only way to drive the horrible transposition from his mind.

After he had got over the shock of seeing the dead girl on Ifeyiwa's face, he said: 'Let's go. It's so dark under this tree.'

The real reason he wanted to go was because he suddenly couldn't remember what the dead girl looked like.

They made their way home silently. Ifeyiwa led them back through a maze of streets, unfinished roads, dirt-tracks, bush-paths, and short cuts. They came to the stall of a fruit-seller. The stall-owner was a woman. She was asleep and her head was resting on her basin of oranges. Ifeyiwa bought some tangerines. As they paid the wind blew out the oil lamp.

'It's going to rain,' the woman said, and hurriedly began to pack her things.

When they got to the street where the party was taking place a strong wind blew over the chairs and paper plates. Omovo watched as a businessman draped in a glowing white agbada, with elegant sacrifications on his fat face, sprayed money on the women who danced. The more the women trembled their enormous backsides to the music the more money the businessman plastered on them. The wind blew some of the Naira notes into the air and the children ran to catch them, screaming. The musicians blasted out their praise-songs through the loudspeakers. Then quite suddenly the rain began to pelt down. The party became riotous with outrage. The celebrants shouted. The men in their fluttering agbadas, which the wind threatened to wrap round them completely, ran in all directions. Some of the men ran straight to their cars. Others ran into houses for protection. People stumbled over chairs and tables. The businessman who had been spraying money on the wind tripped over his voluminous clothing and fell face forward into a basin of fried goat. Children screamed everywhere. The women, with much more presence of mind, dismantled the chairs and tables, carried off the basins of food and the crates of drink. The musicians hurriedly packed up their equipment, carried in the loudspeakers, and stumbled over their instruments. The chaos was extraordinary. The rain became a down-pour, torrential and unrelenting. The lights went out round the arena of the party.

The rain thrashed down. Ifeyiwa and Omovo began running. They ran through the wetness and found nowhere to hide, no eaves under which to shelter. They ran aimlessly. After a while Ifeyiwa stopped.

'The mud is getting on my dress,' she said.

They stopped running and picked their way serenely through the rain. They were soon completely wet. Omovo noticed that Ifeyiwa's face glowed with a wonderful radiance. He held her and she stopped and looked into his eyes. Her face was wild and her eyes were intense. He kissed her. Then they began walking again. They walked through the passions of the season.

Then Ifeyiwa stopped again. Omovo looked round and realised that they had broken through the dream maze into a familiar place. They had arrived at their street. Ifeyiwa was drenched with rain. Her clothes stuck to her body and her hair dripped water. She looked oddly defiant.

'I will always remember this,' she said.

Omovo smiled. He felt as if they had undergone a numinous ritual. He felt as if they had passed through an invisible door which opened only in one direction.

'What will you tell him when you get home?'

Ifeyiwa stared into his face as if she were reading a script with tiny letters.

'Don't worry. He went out to a meeting of his townspeople. He'll be back late.' She paused. Then she said: 'I am so happy. I won't let anyone take it from me.'

Omovo stared into the distance. Then he looked at her and said: 'If you come round tomorrow I will draw you.'

'I will meet you in the backyard,' she said.

There was a half-smile on her face. Her eyes were sad. They were sad in the way that only a deformed kind of beauty can be. At first he didn't understand the sadness. Then he noticed that the rain had washed off her mascara and eye-shadow and powder, giving her an almost ghoulish look. He touched her face. She lowered her head. When she looked up she became the girl in plain blouses and soup-stained wrappers that Omovo had always known. She looked as if she had stepped out of her enchantment, and into her reality.

'Thanks, Omovo,' she said simply.

Then she half walked, half ran down the drenched street. He watched her as she went past abandoned stalls, record shops, provision stores, all shut for the night. The rain had stopped falling. Calmness reigned over the land for a moment. He watched her cautiously approach the patch of bushes. He tried to see beyond the bushes but couldn't. And as she vanished from sight, walking hurriedly, she made the darkness yellow. Omovo felt as if a gift had been snatched from him.

He stood still for a long time. Rainwater collected round his feet. There were no insects around. As he stood there, pondering the collective haze of light above the houses, something happened. Darkness fell over everything like a mighty cloak. There had been another power failure. Disorientated by its suddenness, he shivered. It was as if a light had gone out in his head. The wind rose and the silence hummed for a moment before he plucked up enough courage to make his way home. As he neared the bushes he thought: 'When the darkness is recent there is almost nothing to guide you.' The compound front was empty. The men who had been talking about infidelity had all gone. He went into the compound without looking at Ifeyiwa's housefront. He did not do any painting that night.

TEN

When Ifeyiwa got home she was surprised to find the lights on in their room. When she went in he was just draining a tumbler that was a quarter filled with ogogoro. He had been to a meeting, but because it had ended in quarrels, and because the lights had been seized earlier in that area, he had returned sooner than expected.

He was sitting bolt upright on a chair. His eyes were raw and red. His face had darkened. He looked as if waiting for her had exhausted him. He had bags under his eyes. He looked ravaged. His hands quivered. Ifeyiwa stood at the door, uncertain of what to do. Then, without looking up, he made for the belt which had been lying on the bed. His voice was loud with barely concealed anger when he asked:

'Ifi, where have you been?'

Words failed her. She braced herself.

'Where have you been?'

'I went to see my friend, Mary. On my way back the rain beat me.'

He looked up at her. His hands quivered more noticeably. 'Why didn't you tell me where you were going?'

'You were out.'

'So whenever I go out you go out, eh?'

'No.'

There was an awful tension in the room. She stood shivering in her yellow dress. Her hair was all over the place. He looked at her a long time. It may have been because she was so well dressed, because she had worn her best clothes which he had never seen on her, because she wore her white shoes, her white scarf, and looked like a bright young girl returning from a party that he felt so bad, so excluded. She had obviously

138

not dressed up so well on account of him. It may have been for all these reasons that he got up and shouted:

'If you go on like this I will send you back to your wretched people! I will send you back to your miserable family! When you foolish village girls have small education dat's how you behave, eh?'

His anger overflowed. He lashed out with the belt and caught her on the neck. She screamed, jumped sideways, and crashed into the cupboard of food. He lashed at her again. He tore the shoulders of her yellow dress. He went on whipping her till she grabbed the belt, rushed to the door, and ran out into the wet night with her clothes in tatters.

'Run! Run outside if you like! You will sleep outside tonight,' he shouted.

Then he went and locked the main door and the door to their room.

She stood in front of the compound. She heard the water running in the gutters. Mosquitoes assailed her. The wet wind blew through her. She was standing there when the lights were seized. At first she did not notice. Then the darkness crowded her. She saw a candle being lit in her husband's room. She went and sat on the dirty cement platform. Her clothes stuck to her and she shivered as the wind kept blowing. She listened to the frogs croaking all over the marsh. She was staring at Omovo's housefront, wondering what he was doing, when she saw his lean silhouetted form come down the street and into his compound. If he had looked up he wouldn't have seen her anyway. She sat in complete darkness, desolate in her torn dress and white shoes and faded perfume. Her body itched. She scratched herself absent-mindedly. And when the wind stopped blowing her head dropped. She readjusted her position and rested her head on the cradle of her arms. Then she raised her knees. She slept like a lost child that had cried itself to sleep.

An hour later the main door opened. Her husband emerged and in a half-gentle, half-angry voice he commanded her to come in. She was silent. He raised his voice and woke her. He moved towards her. She turned, saw his menacing form creeping towards her, and ran into the street. He pleaded with her to come in and dry herself and get some sleep. She moved further from him, till all he could see was her white shoes. He stayed pleading for a while. When he saw how hopeless his efforts were, when he saw there was nothing he could say that could make her trust his desire for reconciliation, he went back in. Then he told her he was leaving the doors open so she could come in whenever she wanted.

139

'Watch out for thieves,' he said, and disappeared into the house. But she stayed out the whole night and slept on the cement platform.

ELEVEN

What was it that woke him?
Was it the rush of images, of birds keening and swarming in his sleep, dark birds fighting in a trapped place, with leaves blown to frenzy all about him?

He stirred on the bed, his mind suspended between waking and nightmare. From beneath the table he heard clutching noises amongst the papers. Then several claws scratched under the bed. He got up, and thought: 'Bloody rats.'

With his awareness of daybreak myriad sounds played upon his consciousness. An alarm clock rang. Cocks crowed. He heard the swishing broom of the woman whose turn it was to sweep the compound. A baby cried insistently in the backyard. An argument between a married couple had started. From the road, through the veil of dawn, he listened to the female prophet who every morning clanged her bell and called on people to repent before the apocalypse. Shortly afterwards he heard the newspaper vendor blasting his horn and announcing the most intriguing items of the day's news. And far away, the muezzin called the faithful to prayer.

He lay back on the bed and when he shut his eyes he remembered the events of the night before. How had he survived the intensities of that night? He didn't know. It was when he became aware of the fan blades blowing cool air at him that he suddenly realised what had woken him up. It wasn't the rats. The lights had been brought back. Feeling curiously happier, he thought about the previous night.

It had been a happy place – the walking, Ifeyiwa dancing, her yellow dress, the rain. Then it became a sad place – the black-outs, the parting, the incomplete embrace. His eyes focussed and he found that he had been staring unseeing at the quote he had written on the wall: 'Yesterday is but a dream.'

He turned over and thought about Ifeyiwa. He wondered if she had got home without any trouble. He knew how jealous, how vindictive her husband was. He had heard about the two thugs paid to beat up the photographer who, it was claimed, had attempted to seduce Ifeyiwa. The beating was so severe that the photographer, under cover of darkness, fled from the compound and was never seen again. His shop, with its displays of photographed babies, newly-weds, and hearses, stayed empty till it was eventually turned into a barber's shop.

Omovo tried to not think about Ifeyiwa. Where could all the thinking lead, to what place, what precipice? Occasional companionship, an intense and distant friendship, decorous on the outside, was all he could really ask from her. He wanted more, burned for more. She needed more – anything less would suffocate her. He turned over on the bed again as if the motion would stop him thinking, but the image of the two birds on the banks of the stagnant stream came back to him. When the image passed he found himself thinking about the painting, and beneath the thoughts was the growing panic that he couldn't remember any details of that other night in the park. Then he remembered Dr Okocha's quote: In dreams begin responsibilities. He felt reassured. In loss begins art, he thought. He found himself staring at the wall:

'. . . and tomorrow is only a vision.'

He sat up on the bed. What is a dream and what isn't, he wondered. What is a vision and what isn't? His head throbbed. He could sleep no longer. He stared at a painting he had done to illustrate a poem Okur had written after their mother's death. It was an oil painting of three red birds scattered in a concussive expanse of colours. Okur had said he had written the poem under the influence of marijuana.

Omovo shut his eyes and tried to forget. But one thought led to another. He lay back on the bed hoping to catch a little more sleep, but as he shut his eyes a rush of images poured over him. He couldn't escape them. Birds, keening, swooped on him. Wherever he turned, thousands of white birds were flying into his eyes. When he fought them off and ran he found some of them clinging to his hair. He pulled them off and screamed when he discovered that the birds had all been blinded. He sat up, and opened his eyes. Everything in the room was in place.

His mouth tasted sour. He needed to brush his teeth and he couldn't remember where he kept his chewing stick. Throwing the sheet off him, he stood up. His eyes went to the quote on the wall, as if magnetised by the words:

'But today well lived makes every yesterday a dream of happiness . . .'

He pressed toothpaste on his brush and paused to regard himself in the mirror. He was dismayed at the longish shape of his head. He left the room wondering what on earth Ifeyiwa saw in him. Outside, it was cold and damp. The sky was the colour of an old man's beard. The air was fresh. And as he walked the length of the compound he could smell the day's new odours rising from the rooms. Children were balanced on potties. Some of the women had begun the morning's cooking. Some men, their faces heavy with sleep, stood in front of their rooms brushing their teeth with chewing sticks and scratching their stomachs. Young girls fetched water from the well.

When Omovo came back into the room he embarked on clearing up the profusion of objects on the table. His room was in such a mess that he abandoned the attempt at clarification. Then as he stood there uncertain what to do with himself, apprehensive of what the day held, he became aware that there was something he hadn't completed. Finally his eyes were drawn to the wall:

'. . . and every tomorrow a vision of hope. Look well, therefore, to this day.'

Not long afterwards he heard a knock on the sitting room door. Then he heard his father talking to someone in an irritated but controlled tone of voice. Omovo opened his door and looked out and saw that it was a Jehovah's Witness. His father told the woman pointedly that he didn't want to be preached to and didn't want any of the pamphlets. He shut the door in the woman's face. When he turned round he caught Omovo's eyes. Omovo, flustered, said: 'Good morning, Dad.'

His father nodded absent-mindedly. He didn't move and he didn't look at his son. The wrinkles on his face had deepened further. His eyes had the wandering, unfocussed gaze of one who didn't want to fix his attention on anything. He looked lost, as if he couldn't recognise the details of his own sitting room. Omovo wanted to say something to his father. Anything. He wanted, for example, to ask his father to tell him a story. Any story. A story of ancient African heroes, of heroes that became gods, of gods that were banished from the earth. He wanted, spontaneously, to sing a song in his native Urhobo language. He wanted to ask about his father's business. Was it progressing? Were the debts

turning into profits? Omovo wanted to ask all these things simultaneously: but he was stopped by the acres of frozen emotions, of cold spaces
between them.

The curious thing was that his father stood next to the door with an
expectancy about his stance which Omovo only noticed afterwards.
After a moment his father made a vague gesture, picked up the Sunday
papers from the table, adjusted his wrapper, and went on into his room.

When he had gone Omovo felt a vague yearning, coloured by
sadness. He decided to do some painting. He painted for an hour. At first
the yearning, the sadness, was lost in his preoccupation. Then after a
while he began to feel himself forcing the brush on the canvas. The urge
to paint thinned. He felt no impulsion of images. He had been working
but nothing caught fire inside him, nothing leapt out at him accidentally
from the colours he had painted. He wasn't interested in what he was
doing. Then he heard a voice within him say: 'Why are you doing this?'
He took it as a sign and abandoned the canvas.

Omovo was pacing his room when a boy knocked on his door and told
him that Ifeyiwa said she was ready and waiting at the backyard. He
remembered his promise to sketch her for a painting. The boy looked at
him, waiting for a reply. Ifeyiwa had told him not to come back without
one. Omovo said:

'Tell her I'm coming.'

When the boy left, Omovo felt afraid. He was afraid of the spectacle
of artist and model, made sinister by the fact that she was married. It
troubled him that such an innocent spectacle could be taken as a public
confession, a discreet sign of guilt.

Wishing that she would come and pose in a secret place, he got out his
sketchbook and board. He moved towards the door and then stopped.
He paced the room again. He felt curiously trapped. He felt trapped by
his desire and by his inability, his unwillingness to resist its pull.
Somewhere in his mind he was aware of the possible consequences of
what he was going to do. He didn't want to think of consequences or of
anything else. In a sudden outburst he banged on his table. As the papers
amidst the clutter flew everywhere, agitated by the small table fan, he
suddenly remembered the source of his nightmare.

Eight years ago, as a boy scout at school, he had gone for survival
training in the forests. They had stayed two days in the wilds and had
lived only on what they could get from the bush. On the evening of the
third day they had got lost coming back to their tents. Someone had fired

a gun not far from them and all of a sudden the forest swarmed with a confusion of white birds. Omovo fled for cover. He ran behind a tree and saw a woman staring at him. When she moved, bats flew from her dress into his face. He screamed and dashed to find the others. When they came back from their various covers the sky was calm and the forest was clear, as if nothing had happened. When Omovo went with a group of friends to look for the woman they found nothing except a scarecrow in the shape of a crude masquerade.

The act of reaching the source of memory made Omovo feel elated. Feeling the joy that perhaps accompanies the pull of a strange fate, the magnetism of events being set on course forever, Omovo turned off the fan, picked up the papers, put them on the table, and went out. In the living room he found Blackie sitting on the arm of a chair staring at him. There was no malice in her gaze but she seemed to be staring right into his most secret thoughts. He didn't say anything to her. He rushed out into the compound.

In the backyard Ifeyiwa was hanging out the clothes she had been washing. She looked different. Overnight she seemed to have undergone a disenchantment. She looked pale. She seemed, in a matter of twelve hours, to have lost weight. There was no lustre on her face, and she wore rags. She seemed to have almost no connection with the girl he had walked into dreams with the night before. Omovo burned for her, burned for her secret pain, for her dull eyes, her sunken cheeks. He wanted so much to soothe her. He wanted badly for her life to be better, but he didn't know how he could help her. When she saw him her face lit up a trifle and her eyes became defiant. She smiled at him. Unduly conscious of the eyes of the compound, he didn't smile back.

'What do you want me to do?' she asked.

'Nothing.'

He had wanted to ask her to sit with her washing in front of her, but she had so suddenly become a mood he wanted to capture forever. He decided, instantly, to sketch her, to make several rapid sketches of her as she performed the ordinary actions of washing and drying clothes. The more he looked at her between sketches the more he noticed her beauty. It had become a hard beauty, softened only by her occasional smiles. The sadness, the love she made him feel, made him want to draw everything that was connected with her, as if his mood, her spirit, his love, as if her mystery and his helplessness, as if that instant resided for all time in the objects present. So as he drew her he also drew the cement wall of the well, the rusted buckets and unwashed plates, the collective kitchens behind her, the naked children with big stomachs near her, the faded blue wall of the compound, and the washing lines weighed down with clothes.

As he did these sketches, in furious speed, and in absolute concentration, she became self-conscious. She talked to him. She made jokes and tried to sound cheerful, but he didn't hear her. So after she had dried some of the clothes she sat down on the low stool and began to wash a blue bed sheet. As she washed she started to sing. She sang very sweetly and while she sang her self-consciousness vanished. As he drew her he became aware that she had stopped moving. He stared at her and saw that the bucket was between her legs and her wrapper had been drawn up. He could see her thighs. His concentration diminished and he grew conscious of the fact that a crowd had begun to gather round him. He was irritated. He felt vulnerable. He also felt a voluptuous heat come over him. To get it out of his mind, as it would clearly compromise him publicly, he decided also to capture her sensuality, her curves, the promise of her thighs, the definition of her breasts. This seemed to help, for he was soon lost in work, lost in her pose which best coincided, at that moment, with the private image he had of her.

Omovo worked fast. There was so much he wanted to catch which appeared in his mind and moved away so rapidly. He found it increasingly hard to concentrate. The sunlight grew harsher, the sky was more fiery than golden, and he could feel the sweat breaking out on the nape of his neck. And then there were the spectators all around, watching them in idle bewilderment, watching as if Omovo and Ifeyiwa had stopped in a dance, or ritual, and would commence performance any moment. Children had gathered. They asked questions and laughed when he told them to be quiet. The assistant deputy bachelor walked past and said, in a manner of insinuation:

'Na wa-o! Wonders never cease.'

Omovo went on sketching. He had heard nothing. The pencil scratched on the white surface of the paper. His absorption had the curious effect of making everything still about him, as if he were emanating enchantments. The flies disturbed Ifeyiwa and she brushed them away. Omovo realised that she had stopped singing. He paused and noticed the shadows on her face. When he had re-established the silver line of that unique mood, he continued drawing.

The children became restless. Nothing dramatic seemed to be happening. Their movements disturbed him. One of the compound men came and stood behind him, breathing on his neck, looking at his sketches from over his shoulder. Omovo stopped.

'I am not a photographer, you know,' he said with controlled anger.

'Sorry-o!' the man said, and went to the toilet.

Omovo had to wait to regain his mood. Struck by the relationships between Ifeyiwa, the well, and the bucket, he noticed that the light on her had changed. She looked transformed, as if the sunlight were an invisible kind of water that had washed her face. Her eyes were full of animation. He continued drawing, inspired by the lights on her white blouse. He had worked into a clarity that seemed to absorb everything when from the entrance of the compound someone cried:

'Trouble dey come-o!'

Omovo was the only person who did not hear. Or rather, he heard a few moments later, for when he looked up he noticed that the spectators had moved away. Ifeyiwa stood up suddenly, a scared expression on her face. Omovo followed her gaze and, too late, he saw Ifeyiwa's husband striding through the compound towards them, his face stony, his fists clenched.

Omovo's mind went blank. He held his breath. For a long moment he stood staring, mesmerised by the reality of what was happening. With great speed, and without saying a word, Ifeyiwa's husband snatched the top sheets from Omovo's sketchbook, tore them to shreds, grabbed Ifeyiwa by the arm, flung her forward, and pushed her through the compound towards their house. It happened so quickly that Omovo felt unreal, he felt he had been dreaming it all. Dimly aware of what he was doing, he walked back to the room.

His father was pacing the floor when Omovo went in. His father stopped and, lashing the air with his hands, said: 'What is wrong with you young people of nowadays, eh? Why are you drawing another man's wife? Watch yourself-o! Women are the cause of many troubles. Leave other people's wives alone! You know the kind of man her husband is, and yet you persist in this folly! You foolish young men . . .'

Omovo desperately wanted to say something, to express his innocence, but his voice failed him. Besides he knew his father wouldn't understand.

'There are thousands of young girls out there . . .' his father was saying.

Omovo didn't hear him. In a dream-daze he stumbled into his room and fell on his bed.

147

TWELVE

'Wake up, Omovo, wake up!'

Omovo stirred and opened his eyes. He saw Keme standing over him. He got up.

'I'm rushing somewhere but I thought I should come in and see you.'

'Keme, how are you?'

'Fine.'

'What's been happening?'

'I can't stay long. Left my bike at the other road and someone might steal it.'

'Sit down, man, and take it easy. I haven't seen you for some time.'

Keme sat. He fidgeted a bit and was clearly uneasy about losing his motorcycle. Omovo said: 'Do you want something to drink?'

'Nothing for me, thanks.'

Omovo went out and washed his face. When he got back Keme was pacing the room.

'Why are you so restless?'

'Everything.'

'So look, what happened with the girl? Did you follow up the case?'

'Of course I did,' Keme said somewhat explosively. 'What do you think I am?'

'A journalist. A good one.'

Keme looked at Omovo. Then he sat down. He quietened a little, but his voice took on the tones of anger spiked with helplessness.

'I went to the police station the day after we saw the girl's corpse.'

He paused.

'And?' Omovo asked.

'I went to find out if they were bothering to investigate the murder. And do you know what happened?'

'No.'

Keme paused again. His eyes hardened and took on a faraway expression.

'What happened?'

'They bloody well detained me for a whole day. They threatened to beat me and lock me up. They somehow got it into their stupid heads that because I was taking an interest in the case I must therefore know much more about it.'

'But why?'

'Well, they said that they had got a call about a girl's corpse, they had gone to the park, combed the entire place, and had found absolutely nothing.'

'What!'

'They found nothing – nothing unusual.'

'But . . .'

'I know. It's weird. We saw that girl's body. We saw the blood on her. We saw the cross round her neck. We saw that she was beautiful and young. We saw the expression on her face. But when the police went there the next morning they found nothing. Nothing unusual.'

'But . . .'

'I know. It's strange. I tripped over her. You lit the match. I remember her dress, torn. I remember her thighs, all mashed up. And they found nothing. As if the Atlantic had washed her body away. As if the earth had opened and swallowed her. As if the night had simply wiped her away.'

'Nothing?'

'Nothing unusual.'

Keme paused again. They were silent for a long while. Then Keme, breathing out a deep sigh of exhaustion, said: 'Maybe we dreamt that wicked night.'

'But . . .'

'You would think that something of her remained. Something incriminating. A piece of her cloth. Her cross. Her blood. Her shoes. Anything to show that she had been unnaturally killed. But how do we deal with nothing?'

Omovo stayed silent.

'I wrote a report about it the next morning, but the editor reduced it to a fraction of a column. It read like a filler. I wrote another piece and my editor said he wouldn't publish it. I asked why not and he said he needed hard evidence.'

'Hard evidence?'

'That's right. It's crazy. I mean we print stories about a woman who gave birth to a snake, a man who rose from the dead, a town in which people say they saw a two-headed elephant. We print things like a judge who made love to a madwoman because it was supposed to make him rich overnight. We even print stories about a village where it rained frogs during the harmattan, but now my editor can't print a story about a little girl who was ritually murdered.'

Omovo got up and sat down again. Keme continued: 'As soon as the police let me go, and it took a call from my editor, because they were thinking of holding me as an accomplice of some sort, as soon as I was free I went to the park. I searched and found nothing. Life is so strange. That night everything was dark and we were lost, but when I went back it was still daylight and I couldn't find the place where we found the body. The whole thing is beginning to make me doubt my own sanity. I don't know what to do.'

'Don't doubt your sanity. We saw what we saw. It was real. Somebody must have come back and removed the body.'

'Who? Why?'

'I don't know.'

'So how can this thing be investigated? Where do we start? How do we know that the police are telling the truth?'

'Keme, we don't know anything.'

'So what would have happened if that night we had taken the police directly to the body?'

'You want the truth?'

'Sure.'

'We would have been held for murder.'

'Why does it have to be like that?'

'I don't know. Maybe it's because it's pretty impossible to investigate anything in a society as chaotic as ours is right now. But I feel certain that we'd be in deep trouble . . .'

'And,' interrupted Keme, 'it would be excellent for the image of the wretched police force.'

'I know. They are more corrupt than boils.'

'Scumpools.'

They fell quiet again. Then Keme said: 'When I told Mother about it she broke down and wept. I couldn't stop her. She wept for hours.'

'So what are you going to do?'

'What can I do? I'll stay with it, write another article on it, or I'll write a feature on ritual sacrifices, strange secret societies and blood fellowships.'

'Be careful. One doesn't know who is a member of what.'

'I know.'

'We know so little about the world, how it works, who manipulates things, who makes dead bodies vanish, who suppresses what information.'

'I know. Maybe, then, I'll write a short story about it.'

'But if you write a story about it,' Omovo said, 'will you invent what you think really happened or will you tell it as you witnessed it?'

'I'm not sure. All I can honestly do is tell it as I saw it.'

'But you are doing that already.'

'It's not enough. I'm writing facts. I haven't said anything about how it felt, what kind of night it was, how it affected me, the owl, the moon, the bells.'

'I know. It's not really enough, is it?'

'No.'

'I even dreamt about it.'

'So did I.'

'I dreamt that when you lit the match I saw my missing sister there and that she suddenly, with sleepwalking eyes, grabbed my ankles. Then she began to crush my bones. I woke Mother up with my screaming.'

'I dreamt that she wouldn't stop following me.'

'Let's not talk about it. The thing is driving me mad. How is your painting?'

'Not going well.'

'I'm sorry.'

'Don't be. It's part of the business.'

'Did you see the article that woman at your exhibition wrote?'

'Yes.'

'I thought it was interesting that she used your painting that was seized as a basis for investigating our national psyche.'

'I thought so too. It's just that she could have been describing another painting altogether.'

'What do you mean?'

'I did not recognise my painting in her words.'

'Have you heard anything about it?'

'What?'

'Are they returning it to you?'

'No. I don't expect to hear anything anyway. Let them have the ugly painting, I've come to dislike it so much. I think because our lives are so hard our art needs to soothe, to massage, more than it needs to pry open all of our wounds.'

'Do you really think so?'

'I don't know. I'm not sure. There are some things one never forgets, things one shouldn't forget. The dead girl's body is one of them.'

Omovo paused. Then, changing the tone of his voice, so it became sadder because he had slowed down his speech, he said: 'When I was a kid I used to sit staring at cobwebs and spiders for long periods of time. Mother was rather scared not so much of cobwebs but that I stared at them so much. She thought it unnatural that I should stare at spiders, dying rats, worms. One day, unable to bear my obsession, she began beating me with a comb and then with the heel of her shoe. It didn't change anything – it actually made me more interested in the hidden, the dark side of things.'

'Why?'

'I'm not sure. I wanted to draw them, to know them. They are magnetic.'

'Too many people are afraid to look at the dark side of things, to look at the things that are there. That's the problem.'

'And so we have rituals and stories.'

'And paintings.'

'Yeah.'

'Omovo, I have never heard you talk like this before. You're changing.'

'I don't know. I feel things have been happening to us that we know nothing about.'

They were silent. Keme got up and began pacing again. 'I have to leave town. I am aching for a journey. I want to taste the road. I feel trapped here. And helpless. I want to leave this bloody rat-race. My mind is scattered. I can't seem to focus. I should be doing something worthwhile with this life that one has only one chance with. I should be building something. I need to get away and look at myself.'

He said all this rapidly, moving his arms, his face passionate, and when he finished he sat down exhausted, almost defeated by his own intensity.

'You're right,' Omovo said. 'One gets lost too quickly in the city. We stop thinking. We begin to thrash about. In the end we mistake confused motion for progress.'

Keme had started to sweat. His restlessness returned.

'I better go, you know. Someone might steal my motorbike if I leave it too long.'

'Okay. It's good to see you.'

'And you.'

'We never meet enough.'

'I know. My mother keeps asking about you. Come round to ours sometime.'

'I will. Say hello to her from me.'

'Sure. And by the way, what's happening to the others?'

Omovo smiled. 'Dele is off to the USA in a few days time. He's very excited about it. And Okoro has found himself a new girlfriend.'

'Well, I must catch them in the week.'

'Yeah.'

'See you.'

'I'll walk you to the gate.'

'I enjoyed our chat.'

'So did I.'

Keme stood at the door looking out. And then, moving his head as if the lights outside hurt his eyes, he said in a voice devoid of bitterness: 'It's crazy, isn't it?'

'What?'

'That we print stories about a man that eats metal, about rats that eat up canoes in Egypt, about women who give birth to quadruplets, but we won't print the story of a girl who had been murdered in a park, on the edge of the Atlantic.'

'It is strange,' Omovo agreed.

Omovo saw Keme to the gate and then walked him all the way to his motorbike, which was parked three streets away because of the bad roads. They were silent all the way. Keme got on his bike, started it, waved, and with an introspective expression on his face, as if he were already at his destination, he rode away.

Omovo, walking home through the muted and gay air of a ghetto Sunday, felt himself slightly hallucinating as a result of the things Keme had said. He felt strange. As he neared home he experienced the half-hidden notion that his art was somehow not adequate to describe African reality.

When he got home he sat on the bed and pondered their conversation. Soon he felt his head spinning in a cross-wind of too many things he had to think through. He opened the windows. The air that blew in was fresh at first and then it brought all the smells of the compound. Light streamed in. He decided to paint in order to escape the traffic jam of his thoughts.

He brought out his easel and oils. He mixed the colours, his mind becoming progressively engrossed in the act, the ritual of preparation for work. He breathed more gently. His mind cleared. Then he got out the canvas he had abandoned earlier. He looked at the confused, ugly colours and half-formed images he had daubed there earlier. He looked at the canvas for a long time. Then, curiously, he began to discern the potentialities in the half-formed shapes. He read himself into them. With his natural aversion for shapes that were not anything related to blood and feeling, with his respect for the narrative aspect of painting, his mood guided him to attempt something he would not ordinarily do because he felt it too difficult and demanding. He started to paint a Lagos traffic jam. The moment he realised what he was doing he was happy, he felt light, and he ceased to think altogether. The vision and his mood carried him on their unique stream and he soon wasn't even aware that he was painting. And in the moments when his concentration broke and he became aware that he was indeed painting he began to do something strange, something he had never done before. He began to name the images he was bringing into being, began to chant them, as if he were praying, as if the naming of them in some way guided his hand:

'Metal. Hot road. Copper sun. Sweating drivers. Busy hawkers. Policemen accepting bribes. Lights on painted metal. Yellow and black taxis. Glittering windscreens. Weather-beaten faces. Struggling faces. Suffering faces. A million colours of sun and city. The faces of my people. Hallucinatory sunlight on the green lagoon. Gasoline fumes. Beggars. Soldiers everywhere. Traffic jams everywhere. Noise. Chaos. Everything jammed. Motion. Confusion. Houses jammed. Streets jammed. A child eating mango. Clear above, jammed below. No birds in the air.'

And so he spoke and worked as if he were transcribing images from a cloud.

After a while he felt drained and aching. He took it as a sign to stop. He knew he had finished. He looked at his watch, which he never wore. He had been painting, without being aware of it, for two hours. He felt good. Then he felt depressed. Then he felt numb. He listened to the compound's listless afternoon noises. He sat down on the bed and covered his eyes with the palms of his hands. His eyes ached. He stayed like that for a while, watching the colours dancing in his inward eye. After some time he got up, left the room, and went to the front of the compound. He devoured the street, the world, with his eyes. He stared gently at the hawkers, the children, the old men, the molten sunlight on dusty houses and stalls. He stared at lizards and geckoes scuttling up walls. He stared at the chickens strutting peacefully across the street, the goats munching discarded yam peelings. Then he stared at the forest in the distance, relaxing his eyes.

When he went back into his room he sat down and, after his eyes had readjusted to the level of light in the room, looked at his painting. It wasn't as good as what he had seen in his mind. But it was better than anything he had done for a long time. He was a little annoyed by the poor reproduction of imagined reality. He always disliked the feeling of knowing that what was good in his painting nearly always came from his inability to do what he intended, to catch what he saw.

In his painting the city became a demented maze, clogged and vibrant with bright colours, but seen through an effluvial mist. He caught the truckpushers, the carriers of heavy loads, the hawkers, the traffic policemen in their orange uniform tops. He caught the hundreds of feeder roads, the paths, the streets, wild lines that lead only into confusion. He caught the streets of cars jammed and crooked. He even managed to convey the dramatic gestures of Lagosians in their frozen, angled positions. The agonies and the comedies of the city. Framing the haste and frenzy was the lagoon. It was of the same green as his painting of the scumpool. All roads lead into the maze of the city. The chaos and the frustration of the city. But the only ways out lead to the forests of the interior and to the seas.

He looked at his work and, with despair and joy in his soul, he thought: Art is a poor approximation, but the best we have. He began to clear up his brushes, his easel, and paints. He put the painting away and went to wash himself. When he got back the exhaustion of finishing the painting opened him up to a kind of sufflation of sadness and weariness. All the emotions he had been avoiding, the shame and sorrow he felt on Ifeyiwa's behalf, his fear, his love, the burden of being free while she was trapped, all these feelings burst in on him and left him fairly quivering on the bed.

He got out his brother's letter and poem and read them. He stared out of the window at the wall which marked the boundary of his compound. Broken glass had been cemented along the top of the wall to prevent thieves from climbing in at night. He felt a little as if he were imprisoned. He looked at the clouds above the wall and the rooftops. He brought out his notebook and wrote:

> I wanted to do a beautiful painting of her. To remember her forever. Instead I've gone and probably made her life more unbearable. Why do people think that because I'm drawing her something shameful exists between us? And why is it that I can't seem to do the right thing when I know quite well what the wrong thing is? I feel I am being drawn into a dark zone. I almost seem to be helping myself along. It's hard.

He stopped. He looked out at the wall and continued:

> Keme came by today. Kept saying bloody. Kept pacing like a trapped, intelligent animal. The girl's body has vanished and all we could do was speculate. There we were: individuals helpless in the face of awful events. Who manipulates our reality? And how long are we just going to accept things?
>
> Dele is going to the States soon. He has made his girlfriend get rid of his baby. No. He tricked her. He wants no complications on the eve of his journey to his dream. He says he is afraid. He is getting out of this inferno and he is afraid. Strange.
>
> Okoro has found himself a new girlfriend. Doesn't talk about the war any more. Always talked about the war. The starvation. Soldiers eating half-done frogs. He doesn't talk about the war. I just realised.
>
> I should do a painting of my friends – children of war – children of waste – the war generation – lost in the cities – lost in offices – lost in traffic jams – trapped in the mazes of daily life – the maze of our history –
>
> I am afraid for my brothers, but at least they have shown me that there isn't just one way but many ways into the world – each forges or finds his own – yes –
>
> – the maze mocks the fairytale with nightmare – Lord, may this life always surprise me – fill every crack with light – when we are falling, Lord, make us the spider that can build its own web as net – may good things always flow into us – and when we most need it, Lord, show us a silver way – a secret way –

When he finished writing he felt better. He got dressed and went for a walk. His father wasn't around. The sitting room was empty. The compound people kept looking at him strangely. At the housefront he could see Ifeyiwa through their open window. He went to Dr Okocha's place. The old artist wasn't in. Then he went and watched the cars speeding up and down the express road.

156

THIRTEEN

Omovo had returned from his walk and was in his room, feeling quite peaceful, when he heard sharp voices from the sitting room. At first he thought that Ifeyiwa's husband had come to make trouble. But as he listened carefully, he recognised, to his dismay, the voices of his dreaded relations. They seemed to be reacting to something Blackie had said.

'We don't recognise you! We don't know you! And we didn't come to see you!' Uncle Maki shouted.

'Then get out of here!'

'Why? Who are you – nothing but a second wife.'

'So what? I am the woman of the house.'

'What house?'

'This house. So you go away. If you want to see Omovo go and wait for him at the front of the compound.'

'Wicked woman. This is how you treat your husband's in-laws. Witch!'

'Who are you calling witch? Your mother is a witch. All of you chop shit. God punish you.'

'God is punishing you already with that empty house.'

At that point Omovo, just about to step out and calm matters down, heard the indignant tones of his father's voice, raised high as if he were hammering on a table as he spoke.

'How dare you come to my house and harass my wife? Who do you think you are, wretched clerk! Get out of here before I send my boys to beat you up. Get out! Get out!'

There was a worrying silence. Then the relation's voice, a register lower, said: 'I want to see Omovo!'

'Get out! You can't see Omovo or anyone else. Just leave before I change my mind.'

Omovo stepped out into the sitting room and watched the whole event through the window, waiting for the best moment to intervene without making matters worse.

The compound men had begun to gather round the exchange. It was part of the compound's tradition that neighbours came to one another's aid when it involved outsiders. Omovo watched the women staring at the 'event', missing nothing. Sensation was in the air.

'Oga-o, Captain of the compound, what's wrong?' asked one of the men.

The assistant deputy bachelor joined the gathering. He had a bottle of beer in one hand. Behind him was Tuwo. The younger bachelors, the men new to the compound, came to give their support. They all streamed out of Tuwo's room. They sounded quite drunk and rather keen on the idea of public revelry and argument.

'Captain, is this man looking for your wife's trouble?' came Tuwo.

'Don't mind these wretched relations of Omovo's mother. They don't have any respect. Insulting my wife! Abusing my house! On Sunday – when a man wants a bit of peace!'

The uncle turned to the compound men and tried to explain. For the first time he came within Omovo's view. He wore an old brown tight-fitting coat that must have been bought second-hand years ago. His hair was dusty and had a fastidious parting. And under the terrible heat he had the folded red umbrella which he used like a walking stick. He turned to the drunken compound men. They listened to him with the perversity of those who intend to misunderstand whatever they are about to hear. Almost pleadingly, but retaining his stubborn dignity, Omovo's uncle said:

'I am Omovo's mother's cousin . . .'

'A very distant relation,' Tuwo said.

'I haven't seen Omovo for some time,' continued Omovo's uncle, 'and as I was in the area . . .'

'You thought you would come and make trouble,' Tuwo interrupted, finishing off Uncle Maki's statement to the great amusement of the gathered crowd.

'No!' protested Omovo's relation. He tried to get back to his explanation but was forestalled by Omovo's father.

'Get out of this compound, you thief.'

'I am not a thief. Did I steal from you?' Uncle Maki said, gesticulating

158

with the red umbrella. He looked rather pathetic, with all his blustering and with his kola-nut-stained teeth, and with all the struggling against the confinement of his small coat. Omovo, feeling bad that a relation was about to be made a fool of by the compound men, was going out to try and calm events when his father launched into an unexpected stream of recriminations. Turning to the compound men, he said:

'Look at him, coming here now and talking nonsense. When my first wife, his relation, was ill did he come and visit her in hospital?'

'No!' the compound men answered.

Omovo's dad turned to Uncle Maki.

'When things were hard for us was it not you people who laughed at us behind our backs? Did you come to her funeral? Have you come to console us since, eh? So what are you doing here now, eh? When we needed your help you didn't come. We have done fine without you. We don't need you and your rat eyes judging everyone, looking to see how other people are living so you can go and gossip to the whole world. We don't need your pretence. Why do you come and visit Omovo now? What do you want from him, eh? Is it because you saw his name in the newspaper, eh? I feed him. He lives under my roof. I got him a job. It's now that you turn up to try and win him over! Get out! Now!'

Uncle Maki, moving his lips wordlessly, waving the red umbrella around, looked absolutely stunned at the torrent of insinuations.

Omovo's father finished by saying: 'And to make matters worse you come here, wake me up, and abuse my wife in front of the people of the compound!'

Uncle Maki made a brave effort to speak, but the compound men had begun pushing him. Their eyes were red and their fingers itched for some action.

'Go!'

'Yes, leave!'

'Leave before we roast you alive.'

'Leave with your stupid umbrella,' the men said.

Uncle Maki pushed them back. Then facing Omovo's father, waving the umbrella menacingly, he said: 'Let no one touch me. I am just coming from church and I don't want trouble.'

'Then stop waving that thing at my eyes. Or you want to blind me?'

Completely misunderstanding Omovo's father's mood, unaware of his depression, his financial pressures, his acute sense of betrayal, Uncle Maki said: 'It's my umbrella. I'll do what I want with it.'

Omovo's father's voice changed. 'Is that so?' Then snapping his fingers commandingly, he said: 'Blackie, go and fetch my machete.'

Blackie went into the sitting room. Omovo ducked back in. He heard her fumbling around the cupboards. Then he heard her footsteps go past. When he looked again his father was holding the machete.

'Useless relatives!' he was saying. 'Thieves and gossips. Pharisees! Troublemakers! Hypocrites!'

Omovo felt trapped. He couldn't just watch helplessly and he couldn't go out then because, with his father now riding his favourite grievances, his presence would only be inflammatory.

'Don't call me a hypocrite! And I am not a Sadducee!'

'Pharisee, I said.'

'Eh, I am not a Pharisee. I am good Christian and I pray to my God every day.'

'And then on Sunday, when God is resting,' Tuwo added drunkenly in his most artificial accent, 'you go and make trouble with your umbrella!'

The men burst out laughing. Uncle Maki raised the sharp point of the umbrella at the men in an aggressive gesture.

'You want to fence, eh?' Tuwo said.

'Don't mind him,' someone else put in. 'He wants to jump fence with his old umbrella.'

'You want fence with machete, eh?' Tuwo continued.

The assistant deputy bachelor, balancing his bottle of beer in one hand, knocked the umbrella from under his nose with the other. It hit the wall near Omovo's father. There was a strange silence as Omovo's father gave a cry of indignation, lifted the machete high, and held it frozen in the air. Everyone stayed still. Then, suddenly, Uncle Maki's wife cried out. Omovo's father, letting out air and shouting 'hypocrite' at the same moment, swung the machete at the umbrella. The crowd scattered. The men yelled. The women screamed. The umbrella was knocked clean out of Uncle Maki's hand and it flew open as it touched the ground. The men burst out laughing again. The umbrella was a sorry object, in tatters, rickety, stained with rust, full of holes. Uncle Maki picked it up and kept trying to shut it, but it kept flying open. Eventually his wife came and seized it from him and snapped it shut in a single gesture. Then she began to push her husband out of the compound.

At first he didn't want to leave. He talked. The men talked back. They began to squabble. One of the women said that it was Sunday and that matters should be settled 'amicably'. Blackie hissed and went into the sitting room and followed the proceedings from the window. The men crowded Uncle Maki, who made vague threats at Omovo's dad. Another voice said something which was lost in the confusion. Uncle Maki made another vague comment about money owed him from the distant past by Omovo's father. Silence followed as the fact was digested. Omovo's father erupted again and lunged in Uncle Maki's direction, but was restrained by Tuwo. Uncle Maki began to leave the compound, dragged by his wife who abused him for all the fuss he had started in the name of an innocent visit.

Meanwhile Tuwo finally managed to get the machete from Omovo's dad. As soon as Uncle Maki left the compound, under a hail of biblical abuse from Omovo's father, and blamed by his wife, the men started to chant the compound's work songs, praising and teasing their 'Captain'. Omovo's father, having made his arresting public gesture, stormed to his bedroom. Omovo was obliged to hide again. When he reappeared, with the intention of going out now that things had settled, he saw that Tuwo had brought the machete in. He gave it to Blackie, and lingered. Her face was overcast. Omovo hurriedly passed them and went to meet his talkative relations.

'Eh-heh!' cried his uncle when he saw Omovo. 'This is the person I came to see! I didn't come to visit that witch who drove my sister to her death and that man who asks me to leave the dirty parlour he calls his house . . .'

Omovo stamped his foot and shouted: 'For God's sake, Uncle, you are insulting my own father, you know!'

There was an ugly silence. His relations looked dourly at him, then looked away. His uncle tramped out of the compound front, stumbling over an empty Coke can. The crowd watched for a while and, seeing that the afternoon's drama had ended, returned to their various chores and recreations.

Omovo stood still for a while, allowing his anger to settle. Then he followed his uncle. In the middle of the street his uncle, his uncle's wife, and their three children were waiting. His uncle stood away from his irritated wife. He kept readjusting his coat, which was tight at the armpits, the material frayed and scuffed. He sweated profusely. His white shirt was covered in patches of wetness. His baggy trousers, his dusty black shoes with the sole of his right foot coming away, his frayed umbrella, his kola-nut-stained underlips, the parting in his hair, and the pietistic bearing of his head made of him a picture of stiff-necked provinciality.

His wife and children also looked self-consciously attired, as if they had brought clothes out from the bottom of boxes, meant only for special occasions. His wife's face was sweaty and serious. She wore a gash of cheap lipstick, with cheap beads round her neck. The powder had run on her face. She wore a green blouse, a multi-coloured wrapper, and carried a black handbag. The strap of her slippers had burst and she walked uncomfortably. The two children, clinging to their mother's wrapper, looked miserable and hungry. They were barefoot.

Omovo greeted the wife and children. They greeted him back, somewhat sulkily. Omovo desperately wanted them to simply disappear. He hadn't seen them in years and when he did they always managed to drive him to extremes of distraction. His uncle said, in a tone of complaint:

'We were just coming from our church meeting, we were passing your place and I said as it is Sunday we should just come and see how you are. Then I received that nonsense.'

Omovo said nothing – he merely gritted his teeth.

'You are here in this hell, eh, and you don't come and visit us. But when we come and visit you we receive all that nonsense.'

'Dat's enough, hah!' his wife said. 'Can't you leave something alone sef?'

'Why? The man called me a thief.'

His wife sucked her teeth. 'You talk too much sef. Ah-ha! You go and visit and then begin to quarrel with your in-law's wife, ah wetin!'

'Look, Ester, shut your goat mouth, you hear!'

Omovo stopped listening to them. He fell back behind them and began to concentrate on things around him. He temporarily retreated into another state of being, soaking in phenomena, looking at the street with the eyes of a stranger. A Mini drove past and filled the air with dust and smoke. The sun burned in the clear sky. The ground was so hot that Omovo could feel the heat through his sandals. He wondered how the children bore it. There were heat-mists in the air and the faces of passers-by looked hollow and dried up.

He wanted to be away from his relatives. They made the heat get on his nerves. Their presence intruded on the revelatory moment that seemed about to break on him. Frustrated, he kept fretting with his fingers. And as he looked at the street with the eyes of a stranger, trying to keep the frustration at bay, possibilities of observed details that could be turned into art kept presenting themselves to him. The yellow scumpool, dense with effluvium. The askew lines of sun-bleached stalls.

The face of a child absorbed in its play. Birds dipping past him. Suddenly a swell of rapture, of golden joy, burst on him from within. And for a moment nothing seemed ordinary. His mind stilled a bird's passage through space. It became a black flash of the extraordinary. He saw the white quills within its black ruffs and saw its feet tucked beneath its quivering tail. When he looked down he saw that he had just missed stepping onto a lump of excrement on the ground.

'So, Omovo, how are you, eh?' his uncle said, slowing down.

'I'm fine.'

'How fine?'

'Fine. Okay. Well.'

'Is it true you've got a job?'

'Yes.'

'Good. Where?'

'At a chemical company.'

'That's nice. When?'

'Six months now.'

'Is that so? Good. Is that why we don't see you any more, eh? Now you are earning money you begin to avoid your relations, eh?'

'That's not true. I've been very busy.'

'Too busy to come to church and worship God. Too busy to come to our town's meeting and make your contribution. Too busy to visit us, eh?'

'Things are hard.'

'But you said things are fine.'

'They are hard.'

'But you've got a job, a roof over your head, you're not married, have no children, and things are hard?'

'Yes.'

His uncle gave a short laugh. 'Ester,' he called, 'are you hearing what Omovo is saying?'

'Yes. Yes.'

He turned back to Omovo. 'So what wrong have we done that you don't want to come and see us, eh?'

'Nothing.'

'We are your people, you know.'

'I know.'

'Come and visit us from time to time.'

'I will.'

'Fine.'

163

They walked in silence. Then Omovo said: 'How are the children?'

'As you see them.'

'And how are you?'

'I can't complain. Our life is in God's hands.'

'Is work well?'

'I can't grumble. What God gives we are grateful to receive.'

Another silence. His uncle brought out a filthy handkerchief, blew his nose so hard it sounded like a faulty musical instrument, then he stared at Omovo and drew closer to him. Omovo could smell the camphor balls on his coat and his hair oil.

'Omovo,' he said. 'Are you all right?'

'I'm fine.'

'Are you sure?'

'Yes.'

'And they are not doing anything bad to you in the house? Your father's wife, I mean.'

'I'm okay.'

'And nothing bad has happened?'

'I'm well.'

'So why did you shave your head, eh? People only do that in mourning or when something bad has happened.'

'Uncle, it was an accident.'

'Accident?'

'A mistake. The barber was a fool.'

'Are you sure?'

'Yes.'

'It's not that you've been thinking too much about your poor mother?'

Omovo suppressed an irritated gesture. 'Of course I think about my mother.'

'Thank God.'

'But that's not why I shaved my head. It was a mistake.'

'You said so. But you look old and tired. Lean. If your mother saw you now she wouldn't stop crying. She suffered so much because of you, her children. So much. Bore so much. Fought so much. She was a brave woman. She wanted to make sure all of you led a good life. But if she saw how things . . .'

'Uncle, please!'

'Believe me, if she saw how things have become . . .'

'Please!'

There was a short silence.

'Do you hear from your brothers?'

Perversely, Omovo replied: 'No.'

'What sort of a life is this, eh? But we mustn't complain. Poor boy. Who can tell what this life will bring, eh? Things used to be so good for all of you. We thought your father would be a big businessman with plenty of money. A man who would help us all. You used to live in Yaba, then you moved to the best part of the city. Then when your mother died things began to go badly. What a life! Your brothers were driven out into the world. No news from them all this time. Ah! You must be very lonely in that house. It's clear your father doesn't care about you. He's got eyes only for his new wife. She has dragged him down. Why not come and stay with us instead of suffering where you are?'

'Thank you, Uncle, for asking. You are kind. A true Christian. But I can't accept your offer.'

'I understand. We are poor. We live in one room in a worse part of Lagos than this.'

'It's not that.'

'I know we are poor. Can't give you a room of your own. You would have to sleep on a mat with the children. But it's better than hell.'

'Thank you, Uncle.'

'If you change your mind . . .'

'I will remember.'

His uncle shook his head pityingly. 'Your mother was a good woman. A very kind woman. Died just like that. And meanwhile your father was busy with another woman. Honestly. Poor boy . . .'

His uncle carried on in the same vein, endlessly, as if he wanted the entire planet and the sandy road to bear witness to the depth of his sympathies. Omovo, forcing down the screaming in his mind, said in a gentle voice:

'Uncle, you are wounding me.'

His uncle didn't seem to hear him.

'I know how you feel. I do. So you have not heard from your brothers. You were all so lucky as children. Sent to good schools. We thought you would become lawyers, doctors, engineers. Ah! Only God almighty knows where your brothers are now. America, England, Ghana? What are they doing? Who knows how much they are suffering in some strange country? They could even be dead, God forbid . . .'

Omovo bore his uncle's words till they got to the wooden bridge. Fortunately for him the two children began to cry. They were hungry

165

and they tugged at their mother's wrapper saying that they wanted some oranges. Omovo bought them four oranges and then gave them ten kobo each. They looked at their mother, who nodded, before they took the money. They fell upon the oranges as if they hadn't eaten for days.

After Uncle had paid the fare for their crossing he went over to Omovo, took him aside, and said: 'We are going to visit another of our relatives. You don't have to see us any further. You have the goodness of your mother. If you have any problems come and see me. And be careful what you eat in that house. God bless you.'

Then he turned and, abruptly seizing one of the children by the hand, began to cross the bridge. For the first time Omovo noticed that he walked with an angled movement. He had some sort of deformity, had suffered some sort of wound, and Omovo had never known about it. He felt a little differently about his uncle when he realised that fact.

His uncle's wife came to say goodbye and as she left she began to struggle with her handbag. Then with an expression of quiet sufferance she gave him a gift of a small measure of cloth, enough to make a shirt, and a loaf of bread.

'We are poor,' she said, 'but your mother was a good woman.'

Then she picked up the youngest child, waved to Omovo, and followed her husband over the wobbling bridge of planks.

Omovo watched them go. In spite of being both relieved and moved he knew that it would be a long time before they were going to see him again. He was so disturbed by his uncle that he felt quite shaken for minutes after their departure. His bones ached with frustration, with anger. His fingers trembled and he kept gritting his teeth. To free himself, to loosen his feelings, he wandered round the ghetto without the faintest idea of where he was heading. He wandered through the subdued Sunday noises and the bustling warm life of Alaba. He walked for so long and was so deeply immersed in his thoughts that he ceased to be aware of the lights and the noises and the people. In his profound involvement with the things that he didn't want to face, the wounds he didn't want to look at, he missed most of the finest moments of the changing day. The sky held deep flashes of blue. The clouds took on shapes so splendid that they suggested other countries, suggested journeys to exotic places. The sky was spectacular with oriental red and orange as the sun set over another day. It took the minor drama of bumping into a girl, who pushed him and said: 'Use your eyes, you idiot!' before he realised with a shock that it was evening. And when he looked up and saw the sky he breathed in deeply. His being trembled like leaves sifting the wind. When he breathed out he prayed for the day when he could suggest the beauty and the sadness of the cosmic drama in paint on canvas.

The joy lasted only a moment, for soon he made out the stars of the slowly defining night. Then he realised that Sunday was almost over, that Monday was just around the corner, pitiless and implacable. He felt gloom settling over him with the darkening lights. With his eyes focussed on the road before him, alert to avoid stepping on excrement, and with a cold wind blowing, he made his way back home. And as he went, struck by the fact that the sand was no longer hot, surprised that he hadn't noticed when the blazing sunlight turned and the heat-mists vanished, and musing on how he could have dwelled so long in his mind unaware that time was passing so quickly, as he went he experienced a moment's revelation. And the revelation resolved itself into the thought that he needed to face himself before he could face the facts and the terrors of this world.

When he got home he came upon his father, who stood in the middle of the sitting room, giving vent to monologues about debts, the wicked world, selfish in-laws, unco-operative children. Omovo fled into his room and deposited the bread and cloth on the table. But even in the room he could hear his father droning on about betrayals, injustices, neglect. His father's voice made him restless, frustrated him, communicated failure and despair to his flesh. Omovo could have borne it if his father hadn't come and banged on his door and said, very loudly:

'And tell your mother's wicked relatives not to come to my house ever again. If they are going to cause trouble. Let the dead stay dead.'

His father paused. Omovo began to sigh, but his father continued: 'What contribution have they made to anything, eh?'

Omovo needed to escape from his father's tirade. He got out his sketchbook, three pencils, a felt-tipped pen, an eraser, and he fled from the room. As he rushed out his father said: 'Are you off to draw another man's wife again, eh?'

Omovo had got to the backyard before he realised that being seen with his sketchbook would simply increase the amount of existing speculation. He went to the compound-front. He found one of the children of the compound crying because the others said he was too small to play with them. He did four drawings of the crying child. When he finished he felt he had done something worthwhile. He gave the drawings to the child, who took them off to show to his mother. She soon came to thank Omovo, saying:

167

'They are better than photographs. I will frame them.'

Some of the other children, who were jealous of the boon their outcast colleague had received, cried for Omovo to draw them as well. But he gave them a small amount of money and appeased them by promising to draw them some other time.

He stayed out for a while. The night deepened. The kerosene lights came on at the various night stalls. Electric lights came on in the houses. He went into the sitting room. His father had retired for the night. He ate, read some pages of *The Interpreters*, and made a final attempt to organise his table in preparation for the rigours of another week. He was leafing through an old diary, overcome with nostalgia, when a piece of paper fell out. The handwriting on it was strange at first. It was only when he came to the second line that he realised it was one of Okur's poems – the poem that had inspired the painting on the wall:

> Little birds of the storm
> Struggling in flight
> Was your mother cruel
> To have pushed you
> From such a height?

When he read the poem he thought a little. He shook his head. He didn't want to think. He put out the lights and lay down. He didn't sleep immediately. He was aware of the darkness and the strange sensations closing upon his mind, bearing down on him, blue and alive. Then a sound outside jolted him. He fell back heavily into his body. Then he lightened and the darkness washed over him in irresistible waves and he dissolved into the void that was not really a void.

. . . and then he found himself in a maze and when he looked up he saw her in the distance, one half of her visible, the other half hidden by the corner. Her eyes were sad and she had a brave smile on her lips. He knew that smile so well. It was the way she smiled when bearing a secret pain. It was her masking of trauma.

He followed her through the maze and she kept eluding him, kept disappearing around corners just as he caught sight of her. And because he couldn't reach her he spoke to her, saying:

'O mother who suffered so much in such silence, why did you travel without teaching me how to reach you? Stop escaping from me, running from me. Come and comfort me, come and fondle my hair the way you used to when I was a child.'

She stopped and for the first time in his life he saw her with adult eyes.

She was smaller than he remembered. Her face was full of wrinkles, her jaws hollow, an old woman with the sad eyes of a bewildered child, wide open and bright as crystals.

'Don't just stand there looking at me,' he said, approaching her gently.

He noticed that her feet were covered in a white mist. When the mist cleared he saw that the ground he walked on in the maze was covered in broken glass. Her feet were bleeding and raw. He saw the scar over the shin-bone on her left leg. It had been caused the day his father, beating her in the kitchen, had accidentally pushed her. She had staggered, turned, and fallen into the fire. He couldn't remember why his father beat her in the first place. He was so young then, with his mother always carrying him, that he sometimes became part of the beatings.

'Mother, I need you. I need your spirit and your warmth, for I am lonely. I am in danger of getting lost. Guide me through this maze.'

But she stayed still and said nothing.

'What must we do to save ourselves from the termites and maggots that eat at our dreams?' he asked.

He began to approach her more hurriedly. From the distance she made a sign. Was she making a gesture of benediction or was she waving goodbye? Then he realised too late that the more he followed her the farther away she seemed. Darkness fell gently over everything and he started to run after her frenziedly. He got to the end of a passage and found himself at a place where five roads met. She was at the end of all of them. She had stopped making signs at him: he had not understood the signs when she made them. And, confused, he went down all five roads, feeling a curious serenity and love guiding him. It was only at the end of the last road that he might have found her waiting. But the darkness turned her face slowly into an illuminated hardness. And when the transformation was complete all that was left of her was a mask unsupported in the air, a mask he had never seen before. It had big lips, rugged cheeks, and the eyes were unbearably tender. Feeling protected, he touched the mask. In the flash that followed he saw his mother disappear into the maze, lost to him forever, and he was afraid . . .

When he woke the night was darker than he had ever known it to be. There was something unnatural about the darkness. It admitted of no light. He yearned for living colours, landscapes vibrant with harmonies. He yearned for art, for sustaining memories, for memories of vision. But the night was too dark and it confounded his mind because he could perceive nothing.

Frustrated, drawn by the pull of black streams, he felt himself submerge, felt himself journeying at a strange speed through primeval caves, accompanied by shadows. And as he sank into the new darkness he prayed that he could reach greater powers, greater visions and the intimations of a greater life that flowed somewhere in the landscapes within.

BOOK THREE

ONE

He woke up with the feeling that his face had become like a mask. The mirror did not wholly undeceive him. His bony head with its growing bristles, and the wrinkle on his forehead, which he had not noticed before, made him feel like an old-eyed, lean-jawed stranger.

He took his towel and soap and made for the bathroom. A slight mist covered the compound. The cold air made him shiver. The compound had the muted business of an early Monday morning. A cock crowed somewhere in the distance and a child imitated its sound. The men prepared for work, combing their hair and chewing their chewing sticks at their room-fronts. Children were dressing for school. Women swept the corridor, warmed stews in the kitchen, and fetched water from the well.

In the bathroom, fooling around for many minutes, tentatively getting his body used to the iciness of the water, he began to take his shower. He was covered with soap, and was singing, when he heard her say from the adjacent bathroom compartment:

'Is that you, Omovo?'

'Yes.'

'I could tell by your towel on the wall.'

Omovo stopped singing. He also stopped the shower. He suddenly had an overwhelming sense of his nakedness. He found it odd that, separated by the mucus-infested wall, he was still disturbed by her proximity.

In a voice that was both sweet and strange, she said: 'I'm sorry about yesterday.'

173

'It wasn't your fault. I should have known better. What happened afterwards?'

'He threatened to cut my face with a razor.'

'Why?'

'So men wouldn't bother me and so he can have some peace. And then he whipped me.'

'I'm sorry. I should have been more careful.'

'Don't be sorry.'

They were silent. After a while she asked: 'Did he destroy all the drawings?'

'Yes, but it doesn't matter.'

'Why not?'

'What I drew will stay with me forever.'

'But he destroyed all of them?'

'Yes, but I can paint you now without them.'

'Are you sure?'

'Yes.'

'I do love you so much,' she said simply.

In the midst of the scum and mucus of the bathroom, and in spite of what she had suffered, he felt himself getting warm. He said nothing. Her voice was different when she said: 'My dreams are getting very wicked. I might do something bad. I feel sorrow hanging over me. I don't want to bring you any unhappiness.'

His head cleared.

'I must see you soon,' she added.

Heavy footsteps approached the bathroom. She stopped talking and began to fetch water from the tap. He resumed his shower and washed the soap from his body. The man who had been approaching banged on the bathroom door, almost bursting it free from the nail which kept it shut.

'Who is there?' asked the assistant deputy bachelor.

Omovo, grumbling, showed a soap-laden hand over the door.

'Be quick, man. I'm late for work.'

Then the assistant deputy bachelor went to the toilet. Omovo listened as he urinated for an unusually long time. Then he began singing in a hoarse voice. When he had gone, Ifeyiwa turned off the water faucet and said, almost desperately:

'Omovo, I must see you when you return from work in the evening. I'll be watching for you and I'll make the same sign. I have to go now.'

There was another silence. Omovo waited. The door to the adjacent compartment opened and shut. And then she was gone. For a moment he felt confused, hollow, guilty. The assistant deputy bachelor returned, banged on the door again, and shouted:

'Be quick, be quick! Why you dey baf like woman? Baf like a soldier! Honestly!'

Omovo, taken aback by his sudden return, replied: 'Which one you dey? It's Monday. I want to be clean.'

'Do you need to take so long? Or have you got a woman there with you?'

'No-o!'

'Eh-heh, then baf quick!'

'But the next bathroom is free.'

'Is it? Why didn't you say so?'

Omovo finished his shower in a hurry. The assistant deputy bachelor went into the adjacent compartment and, amidst complaints about women and business, had a showerbath while singing in his voice of a stentorian frog.

When he left home for the office he saw the morning as all mist. He should have hurried to work, for it was always difficult catching a bus at that time of day. But he stopped at his compound front and, breathing in deeply the smell of earth and dew, stared at the crowds of ghetto-dwellers hurrying to their different jobs. The morning was all mist and in the mist people hurried, like shades in an earthly purgatory, to the bus-stop. With heads bent forward, as if they were carrying invisible burdens, they all trudged in the same direction. There was no-one in opposite motion. In the mist he could not see their individualities, could not distinguish their clothes, could not see their faces, or the kinds of shoes they wore. They seemed, curiously, like sleepwalkers.

As he joined them, as he entered the mist, the people ceased to be blurred, the shadows materialised and became real. The abstract crowd broke down into its composite of individuals. He breathed their breath. He smelt the breakfasts that still lingered on them. He saw many different faces. He saw them old and mask-like. He saw them wrinkled and sober, lean and battered, old faces with lines made deeper by the morning. He saw them young with faces bewildered, frantic, unadjusted to the new day. When he saw people he recognised greetings were brightly exchanged.

As he went with the crowd to the bus-stop he experienced a sudden lucidity. He too had become part of the mist, part of the 'exodus', as

175

Okoro often called the passage from ghetto to office. He felt – given the masses of people struggling for few buses, the crush, the hassle – that the passage was another kind of traffic jam, a jam from which there was no escape. Where are we going? he thought. And after all this, after the exhaustion of arriving, what then? He thought about the wrinkle on his forehead: a one-way traffic, a line drawn by a child. He hurried to the bus-stop.

At the bus-stop the frenzy, the chaos, the crush, was as intense as ever. The bus-stop was really a clearing at the roadside, an arena in which every morning masses of hard-working folk fought out a continuity of unjustly balanced struggles. The danfo buses were so few in relation to the demand that whenever one of them swerved into the bus-stop human heads surged to it with a relentless ferocity. People rushed, elbowed one another, necks were squeezed, shirts dragged back, people were shoved, pulled under, or trampled upon. People did anything to get on the buses. It was a pitiful sight, and it was impossible to catch a bus without sacrifice, without pain: a grazed wrist, a broken arm, a torn shirt, a scratched eye, or even roughly massaged breasts. But the sacrifice was worth it if the bus was caught, for there were always the victims, those who struggled passionately, who were wounded, had their clothes destroyed, and who never succeeded in embarking. Omovo always marvelled at people's responses to the first part of a working day. Some seemed curiously to relish the confusion, the rush, the required nimbleness. Some smiled foolishly as they were shoved, others fought back with implacable bitterness, lashing in all directions as if the rest of the crowd were their antagonists, as if getting on the bus was not their real goal. And there were moments of sinister entertainment when fights broke out or when two people, abandoning their attempts at getting early to work, began abusing one another with insults ranging from insinuations of impotence to oblique statements concerning the other person's grandfather's rectum. Omovo had always thought of the bus-stop in the mornings as the perfect symbol of the society, and through that, of life in general. He had always been afraid to tackle it as a subject for a painting.

When he arrived it seemed at first that he was fortunate to have a bus swerve near him. But the driver, relishing the whole drama and his unique place in it, swerved with too much flourish and barely missed knocking over a good section of the crowd. The bus conductor, a boy no more than twelve, bellowed the destinations of the vehicle and leapt from the doorway where he had been clinging. Omovo had calculated

176

where the bus would stop. Then he waited, poised, for the driver's dependable sudden reverse. And then he ducked past a swarm of people, made for the front seat, jerked open the door, and leapt in with a single fluid motion. But then he found he had to wrestle for the only seat with a formidable woman. Using the combination of her massive frame and her huge breasts she attempted to squeeze Omovo against the door, to crowd him out of the competition. But Omovo ducked under her arm and managed to gain the seat. She kept pulling at his shirt, and when this ploy failed, as he was already safely seated, she spat at him. The driver said:

'Ha, madam, he is your son's age. You no get shame?'

Omovo wiped his face. The woman glared at him.

'God go punish you,' she said.

The bus moved suddenly.

'You are a bad loser,' Omovo shouted at her. She made an abusive sign. The bus conductor laughed mischievously at all those who were left behind. The crowd swallowed the woman. The bus was in full motion down the road when Omovo realised, to his dismay, that his new white shirt had been dirtied and that two of his buttons were missing.

'That's life,' the driver said, smiling.

After crossing the wooden bridge over the murky creek at Waterside, he had to get off and catch another bus to Apapa. He had now entered the stage of the journey to work which one of his friends had dubbed 'the great trek'. It was the passage through the residential district of Apapa. This was the district of the rich, of expatriates, with their well-built houses, porches, swings, flower gardens, and swimming pools. The houses lay silent behind hedges and freshly cut lawns. Creepers covered the doors. Tall whistling pine trees scented the air. Birds called. Every house had a shed with a guard. Dogs barked. It was like journeying into another country.

Omovo tramped on with the crowd along the dusty road. An empty danfo bus hurtled towards them, the conductor hollering its destination. The bus turned and parked. People poured at it, Omovo amongst them. He struggled, was shoved and squashed. He wasn't successful. The bus drove away with people clinging to the doorway, others hanging on at the back. Smoke and dust clouded its departure. People who had failed to embark grumbled and cursed the driver.

Omovo pushed on, battered, breathing heavily from the exertion.

When he looked up he saw his friend Okoro, leaning against an Indian almond tree. His friend smiled.

'I watched you nearly get yourself killed,' he said.

'I'm late.'

'I don't bother to rush any more. It's suckers that rush.'

'Suckers, eh?'

'Yeah.'

For someone who wasn't rushing Okoro looked in a bad way. He looked exhausted, as if he had already lived the whole day in advance. His hair was dusty, his shirt rough, his jacket a little dirty, and his matching trousers unpressed, with creases like lines on a map.

'You look as if you slept in the street.'

'I had a great weekend.'

'It shows.'

The crowd surged past. When a bus came along it broke into a kind of hysteria. The sun was out and the mists had gone. Omovo often thought of the crowd as an organism, a single body with many arms and legs. But now he felt certain the crowd was nothing but many separate cells, individual, each dedicated to its own function.

'How was the party?'

'Fantastic. Excellent. Plenty of women, wine, and food. The Yorubas know how to spend money.'

The sun grew brighter, its rays filtering through the branches of the whistling pines. Okoro shaded his eyes. Omovo wiped the sweat off his face with a handkerchief.

'Did you take July with you?'

'Where?'

'To the party.'

'No. She's too precious for that. I treat my women with style. I got my head screwed in the right direction, man. What do you take me for?'

'An American.'

'What?'

'You've got a lot of Americanisms in your mouth these days.'

'I've been reading Hadley Chase.'

'I know.'

'Just read a novel of his called *Eve*. Picked up a lot of phrases and tricks, you know.'

'I bet!'

'But don't bet your right arm to a bad penny.'

178

'Anyway did you know Hadley Chase is an Englishman, not an American?'

'Pull another one.'

'Really.'

'He writes like an American so that's fine by me.'

'Good.'

'Sure.'

'So how is July?'

'Great. Beyond belief. Food to a starving man. Did I tell you we went to the Surulere night club together?'

'No.'

'She paid our taxi fares, paid for the tickets, and even bought the drinks. Too much, she is. Special. A grand chick. We danced and did things. She didn't mind.'

'Lucky bastard.'

'I haven't finished. So, we were at our table when a tall guy came over. He wore dark glasses and looked like a guy with bread. He grinned at us. I grinned back. Then I look sideways and see her smiling at him too. So I say to myself: "Hey, is this a showdown?" The tall guy says, "Hello baby, long time no see. What a place to meet again. Ain't you gonna say hello?" He had this cheap fake American accent and I notice his teeth is kinda too big for his mouth. My woman says to him: "Hello, Amama. I don't think I'm happy to meet you again. I am with my lover so please take your big teeth away from here." The tall guy takes off his glasses, puts them on again, looks at her, then at me, and like a goofy fool he goes away. You know what we did?' Okoro said, turning to grab a surprised Omovo, 'We burst out laughing and didn't stop till the tears rushed out of our eyes.'

Omovo smiled and, propelling his friend forward, said: 'It's a great story. But let's hurry or we'll never get to work today.'

'You're jealous.'

'Because I didn't laugh?'

'You don't have a woman, that's why.'

'You're right.'

They pushed on.

'Have you seen Keme?'

'He came to my place. Said he wants to leave town.'

'Yeah?'

'Yeah.'

'What about the dead girl? He hasn't given up, has he? It's not his style.'

'He hasn't. But the body vanished. The police said they couldn't find it.'

Okoro laughed nervously. Then he was silent. Then he swore and said: 'During the war dead bodies didn't vanish. They simply decayed or were eaten by dogs.' He paused. 'You know, I remember seeing a man's leg under a tree. A burnt leg. No toes. Maggots were crawling out of it.'

He was silent again, then said in a strange voice: 'Some of us were lucky. Bloody lucky. Young and lucky.'

'Take it easy.'

'Sure I'm taking it easy. I forget, that's all. You learn the trick of forgetting. You just dance when you can, get a woman, go to work, and forget.'

'Let's change the subject.'

'Sure. Let's change the world, why just the subject?'

'Let's change it.'

'Change it into wine.'

'Let's forget it.'

'Why?'

'Let's.'

'You know, Dele said he is frightened. What of? His father is rich. He's going off to America. He's gone and got a good woman pregnant. And he's afraid. And me? I wake up on some nights and the war is still going on. Bombs falling. A man, shot through the chest, is calling my name. I look. He's my father. Mines go off. Bullets sounding everywhere. Journalists hiding in shattered doorways. My gun's wet with someone's blood and I'm shooting in all directions like a mad man. I run through the city and see bodies rotting in the streets. I go and report to my officer and he's fucking a woman against the wall in his bunker. I go back to sleep and enter another nightmare. Now look at us. It's supposed to be a time of peace and yet we are frightened.'

Omovo stayed silent. Okoro laughed. His voice lightened.

'Nobodies, that's what we are. People who remain at the bottom, filing documents, running errands, a life of overtimes.'

'We are not nobodies.'

'What a life.'

'We don't have to be.'

'I must read harder for my papers. Must go to university. Must own a car, have a good job, and plenty of money.'

180

'Let's hurry. All those buses and we haven't even rushed for one.'

'It's suckers that rush.'

'Sure.'

'Talking of suckers, you know a really strange thing happened to me the other day.'

'What?'

'I went to one of our town people's meetings and at the end of it we had a dance. I couldn't join them.'

'Why?'

'I found I had almost forgotten how to do our traditional dance. I was really ashamed. All the elders kept mocking me. I mean here I am. I can do any disco dance, but I have forgotten the dance of my own people. It's really strange.'

'I know what you mean. I can't speak my mother's language at all and I struggle with my father's. How did this happen to us, eh?'

'We've been selling our souls without knowing it, I guess.'

'Yeah. Something has been stolen from us, all of us,' Omovo said, echoing Ifeyiwa's words.

They tramped on silently.

'Let's hurry,' Omovo urged.

'Hurrying is for . . .' Okoro started to say, when an old man, his breath heavy with ogogoro, bumped into him.

'Are you mad?' Okoro shouted at the old man. The man began to apologise, but changed it into a curse.

'It's your father who is mad!' he said. 'Is that how you talk to your elders?'

'Foolish old pensioner. Look where you're going.'

The old man stared at Okoro and shook his head pitifully, a ridiculous expression on his face. He had deep wrinkles and a sad, defeated mouth. He dragged up his voluminous trousers, shook his head again, and went on. Okoro started laughing, then he stopped. He became thoughtful. He watched the sad old man who was drunk that early on a Monday morning. He didn't take his eyes off the man till he was completely lost in the crowd.

Buses came, people surged. The buses filled, turned, and sped off.

'So how's your painting?'

'Bad.'

'We have faith in you, you know.'

'Sure.'

'You have a strange talent. I liked the drawing you did of Dele. He said he would frame it. You made him look young and confused.'

'Sure.'

'Now you are saying it.'

'What?'

'Sure.'

'Oh that. It's infectious.'

'How are you getting on with your stepmother?'

Omovo said nothing.

'All right. Bad question. Have you heard from your brothers?'

At that moment a blue danfo bus, old and flaking, swerved near them. Dust rose in the air. Omovo roused himself and dashed for it. He made for the front seat but a man, whose breath stank of sardines, got there first. Omovo struggled for the back and secured a seat close to the sliding door. He saw Okoro belatedly struggling to get on.

'The bus don full!' the conductor shouted. 'Na when chop don finish nai una go rush. People who no get eye for back. Go on driver, go on!'

Omovo, through the little window, said: 'Hi, sucker.'

Okoro smiled sheepishly. 'You bastard,' he replied.

The bus sped on towards the Apapa Wharf. It seemed they would arrive in a short while. But they soon slowed down. The driver took all sorts of trenchant short-cuts, all manner of abominable traffic risks, forced his way in front of other cars, but in the end, like everyone else, he was trapped in the intractable morning traffic congestion. Omovo, looking out of the window, forefelt the insinuations of another tedious day. He was conscious of revolt simmering within him at the remembrances of all the tensions in the office. The mists had cleared completely. Omovo stared at the faces of the passengers. Faces carved on the bitter wood of harsh realities. The faces of those who worked hard at what does not give them pleasure. Faces like masks. Omovo did not look forward to the day's work.

TWO

He arrived late at the office. As he went down the corridor to his department he felt betrayed by his footsteps. He stood outside the office door for a moment, staring at the sign which read CHEMICALS. Bracing himself, he reached for the door handle and went in. It was cold inside. The air conditioning had been turned up to the limit. He shivered.

The moment he entered he felt hostility settle on him. At first no-one acknowledged his presence. As he went towards his table he passed the office supervisor and said, rather too brightly: 'Good morning, Akapko.'

The supervisor, lifting his head slowly from a thick file he had been studying, stared frostily at Omovo.

'*Mr* Akapko, if you don't mind,' he said, in a grumpy voice.

'Good morning, *Mr* Akapko.'

'Much better. From today I want everybody in this department to treat me with respect.'

'Did you have a good weekend?' Omovo asked, smiling.

The supervisor ignored his question and returned to the study of his file. He had been with the company for over twenty years, had started out as a messenger and risen slowly up each rung, and recently had been made a supervisor. It was the crowning achievement of his life. It gave him the pass to eat in the senior staff canteen and the entitlements of a car, expenses, and housing allowance. He didn't want his juniors to forget the fact that he had arrived, but arriving had not taken from him his ingratiating attitude to his superiors. He looked up after a moment. He had the face of a gnome, a face full of suffering, with its dust-beaten beard and hungry whiskers. He said:

'The manager wants to see you.'

'What for?'

But before the supervisor could reply the door to the general office opened and Simon, the office typist, came in. He was carrying a pile of typing paper and office requisitions. When he saw Omovo standing near the supervisor he let out his peculiar brand of whooping laughter.

'Our painter has at last arrived.'

'Hi, Simon.'

Simon laughed again. 'Did you hear him?' he said to the office at large. ' "Hi Simon".' He went round to his table and put down the things he was carrying. 'What's his excuse this time? Don't tell me he's been boozing all weekend. I won't believe it.'

Simon had the vivacity of a cricket and a perpetually famished look. He was lean and alive and full of the kind of humour that seemed to have equal measures of spice and malice. He had an extraordinary face, generously endowed with wrinkles, pimples and spots. He had lively eyes but when he was sombre his hangdog expression, his haunted look, made him seem like one who carried on his face all the woes of his life. When he laughed he looked funny, in spite of the fact that his face took on the quality of crumpled brown paper.

'Shut up, Simon,' the supervisor said.

Omovo went to his desk and brought out his file on the allocation of chemicals to companies. Simon made another remark about his lateness. He was in a mood for teasing. Omovo ignored him. He wanted to get through each day of office routine with the minimum amount of aggression. This meant that he didn't participate, and resented obeying orders. His detachment alienated him, made him vulnerable.

'Honestly!' continued Simon. 'You are the only person I know in this department who can come late on Monday and not be scared. Ten years I have worked in this bloody company, and I've never been late on a Monday.'

The supervisor shouted: 'Shut up, Simon. Get on with your work. It's not your business. And besides the manager wants to see him.'

'Supervisor wetin!' Simon replied. 'You are shouting at me now but after work we will be drinking from the same bottle. Know your people, honestly!'

The supervisor smiled and went back to his file.

Omovo studied his files. Customers would soon start pouring in, each clamouring for attention, for priority treatment, each with complex requests, each with complaints. He had yet to count the chemicals that had come in that morning. He brought the relevant cards from the

184

cabinet under his table and was sorting out the ones he needed when he heard Simon, in the mood to irritate, say:

'So, painter, what made you come late, eh?'

'I woke late. I had problems catching a bus.'

'So that's all you can dream up? You are in trouble. Wait till the manager sees you.'

'Simon, sit down and work,' came the supervisor. 'You have your own problems.'

'Supervisor wetin!' replied Simon a little loudly.

Chako, who was the manager's secretary and the oldest member of staff, banged on the table. He had been so silent that no one had noticed him up to that moment.

'Simon, you fool, you are disturbing my concentration!' he shouted.

At the moment of being disturbed he had been studying the football coupons, hidden under a file, with abnormal industry. He had been playing the pools religiously for twenty years. He had never won a penny and had never given up hope. Every Monday he started afresh. He was a very religious man, in the sense that he attended an Aladura church regularly, and believed in the tenets of his church. In his middle forties, he dressed impeccably but with an outrageous sense of colour combinations. He had quick movements and an oddly twisted face. The curious thickness of his nose, with its entangled filaments of hair, was well suited for, or a result of, his endless snuff-taking. He always looked rough-shaven, as if his hair was wholly resistant to razor blades, and was stricken with a permanence of shaving rashes. He was something of a character in the department. Not even one with the hardiest perversity could fail to tolerate him, if only for his eccentricities and for his antiquity – he had been in the company from its beginnings. Upon banging the table and securing the silence he wanted, he resumed his concentration on his pools forecasts, circling, arbitrarily, the numbers 6, 26 and 36.

But the silence was temporary. Simon was not through.

'Honestly, Chako. Anyone looking at you will think you are conscientious. We all know what you are doing.'

'Mind your business.'

'You are doing your Ph.D in coupon philosophy, after studying for twenty years.'

'Shut up. I warn you.'

'Have you ever calculated how much you have spent on that useless thing?'

Omovo went on with his records. When he had sorted out the cards he needed for the morning's count, he stowed the rest away and stood up.

The supervisor said: 'Have you seen the manager yet?'

'No.'

'What are you waiting for?'

'He can't,' Chako protested. 'The manager is on the phone.'

The supervisor, entering into the prevalent mischievous mood, stared at Chako. 'I wonder why I share the same office with you riff-raffs,' he said.

Simon rattled away at the typewriter. Chako went back to his football coupon, circling the numbers 7, 27 and 37. He settled back in his chair and began to count with his fingers.

'Look at him, look at Chako,' the supervisor said to Simon. 'He's really serious this week-o. If he can study like that, eh, why shouldn't he pass any exam, eh?'

Simon looked up. 'You can say what you want. But when he hits that jackpot don't go near him-o. Even his Aladura church won't make that mistake.'

When Chako heard the last sentence he flung back his chair, stood up and launched into torrential abuse. He was quite incoherent. He shouted in fits and jerks, mixing English with his native Igbo. When he was angry he developed a pronounced stammer which the others found comic. The supervisor picked up a file and hid his face. Simon masked his laughter beneath the clatter of his typing. When Chako had spent himself he settled down, put away his football coupons, and busied himself with a customer's letter.

His timing was impeccable. The door behind him opened and the manager stepped out and scanned the office.

'What's going on?' he asked in Igbo.

The office answered him with silence. He was short and well-built, though in the past, much to his chagrin, he had often been mistaken for a clerk. It was rumoured that he had risen so high, and so fast, with the help of the company's mafia. The truth was that he was a graduate and had recently returned from England, where he had worked in the chemicals arm of the parent company. But like most men who have been surprised by power, and maybe to compensate for his lack of stature, he couldn't tolerate silence.

'I said what's the matter here?' he said again, in Igbo, his voice booming.

186

The office stayed silent. Everyone was still. Omovo had, unfortunately, been caught standing up, on his way to the warehouse.

'Good morning, sir,' he said and made for the door, treading as self-effacingly as possible.

'Omovo, don't try to escape. Come and tell me why you were three hours late this morning.'

'I couldn't help it.'

'And why, if I may ask you, couldn't you help it, Mr Omovo?'

Simon began to type furiously, as if the words were running away with him. He had an expression of studied concentration on his face. The supervisor, engrossed in some recent shipping documents, turned the pages over with noticeable rapidity, his fingers tapping a thoughtful rhythm on his table. Chako, with a bedraggled kola-nut between his lips, ruminated over the customer's letter. Omovo turned the cards in his hands.

'I woke late, was caught in the rush . . . It was hard to catch buses . . . my shirt is torn, I mean my buttons . . .'

'I see.'

'The rush was terrible this morning.'

'So you keep saying. But everyone in this office, apart from the supervisor and myself, comes from Ajegunle. And they get here on time. Besides, what's to stop you from tearing off your own buttons?'

'I wouldn't . . .'

'Shut up! Listen, young man, you are the most frivolous, unserious, uncommitted, unconscientious, and insubordinate member of this department. Look at the rest of them.' And the manager indicated the office at large.

Simon impressively ripped the sheets from the typewriter. Then he read through what he had written. The supervisor picked up a ball pen, turned one of the pages of the shipping documents, wrote a comment on it, and then turned to ask the manager a relevant question about the recent shipments of liquid chlorine. The manager gave a lengthy and resonant reply. Chako, working his mouth, nodded vigorously at something significant he had noticed in the customer's letter. The manager turned to Omovo and was about to speak when Chako blew his nose, the sound of which was like wood being briefly sawn. Simon resumed typing.

'This is an efficient team. You're the odd one out. Always loitering. Consider this your fourth and final warning.'

Omovo stared at him. For the first time he noticed the leer that lurked

187

on the manager's mouth. The manager, obviously disturbed by Omovo's cool reception of the threat, fingered his tie, and strode back into his office.

Chako brought out his football coupons, fished out another kola-nut from under his typewriter, and proceeded to chew. Simon stared at the calendar with the picture of a generously-breasted semi-nude white woman on the wall opposite. Then, grumbling that the office was too cold, he brought out his tea bread and fetched himself a glass of water. He kept dipping the bread in water as he ate. The supervisor brought out his pocket calculator and, with a hungry studiousness, began to work out how much his salary, his overtime, his allowance and other invented expenses would amount to on payday.

Omovo passed out of the cold office and made his way to the hot warehouse. As he travelled these antipodes he was overcome by something more than the intimation of things about to happen.

The day's work progressed. Customers came in such numbers that the chemicals in stock had to be strictly allocated. Often the competition was such that powerful clients went higher up in the departmental echelon to arrange their orders. When that wasn't happening they often resorted to back-door methods, to bribery, to intimidation, or to sheer persistent verbal attacks. The office would be crowded with customers squabbling, attempting to jump the queue, or to get more than had been allocated to them.

It was Omovo's job to make the allocations on a daily basis, to take the customers' orders and arrange for them to collect. This meant interminable trips up and down the corridors, to the warehouse where the authorised documents were deposited, and then to the accounts department where copies of the transactions were submitted and the customers' accounts checked and debited. By one thirty Omovo was usually sweating, haggard and exhausted.

He was on his way back to the department when Mr Babakoko blocked his path. He was a bulky man, a businessman, in a resplendent agbada, with beads and amulets around his neck and gold rings on his fingers. He had facial scarifications and small red eyes. He smelt of incense and corruption. He had sly mannerisms. Omovo had been aware of him in the office. The loudest of customers, he padded about the place with his thick arms dangling beside him as if he were a chief. He was an important customer with a lot of influence in the company. He had a major contract to supply the state's water corporation with liquid chlorine.

'My friend, what wrong have I done you?' he said.

'Nothing. Why?'

'So why are you treating me like this?'

'I don't understand.'

Mr Babakoko at first responded with a look of bewilderment. Then he smiled and put his weighty arm round Omovo's shoulder and walked with him up the corridor. Omovo felt uncomfortable, he felt himself enfolded in a conspiracy he didn't understand. The powerful odour of Mr Babakoko's Arabian perfume, the incense and the bodysmells, made Omovo feel slightly ill. He shrugged his way from under Mr Babakoko's arm. The businessman smiled at him again and Omovo understood.

He was such an important customer that it had become customary for him to get his supplies directly from the manager, who got either Simon or the supervisor to deal with them. But this afternoon the manager was unavailable, the supervisor had gone off to have his car repaired, and Simon was at the trade union meeting. It fell to Omovo to handle his allocation and he treated Mr Babakoko's papers no differently from anybody else's.

'Listen, my friend,' Mr Babakoko said, 'you are young and I understand what you need. Just come out straight with me and don't waste my time. Your friends are straight with me, your manager is straight with me. They get what they want and so do I. Everyone is happy. Fall for me, I fall for you – that's the game. Don't be shy about it.'

'About what?'

'Tell me what you want and arrange my supplies quickly. Your queue is too long. I have five other companies to get to and I can't spend all day here.'

There was a moment's embarrassment. Then Mr Babakoko, drawing up his agbada sleeves, dug his hand into the folds of his voluminous garment and began to struggle with one of his hidden pockets.

'You are making a mistake,' Omovo said, moving towards the office.

Mr Babakoko found what he was looking for and, running alongside Omovo, began to peel off notes from the bundle he had in his hand. It seemed like a substantial sum. He attempted to pass it into Omovo's hand. But Omovo rejected it. All this happened in the corridor, in full view of workers who passed by them.

'I said you are making a mistake,' Omovo said again, stopping to make his point decisively.

'Don't be a fool, young man. Take my offer and do my business quick.'

'You'll have to wait your turn.'

Mr Babakoko peeled off some more notes. Omovo had a sudden desire to knock the bundle out of his hands. Instead he turned, said something incoherent and insulting, and pushed on. Mr Babakoko caught up with him again. The money had disappeared. He stopped Omovo and with a demonic expression on his swarthy face said: 'This world is bigger than you. In this place money does all the talking. I feel sorry for you. Very sorry.'

Then he hurried off angrily down the corridor, his agbada fluttering about him like obscene wings.

Omovo watched him go. He remembered what the men of his compound had said about the massive can of worms. He thought about the entanglement of bureaucracy and corruption that had spread throughout the society. He thought about the older generation, how they had squandered and stolen much of the country's resources, eaten up its future, weakened its potential, enriched themselves, got fat, created chaos everywhere, poisoned the next generation, and spread rashes of hunger through the land.

He thought about all these things, and about his confiscated painting, as he stood at one of the large windows of the corridor. The windowpane was very clean and he looked out into the courtyard. The concrete floor was streaked with light and the factory buildings were painted yellow. He stared at hulks of machinery and at the workers in greasy overalls without seeing them. He could feel the sweat all over his body. He felt his face lean, his head bony. He felt exhausted and realised that he was trembling slightly. He made his way up the corridor, away from the office, with the vaguest idea of his destination. He felt fairly certain, however, that trouble was gathering over his head.

THREE

'Where can we talk?' Joe said to him, at the accounts department.

'Anywhere. Here.'

Joe looked around. 'It's not the kind of thing to say anywhere. And certainly not here.'

'The warehouse then.'

'Fine.'

'But be quick about it or the manager will say I'm loitering again.'

Joe was one of the few people in the company whom Omovo liked. He was tall, he had a moustache, dressed brightly, looked sharp, modelled himself on film stars, dreamed of going to America, and was easy-going. He used to be in the chemicals department before being promoted. He had joined the company a few months before Omovo.

They went to the warehouse and stood like conspirators behind a stack of chemicals. The smell of all the different chemicals was dense and pungent. Omovo found it difficult to breathe. And when he did the pungencies burned his nostrils and shocked his brain. The heat in the warehouse was incredible. Green mists hung in far corners and it was as if the sacks, the crates, and the walls were all giving off their acrid essences of boiling air. Strange liquids coagulated on the floor. Powders and granules had spilled out of their greasy sacks and changed colours as if their inorganic natures were bursting into flower.

'What did you want to say to me?'

'Take it easy.'

'I am.'

'How long have you been with the company?'

'Six months.'

'How much do you earn?'

Omovo looked at him.

'Don't think I don't know. I work in accounts, remember.'

'A hundred Naira a month.'

Joe fingered his fashionable tie. 'Only?'

'Yes.'

'Have you been confirmed?'

'No.'

'Why not?'

'I might be. This month.'

Joe laughed strangely. 'How much overtime do you do?'

'Depends.'

'On what?'

'On if it's compulsory. Left to myself I don't care much for overtime.'

'Why not?'

'I'd rather go home and paint.'

'Sure. But does your salary last you till the end of the month? That is after feeding yourself, transport, tax, the national provident fund, the weekend fun, and, of course, things for your painting?'

'I manage somehow.'

'Do you have old people in the family?'

'Joe, where are all these questions leading? You sound like the inquisition.'

Joe smiled, and then lowered his head. 'I hear things. People talk. They whisper. They say things when you go past. Some people don't like you.'

'People don't have to like me.'

'Sure. But they say you spoil their "business". They say you are too proud.'

'I do my job and go home and paint.'

'Sure. But that's why you're a fool.'

'Take it easy, Joe.'

'You think you're smarter than everybody, don't you?'

'I'm balder than everybody.'

'You think not taking a little harmless bribe makes you special, eh?'

'No.'

'Listen, I'm telling you this for your own good. Your boss doesn't like you.'

'I know.'

'I overheard him talking about you in the canteen.'

'What were you doing in the senior staff canteen?'

'I have my plans.'

'Sure.'

'Your colleagues don't like you either.'

'I know.'

'You keep too much to yourself.'

'I'm left out.'

'You don't give people a chance to get to know you.'

'I try.'

'The job you do is important.'

'Is it?'

'Of course. That's why when you were interviewed for the job the manager asked if you would be co-operative. You said yes, didn't you?'

'I had to. I didn't know it also meant taking bribes. Besides, how do you know what went on at my interview?'

'I have my ways.'

Omovo looked at him again and saw him differently.

'Listen. All of us went through that. You have to co-operate. Look at your mates. Go and see Johnson's place. It's in Ajegunle, but it is virtually a palace. Mark you, he's a clerk like you. Or notice how well Jack dresses. Or look at Simon. You think he is a joker, don't you? But he's building a mansion in his village, and planning to buy a car. Now look at you.'

It was Omovo's turn to smile. Joe looked him over with vague, if affectionate, disdain.

'Your clothes are in bad shape. Cleaners and messengers look better than you. And to make matters worse you went and shaved your hair when there is no death in the family. Do you belong to a secret society?'

'Sure.'

Joe flashed him a glance and decided he was joking. He continued. 'So, like I was saying. How do you think people make it in the company when the salary is so wretched?'

'Hard work, tailored spending. I don't know.'

'Look man, it doesn't mean anything to take a little bribe. It won't stop you being the person you are. It doesn't stop Chako from being a fervent Christian, does it?'

'Doesn't seem to.'

'If you don't want to do it then at least don't make it difficult for others. Don't block people's way. The life is hard enough as it is.'

'So what are you saying?'

'The right hand washes the left. The left hand washes the right. Both hands are clean.'

'You're a philosopher.'

'I heard Babakoko complaining bitterly about you. He said you insulted him.'

Omovo began walking away. He walked over a burst sack of yellow granules.

'Omovo, I haven't finished.'

Omovo went out into the fiery glare of sunlight. He went past the stacks of alloprene, the yellow liquid-chlorine drums, past the noisy machines, and nodded at the drivers who were arguing in a truck. The heat was merciless. The sunglare crowded out his thoughts, deadened his pores, saturated his clothes with sweat. The multiple lights flashed at him from all the metal and the windscreens. He brought out his handkerchief and wiped his face. Joe caught up with him.

'Omovo, don't be a fool. As a friend, I am the only one who can tell you these things.'

'Thanks for telling me.' Omovo stopped to wash his face under the tap outside the canteen.

'Listen man, you are not indispensable in this company.'

'Nobody is.'

'You are a nothing.'

'At least I can't get worse.'

'If you leave nobody will notice, nobody will feel it.'

'You care too much about what people think.'

'Sure. But you are unimportant. They can spit you out just like that.'

'Leave me alone, Joe.'

'You're nobody. They can just spit you out.'

'Leave me in peace.'

Omovo bent down, threw his tie over his shoulder, and splashed water on his face. The water was cool at first and then it became lukewarm. Joe sucked his teeth in exasperation and contempt. He made a gesture which Omovo didn't quite catch. After a while Omovo heard his shoes grating on the cement floor in a supposedly significant exit.

When Omovo got to the office the supervisor said: 'Why haven't you been attending to all these customers who are waiting, eh? Have you no pity? They have been sitting here all morning.'

Omovo said nothing.

'I've seen you loitering about in the warehouse, chatting with Joe. Just watch it-o! So please attend to the customers now.'

194

Chako said: 'Omovo, the manager wants to see you.'

The supervisor said: 'Attend to these tired customers.'

Simon said: 'Omovo, take these papers to accounts.'

Omovo stood bewildered.

The phone rang and Simon picked up the receiver.

'Hello. Ah, na you. Okay. I'm sorry. Omovo? Okay. He will do it soonest.' Simon looked up. 'Well, painter, our boss in the other office wants you to make him some coffee.'

Omovo stared at Simon. He knew that when one request for coffee was made, others would follow till he had made cups for the entire office and even the customers. He said: 'It's break time.'

'So what?' came Simon.

'I'm not doing anything.'

Chako shouted from across the office: 'Omovo, the manager wants to see you now!'

The supervisor, banging on the table, said: 'Won't you attend to the customers?'

'What about the coffee?' Simon demanded.

Omovo went to his table. He felt himself trembling slightly under the attack of conflicting orders. He felt the sweat running down his back. The air conditioner droned. He sat. He thought about the absorption of working, the curious pleasure of losing yourself in business. He also thought about how insidious, how deadening it was to work at something you found neither interesting nor creative. After a moment he got up, brushed past Chako, and knocked on the manager's door.

The manager harangued him. Omovo received his monologue calmly. The manager, sipping his coffee and not looking at Omovo, kept rambling, kept waving his hand in his air. Omovo noticed his gold wrist watch. The manager said he wanted the department to achieve the highest sales figures of the season. He warned Omovo against insulting important customers; they were the backbone of the business, and the company worked by their consent.

'I don't want anyone to spoil this year for me, you hear?'

Omovo nodded.

'Have you taken in what I said?'

'Completely.'

The manager studied him. With a doubtful expression on his face, he waved Omovo out of the office.

During the office break everyone tried to pressure Omovo to go buy meat pies from the Kingsway. He absolutely refused. He sat at his desk, brought out his drawing pad, and started a series of sketches. He began with attempting to draw a section of the office. Simon, Chako, and the supervisor sat round a table deeply involved in one of their interminable discussions about pay increases. He decided to draw them. But he ended up with a set of caricatures. He made Simon's face look like a fractured calabash. He exaggerated his wrinkles as if life had not exaggerated them enough. He drew Chako as a mean-faced old man and gave him a comically long nose. And then he depicted the supervisor as a frustrated man and made his wiry beard into something resembling barbed wire and his ears into coins.

When he finished with the sketches he began to laugh. His colleagues looked at him without saying a word. He stopped laughing and closed his drawing pad. They went on with their secretive discussions about pay increases, their plans, their overtime.

Then, remembering Da Vinci's face-studies, his masterly drawings of old men, of powerful men, Omovo decided that it was too easy to satirise the powerless and the weak, to laugh at them rather than face them, ghetto-dwellers that they were, each face imprinted with its own hardship. He decided to draw his colleagues as they were, to test the edges of his craft by drawing what he saw without being sidetracked by his ego, by his ideas and opinions, his dislikes, and to do this within a limited time. He found their faces difficult to capture and found immense depths of shadows, of tenderness, that he hadn't noticed before. He felt a little ashamed.

Drawing made him think. He thought about Joe, about his lost drawing, his seized painting, about Ifeyiwa. The cold office made him think of a second-rate film he had seen some time ago. The film was about a kind of Shangri-la. Images from paintings he had done, canvases he had rejected, rose to his mind. He remembered a song from the film. The words were idealistic but at that moment they found sympathy in him: For your your reflections reflect on the things you do. And the things you do reflect on you –

He shut his eyes and began to meditate. He remembered another song from the film: There is a lost horizon waiting to be found . . .

He pondered the words, slipping deeper into a curious serenity. The words grew in his mind. They turned into other words and gave way to images, states of being, landscapes of possibilities. The strangest flowers opened up to him. As the sound of his colleagues faded, and the drone of the air conditioner receded, he experienced a sudden sufflation, an expansion of being, and he had a momentary wordless sensation of the underlying unity of things.

Chako, blowing his nose, disturbed Omovo's meditation. He opened his eyes, shut them again, and heard, as clearly as if it had come from behind him, his brother reciting the words from his own poem:

> 'But I found sketches on the sand
> While voices in the wind
> Chanted the code of secret ways
> Through the boundless seas.'

Omovo's heart palpitated with a wild joy. He felt his being include all that was hidden and radiant in the world. The feeling came unexpectedly, like a revelation. Then just as unexpectedly his meditation changed. He remembered the girl in the park. He imagined himself as the victim, imagined himself dead, his organ defiled, lying dead and unidentified in a park. Omovo felt as if he were trapped in a hole, in a well, in a pocket of terror lurking in his mind. He couldn't get out. Then suddenly in the darkness he had another vision. He saw the nation in riot, in the grip and fever of revolution. He saw flames everywhere, saw structures tumbling down, ghettoes burning, towers crumbling, saw people in masses casting about, wailing about their burdens, saw children weeping, women with charred hair, ashes on their faces. He felt the land overwhelmed with desperation, as if living were a kind of inferno, a kind of hell, life as the purgatory of the poor. When he eventually escaped the vision and surfaced to the reality of his office environment he felt tears in his eyes. He brushed them off and carried on with work.

Weighed down with his vision he found the second half of the day's work harder than usual. He felt his vitality being sapped out of him in trivial chores. He also felt joyful to be alive and working in the world, but this didn't stop him being a little resentful of the moments when he felt the overwhelming need to paint, to draw, wasted in performing tasks anyone could do.

Towards the closing time, however, he could not help noticing a young man sitting near Chako's desk. Chako and the others were a little deferential towards him. Omovo later discovered that he was the manager's nephew who had failed his school certificate exams. He was seeking a job in the company. As Omovo went up and down the corridors, sweating under the weight of numerous chores, he could not help feeling that someone's job in the company was about to die.

FOUR

The day's work ended and Omovo went home. The others stayed behind for overtime. They mostly did their own private business. As always Omovo found the struggle to get home worse than that of getting to work. The exhaustion, the heat, the frustrations and attritions of work made people that bit more ferocious.

When he got to the Amukoko garage there was dust everywhere. The dust rose from the untarred roads. Added to the dust and the heat were the many smells of the ghetto. The air was dense with the odours of frying oils and stinking gutters. The street was covered with litter.

The day's work weighed down upon him. He felt depleted. He stumbled along listlessly. The sweat and the dust, caked by the dry heat, made his face a mask of exhaustion, of enervation. The maddening noises of the area preyed on him. He stumbled down the molten street as if he were sleepwalking.

When he got home he was confronted by the lifeless desperation of the sitting room. He became unusually aware of the faded pictures on the stained walls, the large centre table with its anomalous leg, the scanty furniture. He was affected by the smell of indifferent cooking, the dust and the cobwebs and the staleness that settles in a room when the windows haven't been opened for a long time. He even noticed that the chairs were out of place and that one of the cushions was somewhat strangled between the springs. He saw an empty ogogoro bottle on the floor beside a chair. He guessed his father had been drinking.

There was no-one around. Flies buzzed around the scraps of food still left on the dining table. Omovo became aware of another atmosphere in the sitting room. Things seemed all wrong. He was aware of the strange silence, the feeling of doom, a bleak finality. He shuddered. He went into his room. Then he went and had a cold shower. As soon as he got back to his room and touched down on the bed he fell soundly asleep.

'Wake up! Omovo, wake up!'

Omovo stirred and woke, disorientated at seeing the face of a stranger becoming the face of his father staring down at him. He blinked and rubbed his eyes.

'Is it you, Dad?'

'Yes.'

He sat up. For a moment there was a tender silence between them.

'Is there anything wrong?'

His father sighed and for a while he didn't say anything.

'Is there?'

His father, avoiding his eyes, said: 'No. Not really.'

Omovo smelt his breath of bitterness, smelt the drink, the cigarette smoke, the despair that came all at once from his father. He took in his sweat, his smell of deep earth, of trapped animals. He noticed the restrained panic in his father's shifty eyes. Omovo was overcome with the urge to embrace his father, to embrace him and to hold him tight. But his father, sighing, moved away and, sitting on the only chair in the room, his shoulders hunched, his head in his hands, said in an uncertain voice:

'I want to ask you a favour.'

'Anything, Dad. Ask me anything.'

'This is very hard for me.'

'Ask, Dad. Just ask.'

His father stammered. When he had mastered himself, he said: 'I need . . . I am a little out of immediate funds. I need some money to pay the rent. Can you manage the money, I mean as soon as you receive . . .'

'Yes, Dad. Absolutely. Is that all? Oh God, Dad, it's nothing. Sure. I can. I will. As soon as I'm paid.'

His father looked up, a little taken aback by Omovo's response.

'Thanks, my son,' he said, sighing again and straightening himself. Some of his old authority returned. 'I will pay you back as soon as everything is all right. It's just a temporary setback.'

They were silent for a moment. Omovo avoided his father's eyes. Then his father got up and at the door he said: 'Have your brothers been writing to you?'

Omovo nodded.

His father looked down and then lifted his head. Then suddenly he made an odd noise, as if he were repressing a pain that had shot through his internal organs.

'They write to me as well,' he said. 'They write me letters that wound me and make me bleed inside.'

Then, abruptly, he left the room.

Omovo stared at the door, his thoughts spinning.

FIVE

To escape the confusion of his feelings Omovo spent some part of the evening in serene contemplation of the works of the masters. Turning the pages of *Great Paintings of the World* had a calming effect on him. He realised, as he studied the colour prints, often making quick copies in his pad, that he wasn't looking at them as much as bouncing off them into his own world, his own realities. He studied Brueghel, with his quivering world of nightmares; Da Vinci, with his secret mystical signs. He loved the famous Mona Lisa and remembered that it was Da Vinci who wrote that 'perfection is made up of details, but detail is not pefection'. He exhausted himself in art, from cave paintings to the hallucinated visions of the Latin American Indians through to the modernists like Cezanne, Van Gogh, and Picasso – whom he had heard described as a supreme creative plagiarist. But he returned to his four great affinities: Da Vinci, Brueghel, the wild man of the imagination, to Valasquez and his fastidious quest for truth, and to Michelangelo. Then he delved into another book of African art. He looked at reproductions of sculptings, mysterious monoliths, jujus, masquerades and serene bronze busts. But he studied them with too much familiarity, for African art seemed to him to be everywhere. He saw the terrifying shapes, the evil-fighting forms, and the ritual powers as being part of things, part of an order. They were in him. It was only later that he would learn to see them with estranged eyes, see them for the first time and be startled into the true realm of his artistic richness.

Before he stopped off his day's study he returned to Michelangelo's sculpture of David. Omovo never failed to be struck by the fact that Michelangelo chose to represent David at the moment before he confronted Goliath. He never failed to be moved by the inner tensions of that moment: David absorbed, about to step out from obscurity forever, to transform himself from shepherd to hero, about to step into history, religion, myth. Did he feel a current pulling him back, with voices singing to him of the sweetness of anonymity, the terrors of fame? Or was he, in his serenity, reaching to the flood of all origins, the birth of gods, touching forces of the air? What was the weight of that absorption, stone in one large hand, wrist abnormally curved, his life about to be changed forever by a stone, a sling, by the destiny of his wrist, by a timing, a grace, a precision, a fearlessness that could only have been prepared for in an apprenticeship so secret, so agonised, and so undefined?

When Omovo had finished his day's study he got rid of the books and meditated for a while, in order to clear his mind and strengthen himself for his own work which would make one day of his life worthwhile.

An hour later he sat in front of a canvas, afraid. The flat white surface daunted him. He sat in expectant silence, waiting for something, an urge, to rise within him. He tried to make his mind as clear and blank as the canvas.

But the mosquitoes got at him even through his khaki overalls. Isolated whinings sounded in his ears. He ignored them.

As he stared at the canvas, he became aware that the urge to paint wasn't strong enough, but he felt images fermenting within him. And still he waited for the waves to rise, for the tide to surprise him. He waited with absolute faith that the hunger within him would emerge in its own time, when the moods within synchronised with the landscapes without.

But the waiting, the expectancy of being, the preparation for vision, awaiting an inner annunciation, a flow, a command, a direction, an overall picture, a single true detail, a precise image, made him miserable, made him afraid. He waited with all his being for a sign, for the waves of desire to reach an unbearable pitch.

And then he remembered an incident from years before. Okur, while cooking, was peeling off the layers of an onion. He spoke of the onion as a symbol of the mystery of being.

'Look at this onion,' he said, his eyes bursting into tears. 'I will peel it off layer by layer and you would think that because it has so many layers it has a luminous heart hidden inside it. There is only pulp. There is *nothing*, you see.'

He paused and then went on, saying: 'There seems to be *nothing* but the onion left to itself will grow, will sprout. There seems *nothing* but it houses life, irrepressible life. Its mystery can't be dissected. Omovo, we need faith, we need St Paul's faith as evidence of things hoped for. There is *nothing* but it was Neruda who said "Men grow with all that grows". We start with one thing and we end everywhere.'

For some time afterwards Omovo's only memory of that incident was the way his brother stressed 'nothing' and the way his face shone with inspired perspiration. But time enlarged that and as he sat staring at the canvas he began to contemplate a different 'nothing'. He felt there had to be 'something'. He felt human beings must create, each in their own way; and that it was only by the application of vision, only by making things, that we could transform the negative 'nothing'. He wondered if his brothers had really left home because they had perceived 'nothing' there. He wondered what variation of 'nothing' explained Dele's scorn for things African, made Okoro continually mask his suffering, drove him – Omovo – to paint the subjects he did. Was it 'nothing' that murdered the girl in the park, that was responsible for his mother's death, his father's isolation? Was this 'nothing' powerlessness, impotence, failure, failure of vision, the victim's heritage? Was it 'nothing' that was casting the nation continually into darkness?

Omovo's thoughts ran on. He was confused by the complexity of his feelings, confounded by his inability to grasp them, irritated that his urges hadn't transformed into the wild flower of art.

Then suddenly, as if something had burst in his brain, he was assaulted by gusts of emptiness and fear. He was plunged into a negative moment of being, the opposite of sufflation, ambushed by images, halls that never ended, walls that rose up to the skies, Ifeyiwa's nightmares, empty mazes, absyms, a monumental terror of the future. He experienced the feeling of space without end, without trees, without human beings, without the sky. And it was only when he let out a short, animal scream that he began to return to a familiar reality.

The blankness of the canvas remained. At first its blankness seemed sinister, unreal, fragile. Without anything particular in mind, he was about to launch into a free expression of himself, painting anything that came to mind, at the complete mercy of whim and luck, when he remembered something Dr Okocha had said. So long as a canvas is empty its potential is infinite. A mark limits the number of things that can be brought into being. The empty canvas can become a gateway into the landscape of nightmares or a vision of sensual bliss. Every act of painting bears a heavy risk, he had said, because every mark would correspond to the immeasurable moods, the intuitions, the memories, the fears that art unlocks in the viewer. He had also said, at another time, that the act of painting was akin to prayer, and that Omovo must be careful in what attitude he prayed, and what he prayed for.

Omovo, drawing his hand back from the canvas, we relieved to find he hadn't marked it – for, in the good fortune of being true to himself, he knew that he wasn't yet sure what he wanted to bring into being, what he wanted to bear witness to, what he wanted to show.

And his relief formed itself into a temporary creed, a surrogate act of creation. He decided that in his paintings he wanted to create a simple vision, he wanted to start with what he knew, and what had hurt him, what had hurt all the people he identified with the most. He wanted his work to be fed from as many dimensions as made up the human. In it nothing would be too big or too small to include. He wanted his work to awaken the emotions and the inexpressible states that he felt, the states that fed into streams, the streams that fed into great seas. He wanted the simple to contain the complex, and the complex to embody the simple. Above all, with his increasing awareness that the artist is nothing but a higher servant, a labourer, a mediator, a carpenter of visions, a channel – above all, he wanted to be master of as many secrets of art as he was able. For he instinctively believed, and seldom questioned, that the highest function of art was to make people feel more, see more, feel more fully, see more truthfully.

This is a terrible path, he thought, and many have died on it. But in his moment of contemplation he was no longer aware of the blankness in front of him. He was no longer aware of his own presence. His spirit was free. The day's exhaustion had fallen from him. And his mind was clear.

The mosquitoes stung him. He became increasingly aware of them. He slapped one on his arm and missed. As he relaxed back into his serenity the room was suddenly plunged into darkness. Another black-out. He cursed. He got up and changed into brighter clothes. He sprayed the room with insecticide, took the blue hat Okoro had given him, and went out to await Ifeyiwa's sign.

SIX

When she went past the house he felt a quickening of his heart. She wore a cheap lace blouse over a faded fish-printed wrapper, and she had her white shoes on. She looked taller. Her hair had been combed out and it made her look full-bodied. She walked with an erect gracefulness that made her stand apart from the bustling ghetto evening. As he watched he became aware of the agitations in his blood. He attempted a series of karate steps, to give the impression that he had really come out to exercise himself, but he felt awkward and he had a sick feeling in his stomach.

Her ordinary clothes emphasised the restraints on her sensuality. And the way she moved, as if she were floating through the evening, filled him with an irresistible longing. When she made a sign to some imaginary personage in the distance he ached to go after her. Then she slowed down, deliberately, and continued with the sign language, as if she were communicating with everything around and not understanding what was being said.

He burned to go after her, but felt constrained by the presence of the compound people who had been driven out of their hot rooms by the electricity failure. They sat on the cement platform, on chairs, on low stools, in front of the chemist's shop, talking about the latest sex scandals in the city, or arguing about politics. Some of them stood at the house-front, surrounded by their children. Others sat telling stories from ancient lore. Their faces were dark in the shadows. He couldn't tell if they were watching him.

While he stood there, uncertain what to do, Tuwo and the assistant deputy bachelor came up to him. Tuwo, wearing a French suit that was rather small for his plump frame, said: 'Look at this young bachelor, he's going to inherit your title you know.'

The assistant deputy bachelor protested. 'My title? No way, at least not for some time.'

Omovo was irritated with their intrusion, but he smiled. Tuwo said:

'When I was young we used to marry early. Now you young ones marry old. The world keeps turning.'

'A wife is expensive,' the assistant deputy bachelor said.

'What do you think of all this, Omovo?' asked Tuwo, in an oily voice.

Omovo nodded absent-mindedly. The two men began to tease him, about his youth, and about how dangerous young bachelors were in a compound full of women and girls. Omovo responded nonchalantly. But it was only when he began another series of karate movements that he could gradually move away from them. When he felt he had waited long enough, and that the moment was right, he sauntered away from the compound. As he left he heard Tuwo calling him. Omovo ignored the voice and moved aimlessly at first, as if he wasn't sure of where he was going.

Then, with timid resolution, he went in her direction. He pretended that he was trying to buy provisions from the street-traders and couldn't find the right brands. While keeping up the pretence he looked for her and found that she had vanished. Exasperated, he turned to go back home when he saw her under the shadows of the deserted shed where they had met the last time.

He put on the blue hat and, feeling a little more secure beneath the disguise, set out after her. But as he got closer to her she suddenly walked briskly away. He was puzzled. She stopped near the hotel and waited for him. As he approached she set off again, crossing the street, hurrying down a side road. He followed. She kept on, leading him round the area, till they got back to their street. And then she went towards a sprawl of smoke-coloured bungalows mostly inhabited by Hausa and Fulani traders. She had been walking so quickly, taking the most unusual detours, dipping into compounds and emerging at other streets through mysterious corridors, that when they re-emerged at their street he didn't recognise it for a while. He was so confused by what she was doing that when she stopped suddenly and made a sign at him he felt dizzy and a new darkness, exploding in gentle colours, swam before his eyes.

A moment later he saw her go into one of the sinister bungalows. The outer walls were blackened with smoke. There was a patch of mud in front of the disintegrating stairs. In an open kitchen at the side of the house three women sat round a smoke-belching fire. They had deep ritual marks on their glistening faces and they argued in a language which Omovo couldn't understand.

The women regarded him darkly. He jumped over the patch of mud, climbed the short cement stairs, and paused at the doorway. The smells of the compound rose up to him. The smells of dried fish, of roots, of mustiness, of the bucket latrine, of overcrowded rooms, of kerosene lamps, of unwashed rags, and of garri sacks. The hallway was dark. When he looked up he saw masses of cobwebs clinging to the beams. The cobwebs kept moving, kept palpitating. They seemed to be possessed of a strange inner life.

He couldn't find Ifeyiwa in the darkness of the hallway. He was a little afraid. The wind howled gently about his mind. Above him, on the awnings, the cobwebs writhed. Behind him the night was pierced here and there by the lighted lamps of street traders. Mosquitoes whined in his ears. Fireflies fleetingly lit up the darkness, but they didn't help him to see.

It was only when he heard her voice calling him softly that he shook himself. He made his way to the room from which dull lights came through the keyhole and under the door. He tripped on basins and babies' potties as he went.

The room was bare. Ifeyiwa was sitting nervously on the edge of a bed. There was an uncertain smile on her lips that made him look around. The room was unswept and musty. The floor, uncarpeted, had been painted a dull red colour. An oil lamp burned steadily on a stand in a far corner. The walls were half painted, so that the bottom halves were blue and the rest remained the colour of plaster. The white ceiling was stained with the accumulated spirals of smoke from the oil lamps. The smell of old cooking was strong in the air.

Ifeyiwa sat on a large wooden bed on which was a threadworn blanket. When he looked at her again he noticed a mysterious twinkle in her eyes. From the far corner of the room the lamp shone, lighting up one side of her. The other side of her was in darkness. She cast the shadow of an elongated disconsolate giantess. There was an elusive sadness about the way she sat.

'Come in,' she said, eventually. 'There's nothing to be afraid of. This is a friend's place.'

He moved unsteadily into the room. When he had come quite close to her he stopped. He breathed in deeply the air of the room, which he let out at once because the smells sickened him.

'Why are you standing there like that?'

He didn't know. He remained standing, silent, thinking, and not aware of what he was thinking; feeling, and not knowing precisely what he felt. Then a tremor came over him, making him shiver.

'I like your hat,' she said.

The tremor passed and everything in the bare room suddenly became transformed by the wonder of her presence. He took off the hat.

She smiled. Her uncertainty had gone. A soft radiance bathed her features. Her eyes had a gentle, moonlight intensity. Her lips quivered slightly. She stood up, as if to greet him formally. Her elongated shadow bent along the wall. She seemed somehow to control the atmosphere of the room. He moved towards her, and placed his palm on her shoulder. Then, slowly, he withdrew his arm. She looked at him, and looked away. Silently, as if in a ritual, they both sat down. The bed creaked. Mosquitoes whined around them.

Then she sighed. Omovo, feeling the inexpressible mixtures of emotions that the sigh contained, wanted to touch her. But the silence widened the distance between them. Omovo was about to say something when he heard a scream from outside. He stiffened. A child began to wail. Its mother berated it. Women's voices rose on crests of different pitches. And then, when a door was slammed shut, there fell a new silence.

'Omovo?'

'Yes.'

'Are you all right?'

'I think so.'

'Are you worried?'

'Yes.'

'Afraid?'

'A little.'

She touched his arm. Her fingers quivered slightly. 'Don't be afraid.'

'I won't.'

'Are you painting?'

'I can't seem to at the moment.'

'Why not?'

'I don't know. I'm not yet ready, I suppose.'

She was silent for a while.'

'I'm really sorry about Sunday.'

'Forget it.'

'He just . . .' She stopped. Then sighed again. He touched her bare arm. Her eyes filled with tears.

'Why are you crying?'

She shook her head, wiped her eyes, and turned away.

'Why?'

She turned and faced him. 'I remember the first time you kissed me,' she replied.

They were silent for a moment. He felt the sweet and sad upwelling of desire extending itself through him. She moved closer. Imperceptibly.

'I was washing some clothes in the backyard and you came and held my face and looked in my eyes and kissed me.'

He smiled.

'I was surprised. I couldn't sleep properly for days after that.'

'I remember,' he said. 'You were wearing a yellow beret held on with a hairpin.'

'That was another time. Much later.'

'Are you sure?'

'Yes. That day I wore a blue skirt, the same blue as that hat of yours, and a white blouse. I didn't even have my shoes on.'

'Oh. I remember it differently then.'

'You should be ashamed of yourself.'

'But I remember the kiss. I don't know where I got the courage. I walked in a daze afterwards. Kept dreaming about you.'

She smiled. The space around her became charged.

'So how are things with you, my Ifeyiwa?'

The smiled faded. He cursed himself for having asked that question at that moment.

'I'm happy now. But things are bad.'

'What's happened?'

'News from home.'

'What news?'

'The fighting has started again.'

'Where?'

'At home. Between our village and the next one.'

'Is it serious?'

'Yes. They've started killing one another, burning farms. Now men hang around the boundaries all night with cutlasses.'

'Oh God.'

'We've had trouble for a long time, but it's only recently we started killing one another.'

'What's the trouble?'

'It's about the boundary. Many many years ago the white people gave the other village our land and after Independence we went to court and won the case. But they wouldn't accept. So we are now fighting.'

Omovo made an angry gesture. 'Those bloody white people. They interfered too much.'

'It's us. We're too greedy.'

'But they shouldn't have interfered so much.'

'I know.'

'I'm sorry.'

'It's all right.'

'I hope none of your family members have been hurt.'

'No. But I also heard that my mother is ill. They say she is probably dying. I might have to go home and be with her.'

Omovo didn't know what to say, didn't know what could possibly constitute a sufficient consolation. When she made a sound, which she stifled in her throat, and when she trembled, as she repressed her crying, he felt wounded. He held her in his arms tightly. She disentangled herself. He searched her face. Her eyes had hardened a little and acquired a curious unreachable coolness.

'You worry me,' he said. 'You keep changing.'

She looked at him. 'Don't say that.'

'Why not?'

'I don't know. Strange thoughts enter my mind.'

'Like what?'

'I'm not sure. It's not thoughts really.'

'What then?'

'It's hard to say.'

'Bad dreams?'

'No. I've stopped having them. I think it's the way my mind has become quiet. When I'm in the house I don't feel things any more. It's like I'm dead or something, as if I'm not flesh any more.'

'Don't talk like that,' he said, running his hand through the thickness of her hair.

She laughed. A tear rolled down from one eye. She brushed it off and said: 'But when I'm with you I come to life again. I begin to breathe like a woman, but I feel like a little girl. You make me happy.'

'Then let's not talk about bad things for a while.'

'Okay. Let's talk about your hat.'

'Why?'

'Why not?'

'What do you want to say about it?'

'It's blue.'

'So?'

'It's a good blue.'

'So?'

'Where did you get it?'

'A friend gave it to me.'

'I don't know of any of your friends. I sometimes see them when they come to visit.'

'You'll know them. Or they will know you.'

'Which one gave you the hat?'

'Okoro.'

'You mean he gave it to you – just like that?'

'Yes. To protect my head.'

'From what?'

'The sun.'

She laughed sweetly. 'Are you sure it's not another girl who gave it to you?'

'I'm sure.'

'You mean you have another girl?'

'No. I don't.'

She smiled. 'Anyway, the hat makes you look like a crook.'

'So you like crooks?'

'Only crooks like you.'

'I'm not a crook.'

'Wear it.'

'No. You wear it.'

'All right.' She pressed the hat down on her rich black fluff of hair.

'It suits you. Makes *you* look like a crook.'

She looked round. 'There's no mirror in this room,' she said.

'Trust me. You look beautiful with it.'

She took it off and placed it on his head at a jaunty angle. She giggled and tried another angle. He took it off and hung it on the bedpost.

'Now the bed looks crooked,' she said.

He pushed her playfully.

'You'd make a good poet,' he said to her.

'I've often thought of writing poems,' she said. 'But I don't know how.'

'My brother said the best way to write poems is to write them. That, and reading lots of good poetry. He made it sound like painting.'

'You said you were going to show me his poems.'

'I will.'

'Why don't you read one out to me?'

'Which one?'

'I don't know. The one you told me about on Saturday.'

'Is it the one about the birds?'

'No. The one he sent recently.'

'Okay.'

She shut her eyes.

'Why are you shutting your eyes?'

'Because I want to hear your voice better.'

He read out his brother's poem in a gentle, hesitant, conversational tone of voice. When he had finished she opened her eyes wide, clapped her hands together once in delight, and said: 'It's nice.'

Then suddenly she kissed him full on the lips and drew back, her being alive, her face lighted, her eyes clear. 'It's really nice,' she said.

Then he held her face and kept her still and, looking deep into her warm brown eyes, he kissed her gently and hungrily. At first she gave him a startled, almost frightened, look. But he went on kissing her lips, then he kissed her cheeks, and her neck, and her eyebrows, her forehead, her ears, and came back to her lips again and stayed there. Her lips were warm and soft. They quivered. He pulled closer to her. They held one another passionately in an embrace made awkward by the way they sat side by side. Then, as if in a new ritual, in which they each knew their exact roles, they stood up as one. They clung to one another. Omovo breathed in the rich aroma of her hair oils. Then he felt his way down her back with both hands. And he stopped on the soft rotundity of her backside.

After that things happened rather fast. Her hands moved tentatively down his side and found his thighs, and found his trouser zip, and fumbled with it, and retreated to his chest, and played with his shaven head, and were gentle on his neck. He unzipped his trousers and unloosened her buttons and took off her blouse. Then he pulled off his trousers and relieved himself of his shirt and stood before her, naked and proud. He kissed her downwards and she opened her wrapper and tore down her pants and he planted his face in her warm stomach and held her breasts in his mouth. She had beads on a string round her waist,

212

which added immensely to the sensuality of her body, the curvaceousness he could never have fully guessed at. And then there were the wonders of touch. He laid her down on the hard mattress and kissed her from her feet upwards, tracing pictures on her stomach and ribs and inner thighs with his fingers. He traced her undulations, her concavities, and was soft on her cleft, and she quivered with desire. Breathing in her potent smells of desire and earth, he felt her tenderly. Her thighs were hot and he played with her pubic hair and marvelled at the loveliness of her sex. It was so neat, so uncomplicated, that he wanted to cry out.

When he touched her body she trembled. It amazed him, this discovery. Her reaction heightened his feelings and he kept touching her gently, in different places, and her tremulousness got worse, got uncontrollable, and he became a little scared at the power of her feelings and held her to him. He wanted to see, to feel, all of her, to remember her forever. He turned her over and cried out gently at the beautiful sweep of her back and at the marvellous rotundity of her buttocks.

'The God that made you,' he said breathlessly, 'did it with so much love.'

When he turned her back over he saw the ritual marks on her stomach, the scars on her chest. He stroked them soothingly, lovingly, and held her breasts. She sighed and drew a series of descending circles down his chest, his stomach, to his first loose scatterings of hair, and then she paused. And then, suddenly, with a desire and a quickness that can only have come from the ancient streams of loving, she held on to his manhood and squeezed him and rubbed him against her. He couldn't understand his feelings and he made her stop and he took in her bronze-brown complexion, the softness of her skin, her radiant, almost golden, glow.

In that atmosphere suffused with gloom, lost in their acts of faith, they were moving towards the things that would consume them. And meanwhile the oil lamp burned steadily and the cobwebs crinkled in corners of the ceiling. And as he began touching her again, and she trembled on the bed, eyes shut, both hands clenching and unclenching, her mouth opening and closing, her face changed and strangely beautiful in the depths of her ecstasy, they were lost in all the forces which they knew nothing about, and which were there, defining themselves around their love.

When he stopped looking at her, when he shut his eyes, he too began to enter that state of possession. And when she touched him it drove him to frenzies and in order to prevent himself exploding before he had entered her he drew away. He found it difficult to breathe. She looked like a wild strange animal and her lips were full and her breasts heaved with a passion so irrepressible that he was completely magnetised. He drew lines down to her sex and then he widened her legs. With his eyes shut tight, breathing in the heady aroma of her nakedness, he found her wet and warm. A cry of unholy joy escaped from her and she tightened her legs round him. He found her rich wetness again and she relaxed her legs, surrendering to his tenderness. Then he mounted her, glided up her, and moved into her slowly. She threw her arms out and then clasped him tight and relaxed and then gave herself to him totally and with a wild look in her eyes she lifted her head and said:

'I want to bear your child!'

And he went in all the way and stayed there and they cried out as one and he moved gently, swimming on her into caverns of sexual dreams. Her hunger shook the bed and she let out a deep deranged uncontrollable noise of bliss and he covered her mouth. Then as he moved in and out of her slowly, savouring every moment, he felt her interiors pulsing around him. He felt her tighten and relax round his sex and she seemed somehow to be sucking him in deeper and he moved faster, pulled by deep currents of indestructible loving. He moved wildly and she moved with him, and then, her legs wide open as if to receive all of him, all of his love, mouth open, face contorted, he kissed her. And the kissing, the meeting of their tongues, increased the feeling of the lovemaking, and the lovemaking heightened the passion of the kissing. And when he felt himself coming from a great distance, when he felt his joy rushing headlong with insane powers he stopped and sucked her breasts and played her nipples between his teeth and soft inner mouth. Then, when he had cooled a little, he went back in and began to cry into her hair because he wanted to make love to her so completely, to go so deep into her, and to enjoy her so fully, and he didn't know how. And she pulled him to her and turned him over on the noisy bed and she mounted him and he started to kick and struggle and she told him to be still and she moved on him and when he relaxed and trusted her he felt it all so utterly unbearable and burst out into her, exploded into fragments of pulsating being and had started a long deafening cry when he heard the shouting outside the room and the knocking on the door. She went on bouncing on him, riding – a wilful mare – arms out, racing on to her heights, and fell on him and they went on moving into one another, daring the crests, when they heard together, freezing, eyes wide open, absolutely still, the voice of her husband as he said, very loudly:

'Come out! I know you are both in there!'

Bewildered, disorientated, they lay still, listening to her husband ranting outside, kicking at the door, turning the handle insanely as if he were going to wrench it off. Omovo began to panic and she signalled to him to be still. And her serenity, her complete lack of fear, quietened him.

'Come out and let me kill you!' her husband screamed, kicking the door, making the hinges groan. Dust and plaster fell off the door frame. The wood creaked.

'Come out or I will break down this door! I saw you going in! Come out!'

Then other voices joined that of her husband. Children began crying. Male voices, gruff and drunken, crowded out her husband's rantings. The voices swamped him. They heard the men threatening to beat her husband up for coming to their compound and disturbing their peace. Someone suggested the police. Female voices joined the noise. Then a woman's voice, more indignant than the others, joined in and berated him, saying that it was her room and that her sister and husband were in there and Ifeyiwa's husband had no right to kick their door. Someone else suggested a long drink to settle matters. The noises died down a little and moved away.

When the discordance had gone, and the banging had ceased, Omovo and Ifeyiwa hurriedly got dressed. Then they sat beside each other, oppressed by the emptiness of the room. The whitewashed half painted walls seemed to close in on them, and the distances between them suddenly became immense. After a while there was a knock on the door and a woman's voice said:

'Mek una go now-o. Take the backyard. Mek una go quick!'

They looked at each other in silence, as if for the last time. They kissed and got up as one, still bounded by tainted wonder. Sex-smells surrounded them in the seedy room. Ifeyiwa seemed unafraid, defiant, radiant, unashamed. She smiled bravely and, walking briskly, disappeared into the corridor.

He waited a few moments. Then he put on his hat. He opened the door. The wind blew through the dark corridor. He went out with the flickering cobwebs above him. Perplexed and drowsy, he stumbled to the house-front, and wandered into the womblike ubiquity of the night, his thoughts trapped a whirlpool, spinning in confusion.

SEVEN

When he left the bungalow he wandered aimlessly in a liquid, somnambulistic haze. The streets and roads that he knew so well became strange to him. Everything he saw troubled him. As he turned into a street the air suddenly was pungent with nightsoil smells. Then, like figures emerging from the semi-darkness of a curious nightmare, he saw them. Buckling under the weights of brimming nightsoil buckets, their faces swathed with cloths, ritualistic in their impersonality, the nightsoil men came towards him. They staggered to the waiting lorries, rested a while, went into the various compounds light and came out again weighted.

The place stank. People fled from them. People hurried. They ran, covering their noses, averting their eyes. The nightsoil men moved clumsily, their knees trembling, their backs arched. They grunted. The buckets they carried were often too full and things slithered down and took their place amongst the accumulated rubbish on the streets. There were no flies around.

Some children from a nearby house took to mocking one of the nightsoil men. He was the clumsiest of the lot. He carried a very big bucket and he staggered and weaved and made strange snorting noises. The children made fun of him in songs. When he stopped and faced them and made his strange noises to drive them away they ran to their home and disturbed the elders who were engrossed in their drinking and their arguments. After a while the children went back and tormented the nightsoil man and threw stones at him. One of the stones hit the bucket and made a hollow sound. Omovo avoided treading on it.

The nightsoil man stopped again. His eyes blazed and his neck was strong and sweat poured down his forehead. He snorted angrily and tried kicking up sand at the kids, but he staggered, cried out, steadied himself with a phenomenal and pathetic effort, and the children laughed even louder. Omovo wanted to shout at the children. But before he could, the exasperated nightsoil man brought up his free hand, in which was a short broom, then he proceeded to flick the contents of the bucket at the children. They ran, screaming and laughing in innocent wickedness. The nightsoil man followed them. The terrible load wobbled on his head.

The elders, who had been drinking, spitting, unmindful of their children's mischief, looked up and saw the grim apparition. One of them shouted: 'Hey, what's wrong with you?'

'Wetin you want?' cried another.

The elders got up. The nightsoil man chose his moment. With the awkward and sometimes wicked dignity that comes with such labours, the nightsoil man struggled, snorted, and then deposited the bucket right in front of the elders, in admonishment for the bad training of their children. The effect was staggering.

'Hey, carrier, are you mad, eh? You don crase?' the elders screamed.

The nightsoil man, cricking his neck, weaving as if in a hallucination, slouched away from the incredible deposit. When the full implication of his act became clear the whole place erupted. The elders, the neighbours, the women around, screamed and howled. People fled in all directions. The elders fell over their chairs and kicked over their table of drink and kola-nuts in their extreme haste to escape the smells. There was a terrible din of outraged screams, entreaties, curses. The stench was enough to drive a whole village insane.

When the commotion died down a little a delegation, consisting of the parents of the naughty children, was sent to the man. They stood a good distance from him and begged him, in the name of the gods and the ancestors, to carry his infernal deposit from their living places. The nightsoil man stared at them, his eyes quietly contemptuous. He didn't even bother to acknowledge their pleas. He stood very still, like a guardsman, very still and straight, his hands behind his back. The delegation drew closer and pleaded and the women knelt and appealed to his love of his mother and asked him to relent in Allah's name, in case he was a Moslem. But nothing they said dented his impassivity.

The women went and sought and dragged out the offending children and they were flogged mercilessly in public. The rest of the delegation pressed on with their entreaties. They prayed for the nightsoil man. The eldest amongst them prayed for the nightsoil man to become wealthy, successful, to have a happy life with good health. But the nightsoil man, seemingly offended by such excessive prayer, stood away from them, surveying the whole scene with his blazing, indifferent eyes.

Then the delegation went away and, after a short conference, they came back again. They had collected some money, which they hoped would appease his anger. He looked at the amount of money they offered. It was ten Naira. With an insulted expression on his face, he turned his head away. The delegation trundled off again, conferred heatedly, and came back with the money doubled. But it was only after they had pleaded for another fifteen minutes, after they had got the children to kneel in front of him and beg his forgiveness, and after they had raised the money to thirty Naira, that he condescended to acknowledge their request. He took the money, counted the notes carefully, checking each to make sure it was genuine, and stuffed them into his back pocket. Then, cricking his neck, he went and struggled with the bucket. As he lifted it, grunting and farting noisily, he swayed, nearly dropped the whole thing, and the women screamed. But he got the weight under control. He bent down to pick up his broom. Then, with a weird dignity, he wobbled and staggered off into the night.

The stench filled the air. It would hang around the area for weeks, a relentless memento.

Having witnessed all this from a distance, Omovo went on his aimless way.

He came to a narrow lane. There were deep tyre ruts on the verge. Sweet-smelling flowers had been crushed on both sides of the lane. Suddenly whiffs of incense were strong in the air. He heard the clanging of bells and riotous singing. He wondered who had bothered to plant flowers in that god-forsaken area. He was touched with a vague serenity. As he went deeper into the lane he became aware of the trees, the bushes and the peculiar darkness. The night was a forest of signs. The lane widened. The incense grew stronger on the air. He saw a fenced off area at the laneside. There was a house in the middle of it. And all around expensive cars were parked. He heard strange drumbeats and was reminded of the ones he had heard at the beach, long before they stumbled on the girl's body.

He suspected he was in the presence of a secret meeting place, a secret society. The meeting place looked like a ghetto church. After the fenced off area the lane ended. Beyond there was marshland and a wooden bridge. He didn't know where the bridge led.

As he stood near the gates to the meeting place, his spirit restless and curious, he was startled by a vigorous flourish of drums and noises. Masked figures, bearing whips, burst out of the forest. Then the central Egungun, a tall figure with a terrifying mask, emerged from behind them, surrounded by a retinue of men holding ropes attached to their wayward ancestral figure. The lesser figures, whose masks didn't have the size or the fearsomeness of the chief masquerade, began whipping one another. The talking drums pounded round them. The retinue chanted incantations. They whipped one another's feet. They jumped, didn't cry out, and retaliated. There was no malice in their action. They whipped one another's backs to the accompaniment of the drums and danced towards Omovo. They danced round him, the masquerade swaying and then running in different directions and being dragged back by its retinue. They whipped the year's evil from one another, dancing round Omovo, but they didn't touch him. Then after they had circled him, their spirits rising, the Egungun possessed, they passed round a mask for him to wear. He refused and they danced past him, towards the ghetto. He heard women and children screaming behind him at their frightening advance.

He went towards the isolated building. The gate was open. The building stood in the midst of the surrounding forest as if it had somehow emerged from the enchantment of a forgotten fairy tale. He came to a large signboard. Nothing was painted on it. A black cross had been planted beside the signboard. The noise of singing grew louder and more discordant. He heard the deep sound of big drums and the clanking of bottles. Deep in the background he heard the strains of an accordion. He heard screaming.

The wind blew sharply into his face, relieving the smell of incense with the wet familiarity of rotting vegetation. He listened to the cadences of nightbirds. He got to the main door of the building and saw another signboard, on which had been painted what he first thought of as Christ on the cross. But when he looked closer he saw that it was much more complex. It was a strangely beautiful painting, full of signs. It had images of birds with the wings of eagles, the faces of owls, the feet of buzzards. It had flying human beings with green eyes. It had turtles with human faces, women with the bodies of antelopes, men with yellow wings. All over the signboard there were the curious harmonies of Egyptian hieroglyphics. All these images and signs surrounded a black figure on a white cross, a figure who wasn't Christ at all. Omovo looked at the signature of the artist and was shocked to discover that it belonged to his friend Dr Okocha. Something exploded in his mind. He was about to utter a cry of astonishment, of fear even, when he heard the intonement of the most frightening incantations from within the meeting place.

The door opened suddenly – and hit him on the chest. He reeled from the force of the door and from the instantaneous assault of the noise from within. For a moment he was stunned, confused. For a moment, as if peering into a slowed-down dream, he could see what was going on inside. Red lights flooded his eyes. He saw men in rows, making motions slowly, as if in a ritual. They were all dressed in white smocks. In front of them, standing on a triangular platform, surrounded by what can only be described as mystic fetishes, was the Master of Rituals. He was a tall man, clean shaven. His smock was of silk and he had red signs on his chest and one side of his face was covered in native chalk and antimony. Before him was a man kneeling, in the throes of possession and petition. He spread his arms out and his palms, catching the lights, looked as if they had been soaked in blood. Omovo realised suddenly that the noises were an illusion. The gathering was silent and they made their liquid motions as if in a dream.

He had barely recovered from his second shock when the Attendant of the Threshold saw him and came out. He wore a black suit, white gloves, and a black hat. He was of middle height, handsome, straight, and had powerful eyes.

'What do you want?' he asked.

'Nothing.'

'Do you want to join us?'

'Who is us?'

'It doesn't matter.'

'Doesn't it?'

'No.'

Silence.

'Well?'

'No.'

'It's our day of initiation.'

'What initiation?'

'The initiation of strangers.'

'Initiation into what?'

'Mysteries.'

'What mysteries?'

'The mysteries of death, of power.'

Silence.

'Well? You are the first for the night.'

'Am I?'

'Yes. And your appearance is correct. You are wearing a hat and I imagine that you are bald underneath.'

'How do you know that?'

'It doesn't matter. I also know that you are a stranger, a sufferer, lonely.'

More silence.

'You have to decide now. I am expected inside for the next stage of our rituals.'

'I'm sorry.'

'Then please leave.'

'Why? Can't I just watch?'

'No. To watch is to commit yourself.'

'I see.'

'Please leave our premises now.'

'What's the rush?'

'You may be holding up the next stranger.'

Omovo hesitated. The longer he stayed, considering the temptation, the more he noticed the changes the attendant's face was undergoing. A strange expression, almost scavengery, began to take over the attendant's features. Suddenly a strong wind blew and hit Omovo at the back of his neck like an invisible knock. The moment passed and Omovo felt curiously wide awake. He turned round and walked past the signboard, giving a last look at Dr Okocha's astonishing painting. Then he went past the second blank signboard and out through the gate. He looked back and saw the attendant still watching him. After a moment the attendant went back in and shut the door.

Omovo went towards the bridge. His mind whirling, he smelt the vegetation. He listened to the cadences of nocturnal animals. Sweet smells of sanity touched his soul. He was overcome with the wonder of things he couldn't see, and the fear of things he shouldn't have seen. His mind was clear and the night, for a moment, took on a softer hue. Then something cried out in the dark.

He thought the sound came from the marshes and he went in that direction. He couldn't see far. But he could see that the wooden bridge was broken. Its wood had been cracked and only dimly lit strands of plank were left. The marsh was inseparable from the night. Beside the

221

broken bridge there was a bush-path. He took the path. The trilling of crickets overlaid the silence. The bushes grazed him. He tripped over a tree root. When he got up something fell through the branches of a tree. He waited. Nothing happened. The bushes and trees passed through his mind. He kicked an empty tin can. It twanged sharply. He underwent a momentary annihilation and then an intensification of feeling. Another sound extended from the dark. It sounded like a baby crying somewhere in the forest. He hurried in the direction of the cry. Then he heard other noises, the confused crackling of leaves and the footfalls of someone fleeing.

He nearly stepped on it. Whenever it was had been half wrapped up in cloth and left by the bush-path. At first, because it wriggled and moved like a strange animal, he was afraid. Then the baby's cry rose up to him, feeble and desolate. In the space of that moment everything became clear.

He gave chase. He bounded through the undergrowth, stumbled over protruding tree roots, and nearly disappeared into a well that was at ground level by the bush-path. Laboured breathing and confused footfalls sounded just in front of him. At a curve he saw the harassed silhouette of the fleeing woman. He called to her. She looked back and then she tripped over the exposed root of a tree. When he reached her she began cursing him. She screamed at him, making wild motions with her long fingers. Then she blew her nose into one end of her wrapper and became silent. She wore an open-necked blouse. From what he could see of her she looked lean and ill. Her hair was uncombed. Her mouth jerked in ugly spasms. She sniffed, spat in his direction, blew her nose again and wiped her face. She kept looking up at him, her body convulsing. She slapped at a mosquito on her bare arm. He said nothing and stayed still.

The wind moaned softly. There was a flurry amidst the leaves and undergrowth. When the wind died down she began to speak. Her voice was rough, defiant. It kept rising to the pitch of aggression and falling into barely audible whispers. She spoke about her husband, who was an armed robber. She said she had been returning from the market one evening when she saw him dead by the side of the road with a gaping hole in his neck. She spoke of how they had no money and how his creditors came that night to seize their property. She said she had no parents, no brothers, or sisters, and what could she do in the world? Should she die because of an armed robber's baby? Her voice dropped. There was another man, she said, who wanted to marry her, but the baby was in the way, it was a weight round her neck, she had no money to feed it, and she had lied to everyone that it wasn't hers anyway. She said she didn't care if the baby died and it was nearly dead anyway and she went on and on, speaking feverishly, breaking down to cry, talking as if she were replying to different voices that kept interrupting her. Then suddenly her tone changed. She began to rail against everything, and asked a long series of 'whys', and began to hammer her fists on the ground, as if it were a door that wouldn't open. Then she flung herself down and tore at her clothes and pulled at her hair. A line of blood flowed down her forehead, past her eyes and mouth.

He gave her a handkerchief to wipe the blood, but she knocked his hand away. He talked gently to her, trying to soothe her, to persuade her to go and take up her child. The wind rose again. She shivered.

Up in the sky the moon emerged from behind a cloud and conferred a silvery haze upon the trees and bushes. In the new silence the baby's disembodied cry came over the air, amplified by the stillness around. The woman got up, as if she had suddenly woken from a dream. She pushed past him and went stiffly towards the abandoned child.

The cry sounded again, but this time it was lonelier than ever. The woman ran with unbelievable speed through the forest. Omovo followed her. When the woman got there the bundle had fallen over on its side. A black cat stood near it and it fled when the woman snatched up the bundle and hugged it tightly to her, cradling it, dancing sadly, her face suffused with a transformed light. Then she freed the child from its wrapping and brushed away the dirt and ants that had crawled on its body and began to sing a traditional song about the hardships of the world.

Suddenly he heard her catch her breath. She held out the baby. It was utterly still. Its legs were deformed and it had a weird face and its hands dangled. She looked at Omovo with wild eyes and she opened her mouth and let out a piercing wail that resounded its terror-stricken vibrations through the forest. Then she ran off screaming into the nightspaces as if she meant to wake up the dead and all those who slept peacefully in their beds.

He knew it. He knew it so strongly that something arched within him and all kinds of voices babbled in his mind and he had a sudden vision of a bird falling and hitting the earth with a complete absence of sound. He felt exhausted. The bushes and the darkness passed through his mind. And when he broke out of the forest there was just the ghetto and the sky, clear, open, and dream-like.

BOOK FOUR

ONE

She walked briskly up the corridor and through the backyards into a secret passageway. When she got to her street she slowed down. The night was alive all around her. She felt outside it all, condemned by the wetness between her legs. She passed the stalls of the bean-cake sellers and the ogogoro traders. She passed the bustling hotel and the record stores blasting out the latest highlife tunes. Confused by her feeling of having been interrupted in lovemaking, she stopped beneath the eaves of the shed and rearranged her wrapper. The shadows hid her face from the street. She tried to recollect herself, to calm down her anxieties.

A car turned into the street and its headlights exposed her briefly. When the glaring lights passed away from her she broke down and cried. Everything washed back to her distorted by nausea. Things had been accumulating so much in her lately that when she watched her husband undress at night, when she watched him dress in the mornings, when she listened to his sickening endearments, she wanted to scream and throw herself through the window. But as she remembered him banging on the door, remembered his threats, the way Omovo froze, the silence afterwards, a feeling of emptiness crept over her. Something about the musty spaces of the room had opened up all the other things she had been hiding from in her life. Another car turned into the street and she covered her face with her arms and cringed as if from an ugliness she couldn't escape.

The moment passed. A Hausa-trader walked past, swaying with every bandy-legged step. Children raced round the corner. She heard the prostitutes calling to men in cracked voices:

'Sweet time man.'

'I'll give you a quick sweet time.'

'Where are you hurrying to, handsome man?'

Ifeyiwa edged from the shadows and stumbled into the street. Her legs were weak. She felt queasy and wet. She felt old in a bodiless way. Forcing herself on, she came to the dark patch of bushes where abandoned babies were reported to have been found, where people had been attacked and robbed, where women had been molested. She found the darkness there calming. She stood for a while and the wind blew through her hair. She heard a strange whimper from the bushes but she was not afraid. She moved towards the noise, parted the bushes, and saw nothing. People hurried past the dark patch, singing as they went. She remembered a song from school and sang it sadly to herself.

> I'm working for my life
> I'm working for my life
> If anyone comes
> And asks about me
> Just tell them and say
> I'm working for my life.

The song made her nostalgic for her brief schooldays. It filled her with indolent images of companionship, of church services, of wide open fields, the athletics season, and of her friends in their starched uniforms singing with smiles at the morning assemblies. The whimper sounded again. She stepped back and saw a flower on a stalk amongst the bushes. It looked black in the shadows. She plucked the flower, smelt it, and sneezed. It did not smell good at all. She laughed quietly to herself and went on. In the dull light that reached her from the kerosene lamps around she saw that the flower was diseased, streaked with browns, eaten by insects, and it was not black at all but a washed-out pink. She took it with her.

Startled by loud rustling behind her, she turned to find a little dog limping out of the bushes. Hanging up a broken paw, it limped towards the stall of a bean-cake seller. The dog made pathetic noises and attracted the attention of the woman whose stall it was. The woman cursed the dog's ancestors and threw a spoonful of hot oil at its back. The dog howled and ran across the street, its head held low, its paw dangling. Some children who had been playing football and fighting amongst themselves noticed the dog. They laughed at its awkward movement. One of the kids, in an attempt to score a goal, missed the ball and kicked the dog. Ifeyiwa screamed. The dog was sent flying. It landed and rolled over like a grotesque football and began to utter plaintive sounds.

Ifeyiwa rushed to the dog. It still breathed. Its forefoot twitched. Ifeyiwa picked up the animal and found it was bleeding. She hurried away with the dog in her arms and the boys taunted her.

Without thinking she went into their room and put on the lights. Her husband was sitting on a chair. He was a solitary, pathetic figure. There was a half-empty bottle of ogogoro on the table. He had obviously been getting drunk, alone, in the dark. In a hoarse voice he said: 'Put out the light. And get rid of that animal.'

His eyes were red. Apart from pouring himself another drink he made no motion. She put the light out and went into the corridor. As she went she noticed that the dog was breathing strangely and its tongue hung out.

The backyard was deserted. There were unwashed plates, babies' potties, dirty buckets, everywhere. She laid the dog near the kitchen to rest. Then she took up a bucket with some water, went to the bathroom, and washed herself. She had to suffer the indignity of drying herself with a neighbour's towel that hung on the mucus-covered zinc walls. Then she went back to the room.

The lights were on. Her husband stared through her as she stood at the doorway. His mouth was slack and his bared teeth were kola-nut stained. His eyes held the pain of dreadful knowledge. He tried to say something, but he shook his head and sighed. She watched him calmly. He stood up and sat down and then stood up again. He staggered to the window. He opened it and shut it. He seized his bottle by the neck and poured some ogogoro down his throat. The burning liquid ran down the stubble on his face. He grimaced and held his stomach.

She stood watching him carefully, her calm giving way to uncertainty. The more she looked at him the more clearly she saw him. Her pity made her see him, for an instant, as a man that was not entirely ugly. She saw the repressed and twisted goodness on his face, she saw beneath his gruffness and perceived the possibility that he had demons of his own. She knew so little about him, had wanted to know nothing about him. During the marriage ceremony, which had taken place in their village, she had barely looked at him, and had scarcely looked at him since. But for the first time in her married life she saw him as a man capable of being possessed by an inexpressible pain. The fact that he had not pounced on her so far made her feel a little more grateful, more respectful. It made her see his humanity, made her see him for once as one who didn't just threaten her and beat her, didn't just, without explanation, tear down her underpants and feel her roughly to ascertain whether she was wet from contact with another man.

She felt a mixture of kindness and coldness towards him. After what had happened when Tuwo last visited, she more than ever wanted to run away to her village. She had always been afraid she would do something dangerous. But as her wicked dreams ceased she became torn between what she knew and what she couldn't know.

Her husband sat down again. He fretted. He tried to rock the straight-backed chair backwards and forwards like a child. Then he started to cry. It was the first time Ifeyiwa had seen him like that. Seen him so naked. She turned away. She didn't want to see something forbidden to the eyes of a wife. She began to play with the diseased flower. She heard her husband weeping and she wanted to scream and break valuable things just so that he could vent all his anger by beating her.

Suddenly he was silent. Then he said: 'What is that you are playing with?'

Ifeyiwa started. The flower fell from her hands and gyrated to the floor. 'A flower.'

'Who gave you a flower?'

'No-one. It's a dead flower. I plucked it from a bush.'

'Who gave you a dead flower?'

She said nothing. His voice changed. 'I said who gave you a dead flower?'

She remained silent.

'Did that boy give it to you, eh?'

Silence.

'I am talking to you. Did *he* give it to you?'

Her face became abstracted. He got up suddenly and stretched his hand towards her. Ifeyiwa ducked, thinking that he was about to hit her. But he wasn't. He reached for his coat hanging by a nail on the door. Then he struggled into the coat with great drunken difficulty.

'I'm taking you somewhere,' he said.

She looked at him quizzically. The pathos had returned to his face. His mind seemed out of synchrony with his movements. His mouth flopped open, and his forehead creased. He looked at her with sly eyes. A curious lecherous expression contorted his mouth. He staggered over to her and with a perverse look in his eyes he grabbed her, his arms trembling, and attempted to kiss her. His breath repulsed her and she recoiled from him. Obscenely, he kissed the air. He held onto her roughly and squeezed her buttocks.

'You're wounding me,' she said, coldly, gently.

He stopped. Then he grabbed her again and, breathing horribly, squeezed her hard. The only sign of the pain she felt was in the contorting of her face. She pushed him away. He fell on the bed. He stood up, his face suddenly resolute. He went to the door and said:

'Come. I'm taking you somewhere.'

'Where?'

'Somewhere.'

For the first time that night she was afraid. She had an image of unexplained bodies in dark places. He came and seized her hand and pushed her out into the night. He put out the lights and locked the door. Then he pushed her down the street. She was scared, but she couldn't refuse to do his bidding.

He took her on a friend's motorcycle. He rode slowly and with extreme caution down the Badagry express road. They went past the Alaba market and turned off towards Ajegunle. Then he slowed down near the army barracks, turned off onto a bush-path and rode deep into the thick forest.

It was dark. The silence was punctuated by the trilling of crickets and the syncopated croaking of frogs. It was very dark and Ifeyiwa felt overpowered by the smell of the earth and the herbaceous fragrance of undergrowth. Her husband told her to get down from the motorcycle and he hid it behind some bushes with the practised motions of one who has rehearsed his plan beforehand. Ifeyiwa was terrified to the point of stiffness. She saw dread everywhere. She saw masks and demons in the darkness. The palm trees weaved. The crickets seemed to trill louder. The croaking of frogs became unbearable. She heard strange whispers in the leaves and was dimly comforted to hear a car driving slowly down the road, its engine spluttering. When the car increased speed she lost heart. It occurred to her to run to the road and scream for help, attempt to stop the passing car. But she knew that no one in their right mind, in a time so rife with armed robbers, would stop at a place like that even for a woman. It was too obvious a device. They would sooner run her over than stop.

'Come here, you educated fool!' her husband shouted somewhere in the darkness.

She didn't move. She tried to locate his position. She waited, tense, like a trapped animal. He leapt on her from behind, held her, and pushed her up the path. She stumbled and he went on pushing her. She regained her balance and hurried on blindly ahead, the darkness like a wall

231

constantly melting before her. Her heart pounded. Her eyes were wide open. Every sound in the dark made her tremble. She kept looking back and when they came to a clearing where light shone down from a distant top-floor window in the barracks she saw that her husband's face had become impenetrable. The night had lent him a mask. His eyes were very bright. He kept opening and shutting his mouth.

When they got to a clearing he told her to stop. The moon came out. The clearing had stakes and sticks all about the place. She couldn't tell if it was a discarded farm, a rubbish dump, or a ghetto graveyard.

'Are you afraid?' he asked in a quiet, murderous tone.

She said nothing.

'Are you frightened?'

Still she said nothing.

'I see. So you are not afraid?'

He brought out a pocket knife and flicked it open. It flashed terror through her and she stepped backwards. He caught her. She said, desperately, hurriedly, her eyes widening:

'Yes, yes, I'm afraid.'

He chuckled. Then he laughed. Then he stopped.

'What are you going to do to me?' she asked.

His eyes were very bright. His hands trembled. He opened his mouth and shut it.

'Do you want to kill me?'

Silence.

'Do you want to stab me?'

'What if I say yes?'

Silence. Then: 'What are you waiting for? Should I take off my blouse? Do you want to stab my stomach or my breast or my neck?'

Silence.

'Just tell me where you want to stick the knife and I'll help you. I'm tired of this life anyway.'

More silence.

'What are you waiting for? Do it quickly before I catch cold.'

His hands trembled pitifully. The wind stopped blowing. The crickets seemed to have a moment's respite. The trees stopped swaying. The night became darker, the silence deeper.

The wind rose again. Ifeyiwa shivered. Her husband's teeth chattered. Their clothes were whipped into a frenzy. The palm trees swayed like

232

soft-limbed zombies in a nightmare. The frogs croaked persistently. In the darkness, his voice rising, her husband said:

'I want to kill you. I do everything for you, I'll do anything for you, and yet you treat me badly. You treat me as if I am a toad. I love you more than anything in the world, but I want to kill you. What haven't I done for you, eh? I give you a roof over your head, I buy you clothes, I feed you, I work myself to death because of you, I protect you. Because of you I have to pay protection money to an organisation. And in spite of all this you don't behave like my wife. You don't like me touching you. After all this time you are not even pregnant.'

He paused. He played with the knife, drawing closer to her. His face became more definite the longer she stared at him. He was a complete stranger, his face a mask of bitterness and agony.

'I don't know what you do to your stomach. But the other day I looked through your things and saw some pills. Why don't you want my child? Am I deformed? Am I that ugly? Am I a snake, a toad, a goat, a rat, eh? I am a man and I want children. I didn't marry you only for decoration, you know. What wrong have I done you, eh? Is it because I am a bit old? Am I the first old man to marry a young wife? And anyway I am not that old, as you know. I can do it better than any young man, and for longer. Age is experience. Age is wisdom and power. Your trouble is that you have no humility, you're too proud for your own good. Your people told me you were a nice girl, shy, well-behaved, respectful. I don't see any of this. Your people asked a lot of money for you – I paid. I had an expensive wedding for you in the village. I brought you to the big city. Your people are wretched people, dying off one by one, and here you are making yanga, being proud, and only because you went to secondary school. Am I a snake, a toad, that you have to treat me like this? And to add insult to injury, today I saw you and that boy going into the room of a prostitute . . .'

He broke off. He made a strange loud noise. He opened and shut his mouth several times like a beached fish, like a man in the throes of lockjaw. Then he began to weep again. The tears glinted down his face. His body jerked spasmodically. Then he burst into a strange confession.

'I've always been lonely,' he said in a strangled voice. 'Always fought alone. My father had nineteen children by five wives. My mother died when I was a child. My father grew to hate me. It was his wives who made him hate me. They were jealous because I was the eldest. I grew to hate my father back. His wives caused it all. It got so bad I used to run away from home. When they caught me and brought me back he whipped me till I pissed and shat on myself. I was ill for a week. I nearly died. He was a wicked man, a cruel man, confused, a failure. He couldn't support his children and one by one we escaped from the village. Because I escaped first and set a bad example I hear that he cursed me. Of all my brothers I am the most backward, struggling like a madman every day of my life. I have done almost every kind of business. I have been a cement trader, a beggar, a farmer, clerk, lorry driver, a garri trader, and in none of them have I succeeded. The same bad luck followed me. When my father died I was happy. I thought my bad luck would end. I did not go home for his funeral. I sat here and got drunk. Since then things cleared up for me a little. I opened a shop. I was careful. I gave no credit. I became a hard man. I've got money now. Plenty of money. But I don't let anybody know. I pretend I am poor. I live here in the ghetto, pretending, doing my business. Nobody stands in my way. I've learnt to survive by being ruthless and tough. But if you scratch me you will find I am a good man, a kind man, my blood is good, my spirit is good. If you stay with me longer, if you get to know me better, you will be surprised. But look at me. I look older than my age. You will be surprised how young I really am . . .'

His voice trailed off. It became cold. The wind blew harder. Ifeyiwa kept shivering. Her husband wiped the tears from his face.

'I am begging you. Begging you. Just tell me one thing . . .'

Ifeyiwa opened her mouth. It was dry. No sound came out.

'Did he do it to you, did he? Did he do that thing to you, eh, did he?'

'No.'

'Answer me truthfully. I am a man. I can take it. Did he do it, did he do it to you?'

'No.'

He did the strangest thing. He lunged at her with the knife. She jumped aside. He turned, started towards her, screamed an incoherent exclamation in his language, and then stopped. He stretched both hands and sent a searing cry up to the heavens. She had never heard such an animal cry before. It was scary. He was like a completely unbalanced actor, bungling his part, and playing out his deepest fevers.

'All I want is for you to love me a little. A little. Love me like a wife, an ordinary wife, a dutiful wife. Give me a chance. Give me luck and children. Help me fight these battles, eh. Love me like a good wife. Don't make me a laughing stock, don't me me look like a fool in the eyes of this wicked world . . .'

His voice changed. 'You must promise me now, here, that you will

234

be a good wife, honourable, dutiful, and that you will never look at that boy again, never speak to him, never go to that compound, never write him letters, never think about him, and that you will stop taking those pills and before this year runs out you will be pregnant for me . . . '

Ifeyiwa caught her breath. Her hands went to her breasts.

'Or I will kill you here now.'

Ifeyiwa stepped backwards.

'If you try to run you are finished.'

She froze.

'If I kill you here, now, what can you do, what can anyone do, can anyone help you, can that boy help you now, eh?'

There was a short silence. Then he laughed. His demonic laughter became a wail. He bared his teeth, clenched his fist, and began to wrestle wildly with the air, madly, as if he had adversaries everywhere in the darkness, as if he were fighting a legion of spirits. She realised how utterly drunk he was, how possessed. Then suddenly, as he wrestled with the demons, he began to cry out, his thighs quivering uncontrollably.

'Cramp! Cramp!' he said in a low voice.

This had often happened to him while he made love to an ever-resistant Ifeyiwa. It had gripped him now and his legs shook, he gnashed his teeth, pounded his fists on his shaking thighs, and called on Ifeyiwa to help him wrestle with the real devils in his body. The knife fell from his hand. He bent over, then he dropped on the ground, and she went and began to massage his thighs, rubbing them gently, drumming on them, while he wailed and jerked and contorted his face.

When the cramp in his thighs eased he got up and began to pace up and down tentatively. The wind went wild. The branch of a tree cracked somewhere in the distance. And then the rain began to fall. At first it pattered on them like bean seeds. The drops became larger. Then it pelted down on them, lashing the trees, whipping up mud on the path. The rain fell on them without mercy, calmed the tremors of his thighs, and they ran to the motorcycle. He rode with terrible difficulty, wobbling along the expressway. The rain smashed down on them, the wind blew them one way and another, and the journey was so rough that they nearly got blown off into the gutter. But the downpour was a passion that soon shrieked itself out. By the time they got back home the rain had stopped but they were thoroughly soaked.

They said nothing to each other on the way. It was near midnight when they arrived. The lights had been seized. Ifeyiwa felt that the night had changed her in some way. She felt as if a door which she never knew existed had opened within her. She felt curiously light and freed of something.

When she got off the motorcycle, filled with a hard-edged sense of joy, the first thing she did was to light a kerosene lamp. Then she rushed to the backyard to check on the dog. The backyard was soggy. The chaos of plates, buckets and potties had been knocked about and the rain had beaten the mud onto them. She checked the kitchen front and everywhere else she could think of. But the dog wasn't there. It had disappeared.

TWO

Omovo, returning from his aimless wandering, didn't rouse himself when the wind rose. He didn't quicken his pace when it began to rain. He welcomed the downpour. It cooled his agitated spirit. It washed away his excess of feeling. He felt the rain as an undeserved benediction. But when it suddenly stopped he was disappointed.

The lights had been seized by the time he got to the patch of bushes. And when he saw a man standing where the bushes ended he knew the man had been waiting for him. He knew without being afraid or curious. He was tired. He knew Ifeyiwa's husband would do something and he was almost glad that his waiting would soon come to an end.

He looked backwards and saw another man. They both closed in on him. They both wore masks, the terrifying masks of funeral spirits. It didn't occur to him to cry out. He knew on a night like that no-one would come to his aid. The ghetto-dwellers would cover their ears with their pillows, grateful that the night had found a sacrifice that wasn't them or their children.

The men drew closer.

'What do you want?'

They pressed towards him, implacably.

'What do you want from me?'

He moved forward carelessly. One of the men hit him. He made no effort to defend himself. The punch caught him on the chest. His hat flew off. He groaned. Then he began to cough violently. The pain galvanised him. He kicked the man behind him. The man was so stocky that the kick didn't move him. It unbalanced Omovo instead. He tried a karate chop, but something went wrong. His spirit was wrong. A solid punch landed on his shaven head. Another one sank into his stomach. He felt sick. Something twisted inside him. His vision went strange, as if his eyes had been switched round. He sank to his knees. He felt his head wrenched sideways with barbaric force. He hit the ground like a slippery log. Lights probed his skull. Fists hammered down on his body. He curled himself into a ball. They went on kicking him. He felt the flesh of his face burst open. He passed out into a dark realm. He floated back to consciousness, like a shade over a red sea, and in the silence he heard a man say:

'Don't ever see her again, you hear?'

Another voice said: 'Next time run far from another man's wife.'

And another: 'If you want a wife go and marry your own.'

The first man: 'Fool!'

The second: 'Bastard like you. Thief! Adulterer!'

Feebly, he still tried to fight. He struggled to stand up. He staggered first to one, then to the other. He offered them his face. He seemed to want to be beaten senseless. He urged them on. Egged them. Goaded them with words. The men seemed to fear his sudden, self-destructive madness. One of them pushed him. He fell. They laughed derisively.

He tried to get up, but couldn't. He kept passing in and out of a red darkness. Then many colours shot through his head. Every colour was a different pain. The night was quiet except for the crickets.

He clawed the wet earth. The earth released his grip. The darkness closed in. He fought it. He managed to crouch. Then he threw up. He felt for the bushes, grabbed hold of a shrub, and hauled himself upwards. The shrub uprooted and he fell again. He stayed down. The wetness of the earth seeped through him. Mosquitoes descended on him. The wind stirred in the land and acquired its various fragrances.

THREE

Holding the crumpled, mud-stained hat in his hand, and shivering along the way, he made it to his compound. When he got to their house he found he had lost his key. There was no reply when he knocked on the door. Strains of music came from one of the rooms in the compound. He knocked again. Then he looked through the window. There was a candle on the centre table. It had burnt so low that it would soon begin to char the table. He wondered where everyone was.

His head felt large with pain. The cut on his forehead felt like a red hot hole. His lips were swollen, one eye felt unusually big, his jaws twitched, and his teeth felt shaky. Blood slid down his throat.

He held his head in his arms and shut his eyes. The big eye wouldn't close. He felt wet and cold and dirty. He didn't really care. He felt surprisingly calm, contained. Beneath the calm he smouldered with an undefined anger.

A door opened stealthily in the darkness. He heard whispers. He raised his head. Lights danced in his eyes. Then footsteps came towards him. A child howled. The footsteps suddenly stopped, and turned and hurried to the backyard. He listened to the sounds of the running shower. After a while he heard the footsteps again. The darkness danced before him and then became a voice.

'What happened to your face, eh?'

Pain shot through his head. He felt blood trailing down from one nostril. He wiped it off. Her hands went involuntarily to her breasts. He smelt the breath of her body. It was a musky, earthy breath, passionate, and diluted by fresh water. His forehead burned. He indicated the door.

'Why your face swell up like that?'

She had brought out the doorkey from her brassiere. She fumbled with the keyhole.

'No reason.'

'No? Dis stupid key sef . . .'

She fumbled with the keyhole and the darkness fumbled with his eyes. A nerve drummed away in his head as if it were going to burst. She kept struggling with the keyhole. She peered at the key, and then tried again.

'The door doesn't want to open,' she said. 'Omovo, try the key.'

Without moving, Omovo said: 'It's not our key.'

'What! How do you know?'

Her face became a mask. Her eyes widened. Her mouth twitched. Her fingers began to tremble. Then her face became gentle and sad. She threw the key on the floor and picked it up again. 'I must have got the wrong key,' she said.

'How come?'

'I must have take another person's key. I've been watching television.'

Her footsteps crept away. He laid his hands on the low wall, and laid his head on his hands. He did not want to think. He was tired. Thinking brought on more pain. He felt sorry for everything. Then he felt overcome with nausea. He hurried down the corridor. He heard Blackie talking in low tones in a darkened room. He got to the toilet in time and threw up. The nausea hovered and passed. He felt empty. He went to the bathroom, washed his face, and on second thoughts he had a cold shower. He ran back to the room shivering, with water dripping from him. The door was open. He took up his hat and went into the sitting room. There were three candles alight on the dining table. The old candle had burned the centre table. The smell of fried onions and tomatoes came from the stove.

'There's water on the fire for ya face.'

'Don't want any.'

'Why not?'

'Nothing.'

'What happened to you?'

'Nothing.'

'Food will soon be ready. Pounded yam and stockfish stew.' It was a rare offer.

'Don't want any.'

'What do you want to eat? I'll make anything you want. Just mention it.'

'Thanks. I am not hungry.'

'You vex with me?'

'No.'

'You no like me. Na because of me your brothers leave, not so?'

'Not so.'

'You tink say I happy for dis house?'

'Don't know.'

There was a moment's silence. The three candles burned erratically, their flames twisting. Shadows leapt about on the walls.

'I know say I don wrong you. But wetin pass, don pass. I like you. Don't vex with me, you hear? It's not my fault the way tings be for dis house. If I know I no for marry enter the house.'

'It doesn't matter.'

There was another silence. One of the candles twitched, spat, crackled and seemed to be dying. It soon loomed back to its full illumination, burning brighter than before.

'Your face is not too swollen. It's still handsome. But you dey bleed for forehead. Mek I go check the water.'

She went. He opened his room door and dropped the hat in a corner on the floor. Then he sat on the bed, trying not to think.

'The water don ready,' she called.

He waited for a while before he went out. He had just finished cleaning his wounds and pressing his bruises with a piece of cloth soaked in hot water and disinfectant, when the front door burst open. His father staggered into the sitting room. His eyes were liquid, large and red. His shirt stank of beer and sweat. He had a two-day growth of beard which gave him a driven expression. He looked as if a secret taint were rising to his face, as if a bewildered stranger inhabited his body. He looked so thoroughly drunk and undignified, so utterly out of character, that for a moment Omovo took him for a familiar tramp that had mistakenly found his way to their house.

'Dad!' Omovo cried.

His father swayed, tottered, then steadied himself. He glared at Omovo with heavy eyes. His gaze was unfocussed. His mouth flopped open. A thin line of spittle ran down to his chin.

'My son!' he said, eventually, as he struggled with his drunkenness, attempting to focus. 'Am I . . . am I . . . not a chief, eh?'

'You are, Dad.'

'A . . . a . . . big thief . . . chief, I mean, eh?'

'Yes, Dad.'

'No . . . one . . . no one believes me . . .'

'Don't mind them, Dad.'

His father kept blinking. Each blink seemed to make him further unable to focus. Omovo wasn't sure what to do. All three of them stood in their different positions as if they had frozen in a dance that was turning sinister. Omovo desperately wanted to do something, to make a meaningful gesture in spite of the pain of his own wounds, but the distance that had grown between him and his father over the years made it difficult for him. As he stood there he was aware that something was being torn down and made naked forever, and what lurked behind their different masks unnerved him in its terror.

Omovo thought about his father. His business was obviously in serious trouble. Had been for some time. Otherwise they wouldn't still be living in the ghetto. His father, however, had always given the impression that he would forge through any difficulties. Sometimes – and this was one of those times – Omovo saw beneath the veneer so much that it hurt. But his father went on putting a front to the world that suggested his life was a fine strategy, that he was so solid he didn't need to display his power. His reputation increased amongst the compound people by negatives.

Omovo remembered, for example, when the family was intact and when he used to come home on holidays from school. He remembered his anxieties, remembered how he used to ask his mother who had come to collect him whether there was now a television or a radio in the house, whether his father had a car, or whether they had moved to a good house. The questions saddened his mother and she often lied, and after they had arrived and he had survived his disappointment he always forgot that she had lied.

He remembered the angry visits of defrauded clients, the lawsuits, the lies to creditors that his father wasn't in or that he had travelled. He remembered the creditors shouting out the crooked details of debts. He remembered the insults they screamed so the whole world could hear. He remembered his fears, his desire to protect and soothe his father, remembered the stony calm of his mother's face in the midst of all the humiliation. He remembered also how callous all this made his father, how he took it out on the chairs, plates, and on Mother. He remembered one fierce creditor in particular: he had burst into the house, after so many frustrated visits, had shouted abuses; and, not content, had seized his father's books, had even taken Omovo's books on painting, and had left with the grand second-hand clock that Mother had bought to celebrate an anniversary of their difficult marriage. Omovo remembered how he had often cried down the streets at night, alone – and as he remembered all these things now he was overcome with deep sorrow.

'Dad!' he cried again, without purpose.

His father looked at him as if he were a stranger. Then he stared at Blackie. In a most pathetic voice, he said: 'My wife, where have you been?'

It was his first moment of clarity since he had come in. The clarity didn't last. He tottered again.

'I've been watching television,' she said.

The room was utterly silent.

'Where?'

There was a long pause. 'In the compound,' she said.

'I've . . . I've . . . been waiting . . . for . . . for you,' he said. 'Waiting . . . for you.'

Silence.

'Been . . . been . . . so alone . . .'

More silence.

'So . . . I went . . . went and . . . and . . . got drunk . . .'

'I didn't go for long. I came back and the house was empty. So I went back.'

His father stared at Omovo, then at her. He took a few steps and held on to the back of a chair. 'I got . . . got . . . drunk,' he said. 'Mosquitoes . . . mosquitoes have . . . have . . . been . . . telling me things . . . things about . . . you . . .'

'Lies!' she said, moving suddenly, half retreating to the kitchen.

Her face was in shadow. His voice was suddenly, momentarily, clear.

'Is it because . . . because I don't have . . . have television . . . in my house. . . ?'

Silence. The candles spat. Shadows danced everywhere, figures in a grim shadow-play.

'No.'

With undirected energy, his father said: 'I . . . I . . . a big chief. . . will buy . . . buy . . . ten televisions . . . for you . . . tomorrow . . .' Pause. 'But . . . but . . . never . . . never . . . watch television . . . in other . . . people's house . . . house . . . again!'

'Yes.'

243

His father swayed. Incoherent words poured from him. The candlelight touched his face, pitilessly showing up his disorientation. Blackie backed away into the kitchen and stayed out of sight. As Omovo watched his father weaving helplessly, clinging onto the chair, he felt a tragic mood creep into the pit of his stomach. He too needed steadying. The pains raved in his head. He felt as if everything in his life, everything connected to him, was spinning in a weird dance, spinning out of control, in slow motion.

'My son!' his father called feebly.

'Yes.' Omovo went round the chair.

'Get me . . . pour me some . . . more drink . . .'

'You've had enough, Dad.'

'What!'

'Try and get some sleep. You need rest. Let me call Blackie for you.'

'Pour me drink! I . . . want . . . drink!'

'No, Dad.'

'You're just . . . like your . . . mother . . .'

'That's not fair, Dad.'

'Always . . . always trying . . . trying to control me . . .'

'Not true, Dad.'

'More drink!'

'No!'

His father glared at him. Then he broke into demented laughter. 'You want to . . . behave like . . . your brothers, eh. . . ?' his father said after he had stopped laughing. Then he said, making a wild gesture: 'Go away! Run away! . . . Abandon ship! . . . useless . . . Go away . . . like them . . .'

'Take it easy, Dad.'

'No! Why should I?'

He made another gesture, tripped, and fell head-first. Omovo caught him in time and managed to straighten him. His father swore profusely, spraying his face with spit and beer.

'Sons of that witch! Your mother . . . was a witch . . . a witch!'

'My mother was not a witch.'

'A witch, I tell you . . . She made me fail . . . always trying to control me . . . improve me . . . took away my freedom . . . wouldn't let me do what I wanted . . . interfered too much . . .'

'Blackie is listening, Dad.'

'So what? Women! . . . Your mother . . . so far . . . has succeeded . . .

in bringing me down . . . she won't leave me alone . . . leave me alone! . . .'

'She's dead, Dad. Dead!'

'Good!'

Omovo let go of his father and went and stood near his room door. His father staggered, caught the chair, and held onto it, looking round the bare room drunkenly, his head jerking, his eyes heavy, his gestures slow, his speech slurring.

'Good, I said!' He raised his voice steadily, till he was practically shouting. 'Foolish son . . . Your mother was a witch. She is still pressing me down. Was this how I was when she died? . . . Were . . . were we not living in Surulere? Now look at us . . . look at this gutter, this ghetto, that we share with riffraffs . . . with rats and lizards . . .'

'It's your own fault, Dad.'

His father either didn't hear or ignored the statement altogether. 'She wanted to kill me . . . drive me mad . . . "Do this, do that," she would say . . . "Invest in this, invest in that" . . . honestly . . . she wanted to drive me mad and collect . . . collect all my hard work for herself . . .' He gave his weird laugh. 'She is the one spoiling my life now . . . pressing me down . . . driving away business . . . confusing me . . . whispering things about Blackie to me . . .' He laughed again. 'She has now turned into a mosquito . . . gossiping about my wife . . . I can see her . . . pressing me down . . . She sends the tax people to me . . . drives away customers . . . When her witchcraft failed it turned back on her. I sat in the house and watched, yes watched her wickedness eat her up and kill her . . . I laughed the day she died . . . I opened a bottle of whisky . . . She has not let me rest since . . .' Laughter again. 'Have you . . . heard of a person . . . dying of an unknown disease before, eh?'

There was a long silence. It seemed a kind of eternity. The silence was ugly. The candles' illumination seemed to die and resurrect. Omovo could no longer bear it, could no longer restrain himself. His anger burst the banks of his pity. Waving his hands furiously to include everything in the house in his accusation, his voice sharp and loud, Omovo said:

'I am ashamed of you, Dad. You don't see what's right in front of you. You are blind. And deaf. And a coward. That's why you have failed. You've failed all of us. Your life has become one big empty pretence and now you blame a dead woman!'

Omovo was angry but what he actually said surprised him. He had voiced an emotion but in the end he had said the words. And in saying the words the emotion betrayed itself and then dissipated. Omovo felt

245

hurt. He felt rotten. He wished he could take the words back. But the damage had been done. The pain dulled in his head. His thighs trembled. A sickening void opened up inside him.

'Me, me, a failure. . . ?' his father said incredulously in a weak voice, a pleading voice.

At that precise moment Omovo suffered an absurd revelation of love.

'Omovo! My son! You call ME A FAILURE?'

He blinked. Then he staggered to a cushion–chair and sat on the armrest. Tears rolled down his drunken face. He cried like a child unsuccessfully fighting down its humiliation.

'Daddy, I didn't mean it . . . I didn't . . .'

His father, regaining a shred of his dignity, raised his palm, commanding his son to be silent. 'Don't say anything. Just leave the room . . . leave me alone . . . please.'

Omovo stayed still. After a moment his father slid down from the armrest onto the cushion. He convulsed. Tears ran down his face. The convulsion soon stopped. His mouth flopped open. He began to snore, awkwardly asleep on the chair. He looked more haunted than ever. But he also looked like a child that had lost something and had cried itself to sleep.

Omovo called Blackie. He knew she had been eavesdropping. She came and dragged his father to their room. He didn't wake up. Omovo went to his own room, dismantled the blank canvas, and wrestled with insomnia.

FOUR

The morning after her return from the forest, Ifeyiwa fell ill. For three days she hallucinated about her mother, about returning to her village. The ghost of her brother hovered over her. The prostrate figure of her father, begging for forgiveness, tormented her. She couldn't bear being bound to the bed. The room suffocated her with the smells of dust and camphor balls. The toilet made her feel worse. The corridors, with its clutter of baskets, brooms, and stained three-legged tables, the noise of squabbling tenants and screaming children, of radios loudly blaring, made her head and eyes burn. She could find no peace anywhere.

On the first day of her illness her husband kept away from her and stayed at the shop. When he appeared he had a brooding but softened air about him. In the evening she roused herself to prepare his food. She couldn't eat and sat huddled on a chair, covered with blankets, shivering, and watching him with dull eyes. She couldn't sleep all night and she cried for her mother.

On the second day some of her husband's people came to her. They all looked like wraiths. They were poor, hunger and bitterness had ravaged their features, they looked lean, their eyes were pitiless, and when they touched her – to comfort her – their hands were so cold and bony that they seemed to increase her debilitation, seemed to draw strength away from her. They frightened her. Their poverty had deformed them. The women were like reformed witches and the men were severe and odd. When they left she realised for the first time that they resented her, that they were suspicious of her, and had pronounced judgement on her in some way. In her confused state she understood that they somehow blamed her for not being pregnant, for keeping her husband from them. She even suspected that they hated her and thought her responsible for her husband's meanness. She was relieved when they were gone.

Tuwo also came to visit. He wore his favoured French suit, he stank of cheap aftershave, and he made long speeches about politics while her husband sat chewing his chewing stick, listening with an abstract look in his eyes. From their conversation she gathered that Omovo was also ill. She heard them talk about sending her to the doctor, or taking her home to the village to recuperate. When Tuwo left, her husband sprayed the room with insecticide and lit two candles, one on the table, the other at the door. Then he made strange rites with a juju she never knew he had. He wore a white wrapper, got her out of bed, smeared her with herbal paste, made libations, prayed fervently to his ancestors, sweating profusely. Then he went out, brought in a squawking white chicken, slaughtered it, and let its blood drip on the door, on the plate of candles, and on the juju which he had hung up above the door beam. When the chicken had stopped flapping, her husband dumped its severed head on the plate, and then he mixed its blood with the herbal paste and smeared the mixture over her stomach and on her breasts. He made her repeat certain solemn words after him. Then he carried her to bed, gave her a stiff portion of ogogoro in which roots had marinated, and disappeared into the backyard, taking the headless chicken with him. She dozed for a while. In her sleep she dreamt that her husband was going to sacrifice her for his relatives. She saw him, completely naked, wholly erect, and with a frightening knife in his hand. Everywhere she ran she was blocked by his relatives, by the women with small bitter faces, and hard eyes. She screamed. She saw a clear road and made for it – but her father, headless, his dane gun in one hand, appeared suddenly. She stood still, sank on her knees, and waited for her husband. He approached with a smile on his face, his neck weighed down with golden necklaces, the knife in his hand. Behind him, through an open door, she saw Omovo painting. Her husband raised his hand to strike her with the knife. She felt calm for a moment. Then, overcome with panic, she made a sudden movement in his direction and accidentally felt the coldness of the knife slice into her. She didn't know whether she had died or not when she woke up.

He stood over her, his palm on her forehead. There were strangers in the room. They were all in shadow. All she could make out of them was the raggedness of their clothes, the roughness of their skins, and the shadows they cast. She began to scream. Her husband calmed her. She had no idea how long she had been sleeping.

One by one the strangers left. They went but they left curious smells in the air. They left negative feelings, unspoken thoughts, moods of bitter presences. They left their shadows behind. She complained of the darkness. Her husband lit five more candles. Then she saw the white basin with steaming water on the table. And beside it a glittering knife, still stained with the blood of the slaughtered chicken. On the cupboard she noticed a new pot, steaming with food. On a chair she saw a white cloth. On the floor, the dead flower she had brought in the last time she saw Omovo.

'Where am I?' she asked.

'You're getting better,' he said.

She couldn't see his face. His voice sounded a little different.

'But what has been happening?'

'You have been ill. Now you are fine.'

She tried to sit up, but couldn't. He sat staring at her for a long time. He said nothing. She slept and woke again to find him in the same position. There were now three candles alight.

'Do you feel stronger?'

She sat up.

'Good.'

He got up and brought the basin over to the bed. He covered her head with the white cloth, then he poured some hot water into the basin. The steam engulfed her.

'Breathe in the air!' he said.

She breathed in herbal essences that stung her throat. The steam blinded her. Its pungencies, its bitter power, made her dizzy, and when she breathed she seemed to be falling into a pit of smoke. After a while he took the cloth off her and made her lie down. He went and poured the water away. When he came back he got out a bowl and a spoon. Then he served her from the freshly boiled pot of pepper soup. She refused to eat or drink.

'What's wrong with you?' he said sternly.

'I don't know who prepared it.'

'My people.'

'I'm not hungry.'

'Drink, it will make you better.'

'I'm not thirsty.'

He tried to force a spoonful of the pepper soup into her mouth. But she kept her lips shut tight and her tremulousness made the soup spill on the bed. He started to get angry, but quickly quietened down.

249

'It's not pepper soup I want,' she said.

'What do you want then, eh? Don't you want to get well?'

'I want to go home.'

'This is your home.'

'I want to go home to my people.'

He stayed silent, watching her, the candles burning, dawn creeping through the window chinks. His eyes were heavy with sleeplessness.

'What for?'

'To see my mother.' She paused. 'Before I die.'

'What's wrong with you, eh?' he said vehemently, in the tone of his old self. 'Why are you talking rubbish? What die? Who is dying? Drink this medicine, Ifeyiwa.'

'No.'

She lay down and covered her head. She heard him breathing heavily, muttering strange threats, heard him pacing, moving objects about the room, like a clumsy old woman. She drifted off to sleep again and woke to find him shaking her.

She looked up. Dawn had broken. The roosters were crowing. Footsteps were busy along the corridor. The noises of the ghetto came to her. The radios, the voices of old women, of little girls. Her husband had bathed, combed his hair, and put on new clothes. He had a bright, hopeful look on his face. He made her sit up, served her food, which she still refused to touch, and began to talk to her. He was curiously, distantly, tender. Then, as if he wanted to prove to himself the fact of his love, he showed her the imitation gold chains, the bronze plaited bangles, and the dyed cowries he had bought to give her when he felt that her spirit towards him had changed. He showed her the chest of clothes, the lace wrappers, the red shoes, the expensive white blouses, and the starched head-ties he had acquired and kept secret. He said he intended to give them to her as a present when she became pregnant. He wanted her to have all these gifts now and to rest content in his house as a wife and to recover soon. She fell into a long sleep, hallucinating, sweating, gnashing her teeth, while he talked.

When, on the third night of her illness, her husband came through the door, she leapt up and stabbed him in the heart and twisted the knife. His chest was bare and she was totally naked. He didn't fall. She stabbed him repeatedly, in the chest, in the ribs, in the stomach. At first he didn't bleed. With increased detachment, she hacked at him. Then she dug the knife into his eyes. He fell forward and hit the floor without a sound. When she turned him over his face had changed. One of his eyes had grown blue and big. It wasn't her husband she saw, but Omovo. She woke up screaming.

When she woke up from her nightmare she realised that she hadn't uttered a sound. She was breathing heavily. The room was quiet. She didn't move. Her husband lay snoring beside her. She mistook his profuse sweating for blood. Horrified, she got out of bed with a silent panic in her heart, wound her way down the dark corridor full of obstacles and heavy with stale smells, and washed herself in the backyard.

Her husband's snoring had subsided when she got back. She spread the mat, took her pillow, and lay on the floor. She was afraid of her calm; she feared she had entered a forbidden zone, an inner area of madness. Everything in her had taken on new dimensions. She looked around the darkness, listening to the rats scratching, wondering what it was in her brain, in her soul, that had made her accept the obscenities of her life. She searched her mind for reconciliations, for things that made sense of her life, that redeemed her existence, and she found none. The unreality of everything struck her suddenly with the force of a witnessed act of cruelty. In the darkness, beside the mat, she made out the flattened shape of the flower. It was like a piece of rag.

Lying face up on the mat, she asked herself what were the realities of her life. She made a mental list: fevers, bad food, overwork, a total absence of freedom, her domination by her husband, unrealised dreams and desires, never enough rest, no play, no dancing or music, no association with people her own age, an unending series of household drudgeries, an unending list of new rules and edicts from her husband to be endured, a repression of the juices, the youthfulness bursting in her, attrition, exhaustion, a lifetime of pretending, of being humble, of holding back her abilities, and a hundred other things. Her list made her dizzy, wearied her. She turned on the mat and shut her eyes.

She had never told Omovo the things she really suffered. She had only hinted. If he knew how to interpret sighs, if he could calibrate their depths, and imagine from what endurances, what silences, they came then he would know, she liked to think. And if he didn't know, if she had to tell him, then he'd never understand anyway.

She thought about herself and Omovo, about how close they were in space and yet how vast the distances were between them. She thought about the atmosphere into which they had been born and in which they must survive: an atmosphere of confusion, acquisition, an age of corruption, poverty, ghetto dreams, a period of waste and loss, a generation betrayed by their parents.

She felt angry at the feeling that in a better world, a different one, a love story would have been possible between her and Omovo. But the age had thwarted them and she had been married off against her will and without her knowledge and only after she had accepted did she meet the only person she would rather have married. She wished, for a moment, that she had remained a village girl, that she had never been exposed to books, to school, to films and popular records, to the desires and yearnings that the society wouldn't allow her to fulfill. Things would have been simpler. But – there he was and here she was, in the darkness, with love between them and the whole world separating them.

Her eyes had become used to the darkness. She stared at the rag. With shadows in her soul, she thought about the troubles burning up her village. She felt bound to the troubles in some way, in some ancient, secret way. Not being able to fathom how this was, or why, she allowed herself to feel that she could help, that she could spread peace for a change, play some surprising and meaningful role. She saw herself that night, in a strange fantasy, as a sort of a peacemaker, as one who could cross boundaries, and go between the villages, giving speeches that would move the people to stop fighting. She felt the urge of a great pull, an unknown gravity, as if something were pulling her spirit home.

She remembered the day at school when she had taken part in a debate. The topic was: what is the role of women in the Africa of today? She had been one of the two main speakers. Her opponent had trotted out the old lines that women should be great mothers, should help Africa retain its traditional ways. Ifeyiwa had said that women should change with the changing times. They should be both mothers and leaders. They should be healers, pilots, priests, and that if God gave them intelligence they should use it to the fullest. She spoke with awkward passion, a little too brashly, and she was extremely nervous. She was inflamed with her embarrassment and nervousness and this made her bolder, pushed her beyond her intended motion. Her opponent won the debate, but Ifeyiwa never forgot the curious excitement of that passion, of going over the edge and carrying on, stuttering, fighting the words, defiant, completing her speech. She never knew she could do it and her friends and teachers regarded her differently afterwards. Her triumph always secretly fed her pride, her sense of herself. After that she began to suspect that she was special in some way.

Her thoughts became confused. She began to plan one set of things, one course of action, and then it would be superseded by another. She decided first that she would escape from her marriage, go home to her village, persuade her family to return her bride price, and then return to the city, and to Omovo. Then she decided that was too much like a dream. Instead she would simply return home, make peace between the villages, and fulfil the vague notions she had about her destiny. But shadows leapt about inside her. Filled with sudden foreboding, she shut her eyes. She couldn't hide from the shadows. They were everywhere inside her, large and unformed, monstrous, intent, like shapes that can never be deciphered. The shadows formed themselves into the face of her father, blinded and decrepit from his accidental infanticide; into the face of her brother with his unfocussed eyes, and into that of her mother, with her mouth stiffened into the shape of a plea. Their faces were all like spirits departing the earth forever.

And because of them – those faces – her decision to leave her husband grew stronger. She saw him now not just as a frightening man, but as an ancient, unyielding force that stood between her and her destiny, as an incubus who kept pressing her down, hiding her books, trying to make her illiterate, trying to make her like all the other women around. For the first time in her married life she saw her husband as a natural enemy, whose domination she would have to free herself from if she was going to have a chance to live.

She saw fully how her initial compromise had betrayed her. She should never have accepted in the first place. She might now be living her real life. She could see the true destination of her acceptances: she would become the sort of old woman of the ghetto, with a stinking wrapper round her waist, her mouth toothless, her breasts flat and drooping, whom the children think of as a witch.

It saddened her that, apart from her mother and the uninspiring teachers at school, she had met no other woman to look up to, who could have guided her. Then she became angry that she had allowed herself to be so cheated of living. Revulsion seethed within her. Her mind teemed suddenly with images of death, of drowning. She was torn between what she didn't know for sure, and what she might now never know.

She felt deserted. Shipwrecked. She thought sadly that not even love could save her or help her avoid the lacerations that kept swooping in her like a large predatory bird. She felt that love had betrayed her even more, had made her accept more in its name, made her suffer and endure more, had kept her in the ghetto, in her husband's house, a servant and a possession. Besides, she knew only too well that Omovo had his own dragons to fight, his own demons. The landscape of losses had trapped

253

them both in simple acts of existence. She thought of the dead, mutilated girl in the park. She felt a little like that girl, mutilated and no-one noticing. She felt she went around mutilated and no-one saw just how the world, how her husband, was wounding her every day. She had to run away. She knew this calmly. Her spirit was forgiving. She forgave everything, everyone, and even herself. And then she cursed everything, everyone, and even herself.

In the dark she planned the day ahead. She gathered her things. Her husband stirred on the bed. He began to snore again. She saw her homecoming. She saw herself receiving a heroine's welcome, with people she didn't recognise rushing to greet her and touch her, singing her name in praises, urging her spirit on to possibilities of greatness. She imagined it would be a bright day after rain when she arrived. She saw the trees swaying in the warm, earth-scented wind. Her husband stirred again. She listened to the changed gear of his snoring while she let the certainty of her decision sink into her nerves. She drifted off into her last night's sleep in the city.

Her husband spoke lovingly to her in the morning. His mouth stank. He kept smiling. Kept petting her. He was unusually kind, paid attention to her moods, and kept asking if she felt better after the night's rest. He even gave her fifteen Naira to buy things for herself. She accepted the money in the humblest spirit. He talked about the future, how he was going to open out. He talked about the beautiful children they would have together, the house he was building, the car they would drive.

'I want us to enjoy life more,' he said.

She nodded.

While he spoke he cleaned his teeth with a chewing stick and spat the mangled wood fibre on the floor of the room. She fetched water, and warmed it over the wood fire. While he bathed she listened to the rats scratching in secret places of the room. She made his food, the choicest dish she had ever cooked in the house – fried yams and plantain, stew with crayfish, and soft goat meat spiced with herbs. He ate happily. He told her amusing stories about his various customers. She laughed where she was expected to: her laughter surprised him. She told him the story of the debate at school.

'I agree with you,' he said. 'You should have won the debate, my good wife.'

When he had eaten he lingered about the house. She became silent. Reluctantly, he went out to the city centre to buy much-needed provisions for his shop. When he had gone she sat on the bed and looked around the room she had hated all these months. She looked at her little table, her clothes on the ropes, his big shoes and torn slippers, the cupboard, the single bed, the chairs, the door, the window. It made her feel strange that she actually felt sad at leaving them behind forever. She was surprised that she had, in spite of it all, come to feel attached to some things in her condition.

She thought of the first day she had arrived in the city and in her husband's room. She wondered at how it could be that at the time she had missed her village from which she wanted to escape, and now she was missing in advance the details and moods of the room she had to escape from. Life is a terrible mystery, she thought. She wondered why no one ever told her things she needed to know, why no one gave her the keys with which to unlock doors of understanding.

She swept the floor. She sang in a sweet sad voice. She made the bed, cleaned out the cupboards, washed the dirty plates and pots, and ensured that everything in the room was neat, tidy, and bright. That morning she felt she had mysteriously recovered. She felt a new lucidity, as if she had been asleep all her life and was just waking up.

She took up a pen and began a letter to Omovo. But she couldn't think of what to say. Or rather, she had too much to say and didn't know where to begin. He should understand, she thought. Then she left a note to her husband. 'I have gone,' it read.

She packed hurriedly. Dressed in her ordinary clothes, as if she weren't going anywhere special, she left the room and put the key under the doormat. Her box was light. She took only her books and a few clothes. It saddened her that she had nothing of Omovo, no photographs, not even one of his drawings. She went to the backyard and looked at everything. She greeted the neighbours in a bright voice. They didn't notice anything unusual about her.

When she left the house she didn't look back, didn't even look at Omovo's place, didn't dare hope to catch a glimpse of him. But she felt certain she would see him again and that they would be together. All around the children played. The wind blew the ghetto litter at her, round her, in swirls. She saw two dogs making love, stuck together. She saw old men sitting on chairs, staring at the street with rheumed eyes, clutching at their cigarettes and their bottles of ogogoro as if at things that would prolong their lives. She noticed how aggressive and confused the young unemployed men were. No one seemed to notice anything, any

255

betrayals. Everyone seemed to accept that this was the only way life could be, the way it always would be. For the first time this realisation shocked her: that no one could see alternatives, the other ways to the seas that Omovo's brother's poem had talked about. She felt sorry to leave things behind. But she also felt as if she had been living on a river and that the water had drained away from her existence.

She felt sorry for Omovo and she said a prayer for him. It was a bright afternoon and mirages shimmered everywhere. As she left she felt sure she saw ghosts everywhere, that the ghetto was becoming a ghost town, that things were changing without people's knowledge or consent, and that the ghetto-dwellers were becoming ghosts and shadows without voices.

FIVE

Omovo had also been ill for three days after the beating. He couldn't send a message to the office and he was certain he had been sacked. He developed a high fever, his eyes kept pulsing, and his head seemed to keep expanding as if his brain were about to burst. He slept badly and things got so mixed up in his fever that he wove in and out of strange mental territories. He hallucinated about Ifeyiwa, and about his mother. He dreamt that his brothers had returned and ransacked the house, kicking things over, destroying tables and chairs, and pursuing his father round the compound with an axe.

Blackie frequently came in to treat him. He tried to repulse her attempts, but in the end his energy failed and he had to submit to her pepper soups, her hot compresses and her ointments. While she tended to him she was vaguely solicitous, she seemed to keep trying to formulate a plea, but his silences distanced her and when she left he lay sprawled on the bed, thirsty, worn down and shivering.

On the second day of his fever he was no longer sure if he was hallucinating or not. His father kept appearing and disappearing, dressed in the full regalia of his traditional clothes, with his long wrapper, his duck-tailed shirt, a fan of eagle feathers in one hand, cowries round his neck, and a flywhisk in his other hand. When he appeared, like an apparition, like a descendant from a powerful line, he would exhort Omovo, boosting his spirit with deep proverbs; he would start to tell stories of magic rivers, and mermaids, of ancient heroes, but he would never complete them.

Later that day, weakened by the heat, his head throbbing, he had another hallucination. Dr Okocha appeared to him. He wore his agbada, and on his back was the burden of all the signboards he had ever painted. He looked very sad, his eyes were deep, his forehead was crinkled and sweat ran over the cracks. With his pained expression he stood over Omovo and said in a quivering voice: 'Everything that is happening to you now is only part of your preparation.'

'What preparation?' Omovo heard himself say.

'For living. This is merely a secret apprenticeship.'

He stayed silent. Omovo watched him.

'Why do you have all those signboards on your back?'

'I'm going to destroy them. I've been going round collecting them. They shame me. They have weighed me down for thirty years. If I had done five paintings I wanted to do instead of all these I would be dead now, but the five paintings would be living. So I am dying now.'

'Why did you do the signboards?'

'To feed my family, why else?'

'You mean . . .'

'Yes.'

'You mean the signboard at the hotel . . .'

'I've torn it down.'

'And the one for the tailor . . .'

'Wrenched from the door, yes.'

'Didn't they try to stop you?'

'No. I took them at night. I've never felt so free. I will never paint another signboard.'

'But you do the best signboards in Lagos.'

'And I could do five of them a day. But I'd rather do a small portrait of an eagle, or the face of the old man of the ghetto . . .'

'Who's he?'

'He's our destiny. If we're not careful. He's my friend. We drink palm wine and play draughts once a week. He's full of tricks. I have never beaten him and that's why I go on playing him. He never laughs. One day . . .'

'Can I meet him?'

'One day. Not yet. Not for a long time.'

'Why not?'

'The young make him weep.'

'Why?'

'I've never asked.'

'Is he jealous of youth?'

'No. He weeps for youth.'

'I don't understand.'

'You're not well. Get some sleep.'

Then the old painter disappeared. Omovo slept soundly and woke up in the middle of the night, convinced he had been talking with dead bodies he had seen during the war. He lay on the bed, watchful, till dawn broke.

On the third day, as he got a little stronger, he heard songs that reminded him of his mother. He wandered through the compound. Everything seemed a little strange to him. His father was nowhere around. One of the compound women told him Blackie had gone to the market. He encountered Tuwo in the backyard, washing his clothes, his underpants, and his socks. Tuwo started to say something to him, but Omovo, unable to confront his eyes, fled back to his room. In the afternoon he ventured out of the compound and went to see Dr Okocha. His workshed was locked. The people around said they hadn't seen him for days. Wandering back through the heat and dust, the noise of blaring record shops, the smell of garbage in the streets, and the sight of old men and women, increased his debilitation. He went back home. He tried to paint, but felt too weak to hold a brush, and the effort of concentrating wearied him. His eyes still hurt and his perception of objects in space had become temporarily distorted. He lay in bed and read and slept till evening came.

He was half asleep when he heard an argument raging between his father and Blackie. He heard his father shouting about Blackie's mysterious absences, heard her defending herself. She said she had gone to the market and couldn't get the best choice of food items which he especially liked and that she had to go back in the evening. She said as she returned she met one of her relatives and went home with her to see her new-born baby. Omovo stayed in the room till the argument burned itself out. When the house was silent again he ventured into the sitting room. No-one was around. He went to the compound front and sat with the compound men, hoping to get some word about Ifeyiwa. He learnt nothing. The compound people, offering their sympathies about his fever, were curiously distant towards him. Tuwo wasn't amongst them.

That night as he lay in bed, weakened by the day's heat which seemed to have stoked his fever, Tuwo appeared to him. Omovo tried to escape his presence. Tuwo kept reappearing, begging his forgiveness. Omovo woke up and found that the lights had been seized. He lay down again, shut his eyes, shivering. Tuwo appeared again. He was completely naked, he had an enormous erection, and before Omovo's gaze he began to make love to Blackie. They both begged his forgiveness as they made love with urgent lustful intensity. And as their enjoyment mounted, as their motions got more frenzied and peaked, so did their pleas. When they had exhausted themselves, when an expression of disgust appeared on both their sweating faces, they found they were stuck, like dogs, and couldn't separate themselves. They tried and they couldn't. Blackie became terrified. Tuwo turned a frightened gaze to Omovo. They both began to beg him to help them separate. Omovo's mother appeared and began to laugh dementedly. Then suddenly his father materialised, with a machete in his hand. The couple started running clumsily around the room. Blackie was bent over, Tuwo behind her. They looked like trapped animals, bound. Omovo's father followed them slowly, with dreadful dignity. He came up to them where they stopped. He lifted up the machete with both hands, a mad and serene expression in his eyes. Tuwo yelled. Before his father cleaved them apart Omovo woke up. The lights had returned. The fan was whirring. Omovo didn't sleep well the rest of that night. He didn't see his father or Blackie in the morning. In spite of feeling weak, his limbs aching, his face still swollen, he decided he had borne enough of being bed-bound.

For the first time in weeks Omovo went early to work. He found that no-one else had arrived in the office. It was nine o'clock. He sat at his desk, confused by its new arrangement. His documents were mixed up, some were missing, the files and cards were in utter disarray. He saw errors in allocations, he noticed that the handwriting on letters was completely strange to him. Alarmed by huge mistakes in the counting of chemicals, he went to the warehouse. Everyone looked at him as if he were a ghost. The warehouse manager hadn't arrived at work either. He went to the accounts department. Only two people were in. Joe was nowhere around. He went to the canteen and had breakfast. It was nine thirty when he got back to the office.

The place was cold. The air conditioner had been turned up to its limit. No one looked up when he came in. Simon was eating his tea bread, dipping it in a glass of water, and staring at the semi-nude white woman on the wall calendar. He had a far-away expression in his eyes. The supervisor tapped away intensely on his pocket calculator, as if his life depended on the figures it produced. Chako paused from the scrutiny of his football coupons to snap off a bedraggled piece of kola-nut. Then he blew his nose. He looked very sober. It was clear he had lost a lot of money on the previous week's betting. He looked up at Omovo, looked right through him, inhaled a thumbful of snuff, shook his head vigorously, and sneezed. At that moment the kettle began whistling. The steam kept lifting and dropping its metal flap.

Omovo hovered around his desk, feeling curiously displaced. The mood of the office had changed. Omovo felt a shiver go through him. The supervisor sighed and then put away the calculator. He seemed satisfied with his manipulation of the figures. Turning in his chair, his features now set in his mask of new authority, he said to Omovo:

'What happened to your face?'

It was only then that the others acknowledged his presence in the room. They looked up and studied the disjointedness of his features.

Chako said: 'Or were you caught stealing?'

'Maybe he was in the wrong place at the right time,' came Simon.

'Abi you painted the right picture of the wrong woman?'

'Or maybe he refused to pay a prostitute and she punched him?' came Simon again.

'Hey, Simon!' the supervisor shouted in mock disbelief. 'So you sabi how prostitutes dey punch, eh?'

They laughed.

'Maybe he got a friend to do it?'

'Why?'

'After all he didn't come to work for three days. You never know the tricks of these young boys of nowadays.'

The supervisor directed the next statement at him. 'You better have a good excuse.'

'I was attacked at night.'

They all burst out laughing again.

'By women?'

'Thieves?'

'Did you try it on a neighbour's wife?'

'Or did you go around with your notebook, drawing people unnecessarily?'

'Did you stay up too late?'

'Or did you get drunk and forget yourself?'

'I was attacked,' Omovo said firmly.

'It shows,' was Simon's verdict.

'It doesn't,' said the supervisor.

'And then I came down with a fever,' continued Omovo.

'A fever?' said an unbelieving Simon.

'He actually came down,' added the supervisor.

'Down to earth,' said Chako.

'I couldn't move for two days.'

'Two days!'

'Two whole days!'

'Yes.'

'And on the third day?' mocked the supervisor.

'I began to recover.'

'You recovered.'

'I began to.'

'He began to,' said Simon.

'Yes.'

'I see,' said the supervisor.

'We see.'

'You better go in and see the manager.'

'Yes. You better go and see him.'

'Not without my permission,' shouted Chako.

Omovo looked round at them, his heart beating fast. He felt rage simmering within him. Rage and defiance. He was about to say something insulting to the entire office when the main door opened. The manager's nephew, who had failed his certificate examinations three times in a row, hurried into the room. He bustled towards the kettle and began tinkering with the cups. In the silence Omovo understood why the office mood had changed. The manager's nephew was young, he looked fresh. He wore black trousers, a white shirt, and a red tie. He looked as if he was full of ready obedience. They nodded at one another.

Omovo turned and, without knocking, stormed into the manager's office. Chako tried to stop him, but was too late. Omovo went in and shut the door behind him. The manager looked up once, his face expressionless, and proceeded to finish his cup of coffee, nibbling on a biscuit. Omovo approached his desk and stood there silently gazing at the manager.

After a few seconds Omovo discerned a certain pungent smell in the office. He wrinkled his nose. He knew. The manager, squirming in his seat, knew that he knew. The silence remained. Omovo brought out his handkerchief, covered his nose, and took two steps backwards.

'That's why I have a secretary,' the manager said, eventually.

The smell grew worse, as if it too were positing a new law of corporate physics: that hot air rises to the top. Omovo refused to speak for a while. He held his breath, released it, and then breathed in measured shallowness. He looked round the manager's office. He studied the table. He noticed the framed picture of his young wife, his gilded nameplate, his thick brown wallet, and thousands of documents. On the wall behind him, next to large portraits of the Head of State and the Director of the company, was a photograph of him in England. He was with other English officials of the company. He was in the background and distinguishable only because he was a lone black face amongst white ones. The rest of the walls had many calendars, some of the company, all of them depicting romantic scenes of Western capitals.

'Sit down, Omovo,' the manager said after a long silence.

The air conditioner droned softly. The smell had gradually diluted.

'So what do you want?'

Still standing, Omovo said: 'I want to know if I have been sacked.'

The manager smiled for the first time. 'No, not at all. As a matter of fact your salary has been increased.' He paused. 'But you have been transferred to our Mile Twelve Branch.'

'The department is very kind,' Omovo said, changing stance.

'What do you mean?'

'What I said.'

'Listen, you failed to turn up for work for three whole days. You had no sick leave, nothing.'

'I was ill. I had been beaten up.'

The manager continued as if he hadn't heard anything. 'I could easily have recommended your being sacked. But I am a considerate man and our department is nothing if not accommodating. We are giving you the benefit of the doubt. We are giving you a chance to change your bad habits.'

'Meanwhile you give your nephew the benefit of employment.'

The manager looked at him, anger flashing for a moment in his eyes. 'These things happen, you know.'

'Sure. But what if I refuse your offer?'

'I'm afraid we'd have to lay you off. Millions out there are waiting for a job like yours.'

'Well, I'm not accepting the transfer. It's spiteful. You know I could never make Mile Twelve from Alaba even if I woke up at five o'clock.'

'Excellent. You have spoken your mind. All is well taken. As I said, the department is accommodating. Put in your letter of resignation with

263

immediate effect, claim your salary and allowances, and go. Good luck to you. I have work to do, if you don't mind.'

The manager picked up a file, indicating that the meeting was over. Omovo glared at him, then said in a voice of controlled rage:

'I can see right through your pretence at good office relations. I'm not impressed. You don't have to try and frustrate me any further. You're very civilised, very decent. You're shit. Time will wash you away.'

The manager threw down the file and exploded. 'You're mad, Omovo. God punish you for what you have just said. Take your money and get out. We don't want people like you anyway!'

Omovo smiled, and left.

He collected his month's salary along with a pro rata payment of his leave allowance, his overtime and his Christmas bonus for that year. It came to quite a substantial amount. He had never held so much money in his hands before.

He went back to the office. No-one spoke to him and he addressed no-one. He went thought his desk, taking out his things, his notepads, his felt tips, the various objects he had accumulated which would be of help to his painting. He put them in a plastic bag. The manager's nephew stayed away. Simon left the office. The supervisor went off for an early lunch. Chako sat stolidly considering his football coupons. When Omovo had finished clearing his desk he left a note to his successor about the errors in the records. As he was about to leave Omovo suddenly felt sad. He felt that sad sickening feeling of being sacked, of uncertainty, of the faces he was leaving behind and might never see again, even of failure. He felt a twinge of loss at the little things about the office, the air conditioner always on high, the coolness of the place when no one was around, the serenity of drawing there after work when he was supposed to be doing overtime. He also felt, in advance, the loss of special relationships, the overheard gossip, the resentments that had become redundant, the parts of him that only the office brought out, the parts that die with the leaving.

But in spite of the difficult shedding of a skin that couldn't grow with him, he had to leave. His shoes grated as he went down the corridor. The walls were yellow, freshly painted, clean. The corridor was empty. When the doors were opened he felt the cool air from the offices. A fine excitement, an almost defiant joy, grew within him at escaping from the grinding wheels of the company. He felt free. His mind was clear. He had decided never to work in an organisation again, never to be a cog in a wheel. He had sworn to set his sails to the fortunes of art. How was he to know what cruel and difficult seas his ship would travel?

As he passed the last of the offices, the door opened and one of the sales representatives stuck out his head. He was heavily bearded and rather fat. He saw Omovo and said urgently: 'Omovo! Make two coffees for me and my girlfriend! Quick! And when you've finished get us some meat pies. We're starving.'

Omovo took a few steps backwards, a mischievous smile on his lips. Through the open door he saw the sales rep's girlfriend. She was very thin, wore a long silk gown, and was all pasted up with eye-shadow, rouge, and lipstick. Her skin had been unnaturally bleached with skin-lightening creams. She was peering at her bony face in a small mirror.

'What are you looking at? Hurry! I don't have all day. Or do you want me to bribe you first, eh?'

Omovo grinned. 'That won't be necessary,' he said.

'Good.'

'Because you and your girlfriend can drink piss – and enjoy it!'

The rep's mouth hung open in astonishment.

'And watch your mouth. A fly might dive into it,' Omovo added.

Without awaiting a reply he pushed on. He left the offices and said goodbye to the gateman. He didn't feel so sad any more. He felt brave. Outside, the dense heat startled him. The smell of diesel oil rose from the overflowing gutters. There were traffic jams on all the roads. Two men were fighting near a shoe shop. He noticed a policeman secretively accepting a bribe from a defaulting taxi driver. There were many flies and midges in the air. But he felt the double liberation of having quit work and of recovering from his fever.

He stopped outside Valentino's Restaurant. He had always gone past it, looking in wistfully. The windows were tinted and it seemed plush inside. He had always wanted to go in and order himself a lavish three-course meal. For the first time he had enough money. 'Why not now?' he thought. He pushed open the doors and went in.

The air conditioner blasted cold air in his face. The restaurant was as comfortable as it looked. It was elaborately decorated. Bad paintings hung on the semi-marbled walls. The lights were blue, the music tinkled from the ceiling, and there was a glass goldfish tank. There were armchairs, sofas, and cushion chairs covered with imitation velvet materials. He found a table and sat. A waiter soon came over.

'What will it be, sir?'

'I haven't looked at the menu yet.'

'Take your time, sir.' The waiter, a middle-aged man in a blue and red uniform, bowed away stiffly.

The menu was almost entirely alien to him. He was a little confused by the exotic food names. Starters: pâté maison, mushrooms à la Grecque, stuffed courgettes. He decided to skip the starters. Main courses: poussin chasseur, tournedos maison, escalope de veal à la crème, entrecôte poivre, eminces de cabestu, scampi Provençale, avocado vinaigrette, pizza, chicken salad, jollof rice and pounded yam. He cursed his poor knowledge of international cuisine. And yet he didn't want to settle for the merely familiar.

'Have you made up your mind now, sir?' the waiter said, mysteriously reappearing in the midst of his confusion.

'Oh yes. Emm. I'll have pizza, chicken salad and jollof rice.'

A mocking smile crossed the waiter's face. 'Any wines? Starters? Sweets?'

'Sweets? What sweets? Oh. No sweets for me.'

'Fine, sir. Wines? Starters?'

'No starters.'

'Can I suggest the stuffed courgettes, sir?'

'Nothing stuffed for me, thank you.'

The waiter coughed. Discreetly. 'Wines, sir?'

'Wine?'

'That's right, sir.'

'Emm. Red wine. No, white wine. Cancel that. Just a glass of water, please.'

'Just water.'

'That's right.'

'Fine.'

'And please . . .'

'Yes, sir?'

'I am not a sir.'

'As you please.'

The waiter bowed away. Omovo gave a sigh of relief. He had begun to sweat. As he sat waiting for the food he remembered something Dele had said:

'If you ever despair of going abroad, just step into a good restaurant and you are as good as there.'

He smiled at the memory. Who despairs of going abroad? he thought. He wondered if Dele had gone to the USA. He wondered how Okoro, who desperately wanted to join him, was taking it. He thought about how intensely the new symbol of progress had become going abroad – to the USA, to London, or Paris. He didn't have the desire to go abroad. He wanted to stay home and bear witness. His brothers had both gone: if he went too who would keep the home front? Who would provide the continuity? Besides: where would he go, what would he do, who would pay his college fees? He envied the solidity that could belong to people like Keme: that of knowing the landscape, being seasoned by it, wrestling with its changes, watching its unfolding history, staying the course. It was the solidity he needed – that of working a fruitful but demanding tract of land. Yes. He would set his sails to the fortunes and rigours of art. He would grow in the landscapes, earth himself. How was he to know that he had chosen the most terrible path?

He looked around at the other clientele. A group at a big table caught his interest. Three white men seemed to be having a confused discussion with two Nigerians. They mixed badly. The white men were lightly dressed. The Nigerians wore suits and ties and they sweated. They were businessmen. The white men sat in a semi-circle and wholly dominated the table. They crowded the Nigerians with words in strange accents and with the tone of their voices. They were all sunburnt and they spoke loudly, in the manner of people who think that what they have to say is intrinsically interesting. Omovo picked up bits of their conversation and was amazed. One of the white men had come to work with an oil company. He said:

'Our people still think of you as savages. You are remarkably civilised.'

One of the Nigerians, who obviously hadn't understood what was said, burst out laughing. The other one said: 'Pardon me?'

The second white man, Scottish, was returning home.

'Had enough of this place. It's a mess. You could run your country better,' he growled.

The first Nigerian laughed again, beating his hand on his thigh. The second one looked away.

The third white man was a journalist. He wore a massive wristwatch. Turning to his companions, a bored disdainful expression on his mean face, he said: 'I've come to write about the English abroad. For *The Times*, you know.'

'What about the natives?' the oil worker asked.

'Who? Oh them. They've got their independence now. They can take care of themselves.'

'But their country is a mess.'

'Still very civilised though. A friendly people.'

The Nigerian businessmen smiled through the exchange as if they were being polite at uncomprehended jokes. They kept looking around the restaurant as if they hoped someone who knew them would see them in their elevated company. And when they spoke, trying as they were to sound like the white men, they got their accents mixed up. The whole exchange at the table was composed entirely of misunderstandings. It was only the embarrassed laughter of the more unctuous of the two businessmen that relieved the uneasy atmosphere.

By the time the waiter brought Omovo's food he was furious. He burned with rage. He thought about Ifeyiwa and the border clashes involving her village, how the ancestors of these white men had created the problem a hundred years before. He wondered at their insolence, their arrogance. Their exchanges had all but destroyed his appetite. Who despairs of going abroad? he asked himself again. If the white men were so insensitive in other people's countries how would they be in theirs? He was furious and he wanted to get up and scream at them, insult them, but managed to control himself with a great effort of will. His hands trembled. He drank the glass of water and breathed deeply. When the moment passed he tried to concentrate on the food. He was disappointed with the pizza, which he couldn't finish. In the end he ate very little. He ordered a Chapman. He drank and tried not to listen to the loud voices from the other table. Suddenly he wanted to escape, to get some air. He called for his bill.

When he saw it he could have fallen off his chair. The bill came to a fifth of his salary. With a set face he collected his change. The waiter stood beside his table longer than necessary, attracting attention to him. The white men stared at him. Omovo ignored them. He wiped his mouth with the serviette and smiled at the waiter. As he got up one of the businessmen released again his explosive laughter. The white men looked at one another, bewildered.

The journalist said: 'I might put in a word or two about their sense of humour.'

'You need one in a place like this,' the Scotsman said. 'Or you'd go bloody bonkers!'

The quieter businessman said: 'When I was in London . . .'

The whole table, indeed the whole restaurant, went silent.

'. . . I saw a fat woman dragged across the road by a small dog.'

The voices resumed their conversation. The pointless remark was ignored. The waiter blocked Omovo's exit. His neck retained its stiffness, his eyes were determined, and he stared at Omovo. When Omovo dropped twenty kobo on the plate the waiter smiled.

'I hope you enjoyed the dish – sir?'

Omovo, convinced that the waiter had rigged the bill, swearing that he would never eat there again, fled from the restaurant with the supercilious voices of the white men ringing in his ears.

As he went home, he felt himself sweating. When he got to the Apapa residential area he found that he had to struggle against the current of the second wave of the 'exodus'. The workers were pouring out for their afternoon and night shifts. He pushed against the grain of the people, against the mass of the crowds. He felt their urgencies, their violences, their fears. It took him a long time to get to Waterside. The crowd pushed him this way and that. He watched their faces, noted their infinite permutations of resilience and suffering. He noted the muscles beneath their clothes, the shapes of noses, the shadings of eye colours, the ruggedness of their jaws, the curious stains on faded shirts. He looked at the affluent surroundings, and through the well-cut hedges and whistling pines he saw the expatriate white kids watching the crowd through binoculars, secure on their balconies.

As he struggled against the waves of bodies that could easily have trampled him underfoot, he felt his armpits getting wet, felt his shirt sticking to his back, felt the dampness of his socks. Then he felt something drop on his shoulder, a wet weight. He looked and saw birdshit. He glanced upwards and saw nothing in the immediate expanse of the sky. He felt marked in some way. It was a very bright afternoon.

SIX

When he got home from the office, Blackie met him in the sitting room.

'Do you know Ifeyiwa has run away?' she asked, gently.

Omovo's face contorted. He felt sick. 'When?'

'No one knows. Her husband thinks it was this morning. He came to look for you. I hope say he no go make trouble.'

Omovo was silent.

'She was a fine girl.'

'She was unhappy.'

'Why?'

Omovo didn't say.

At the backyard the compound people were gathered. Takpo was wailing about Ifeyiwa's abandonment. His voice quivered. Tuwo was trying to comfort him with proverbs. The women advised him to go after her and 'iron' things with her parents. It was a noisy gathering; everyone contributed their opinion of where she might have gone, what should be done. Some suggested he go to the police. Others thought he should be patient. Omovo, unfortunately, went past on his way to the toilet. There fell an immediate accusatory silence. All the faces turned on him, the eyes bored into him. Someone said:

'Men of the compound! Watch your wives-o! There are thieves around-o!'

Someone else said: 'Hah, quiet people are the most dangerous.'

Takpo pushed through the gathering. The women screamed. The men tried to hold him back, but he shook them off. He stood very close to Omovo, their faces almost touching. He breathed heavily into

Omovo's nose. He smelt of ogogoro. His eyes were bloodshot and wide open, his mouth twitched. His face was pitifully shrunken.

'Omovo?'

'Yes?'

'My wife don run leave me, you hear? Ifeyiwa has run away, you hear?'

'Yes.'

'She run away and leave me one small note on paper, you understand? You see what you've done to my life? You see wetin you don cause, eh?'

Omovo was silent. He lowered his head.

'I saw both of you when you entered that house. I saw you with my own two eyes, you hear me so? You see what you've done to me, eh?'

Omovo moved backwards.

'Okay, I'm an old man. Now I'm finished. Are you satisfied, eh? Are you? So what did both of you plan, eh? What's the plan?'

Omovo shook his head. Tapko continued, blasting his hot breath at Omovo.

'Do you know how much I paid on that girl's head, eh? If you sell all your things you can't pay her bride price. I try to make her happy, I try everything, I gave am money, I buy am jewellery, I open shop for am, I give am gold, I buy am clothes, I take am go out, I send am to school, I buy am books, I look after am as if she be princess. But look now. Because of you she take my money, took all my money, took all the things I do for am and then she run away. You see what you've done to my life, eh?'

Omovo stayed still. He held his breath. He was baffled.

Takpo turned to the crowd, raising his hands, lifting his voice, in gestures of great agony. 'How can a man know what's in a woman's mind, eh? How? How can a man understand a woman, tell me-o! I want to know!'

He turned back to Omovo. 'All that time she was with me, all that time it was you, YOU, she was thinking of, eh? Maybe that's why she refused to be pregnant! What was your plan, I want to know! I want to know . . .'

Suddenly, overcome by anger, Takpo fell on Omovo and slapped him, kicked him, scratched him, spat on him, wailing like a madman. Omovo bore it all without moving or flinching. Tapko began lashing out with his fists and shouted: 'I'm going to kill you! I'll hire people to kill you! Bring back my wife-o! Bring her back!'

The compound men swarmed in and pulled them apart. Omovo bled from the wound on his forehead. Long scratch marks ran down his cheeks. He went to the bathroom and washed his face. Then he went past the crowd again to his room. He sat and stared out of the window.

He sat motionless for a long time. The voices died down in the backyard. But Tapko went on shouting. After a while his voice also quietened. On an impulse Omovo got up and packed a bag. He, too, would go away. Some time ago Keme had given him the name and address of a friend's family in B—, a seaside town outside Lagos, who might rent him a room. Omovo had often told of his need to find somewhere outside the city where he could paint.

While Omovo sorted out his clothes he came upon the ring Ifeyiwa had given him. He put it amongst the masses of his hair in the cellophane wrapping. (Much later he would keep the ring in a special place, as if it were a lucky charm. Then, later still, he began to wear it on his little finger. He kept the ring for the rest of his life.) The loaf of bread his relations had given him had turned mouldy. He threw it out along with Okoro's hat. He packed his clean shirts and trousers into a leather bag. Then he concentrated on the items he needed for his painting. He took a few books – none on the visual arts. When he had finished he zipped the bag shut. He tested its weight, and was satisfied. He went and sat alone in the sitting room. He needed to gather himself. Too many things.

The mood of the sitting room seemed the same as ever. The same underneath. He tried not to think about anything.

Memories of childhood invaded him. He remembered being locked up in a room with his brothers while his parents quarrelled. Chairs were being thrown about, glasses were broken. Cruel words were shouted and endlessly repeated. He remembered one night in particular. His parents had been quarrelling bitterly while a storm raged outside. That night Omovo lay wide awake listening to the fury of the storm and the destructive passions of his parents, feeling the immediacy of doom. His mother howled. A door was banged shut. Outside the wind twisted the zinc roofing. Omovo began to cry. Okur picked up a book and threw it across the room.

'It's okay, Omovo, it's okay,' he said.

'It will pass,' Umeh added, getting up and looking out of the window.

Omovo went on crying. Okur got up and slapped him. For a moment there was silence. The storm wailed and thunder growled. Omovo felt his neck muscles twitch as he tried to control his terror. Then Okur embraced Omovo. Umeh embraced them both.

'It's okay,' Umeh said.

Omovo suppressed the urge to break into a greater intensity of weeping. Too many things.

And then there were memories of his mother. He was at school when she died. He was playing football when he received a message that someone had come to visit him. It was one of his mother's sisters. She had come to take him home. She was cheerful during the whole journey. At the funeral she wept so long and violently that it took six men to tie her up till she quietened down. They said she didn't speak for nine days. That was the first time Omovo's head had been shaven.

How did his mother die? No one seemed to know. The doctors said it was a heart attack, too much stress. Their father chose to believe she had an incurable disease. His brothers swore she had been poisoned, that a curse had been put on her. It did not matter in the end. She died, that's all.

For a long time, thinking of her constituted a bitter, futile exploration of memory. How does one remember a mother who has died? By her face? Her eyes? As a half-forgotten, selective series of acts? Her voice? Or a spirit, a mood that never leaves? The intangibility of his memory of her made it more painful.

She was a hard-working woman, determined, proud, on her way to prosperity. She had a shop that sold provisions – biscuits, cigarettes, sweets, kerosene, water. She had begun to branch into selling clothes. She was active in her town's people's meetings, was respected by the women of her village association, was invited to the naming ceremonies, the funerals, the weddings of the market women. People feared her. She had strong eyes. She was lean, even bony, but had an odd irrepressible power. She had a sharp voice and always said what she thought. She was quick to enter quarrels and could shout down any adversary. But she was also a good mediator in other people's quarrels and was known to be very kind. Omovo's father, envious of her, scared of her, treated her badly. The more she succeeded the worse he treated her. Then there came talk of another woman. His father wanted a second wife. Sometimes the woman was seen in the street. Then one day his mother fell ill. The expression on her face changed. Her spirit lost its fire. Her moods became strange. She complained of headaches, of seeing spirits at the shop, of nightmares. Her business dwindled. Her customers went elsewhere. She grew lean, her appearance became careless, a baffled expression entered her eyes, and she began to go around barefoot. She started to look slightly mad.

A mood of hope entered the house when his father announced that she would soon have a baby. Omovo remembered the afternoon when they were driven to the hospital by one of his father's relations. As they sat in the lounge waiting for the good news of another baby Omovo and his brothers made bets about its sex. They were taken home in a strange atmosphere of gloom. They learnt that something had happened to the baby, that it had refused to live. When they got home from the hospital they found another woman in the house. She was spirited out through the backdoor. Her brown undergarment was found beneath the pillow.

Afterwards, as the quarrelling grew more feverish, Omovo's father took to physically throwing his mother out of the house. She slept in front of the house, with her children huddled to her, with her possessions scattered all around her.

Sometimes she went away for months. Her absence made the silences in the house unnatural. Once, when she came back, she gathered Omovo and his brothers together. She stared at them with wide frightened eyes, as if she wasn't going to see them again. She just stared and didn't say anything. Okur and Umeh began to cry. Omovo went out of the house. He wandered about the streets for a long time and he did not cry. It was a Sunday. Everything was quiet. He walked till he was tired and when he stopped he couldn't recognise where he was. Everything turned strange. He felt as if he had strayed into a dream.

He sat down at the roadside and fell asleep. It was dark when a strange woman woke him up. Her hair was white, her limbs were graceful, her face was beautiful and long. She took him by the hand and led him to his street. Before he got to his home she had vanished into the darkness.

When he got home his parents weren't in. They had gone out searching for him. His brothers asked him angrily where he had been. Okur was about to hit him. Umeh stopped Okur. Then they held one another, embraced one another, in fear.

Omovo pulled himself away from all the memories. He got up and went to his room. The day passed. Evening came. He slept a lot and read. Night darkened his windows. He kept staring at the blank canvas, feeling the urge to paint rising in him, but not overflowing. The urge didn't reach that pitch beyond which he had no choice. In between the waxing and waning desire to paint was the hunger to see his father, to

274

talk with him, re-establish an old harmony. He didn't see his father that night or the following morning. He didn't venture out of his room. He felt he had somehow imprisoned himself.

He had been asleep, he hadn't been dreaming, when he suddenly woke up. In the darkness, having woken up for no perceptible reason, he was confused about where he was. Had he strayed into a dream? Everything was stripped of meaning, of function. In that moment there was no relationship between him and the objects in the darkness. The bed seemed to be in the air. The chairs, the walls, the ceiling, the shapes of his paintings, the sprawl of his clothes, nothing had any connection with anything else. The capacity for linking things seemed to have dropped out of his consciousness. He felt he was floating on a black sea, he felt he was in a cave, in a dark space on another universe, in a different, unrecorded time. There were ghosts and shadows all around him, the humped figures of prehistoric rocks, of alien beings. He couldn't think, couldn't move. An invisible weight held him down. He tried to be calm. He tried to enter a state of prayer. The moment deepened. Something in him, a formless insurgent spirit, an energy the exact shape of his body, kept straining against the borders of his being as if it would burst out and devastate his senses, burst out into flame, into unbearable intensity. He breathed deeply. Then slowly. His mind freed itself. He prayed for everything. He prayed for all the faces he had ever seen. He began to recall the faces, to shore them against his terror. And the faces became crowds. He could not name them, could not give the faces names, nor name their features, so that each feature would make his seeing them more definite. Language failed him. There were things he wanted to say, songs that were breakers of spells, songs his mother had taught him, songs that were parts of stories told under moonlight in the village. He couldn't sing the songs in English. The space that the language filled created a new emptiness. He couldn't sing them in his language either. And so he could not keep back the crowds he had imagined into being. The crowds welled up in him, talking all at once, shouting, arguing, but no words came from their mouths. Their gestures were dramatic, they were passionate, they spoke three hundred and fifty-six languages simultaneously, and were not heard.

The yearning to hear them, to be heard, the desire to speak and to be understood in a language that flowed naturally, clamoured in his being.

A voice within him said: 'You need a new language to be heard.'

The crowd disappeared. Colours replaced them. The colours flowed in startling configurations. The configurations grew brilliant with strange energies. Then the crowd returned, became concrete, remembered faces. Crowds at Waterside. At the garages. At the marketplaces. The bus-stops. Crowds of the ghetto 'exodus'. Pouring down the roads. Masses of people silhouetted in the late evenings, streaming down the main roads. The roads jammed with cars. The cars surrounded by hawkers of boiled eggs. The crowds of the apocalypse. They had gathered somewhere. Then they froze in their gestures, in their shouting and arguing in the different languages.

Then they began to rampage. They tore down the houses on the exclusive lawns. They destroyed the whistling pine trees, the hedges. In the burst of their rage, their hunger, they vented their fury on all images of power, burned down petrol stations, government vehicles, they overturned lorries and oil tankers, and then they themselves caught fire, their bodies incandescent, their hair yellow, their clothes burning green and blue, the crowd turning into colours blinding and without language. And as the fires swelled, shadows writhing within them, something swelled in him and suddenly snapped and burst out through his skin and escaped into the air as if a spirit had been blown out of him, and for the first time he heard himself scream. The invisible weight lifted off him. A wind blew over his head. From somewhere in the darkness he heard the elliptical beats of talking drums, he heard strains of an accordion. Intimations of meaning flowed in him. The moment of unreality passed. He slept soundly afterwards.

Morning came. Geometric points of light played on the bed. He listened to the sounds of the compound. He smelt the rising odours and fragrancies of another day. He re-experienced the sensation of being trapped in his room. He stared at the objects on the walls, the shapes of broken calabashes with his engravings on them, his paintings and those of favourite artists, the Buddhist Chant 'The Salutation to Dawn' which he had written on a paper in his finest calligraphy, the coral shells dangling from the ceiling. He got up, washed, ate, and tidied his room. It was the morning of his departure.

When he had finished with these tasks he took his leather bag to the sitting room. His father was not around. Omovo suspected he had gone out on some obscure salvaging mission. Blackie had gone to the market. Omovo stood at the threshold of the main door. He looked at everything in the gloomy sitting room. For a deceptive moment he looked with the passivity of new eyes, as if he sensed better ways of using things about him, elements within him. But he felt the strange silence of the house and fear came upon him, the shadow of a large bird. The sensation was soon gone. But the shadow of the fear lingered, like a sudden wailing on a lonely night projecting itself into the recesses of the mind.

Before he left he wrote a letter:

> Dear Father,
> I have resigned from work. By the time you get this I will have gone to B—. I've no idea how long for. I need to be by myself and gather things together inside me, need to think. Besides I want to escape from the traffic jam of our lives. Don't worry about me. Hope your business improves and that your spirit is well. I'll see you when I get back. Enclosed is the little something you requested. Hope it helps. Good luck, Dad.
> Your loving son,
> Omovo.
> PS: I really would like you to see my new paintings.

He left the letter on the table and set off on his journey.

Late that evening, surrounded by the lingering perfume of his wife's absence, Omovo's father read the letter. He saw hidden emotions, hidden meanings. He read it twice.

He remembered the day he threw his two sons out of the house. He remembered with shame the words Umeh had said that had made him so uncontrollably angry.

'You always win arguments and lose battles, Dad. There's nothing solid in our lives. The years have left the family behind. I'm frightened for us.'

His sons had struck a raw nerve. Instantly, for daring to criticise him, they became inescapable symbols of his failure.

They haunted him now that they had gone. Lately he had begun to have nightmares in which Okur bore down on him, a knife sticking from his throat. Nightmares in which Umeh kept laughing from behind him. When he turned he would see his first wife, with silver eyes and a toothless mouth.

Since their departure, his sons had been writing him letters which seemed calculated to unhinge him with guilt. He read them all. They wrote about their sordid lives. They sent photographs in which they were virtual tramps, with their eyes of deranged rebellion.

They wrote about their illnesses. Their debts. About getting into fights, their imprisonments, about being set upon by gangs of white men who hated black people. About the ships on which they stowed away. They spoke of themselves as homeless orphans. They wrote of their fights among themselves, their splits, their reconciliations. They never accused him and were utterly without self-pity. They didn't seem to know why they wrote to him. Their letters had no addresses and tended to come from different cities, different countries. The last he heard from them was that Umeh had been stabbed in the chest during a gambling session. He didn't know if Umeh was alive or not. In that last letter Okur said he had decided he wasn't coming back home, that there was no home anywhere, except on the road.

The last letter also said they'd grown sick of writing to him and would do so no more. They hoped Omovo would take care of himself and carry on with the development of his talent. They wished their father the best.

He depended on those letters. He waited for them. They kept him hoping. He hoped that whatever it was that made them write to him would some day make them come home. He dreamed of a magnificent reconciliation, a mythical homecoming for his prodigal sons. Their last letter devastated him. For days he went around as if something had evaporated inside him. He acted strangely. He became forgetful. He began to have bad dreams. He functioned badly: business suffered. His concentration wavered, his eyes began to fix vaguely on the horizon, he stopped noticing things happening around him. And this drinking got worse. He drank in order to sleep. Drank in order to clear his head. Drank to celebrate. Drank to forget. Drank to survive the failure of his company.

To Omovo he behaved the exact opposite of how he felt. He became a little hostile to his paradoxically named son. He became colder when in fact he felt a greater tenderness for Omovo. But at no point did he concede, or contemplate conceding, that his sons were right. His life was not empty. As far as he was concerned things were too complicated for the young minds of his children to understand. Their time would come. He would see if they would survive the confusions in which life makes everyone flounder.

He had always had a special fondness for Omovo, the son who had opted to remain at home, the son in whom he had nurtured a love for art. Over recent years he understood Omovo's paintings less. They had grown more grim and uncomfortable. They, too, seemed to accuse him.

He often wondered why his son couldn't paint happier subjects. Now he had lost contact with the only son who was close to him, lost contact with most things, it seemed, apart from Blackie, centre of his life. How he needed her, relied so much on her.

But Omovo's letter had touched him. Much as he tried he couldn't deny that it was, in a curious way, a gesture of love.

He had often wanted to ask Omovo why he had shaved his head. What was he mourning? It troubled him that his own son looked so strange, bony, awkward, silent. He had often wanted to embrace Omovo suddenly, to tell him stories. He had sometimes sensed Omovo wanting to talk to him: he had seen the words struggling across his face. But, unable to bear his own sadness, he had always turned away before Omovo could speak. He couldn't control this reaction.

The day that he gave Omovo the letter from Okur he had strongly resisted the urge to break down and off-load his problems and fears, to ask his advice. On the day that he was reading the last letter from Okur and Umeh he was truly startled when Omovo had stumbled upon him. It was as if his sons had returned to renew old quarrels. When he read in the newspapers stories of riots and racial violence in Western lands he feared for his sons, he prayed for them. He feared for them but he was essentially afraid of them. He was afraid of their power to hurt him.

He stared at Omovo's letter. Then he stared at the bottle of ogogoro on the table. Then, suddenly, as if he had been hit on the head from behind, he felt himself plunge into darkness. A moment later he realised that the lights had been cut. The mosquitoes found him in the blackout. The heat rose in his skin. He became aware of Blackie's perfume faintly scenting the air. She had gone to the market and yet her perfume lingered. He wondered what had happened to her. He felt lonely enough as it was. But her perfume made him feel lonelier.

SEVEN

Ifeyiwa travelled with her illness; she travelled in a state of extended hallucination. Her journey seemed a kind of dream. She still felt feverish when the lorry dropped her at the village junction. The lorry driver would go no further. The women in the lorry advised her not to go to the village at that time of the night. They suggested that she should find a place in town to sleep till dawn. One of the women even offered to put her up.

But Ifeyiwa had travelled three hundred and twenty miles, and her legs were stiff. Her back ached. She hadn't once thought of her husband. She had thought only of her liberation. She remembered that she had always been able to walk free in the environs of her village. As far as she could see nothing had changed. While she got her bag off the back of the lorry she noticed a file of women with firewood on their heads, lamps in their hands, staggering along the dark road. She had come this far and could now breathe the air of her oldest dreams.

When she made her decision to walk home to her village from the junction, she experienced a moment of lucidity and resurgence. She wanted to surprise her family, she wanted an unexpected homecoming. The women's advice only had the effect of convincing her that her decision was the best one. She could no longer fully trust other people's statements about how she should live her life. They had deceived her too often. They had led her here. Overcome with the freedom that lay just ahead of her in the darkness, along the beaten track that wound past the village shrine to her home, she felt certain she would now make her own decisions, go her own way, wherever it led.

And her mother lay ill just a walking distance away.

As Ifeyiwa stepped back from the lorry the women warned her again. 'Don't go-o!' they said. 'There is trouble in the air.'

Ifeyiwa felt the tug of their concern. The moon was bold in the night sky. The wind made the leaves rustle. She smelt woodsmoke on the night air. She experienced the mysterious lucidity of convalescence, the great pressure of its hopes. In that moment she had a belief, a faith, in the goodness of the world. She had faith in her freedom. It will not be in vain. The women said a traditional prayer for her and wished her luck. She wished them a safe journey. The lorry started and drove off slowly, its tail lights like two red eyes vanishing in the distance.

Alone on the beaten track, in the darkness, with the moon above, she experienced an ecstatic sense of liberation. She jumped. She ran. She sang. She was young. She was almost home.

The smells of firewood burning at night, of fish drying on racks, came strongly to her. She was overwhelmed with the herbal aroma of the farms. The earth breathed out its deep essences. The wind rose and blew frenziedly. Branches cracked as if unnatural forces had wrenched at them. Suddenly questions began to nag her. What had she been freed into? The lorry had gone. Had she made a mistake? She stopped. Her mind was calm. She heard her mother's voice in the wind. She remembered the feelings of being a child and singing or playing under the supervision of moonlight. She remembered the nights of storytelling. The nights of rituals, when goats were slaughtered and the blood from their necks fertilised the darkness of the earth. She remembered the festivals that went on for seven days, culminating in the night of the unpredictable masquerades – the masquerades from which the women and children had to be protected.

She remembered her father's farm with the large obeche tree right in its centre. Strange birds sang intermittently in the dark. The sky turned violet. Bursting with clarity, she hastened home. Those birds, yes, those birds. She listened to them. Birds of the moon. Birds of omen. She had heard them in her dreams. As she went past the village shrine, housed in a hut without a door, she had another vision of how she could live, of the person she could be. Shortly afterwards she heard a man's gruff voice say:

'Stop! Who goes there?'

Wrenched from her thoughts, the night hazing, the bushes suddenly coming alive, she found she couldn't get her words out. Her throat went dry. Thinking it all a horrible dream she turned and saw her dead father staring at her, his face bold as the moon, his eyes empty. She heard rapid voices.

'It's a spirit.'
'An animal.'
'An enemy.'
Then a shot was fired.

Two days later her body was found on the shores of the brackish stream near the neighbouring village. No one was sure who was responsible. But her people took it as a sign of unforgivable aggression and the fighting between the villages reached new heights of bloodshed. Three days afterwards a young man returning from the farms was shot. Ifeyiwa's mother sued for peace. Meetings were held. A ceasefire was heeded. For a while peace reigned along the village boundaries.

Both villages had other problems anyway. The government was going to build a major road right through them. That meant unacceptable resettlements. The yields from crops had been poor for many months. They had no electricity and no water supplies. The youths were leaving for the cities and the villages had become rather ghostly, inhabited only by the very old and the very young.

Time passed. Ifeyinwa's death acquired other dimensions. Some said she had killed her husband and was on the run. Others said she was sick of life and had offered herself as a sacrifice. For a while, amongst those who didn't know the true story, it seemed as if her death would give birth to a legend.

At one of the meetings intended to effect a permanent reconciliation between the villages, an elder said: 'We are killing ourselves over a problem which the white man caused in the first place. Let this innocent girl's death be the final sacrifice. Let us solve this problem in our own way.'

The peace lasted till other things came along and fuelled the old hatred which had never been examined, never exorcised. At another futile meeting just before the outbreak of fresh violence the priest of the village shrine said the spirits of the land had been angered. No one listened.

'What was her sacrifice for?' he asked. No one answered.

BOOK FIVE

ONE

When Omovo set out on his journey he had no clear idea what he was escaping from or what he expected to find. He arrived in the town of B— disorientated. The address that Keme had given him seemed clear enough, but finding the place exhausted him. He had to walk halfway round the ancient town, he was frequently misdirected, and the heat was excruciating. The town confused him. He didn't understand its transport system. And the name he had been given was spelt wrongly. It turned out that he was to stay with one of the most important chiefs. And to make matters worse, the address was of a place quite close to the garage.

The chief wasn't in when he arrived. He had to wait for hours sitting on a bench in the corridor, hungry and confused, before one of the women of the house took it upon herself to show him the room. She was the chief's youngest wife, and didn't speak English. She too was new to the town and didn't seem to know where she was going. She led him through the market, down all sorts of dirt tracks, took him through large compounds full of children and old women, stopped to talk many times, and effectively took him round the town again to three different houses before they got to the place. It was a small house that was really just a room. At first Omovo thought it was an abandoned shrine house. In the backyard there were masks and jujus on sticks. Not far from the house was a graveyard. Beyond that could be heard the lispings of the wind on sea.

Omovo was totally exhausted when he arrived. He was virtually sleepwalking. He felt as if his identity had in some way been scrambled up. The chief's youngest wife showed him the room. He didn't understand a word of what she said. He hadn't understood anything of what he had been through that day. It was as if he had been in a dream

285

and someone had tied up his legs. He was relieved when the woman left.

The room was small. It had a small bed with creaking springs. It also had a red–topped centre table and an old cane chair. The air in the room was musty. It smelt ancient. It also smelt of death and rituals. He threw open the windows. Fresh air and oblique light came in. Cobwebs clung in high corners of the ceiling.

Omovo was so exhausted that as he stared out of the window he suddenly found himself wandering down a corridor. After a while he realised he was lost. As he wandered aimlessly he passed an ordinary blue door. Through its opening he heard the most intensely beautiful music. He had seen lights swirling within, lights of violet and silver. It was only after he had gone past the door that he realised how blissful the music and the vision beyond had made him feel. He had glimpsed something quite magical and the door had turned golden in his memory. But he carried on wandering. He couldn't stop. He didn't know how. He felt restless and incomplete. He felt he had cheated himself of something. The years passed. He wandered through strange towns down whose streets slaves were dragged screaming, towns with old seaports, towns where the fishermen cast out their nets and threw the fishes back into the sea. He passed cities of ancient rocks, where sacrificial victims sang before they accompanied kings to their deep ancestral graves. He travelled through places where the populace dug the earth for gold and where the elite ate the gold, trampled on it, burned it, made clothes out of it, sold it to strangers across the seas for mirrors and bitter coffee, places where the young went around hungry and confused, where women bore thirty children and chased headless chickens. And with the passing years he hungered more for the sensation of passing that blue door, he yearned for the room. He went back to seek for it and met an old woman who was dumb. She made a sign to him and he followed her. But then things changed and he lost sight of the woman and got distracted by a market place so vast that the deeper he went into it the bigger it became. The road closed up behind him. He got distracted by strange animals, ostriches with the eyes of owls, sheep with the heads of hyenas, and green cats with eyes of blazing silver. He saw beggars with dramatic deformities. Some were like contortionists permanently set in their moulds. He saw legless magicians, armless musicians in dark glasses who played their instruments with their teeth.

Through all this he was occasionally and unbearably haunted by the blue door and its undiscovered interiors, by the bliss he had experienced. And when as an older man he managed to free himself from the familiar distractions, he sought the room afresh. He wandered many years. He wandered through earthly music of sensual delights, through bars where the drinks were free and addictive, through images of the past. In one city he saw Ifeyiwa fleeing down the streets. He pursued her, but she outran him, and when at a closed-off road he finally caught up with her – she turned into a shadow and melted through the walls. Lost in the city, he spent his time listening to the colourful tales of old men and pirates, who told him of circuses that floated on seas, of bazaars in the air, of towns that reincarnate in different places through time. The old men died, the pirates answered the call of salt-sprays. He followed the pirates and noticed that they got on ships which never set out across the seas.

Time accelerated. His yearning turned to bitterness. The years became deserts. Maggots ate at him. Flies clung to his honeyed brows. Crows followed him patiently. And then on the day he discovered that he had become an old man he found the corridor. As he went along, it multiplied. The floor shone like a blue mirror. His eyes had grown tired. His feet erupted with blisters and boils. Confused, infirm, increasingly blind, it occurred to him that he was now a spirit, that he was joining the dead. He had begun to be overcome by a nauseating panic when, in the distance, he saw the door. A strange dawn shone through its golden crack. The flies had left his honeyed brows. The crows had gone. He felt both too heavy and too light. The door started coming towards him. He heard the music of unbearable bliss. The illumination from the door's opening got intolerably phosphorescent the closer it came. He woke up before the door opened its terrible splendours to him. He woke up scared. The sun burned on his face. Outside the birds twittered. He lay on the bed disturbed. All through that day and for many years afterwards the disturbance remained. He had been asleep for eighteen hours.

The chief called by the room that afternoon. He looked two hundred years old. He had the face of ancient masks, wrinkled, ravaged with age, stamped with power. He had beads round his neck, he wore a faded duck-tail shirt over a baggy pair of trousers, and had on rubber shoes. He bore a large fan of eagle feathers in one hand and a walking stick in the other. He came with two of his servants. The chief didn't sit down and didn't stay long. Omovo knew he was dying. Omovo listened intently to his heavily accented Yoruba. And as he listened he felt things stirring within him.

★

In the evening one of the chief's sons came to show Omovo the bathroom and where he could get the things he might need. He informed Omovo that feeding was included in the rent. The chief's son attended the local secondary school. He had sensual lips, fine marks on his forehead, and his eyes were full of mirth and brightness. He wore khaki shorts and a blue check shirt. He said:

'My name is Ayo. My father told me you would be staying here for some time. I will be bringing your food. Your are a painter? They teach us art at school, but we have a bad teacher. I am in Class Four now. I like physics and maths. Have you finished secondary school?'

Omovo liked him immediately.

Night fell. Alone in the room, Omovo listened to the sounds of the town. The sounds were of a kind he had almost forgotten. He listened to them with a hungry rapture and felt the secret awakening of countless sensations. He listened to the wind and sea, to human voices that seemed to have minimal undertones of tension, to the children playing hide and seek, to the elders playing ayo and telling stories, to mothers settling quarrels. He listened to girls whispering with secret lovers. They made the darkness alive with their tiny peals of mischief. He listened to the dogs, the goats, and the birds. He watched the moon, bold in the sky, with clouds sailing across its face. The sounds drew him back to a period of magic twilights. He was happy that night, but he didn't sleep well.

Ayo took him to his favourite parts of the beach. Omovo watched the lights on the sea, watched the shimmering water, the lights turning delicately into intimations of rainbow through the spray. He was overwhelmed with the freshness of the air, overcome with clarity. The sea glittered in the dying lights of the evening. He watched the floating clumps of seaweed and listened to the distant songs of fishermen returning from their day's work. The sky turned grey, the sea turned brown. The lights of the town converged above it like a collective halo of red and grey. Sensing that Omovo wanted to be alone, Ayo slipped away and left him enraptured in his contemplation.

The days came, were heightened, went, and were lost. Omovo, drenched in sunlight, roamed the beaches. He roamed the bush-paths. He paced up and down his room. He was restless. He felt vaguely aware that different things in him were coming together in images of clarity and terror. He felt strange energies ready to burst in him. But the coming

288

together of things within eluded him. He watched, listened, waited. The days crept away, leaving his life-wish unrealised.

On the third day there was a black-out. In the darkness, fighting off the mosquitoes, he suddenly remembered a moment from his childhood. During the civil war, federal soldiers had been stamping through the town hunting out the Igbo people. They went to shops and kiosks owned by Igbos, broke their way in, dragged them out, and took them away. Sometimes particular townspeople, who had grudges against particular Igbos, gave away their hiding places. Often the townspeople took it upon themselves to do the job of the federal soldiers for them. It was a sick time. That day the soldiers had stormed into the beer parlour next door. Everyone in the street knew an Igbo undergraduate had been hiding there under the protection of a prostitute. When the soldiers went in the undergraduate ran out. The women screamed. The young man ran into the street shouting: 'Chineke! Chineke!'

One of the soldiers shot him in the back and the undergraduate buckled, staggered, his arms flailing. The soldier shot him again and the young man cried:

'Hey God!'

Then he fell on his back and stayed there twitching and died with his eyes wide open, his fingers clamped between his teeth.

The soldier who had shot him went over, stared down at him, spat, his gun ready. Then for some reason, maybe to make sure the young man was dead, the soldier tried to pull the dead man's fingers from between his teeth. He pulled the arm. Kept pulling it. But he couldn't get the desired result. Instead of the fingers being freed, the dead man's upper body kept rising and flopping as if he were in the grip of obscene spasms. His death grin, his burst chest, his shirt swollen with gore, and his wide-open eyes, made him look horrifyingly inhuman. The soldier, having failed in his intention, frustrated, annoyed, dragged the body to the roadside and kicked it into the gutter. The rest of the soldiers joined him. They lit a cigarette, shared it, and discussed their next destination in rough voices. When they'd finished the cigarette they pushed on down the street, waving their guns in the air like conquering heroes, and carried on with their task of Igbo hunting.

The street was silent. The townspeople had watched the event from the protection of their windows. No one moved. Then not long after the soldiers had gone a wailing noise, more piercing than the sirens, came from the beer parlour. The prostitute rushed out, cursing and screaming, her hair in disarray, her clothes torn. She wept and threw herself down on the street inconsolably. Then she stopped and lay there. She lay still as if dead. Then she got up and with a strange calm, tears running down her face, emptied her purse onto the body of her dead lover. She emptied all her coins, all her pound notes, on the body. Then she disappeared down the street, staggering, pulling at her hair.

That night the people of the street saw her return. She dragged her lover's body from the gutter, dragged it down the street, and rumour had it that, without stopping, she carried the body three miles to the graveyard and buried it. She was never seen again.

By morning word had gone round and gangs of boys from all over town came to scavenge in the gutter for the prostitute's money.

Omovo saw it all from the sitting room window. He hadn't slept all night. Fear had kept him awake. He saw the boys his own age struggling amongst themselves, kicking around in the gutter, trying to retrieve the coins and pound notes. He saw it all, but he didn't understand what he had seen.

He understood now. Sitting in the darkness of a strange town, fighting off the mosquitoes, the memory brought a bitter understanding. His mind was calm as he thought: *'That is my generation. Scavenging for blood money. Corruption money. Scavenging for the money of the dead. The money of corruption. Curse money. Scavenging our futures, our history. A generation of guilt, and blindness, and infernal responsibility.'*

Hours later the lights returned. He heard the children of the town cheering the return of the lights. He heard activity, music, noises of hope. But for Omovo the lights merely provided an escape from memories of cruelty.

Later that morning Ayo brought his food. After he had eaten they both went to a sea inlet. Omovo sat on the ground staring at the sky. Ayo tried to catch fishes with his bare hands. The wind blew criss-cross ridges on the water's surface. Ayo gave up on catching fish and suggested a swim. Omovo didn't want to. Ayo pointed to something in the water. Omovo got up and looked. He saw a coral shell of lovely colours entangled in seaweed. As Omovo marvelled at this vision he slipped and fell into the water. Ayo laughed and jumped in after him. They splashed around. Ayo dived down and when he came up he was holding the coral shell. It was such a beautiful sight. The coral shell, marvellously streaked, had been strangely eaten away at the centre, like an imperfect heart. When

Omovo took it in his hands, turned it round, studied it, holding his breath, something went through him. He shivered, twisting, and cried:

'I've got it! I understand!'

Ayo said: 'What?'

Omovo was silent. The illumination dwindled on his face. He sank to the ground. With his face on his palms, he said in a disappointed voice: 'It was nothing. It's gone.'

Soon afterwards, both dripping sea-water, they headed home.

On the way back they were silent. Omovo kept looking at the lovely shell as if it were the undeciphered emblem of a mystic understanding. In a voice both calm and desperate, Omovo said: 'Ayo, your name means "life", right?'

'Yes. But it's short for Ayodele, which means "life has come into the house".'

'I know.' Omovo continued: 'Well, I want to tell you a story.'

Then Omovo told of the strange dream he had about the door and the room. When he had finished Ayo said:

'And what happened? Did you get to the room?'

'No, the room was coming to me.'

'Did it?'

'I'm not sure.'

'But did it?'

'No. I don't think so.'

Ayo was silent. His youthful face took on a disturbing aspect of wisdom. He said, eventually: 'I'm happy it didn't.'

'Why?'

'My father has been having dreams like that. Different, but similar.'

'So?'

'If it came to you, it means you will die soon,' Ayo said.

Omovo said nothing. After a moment, Ayo asked: 'When did this story happen to you?'

'It happened on the first day I arrived in this town.'

Ayo said: 'It's sad.'

They parted company. As Omovo went to his room he experienced a curious sweetness as he pondered the dream. It wasn't long before the indefinable sadness of a premonition swept over him.

That night he bathed for a second time and went to bed. He kept tossing and scratching himself in places where the bedbugs bit him. He shut his

291

eyes tight, as if the darkness were a blight he did not want to face. He heard the noises of the town. The sounds were not as enchanting as when he first heard them. The mustiness, and the smell of death, in the room, scared him. The constant power cuts filled him with impotent rage. The bedsprings creaked with his every movement. Areas of colours danced before his eyes. The colours became menacing forms. When he opened his eyes he thought he saw ghosts in the room. He thought he heard the rattling of chains, the wailing of gagged slave voices. He turned over and covered his face. The menacing shapes returned and oppressed him. He tried to will them away. But doing this only kept him awake. He felt his muscles palpitate. His shoulders were tense. He felt himself arching his back, felt throbbings in his neck. The moving colours became voids that opened inwards into deep, unfathomed interiors. Things were coming together within him even as he slept.

He woke up suddenly. He heard a sound. A movement. The syllable of a repressed scream. The wind outside rattled the corrugated zinc roof. He heard an explosion somewhere in the darkness. He sat up. Afraid. He waited. He watched. He wondered. And his wonder infested his silence with motion. In the semi-darkness he could see the coral shell. It was on the table. It seemed to float on waves of darkness. As he stared at it something happened inside him. He got up, put on his shirt and trousers, took the shell and left the room.

At first the town seemed quiet. It seemed quiet in its ancient ravagement. The wind was fresh on his face. The dawn was crisp. Skeins of mist hung in the air. The wind roused the leaves and made the branches of the palm trees weave. He passed the silent houses. He crossed fields. He listened to the cock-crows, the bleating goats, the limpid cries of birds. He wondered if it were possible to create music using only the different sounds of animals. Crossing fields and farmlands he smelt the grass and noticed the different shades of their greenness. He wandered the bush-paths. He was barefoot and the feel of the earth, the wetness of dew, the assenting sound of every footstep, were sensations etched out in moments of shimmering clarity. As he wandered in the limpidity of slowed-down time he began to see the town as it might have been – a place ravaged by history, a place for the transit of slaves, a place of old feuds, dead kingdoms, of strife and internecine wars.

The sky lit up. The sea, changing colour, took on a subdued lucency. Then the air became full of birds, eagles, dawn-birds, birds of strange songs. Something wonderful happened everywhere around him. The fishermen sang in the distance as they launched out to sea in their dug-out canoes. Then an illumination settled in him. He breathed deeply the dewy air and shut his eyes and saw a face bleeding a curiously quivering – blinding – light. As he breathed in, energy was drawn inwards and he felt oddly faint, felt himself falling into a vortex of primordial, volatile being. Then as he let out his breath he felt as if he had hit upon a discovery, a secret that had been apparent all along.

He shouted triumphantly: 'THE MOMENT!'

And he gave himself over to the wonder that had awoken in him.

His illumination became a tumble of words spinning in him, erupting in thoughts and speech, in being and words, in visions and emotions deeper than the urge that made him paint. Bursting in this state he saw time enfission into every moment, into endless possibilities of life. Time was the sea – a million lights revolved on every crest – past met present, present met future. Quivering with excessive love, he had the vision of a terrifying and unfinishable portrait of humanity –

He felt the purity of helplessness, the subversion of hope – he saw caves of unmeasured corruption, felt the burden of desperate prayers uttered, unheard – the prayers of slaves – the betrayal of ancestors – the treachery of leaders – the lies and the corruption of the old generation – their destruction of future dreams – they raped our past, we rape our future – we never learn our lessons – history screams and ghettoes erupt with death and maddened youths – they scrambled for our continent and now we scramble for the oil-burst of Independence – traitors and disunity everywhere – those who are deaf to history are condemned to be enslaved by it – enslaved by ourselves, our attitudes, our tribal madness, each for himself – the smiles of the rich grow more predatory while children weep their lives away burning in infernos of hunger and disease – our history hasn't hurt us enough or the betrayals would stop, the streets would erupt, till we are overcome with the inescapable necessity of total self-transformation – we burn for vision – clear, positive vision – for vision allied with action – for want of vision my people perish – for want of action they perish – in dreams – in dreams begin responsibility – for we have become a people of dream-eaters, worshipping at the shrines of corruption – we can't escape our history – we will dwindle, become smaller, the continent will shrink, be taken over, swallowed, pulped, drained, by predators, unless we transform – in vision begins – in vision begins responsibility – and even as we die, and shrink, and are taken over, reduced, seen as animals, as invisible, even as the streets spill over with the poor, even as we dance our lives away, and celebrate the powerful, worship like servants at their vulturous shrines, we can utter psychic decisions and set forces into motion that could change our lives forever – in vision begins action – in action begins our destiny – for the things that you do change you

– and the changes affect the things you do – to him that hath shall be given – seek and ye shall find – to him that hath not shall be taken from, even that which they haveth – you either become, or you die –

Omovo's moment of illumination tumbled on within him.

I came here to escape and I find our past waiting for me on these shores – now we are the trampling ground of foreign powers – we don't affect the world – we bear suffering too much – our resilience is our weakness – for want of sugar the whites colonised half the world – we have suffered slavery, the loss of our art, we suffer droughts, we inflict wounds on ourselves, and yet we do not conquer our weaknesses – our blood fuelled their industrial mills – all for the bitter taste in their mouths, the taste of bitter coffee – the bitterness in us should long have festered and turned to acid and turned round into the sweetness of transformation – transform, or die – in dreams begins responsibility –

– the moment breaking down into prayers unheard – cries unheeded – warnings unaccepted – visions unseen – the moment dissolving into steps upon broken bridges, directions untaken, signs unread, prophets silenced – artists destroyed – the moment is self losing its centre, finding new ones – rashes of insanity – wandering in wilderness of lost possibilities – and I am here on these shores, in this strange town, weighed down by soul-clogs of useless knowledge, other people's opinions, the creative dangers of thinking in an imposed language – betrayed by language – erased from history – deceived – as children, we read how the whites discovered us – didn't we exist till they discovered us? – weighed down by manipulated history, rigged history books, rigged maps of the continent – weighed down by lies – and then believing those lies – swallowing them – force-feeding ourselves with them – gorging ourselves – my generation is one of losses – inheriting madness, empty coffers, colossal debts, the vanities of the old generation, their blindness and greed – inheriting chaos – confusion – garbage – fumes everywhere – violence – coups upon coups – but chaos is the beginning of creation – God created chaos before he created order – a greater order – chaos is rich in possibilities – in vision begins responsibilities –

And as Omovo's being swirled a word kept repeating itself to him:

transfiguration – transfigure the deception multiplied by education – all education is bad until you educate yourself – from scratch – start from the beginning, from the simplest things – assume nothing – question everything – begin again the journey from the legends of creation – look again at everything – keep looking – be vigilant – understand things slowly – digest thoroughly – act swiftly – re-dream the world

— restructure self — all the building blocks are there in the chaos — USE
EVERYTHING — USE EVERYTHING WISELY — EVERYTHING HAS SIGNIFI-
CANCE —

And as lights in the sky, from the sun, grew more intense, the points of
illumination within him grew dimmer. As he tumbled deeper into the
wells of knowledge and understanding he didn't know he had access to,
his moment of vision became more incomplete. But his contemplation
rose beyond words. Rose into higher dimensions within, opened doors,
and broke down walls, and expanded the spaces within him, into new
states of being. Points of light forever vanish. Visions are always
incomplete. Between the chaos and the clarity, the ever-moving
motionless being, between the interstices and the clamours of the
moment, a secret self was forming, a new man emerging. He had been
given an unnamed sufflation and like most of us he didn't know how to
experience it fully.

The wonder was soon gone. His head felt empty, as if all his energies had
been expended in a hurricane he himself had generated. The moment
had passed. The wind blew hard and he felt lighter than ever, as if he had
lost weight with the moment. Veins throbbed on his forehead. He felt
devastated, wrecked, he had a terrible headache. He felt cold and
vulnerable, afraid of what had happened inside him. The dawn had
turned. He felt weak and the afternoon sun seemed to weaken him
further. He sank to the ground and lay there, staring at the sky.
    People going to the farms, on their ways to work, marketwomen,
petty traders, praise-singers, carpenters and blacksmiths, people of all
trades, passed him as he lay there on the ground. He saw the looks in
their eyes. He heard them say things about him. He heard them mutter
about him being a stranger, strange and mad. They hurried past. After
some time he got up. He felt sad that he had thought and soliloquised
away the beauty that had come into him with the dawn.
    He wandered down to the beach. He came upon a little girl who was
singing to the egrets, playing on the shore, building shapes out of sand
and stones. She seemed happy and unaware of it. Omovo knew
intuitively that she was Ayo's younger sister. When she saw him coming
she smiled at him and then ran away, her laughter on the wind. He
turned and went to his room, walking against the wind, the salt of sea
bringing tears to his eyes.

★

In the afternoon Ayo brought his food and said: 'My father is ill. He has been ill for about six years. He still goes to the farm. Now he's in bed and cannot move his legs. He looks very strange.'

Omovo consoled him, saying: 'He is a good chief and a strong man.'

Later Ayo remarked: 'You look lonely sometimes.'

'It's a lonely business.'

Ayo was silent. Omovo said: 'We're all alone. We all carry aloneness inside us whatever we do.'

'Do we?'

'I think so. Sometimes we're aware of it and sometimes we're not.'

Another silence.

'What happened to you?'

'What do you mean?'

'What happened to your head?'

'My hair, you mean.'

'Yes.'

'Nothing.'

'Why did you shave it?'

'I didn't. A barber did.'

'It's growing a bit.'

'Is it?'

'Yes.'

'I don't notice. But that's good.'

'Do you know the story of Samson and his hair?'

'Yes. It's a good story.'

'Do you think when your hair grows you will be strong?'

'Am I not strong now?'

'But you look lonely.'

'I'm not really.'

'You're sad?'

'Sometimes.' Then: 'I may get stronger. If I'm lucky.'

'I hope you're lucky.'

'Thank you. I hope I use it well.'

'I think you will.'

'You're a nice boy. I hope your father gets well.'

'I hope so too.'

'How long will you stay?'

'Not long.'

'I will miss you.'

'You'll be okay.'

'When you've finished eating I want to show you something.'

Omovo looked at Ayo. Then he nodded.

When he had eaten they both set out. Ayo led the way down the dust tracks. He took Omovo to a ruin of a house. Omovo had passed it before and had often seen the old chief standing in front of it looking sad. It was an old single-storey building, unpainted, uncared-for, unlived in: a sad house, decrepit with shame, unremarkable, in a state of collapse, sinking into the soft soil.

'That's where the chains of slaves are kept. I've got the keys. Do you want to see them?'

Omovo looked at the house again, noticed how it seemed to be leaning over, noticed the unpainted door, the slightly rusted padlock. Then he looked at Ayo's young face, eager, unknowing. Madness turned in his brain. He shook his head, turned, and wandered off by himself, and left Ayo standing there, staring at the keys in his hands, wondering what he'd said that was wrong.

Omovo was returning from the house of shame when a madman jumped on him from the bushes. Omovo screamed. The shock had almost made him faint. The madman laughed and went a short way up the path, blocking Omovo's passage. Omovo regained his serenity. The madman was naked from the waist down. He had cuts all over his legs and feet. His organ was thick-veined, his pubic hair dusty and matted with wild flowers and grass. He wore the blackened remnants of a shirt. His eyes were passive and unfocussed. His beard was rough and covered with bits of chewed-up food. His hair was covered with detritus. Suddenly he began to shriek, to repeat strange words, as if he were warding off demons. He threw himself to the ground, lay still, then rose with the demonic rectitude of a sleepwalker. Then he started scratching himself, dancing curiously. He scratched at his ears, till they bled. He scratched as if he were trying to pull out some minuscule antagonist. Then he began to scream, as if he couldn't hear himself. Words poured from him. The birds around flew from the trees.

When the madman had jumped on Omovo his first impulse was to flee into the bushes, screaming. After he had shaken off the madman and noticed how unviolent he was, Omovo calmed that impulse. The man's madness seemed to him to take the form of words, incoherent words.

297

His mouth frothed while he kept uttering an unending stream of words. The madman regarded him with blank eyes, eyes without intent, without the slightest recognition of a fellow human form. As Omovo neared the man, to go past him, home, he was surprised that he felt protected by a vague and tangential affinity. The madman looked at him with fractured eyes that seemed to suck in Omovo's spirit. Drawing tightly about him his cloak of electric awareness, Omovo passed the madman. Calmly.

That night the chief died. Omovo knew. He had been woken up by the talking drums, whooping noises, bells, and cultic dances. Then later there came the unmistakable wailing from the town. The wailing sounded all around him, as if it had communicated to all the precise nature of the grief from which it had sprung.

At dawn Ayo knocked on his door. He brought food. Omovo asked him to come in, but he wouldn't. He sat on the threshold. He looked different. His hair had been shaved off. Sobriety weighed on his face. He had the disorientated expression of one who has been woken from a deep and beautiful sleep. He didn't seem to know what had woken him up.

'Ayo!' Omovo said.

The boy was silent.

'Ayo, come in.'

Dazed, the boy got up and began to stagger away. Omovo called him again. But the boy, activated – it seemed – by his name, started to run. His arms flailed in the air.

Omovo did not see Ayo for the rest of the day. The death of the chief hung over the town like an ominous cloud. He had heard the women in the market warning their children not to play out at night, that the old chief was dead. He had heard them say that for the next seven nights fearful figures would take to the streets looking for children and strangers.

Omovo thought about the chief. He had often seen him, fly-whisk in hand, wandering through the compounds, meandering through the clamour of his many wives. He had often seen the chief arguing with the elders of the town, or sitting on a cane chair, chewing on a kola-nut, drinking ogogoro, with one of his children fanning him, while his eyes remained fixed on the horizon, where the sea-spray touched the sky.

And one day he had seen the chief standing in front of the house of shame like an unwilling pilgrim, a hostage of history. He stood, head bowed by an invisible, indescribable weight. Perhaps his ancestors had helped sell slaves. The vision of the chief standing in front of the decrepit house never left Omovo. The chief had been a walking way of life. He was also a walking inheritor of death and chains and bad history.

That same day Omovo packed his things. He paid the rent to the chief's youngest wife who had shown him the room the first day he arrived. He left a note, his address and some money for Ayo. As he made his way to the garage he saw the town differently. He saw it as a small town, reddened with dust, a town of huts, zinc abodes, isolated single-storey buildings. An ancient town in ruins. A town haunted by the slave cries from its shore, marginalised, as if its history had ravaged its spirit.

Thinking about the inescapable vengeance of time, Omovo caught a bus. Those moments would pass forever. The journey home was uneventful. He slept throughout.

TWO

When he arrived at his compound people greeted him mournfully. There was a dismal mood in the air. Everyone stared at him as if he were a stranger, a ghost. The front door was locked. The curtains were half-drawn. He looked in through the window on which films of dust had accumulated. Apart from a lizard scuttling over an uneaten meal on the dining table, nothing stirred inside the room.

With the furtive movements of a purveyor of bad news, the assistant deputy bachelor came to him and said: 'Omovo, where have you been?'

'Away.'

'Haven't you heard?'

'Heard what?'

'Have you eaten?'

'Yes.' He hadn't.

'Don't you have the key?'

'I have the key.'

'Then open the door. Let's go inside. There's no point talking in public.'

'What's all this about?'

'Open the door. Something terrible has happened.'

The chief assistant deputy bachelor didn't tell the whole story. What had happened was that because Omovo's father – 'captain of the compound' – and two other men weren't around, the regular cleaning on Saturday had been postponed. To compensate for this and to placate the women, Tuwo had proposed an evening of drinking and celebration. The event became an impromptu party. All the members of the compound had contributed food, brought chairs and stools, soft drinks. Guinness, and ogogoro, and all had crowded into Tuwo's place. He had the most impressive rooms in the compound. He had an old stereo in a glass cabinet. He had various trophies for dubious sporting victories from his school days. He had exotic calendars and enlarged photographs of himself in a place that, snow-covered, was evidently England. Certificates of merit, top hats, chinoiserie decorated the walls.

Tuwo dressed in his finest French suit. The trousers, tight around the thighs, emphasised his virility. As the compound people poured to his room he came into his element, welcoming everyone with his most flowery phrases delivered in falsetto accents. Tuwo laid on drinks. Omovo's father visited briefly, and was given a drunken and tumultuous welcome. He drank a little, spreading silences around him with the gravity of his presence, and then, as befitting great men on small occasions, left for some other unspecified engagement. When he was gone, leaving Blackie behind with instructions about what he'd like to eat when he returned, which might be late, the party resumed its earthy rowdiness. The drinks flowed. The men brought their favourite records. The women hurriedly made themselves up and dressed in fine clothes. Tuwo told amusing stories of his adventures in England, his amorous escapades with white women. Very much the centre of attention, he held court charmingly, sent for more drinks, played records, and performed imitations of white people and their mannerisms. He had the compound people in fits. The women teased him about taking a wife and not being a danger to all the women of the ghetto. The men mocked him. Everyone got drunk. Even the assistant deputy bachelor, much against his reputation, brought a woman and started noisy rumours of an impending marriage, rumours which delighted everyone except the woman herself, a shy village girl, new to the city, who disapproved of such behaviour.

The party grew rowdier. Glasses were broken. Salty jokes stung the air. Dancing started. The men danced with their wives, danced with one another, shaking the floor with their heavy stamping, steaming the place with their heat and sweat. The men danced with one another's wives. More drinks were bought. One of the men began an argument about who were the best dancers in the compound. The assistant deputy bachelor, much to everyone's surprise, declared that he was a finer dancer than anyone he had seen that night. The other men all spoke well for themselves. The women suggested a competition in which they would be the judges.

301

The men danced. The assistant deputy bachelor utterly delighted everyone with his transformation from a serious money-hoarding shopkeeper to a sprightly, vigorous dancer. He leapt about the place, quite drunk, inflamed by the presence of a woman in his life. He danced with traditional zeal, a little rusty perhaps, but quite captivating. Everyone poured praises on him. Even his shy woman was proud of him. The other men danced, some better than others, all of them drunkenly, with more stomping than rhythm. Then it came to Tuwo's turn. Very much the women's man, Tuwo launched into an ambitious series of movements. His repertoire was impressive. He danced to traditional records, to modern music, to golden oldies. With his virile pelvic thrusts, his trembling thigh movements, his mock Charlestons which raised much laughter and approval, with his bravura, his eloquent running commentary on events, his brio and hospitality, and in spite of the fact that he split his trousers while improvising old steps, it was quite clear he was much the best dancer in the compound. When the women made their declaration everyone shouted, some of the men protested, others insinuated favouritism, the assistant deputy bachelor left in anger, but returned soon afterwards, and general dancing was resumed, drinks consumed, till the early hours of the morning. Even the children, weaving between the bacchanalia of adults, managed to steal bottles of beer and ogogoro and experience the first euphoria of drunkenness. It was the most lavish party yet staged in the compound. Everyone seemed happy.

The dignified exit of Omovo's father merely concealed the fact that he had set off on a desperate round of visits to relations he had long ignored. He had gone to raise money to aid his ailing company. It was a last resort. His relations quoted obscure proverbs which amounted to the statement that they couldn't help him. They told him of their problems, their desperation. Their problems were more serious than his. One relation had two children ill in hospital, one needing an urgent operation. Another owed three months' rent and was being evicted. A third had just had a baby and had spent all his money on necessities. And so on. Omovo's father saw all these as excuses to humiliate him further. He came back home, furious, frustrated. He stopped off at three beer parlours and got progressively more drunk as he neared the compound.

It was late and Omovo's father came home to a compound in the last stages of its celebrations. Drunken quarrelling voices sounded from the rooms. A few men, supporting one another, staggered out past the wrought-iron gate singing loudly. His door room was wide open. His food had been laid out on the dining table. The food was uncovered, it had gone cold, and a fly had died in the soup. Strange children ran in and out of the sitting room. He learned that a few drinks at Tuwo's place had developed into a sensational party. He called for Blackie. She wasn't around. Everyone, it seemed, had seen her a moment before. They told him of how Tuwo had won the dancing contest. He drove the children out of the living room. Caught in their first intoxication, they abused him, laughed at him. He went and fetched his famous heavy-buckled belt. The children ran. He waited. Then he went to the bathroom to urinate.

He heard low voices in the bathroom. When he knocked and inquired about how many people were in there, the voices stopped. He knocked again. There was silence. Then Tuwo said he was having a wash. Omovo's father went to the toilet, found it occupied, was about to go back to the room when he smelt his wife's perfume. Without thinking, he banged on the bathroom door. Two voices cursed. He pushed his way in, tearing the door from the flimsy nail that shut it inside, and saw Tuwo clasping protectively the complete nudity of a woman. Man and woman were stuck together and when Omovo's father cried out in horror, the woman broke into a panic. She began to shriek, unable to free herself, unable to escape, trapped in the tight space. It took a long moment for him to recognise the ripe, alien nakedness of Blackie. It took him a long moment to adjust to the dull light glistening on their sweaty bodies. They stood ankle-deep in scum water. Blackie had her back to the wall, which was covered in a liverish coating of slime. Stunned by the overpowering smell of their arousal, his drunkenness cleared by the stench of the stagnant water, Omovo's father stepped backwards. He let out a mad yell. Then he rushed back into the bathroom and lashed at his wife, tore at Tuwo's neck, kicked them, hit them, and slipped, falling into the slimy water. The naked couple fled out of the bathroom, trampling over him, and out into the compound.

Omovo's father rushed after them, shouting dementedly. He pursued the naked couple down the corridor. Tuwo fled into his room and bolted the door. Blackie was seen running away up the street with only a flimsy blouse, which she had snatched from the clothes line, covering her. Omovo's father stormed to his room, came back with a machete, and broke down Tuwo's door with a few hefty kicks. He chased Tuwo round his room. The compound people rushed in, but were too late. Omovo's father cornered Tuwo near his stereo equipment. Frothing at the mouth, wreaking his terrible rage on everything in the room, destroying the television set, the stereo, the table, he was a truly frightening sight. The compound people saw him lift up the machete. Tuwo tried to jump on him, missed, and fell. As he got up, Omovo's father brought the machete down on Tuwo's neck with an elemental force. There was a mighty wail, cleaved off before it reached its pitch. Then silence. Omovo's father, vented of rage, bloodied machete in hand, eyes deranged, pushed through the crowd. Everyone cleared a way for him. He went to his room and locked himself in. The compound women began to scream. There was blood everywhere.

Not long afterwards Omovo's father emerged. He wore his best suit, his feathered hat, he had a fly-whisk in one blood-covered hand, a walking stick in the other. He was dressed as if he were going on an important mission, as if he was going to welcome a powerful dignitary. He announced that he was off to the police station to give himself up. He announced it calmly. They stared at him as if he were a complete stranger. He departed. Two of the compound men followed him to make sure he wouldn't run away or escape. The chief assistant deputy bachelor was one of them.

Omovo listened in complete stillness. When the assistant bachelor had finished, Omovo remained silent. Apart from the hardening of his eyes, and the twitching of muscles on his face, he didn't move. It was as if he had heard nothing. The assistant bachelor, like all insensitive purveyors of bad news, thinking that Omovo had taken it all so bravely, went on to make a terrible mistake. He added the information that Ifeyiwa was dead, he told of her bloated body, of how she had been buried in an unmarked grave. He said Takpo had gone home to her village, learned what happened, came back to the city, and wailed in the streets for days. Then he closed his shop, packed up, moved away from the area, and hadn't been seen again.

Suddenly Omovo began to tremble. His teeth chattered. He sat down and stood up. His eyes widened. For the first time he saw that while he was being told all this the compound people had gathered in the doorway. They peered in through the window. Some of them had spilled into the sitting room. He shut his eyes, held his neck, twisted, staggered, and fell. He heard the laughter of a child. He got up. Nausea flooded him. His eyes filled with tears. He sat down, the chair tilted, he jumped off, groping like a blind maniac. His eyes cleared, he saw the intrusive presence of the compound people, the men with hungry faces, the women with eternally inquisitive eyes, the children with protruding stomachs, and he yelled.

Shouting Ifeyiwa's name, his mind seething with uncontrollable rage, he rushed to the kitchen, scattered the pots and pans, overturned the cupboard, and emerged with the blood-engrained machete in his hands. Swinging wildly, he launched at the assistant deputy bachelor, chased him round the sitting room, lashing out at the windows, at the over-large centre table, at the faded pictures on the walls. Then he screamed at the compound people jostling at the doorway:

'Get out, you voyeurs! – you vultures! – you spies! – voyeurs of other people's tragedies – get out!'

They stared at him as if he were merely a deranged performer. Then he charged at them. He pursued them into the compound, running in all directions, creating an incredible commotion.

'The boy has gone mad!' voices said again and again.

'Hold him!'

'Tie him down!'

'Seize the machete!'

'No, you seize it.'

'Hold him before he repeats his father's crime.'

Omovo tore after them relentlessly, following them to the backyard, clashing the machete against the zinc door of the bathroom where some had taken refuge, then chasing the rest towards the housefront, hacking at the room doors of those who had locked themselves in. He shouted and yelled, storming to the housefront. When he clanged the machete against the wrought-iron gate, sparks flew, and the machete spun out of his hand. The compound men swarmed over him and temporarily overpowered him. But in his rage his spirit was uncontainable. He fought himself free, spitting and lashing out, wrenching himself from the metallic grip of the men.

'Hold him!'

'Tie him down!'

'Get some ropes!'

'Where is he going?'

'Send for the doctor.'

'Which doctor?'

'Doctor Okocha, his friend, the sign-writer.'

'Catch him first.'

'He's gone!'

'Thief! Thief!'

305

'Grab him!'

But Omovo ran up the road towards the bus-stop. With rage and grief mixing in his brain, he ran without a sense of direction, utterly unaware of what he was doing. He struggled and got onto a danfo bus, and when the danfo moved, he jumped off. He ran into the main road without looking, raving. He heard the dim blast of car horns. He heard wild screeching, a distant crash, and several human cries surrounding him. He had almost been run over. Walking round and round on the road, as if in a dream, he did not register the fact that the car had stopped a few inches from him, till he smelt the sulphurous heat of its engine. The sky seemed to lower. Out of it he saw a host of blackbirds flying towards him. He saw eyes fixed on him. They disappeared when the car owner stuck his head out of the window and shouted:

'Get out of the road, you madman! Get out! If you want to die it's not my car that will kill you!'

He staggered across the road and fell in front of a kiosk. People gathered. Muttering gibberish, kicking about on the ground as if he had indeed gone entirely mad, he cried himself miserable. And the crowd stared at the bald young man, bewildered at the depth of his sorrow.

The compound men found him in front of the kiosk and tried to carry him home. Doctor Okocha was with them. They tried to get Omovo to stand up, but they found it impossible to move him, so strangely weighted had he become.

'Fuck off! Get away! You voyeurs, bastards!' he cried.

Doctor Okocha told them, with deadly authority in his voice, to leave matters to him. The compound men drew back. 'Let the sign-writer handle it,' they said.

Doctor Okocha approached Omovo gently, as if he were a dangerous, unpredictable animal. He leant over and said something to Omovo. There was a moment's silence. Then Omovo, lashing out, shouted:

'Voyeurs! Spies! Ifeyiwa is dead! My father is a murderer! What more do you want from me! Vultures! Leave me alone! You can't help me!'

Then Okocha slapped him. For a moment Omovo shut up. His eyes became bright and mad. The old painter slapped him again. Harder. Tears burst into Omovo's eyes. The blood vessels in his neck stood out. He did not cry. The old painter said:

'Are you mad, eh? You haven't even been born yet. Have you

306

forgotten – have you forgotten your responsibilities? Pull yourself together. You're a man – an artist – a warrior.'

THREE

Omovo did not go home with the compound men, but was led by Doctor Okocha to his workshop. Omovo spent the night there. Doctor Okocha cleared the signboards from the floor space, fetched a mat and some pillows, and tried to make Omovo lie down. Omovo sat, eyes distracted, silent. Doctor Okocha sent a message to his wife to prepare a strong bowl of herbal soup. Then he bought a bottle of ogogoro and some beer. When the pepper soup came Omovo drank it. Doctor Okocha poured stiff drinks for both of them. He downed half a tumbler of ogogoro and sighed. He suggested Omovo do the same. He did. He still hadn't spoken. It would be many days before a word would pass his lips. Doctor Okocha waited a moment, poured some more ogogoro into the tumblers, then he began to speak.

'My son,' he said, 'I am aware of all that's happened to you. More is yet to happen. And more on top of that. Remember: even this shall pass. Bad things will happen and good things too. Your life will be full of surprises. Miracles happen only where there has been suffering. So taste your grief to the fullest. Don't try and press it down. Don't hide from it. Don't escape. It is life too. It is truth. But it will pass and time will put a strange honey in the bitterness. That's the way life goes.'

Doctor Okocha paused. He sipped from his tumbler. Omovo was still. His eyes blazed. Doctor Okocha got up, rummaged around on his cluttered table, got some kola-nuts and alligator pepper. He gave some of the latter to Omovo, who chewed on them mechanically. Breaking a kola-nut with the slow deliberate motions of a diviner, the old painter continued:

'Look at me, for example. I have buried two of my children. Both boys. They were Abikus, spirit children. The native doctor made marks on the body of the last one that died. The exact marks are on the body of my child that has been ill. We are still trying to get his spirit to stay in this world. That aside, I saw my village burn down during the war. I heard my brothers, my sisters, my mother cry out when a grenade fell near our house. It has not been easy. This heart is small but I have never been able to understand how it can take so much suffering and still go on beating. But it does. It does. I don't know how.'

When Doctor Okocha broke the kola-nut he threw the lobes on a plate and observed their formation. He got up, stumbled on a signboard, and searched around for his glasses. He found them, put them on, and studied the lobes on the plate more intently. The glasses transformed his face of solid teak, introduced an ancient unearthly wisdom on his features, made his eyes curiously bigger. As he divined the kola-nut lobes he said without looking up:

'And apart from me, look at this ghetto, this Ajegunle. Anybody's story here is worse than ours. This place is a big wound. My eyes get raw when I look at it, look at our hardship, the way we manage to live. People live in houses with no roofs. Their children die every other year. Huts of zinc, full of holes. Big families who eat only one meal of garri every day. They can't get medical treatment. Quack native doctors take the little money they get. Their children sell empty bottles and old newspapers from daybreak to night time. No jobs. Families ridden with disease. Their children shit worms. The young boys run off and become garage touts. Children suffer from malnutrition. And yet. And yet the heart of the ghetto beats. They suffer and smile, as the musician put it, they go on, fighting. I see it all with my eyes. Day to day. Day in, day out. This is my responsibility. I tell you, one day this place will go up in flames. All the ghettoes. In flames. The day the spirit of the people wakes up. I want to paint the ghetto. I want governments to see how their people live. I want us to wake up. I paint signboards free of charge for one-armed men who open up barber's shops. For tailors with tuberculosis. Men with sick children. What else can I do? Looking at you makes me feel ashamed of myself.'

He threw the kola-nut lobes again. He touched them, noting the ones that were facing up, the ones that were facing down. He read their significations, working his mouth, the sweat gathering in the crinkles of flesh on his forehead.

'In seeing clearly begins the real responsibility. I feel ashamed, yes. I am in my fifties. I have been painting for thirty years. All I have is a workshop. My real responsibility has been staring at me in the face, burning my eyes, wounding me, and I haven't even noticed it properly. It takes you, a child of a new generation, to come along and make me realise this. I have been asleep. You have changed my life this night, do you know that? I want you to stay here as long as you want. Paint here. I will make copies of the key for you. Treat this as your workshop too. But don't let grief kill you. You are not born yet. You haven't painted enough. You haven't had an exhibition of your own works yet. You owe it to what you're suffering now to make sure you survive. You owe it to us, your people. The Greeks have a saying that the skylark buried its father in its head. Bury this girl in your heart, in your art. So live, my son, live with unquenchable fire. Let everything you're suffering now give you every reason in the world to master your life and your art. Live deeply, fully. Be fearless. Be like the tortoise – grow a hard shell to protect your strong heart. Be like the eagle – soar above your pain and carry the banner and the wonder of our lives to the farthest corners of the world. Build your strength. Destiny is difficult. The people without knowing it will always be on your side. They will nourish your soul. Never forget that the people suffer too and struggle, and you will be safe in art.'

He threw the kola-nuts a third time, shook his head, smiled, took a lobe for himself and gave Omovo one. He uttered a prayer, drank, and looked at Omovo. His eyes were neutral, deadened. Omovo took a long sip from the ogogoro, his head moving round and round, inscribing invisible circles in the air.

'We all have to carry on, to continue the unfulfilled dreams of our fathers and mothers. Their dreams gave birth to us. Their dreams and failures are our mandates. To them we add our own ideas, we try to be better, we pass on the responsibility, we die.'

Okocha stopped. Sitting upright, his head drooping, Omovo had fallen asleep while the older man was talking. Okocha stretched him out on the mat, laid the pillow under his head and, drinking his ogogoro stolidly, geckoes running up and down the walls, he went on talking to the sleeping form.

'I wanted to be a priest when I was a child. The priest of our village shrine. I couldn't. Then I wanted to be a herbalist. They wouldn't allow me. Then a doctor, but there was no money to send me to school. Now I am a painter. Signwriter. They call me Doctor – Doctor of signs. They say I paint the best signboards in this city. I used to.'

Okocha laughed wryly. 'You were right, my son. I can't help you.

Words can't fill a calabash. Only you can help yourself. But be like David in the Bible – use your own weapons.'

And so he went on talking to Omovo, who was fast asleep, till he himself became tired and drowsy. Then he put out the lights in the workshop, shut the door behind him, and staggered out into the ghetto on a mission of his own.

Omovo woke up suddenly. It seemed as if many days had passed: he had no idea how long he had been sleeping. Time had become disjointed, had changed in some way. It had been raining and now it had stopped. Everything was charged with the silence of the air after a storm. A steady noise, like a stream of murmured words, started in his ears. He got up from the mat and stood staring into the underwater darkness of the old painter's workshop, wondering where he was. He felt curiously lighter. He felt he had entered a new universe of being. And he was afraid.

His eyes got used to the darkness. He did not put on the light. He saw a white juju pouch, weighed down with its sacrificial contents, above the door. He saw that the workshop had become even more cluttered and he was struck by the new presences of worn-out Egungun masks, carvings of teak, sculptings of ebony, forms of reincarnated mothers, sculpted panels, of Abiku babies all contained in the womb of agonised mothers, their heads upside down, their eyes large with mischief. He saw signboards stacked against the walls. He lit a candle and was bewildered by the quantity of new paintings, all fresh, all frenzied, on the walls of the workshop. Large paintings of crowds, of women with big stomachs, garish paintings of crowds at bus-stops, of laughing demented children, and he saw a painting of himself lying asleep, with the form of an old warrior watching over his sleeping form. He saw the cobwebs, the rafters, and the spiders. He blew out the candle and waded through the darkness. He opened the door and shut it behind him. He stared at the painted eye on the door, the eye with the red teardrop. He wandered into the twilight of the ghetto, seeing everything with new eyes, feeling as if his eyes, his senses, had been unbandaged.

The landscapes passed through him. He saw the scumpool, the immense heaps of rubbish in the streets. He saw the crumbling half-made houses, the perforated zinc abodes, the sinking bungalows, the huts entirely soaked through with rainwater. He passed the beggars who were huddled together, asleep by the roadside. He passed the drunken old men, with faces like crushed metal, who stumbled from stall to stall, coughing their lives away; the old women with eyes of bitter rheum, mouths like sores, with their flattened breasts that nourished a generation chained to hunger and poverty, their hands like the pulped branches of indeterminate crucifixes. One of the old women was clutching at a bottle and crying out about how her children had betrayed her. Further on he came to a man with a beaten face who clawed the wet earth for his fallen cigarette. Not far from him a baby had fallen, unnoticed, into the scumpool. It thrashed about hopelessly. Its mother was nowhere around. Omovo picked the baby out. It didn't stop crying. He went on and encountered a young madman drinking from another scumpool as if it were an oasis in a land of bitterness. The wind blew the dirt along the unofficial rubbish dump of the street. It was dark. The landscapes passed. Beyond the ghetto, in the distance, shone the lights of multinationals, the lights of the rich, the flares of oil terminals burning precious unused gases away into the night air. Little whirlwinds cascaded round him as he walked and listened to the paradoxical heart of the hard and vibrant city.

Lightning cracked the sky. Thunderpeals detonated above him. The rain came pouring down. He was exhausted from seeing so much. He started hearing in his head noises like the gnashings of bad teeth. The rain soaked him. He slipped and found a curious sweetness in his fall. Darkness drifted past his eyes.

He lay down for a long time. Footsteps occasionally passed by in his mind. The rain had stopped. Something broke inside him, broke into calmness. And he saw himself in the midst of a field. A withered orange tree stood in the expanse. Then he saw a naked child running in the field. It stumbled, fell, and went on running. The earth was its treadmill, for hard as the child was running it did so on the same spot, getting neither closer nor further away. But it went on running, the spirit of unconquerable being.

The noise of an engine approached. A lorry went past and splashed water over him. He lay down, twice soaked, listening to the sounds of running water.

Time passed. An old beggar, with a wasted wound of a mouth, an unlit cigarette end on his lips, came and shook him. He tried to get up. Everything swayed as if the world were in a bowl of transparent liquid. He saw the running wounds on the legs of the beggar and he developed a headache. The beggar flashed Omovo a smile which only made him look uglier. Omovo got up, searched his pockets, found a coin, and dropped it into the beggar's proffered bowl. Picking one step after another, his muscles stiffened, he moved with the awkwardness of one learning to walk for the first time.

He wandered back to Okocha's place, raving. As he went he realised something was missing in the streets. The place had an unfamiliar nudity. He couldn't place the feeling. But the streets looked starker, as if some vague beauty that made the place almost bearable had been stripped away. The bright, hallucinated murals of dancing clientele that adorned the hotel were now covered in plain blue paint. The signboard of the tailor had gone. The unusually colourful roadsigns had disappeared. Omovo was baffled. The streets had been entirely stripped of signboards. The murals of seedy brothels were painted over, the signboards of beer parlours, hairdressers' shops, barbers' saloons – with their comic hairstyles – the signboards of betting shops, with their depiction of the wicked pleasures of losing money, had all vanished. They were gone. Suddenly the place looked bare and frightening to Omovo, as if a malign whirlwind had swept away the identities of places. Omovo wandered on, feeling lost and displaced.

He found himself taking the path into the forest. When he recognised where he was he gave a start. He was near the broken bridge, not far from where the woman had discarded the baby. He turned round and went back. The lane was empty. He came to the gate of the strange organisation. The blank signboard at the gate had gone. The signboard with Okocha's bizzare painting of a black messiah surrounded by hieroglyphics and birds with human faces was left standing. It stood alone, without reference. It stood alone in a vacant lot. The building that was behind it, where he had had the odd encounter, had completely vanished, as if he had only dreamed it.

He rushed back to Doctor Okocha's workshop. All around the shop, in all sorts of piles, were the signboards of the ghetto. At the back of the workshop a bundle of them smouldered away in the remnants of a fire. The door was open. It was dark inside. Doctor Okocha wasn't around. Omovo tried the lights. The electricity had been returned. Over-whelmed by a sudden rage, his mind a mixture of sadness, wonder, and bewilderment, Omovo dug out a blank canvas, set it up, prepared a palette of paints, and waited.

He was hungry. He had been hungry all day. He drank some water. The water made his hunger more intense. He stood in front of the canvas, staring at a spot on its blankness. The spot began to move and then it grew bigger. Mists clouded his eyes. He shut them. Then something opened within him, illuminated by his expectant anxiety.

He began to paint. He painted a slightly unreal parkland. It was idyllic but tinged with menace. A night sky, faintly lit by an absent moon. Strips of water with moonbeams. Through the screen of trees he painted the Atlantic Ocean, its mighty waves rolling. Landing on the beach were strange green ships enclosed in mist. Around the ships were the forms of invaders. Predatory birds in ominous shapes emerged from the sky.

In the foreground of the painting was a tree withered like the biblical fig. Near the tree was the most central figure, the corpse of the girl. He made her skin tone luminous, phosphorescent, as if her body were blazing. She was like a hallucination, a dreamed being, in a naturalistic landscape. A beautiful, bloodied, intensely coloured being. Her dress is torn. There is blood on her breasts, on her clothes. The area of her upper thighs is a stylised mess of mutilation. He painted a glimmering cross round her neck. Omovo worked intensely, hurriedly, not wanting to lose the flow of intimations. Then he stopped. He had trouble with the girl's face. He had entirely forgotten what the girl's face looked like. So, keeping Ifeyiwa's face in mind, he painted and re-painted the face. He kept changing the features. First he gave her a tortured smile. Then a madonna's grimace. He gave her a peasant girl's face. A scarified face. A stylised face. None of them worked. He wanted to scream. His inability to give the girl a face seemed to be driving him out of his mind. Then, after a while, he wiped out her features, and turned his attention elsewhere. He was about to add some touches of colour to her bright check dress when darkness swam before his eyes. He gave a shout, dropping the brush. Then he screamed, fearing that his brain had snapped, that his mind had unloosened and now floated in some terrain of madness. After a moment he realised the lights had gone again. He lit a candle. When he looked at the painting something twisted inside him. He realised, instantly, that the work could only ever remain unfinished, beyond completion, and that the girl would have to exist without a face.

He lit two more candles, because he had become a little afraid of the darkness and of what he was painting. He gave the work a title: 'The Beautiful Ones' . . . He was about to complete the sentence, but changed his mind. He wanted to use his own words. After a few seconds he wrote, 'Related Losses'.

But seven years later, after he had completed his seven Ifeyiwa paintings, when he had seen more, suffered more, learned more, and thought he knew more, he made certain changes to 'Related Losses',

314

vainly trying to complete what he knew was beyond completion, trying to realise a fuller painting on a foundation whose frame was set forever. Succumbing to the dangerous process of looking back, making himself suffer a long penance for a past artistic shame at a work unrealised by youthful craft, and under the pretext of wanting to re-educate himself in the form, he quite radically altered the painting. He got rid of the ships, the invaders, the turbulent Atlantic. He erased the predatory birds in the sky. He blotted out the unnecessary symbols that were not part of the original experience. He made the trees denser, and allowed the girl's body more dominance. He made a phantom figure brood above her, the figure of an ancestor or of the unborn. Then he painted for the girl a bright yellow dress. He made her mutilation obscenely beautiful, as if she were giving birth to a monstrous mythic force; a messy, almost messianic birth from a flowering wound. Then he made her feet bare, small. He gave her cuts, buises, spikes. But her feet were bright, as if ochred, as if she might have walked on magical roads. Then, finally, he created for her a sweet pair of eyes, a beautiful little nose, the nose of a gifted princess, and thick proud lips, sensual, silent, beyond speech, self-communicative.

But that night his hunger was virulent. His hunger ached like an acid in his stomach. He had no appetite. When he had finished, full of sorrow for the faceless girl, he sat down on a chair in utter exhaustion.

Later he went to Keme's place. Keme's mother was not surprised to see him. She embraced, him, took him in, made him bathe, coaxed him into eating, and laid him down on the best bed in their poor household.

FOUR

Weeks passed before he could see his father. He was allowed only a short space of time. He was wearing Ifeyiwa's ring. There had been rumours that his father had refused to speak, hadn't spoken all the time he had been held in prison. It had caused problems. The police had become a little testy and had beaten him a few times to open his lips. The lawyer had found the whole business frustrating, to say the least. Omovo hadn't come to get his father to talk. He had come to talk to his father. The short time they had was running out. Now and again, with no particular relationship to what was being said, his father nodded. He kept staring at the window behind Omovo. His eyes were deep and red-veined. His cheeks were mottled and he had a growth of beard which gave him a haunted expression. His fingers trembled.

Omovo could not bear his father's twitchiness and so he began to talk about whatever came into his head. He told his father about harmless, unrelated events in the compound and the ghetto. The assistant deputy bachelor had got married and had lost his fabulous name. A pregnant woman in the compound gave birth to triplets. A lorry, reversing in front of the house, had accidentally destroyed the water tank. The nightsoil men had been on strike for three days. Omovo told his father about the vanished signboards and the subsequent outrage of the shop-owners. They had set up vigilantes to catch the thieves. The story had been humorously reported by the newspapers. Omovo told about the barber's apprentice who had shaved his head. Apparently he had gone and done the same thing to someone else, someone who had turned out to be a widely-feared thug. The thug had beaten the apprentice in full public view and then had proceeded to give him a taste of his bad craft by shaving his head with a blunt razor. Then his boss fired him. The poor apprentice now roamed about the streets, provoking laughter wherever he appeared.

His father's expression didn't change. A policeman came in and went out. There was silence. Wanting to fill that silence Omovo said Umeh had written him. A trapped look entered his father's eyes. Omovo then told him Umeh had written to say he was being deported home. His father remained silent, a picture of solicitude.

'Our time is up, Dad.'

His father looked old. The police guard came in and hovered. Omovo leant across and kissed his father on the cheek. He felt the bristles and smelt his sweat.

'I'll come and see you often. Everything will be fine.'

His father nodded. He went on staring at the window. Omovo turned and saw the window. It was cracked and stained, but beyond it could be seen a dusty guava tree in bloom, and beyond that was a framed view of the turbulent city.

'Dad . . .' he began.

But he could not find the words. So many things clamoured within him. He wanted to say, in the clearest possible words, how much he loved his father. But he shook his head. Then he felt the policeman's hand on his shoulder and said:

'It was my birthday yesterday.'

He got up. Suddenly, his father caught his hand and held it between the tough hide of his palms. Omovo didn't move, caught between the policeman and his father's grip. He sat down again. His father squeezed something into his hand.

'Your mother gave it to me. It's supposed to bring good luck. I never wore it.'

It was a chain with the bronzed representation of a heart. Within the heart was another one, upside down. Omovo stood up again, flooded with confusion. As Omovo left he thought he saw on his father's face the faintest outline of a misted smile, momentarily freed. Nothing else mattered. He went out of the stuffy police station into the heat, the noises, and the smells of the city. The traffic jams still clogged the roads and the hawkers filled the air with their numerous voices.

Keme, with his inseparable motorcycle, was waiting for him up the road. He was finishing off a bottle of Fanta. They walked for a long time in silence. They went to a bar and got drunk and were silent. As they made their way home, Keme pushing his bike, Omovo said:

317

'It's a hell of a life.'

'How is he?' Keme finally, and tentatively, asked.

'It's a hell of a life.'

'How did it go?'

'Painfully. He didn't say a word. Till the end. He kept nodding. Then the policeman came. I wanted to say millions of things and I didn't. But as I was leaving he looked at me and I understood something for the first time. But I'm not sure what. The lawyer says he stands a good chance. *Crime passionel* and all that. A useful lie.'

Keme changed the subject. They talked instead of their friends. Keme told Omovo that Okoro was in hospital.

'What happened?'

'He was standing by the roadside when a military vehicle trying to escape the traffic jam sped past and knocked him over. It didn't even stop.'

'Was he badly hurt?'

'Yes. His leg. He's in a bad way.'

'Oh God!'

'Yeah.'

'We'll have to go and see him.'

'I have. The first thing he said was that his girlfriend had deserted him. Left him for some other guy. A guy with big teeth, a disc jockey. Poor Okoro had spent all his money on the wretched girl.'

'I met her. I thought things were fine between them.'

'So did I.'

They were silent.

'It's odd,' Keme then said, 'but he just kept on talking. He went on about Dele having gone to the USA. He said Dele had let him down, that they had planned to leave together. Then he kept on talking about the war. He said he had fought for a year, hadn't been wounded, and now when there was supposed to be peace a military lorry comes and knocks him over just like that. He said strange things.'

'Like what?'

'He said all the doctors in the hospital were spies, ex-soldiers, dead soldiers. He said they were conspiring to cut off his leg.'

'Is it true?'

'No. He's in a plaster cast. He said he dreamt he was an old beggar, dragging himself along the crowded streets, his only leg contorted round his neck. I've never seen him so frightened. He wouldn't let me go when

I was leaving. They had to sedate him. He kept jerking and twisting. I couldn't bear it. I fled and wept and haven't been back.'

After a short, poisoned silence, Keme continued: 'Dele sent Okoro a letter.'

'A letter?'

'A short one.'

'What did it say?'

'Guess.'

'That he'd robbed a bank?'

'No. It said: "States is fun. Had my first white woman today." '

'Oh!'

'Quite. And his father has disowned him.'

'Why?'

'For disobeying him, I suppose.' Another silence. 'Do you still think of that dead girl we saw?'

'Yes. I did a painting of her. My first real painting. Did anything develop?'

'No. I couldn't discover anything more. I wish things happen like they do in films. You know, where a journalist digs around, finds a clue, then is on to the killers, and then brings them to justice.'

'So do I.'

'But it's old news now. My editor yawns whenever I bring up the story. Every day we have news about scandals of corruption in government circles, massive embezzlements, our docks crammed with tons of uncleared cement, government housing projects where the houses haven't been built, a journalist murdered by the secret police, students rioting, union leaders gone missing and turning up dead, secret executions of coup-plotters and of innocent protesters. What can a man do?'

'I don't know.'

'But I still dream of her. This country's in a bad way. Something is hanging over us. We can't have all this chaos without something terrible happening. It's impossible to investigate anything. Things are getting worse at an incredible rate. The problems got bigger than all of us before we knew about them. No-one listens. Our history is turning into our worst nightmare and we aren't doing much about it. The whole thing drives me mad.'

Short silence.

'And then there was Ifeyiwa.'

'Who is she?'

319

'Didn't I ever tell you about her?'

'No.'

'I can't go into it. It's too terrible. Too close. Can't.'

'Fine.'

'She suffered. Maybe I also loved her because she suffered. A dangerous reason to love.'

'Does love need reasons?'

'I don't know. But maybe love is dangerous.'

'I'm not sure. We carry too many fantasies inside us.'

'And fantasies are a mirror.'

'A shield.'

'A blindfold.'

'It's hard to see people for what they are; and maybe to love them for what they are.'

'I know. To love simply is a gift. Ifeyiwa had that gift, and is now dead.'

'Tell me about her.'

'I can't, I can't, it's too painful.'

'Did I tell you about the policeman who seized my motorcycle?'

'No.'

'I was on my way to work. He stopped me. I discovered I had left my licence and insurance at home. He asked for a fifty Naira bribe if I wanted back my bike.'

'Did you give it to him?'

'Of course not. After two hours arguing he let me have my machine. He said they pay them badly. He's got five children and a wife to feed. He's all right.'

'Yes. It's hard for people. That's all.'

This provoked Keme into an uncharacteristic outburst.

'That's true. You know, Omovo, we are a betrayed generation, a generation of burdens. We will be the inheritors of bad faith and the cost of all the waste and the corruption. We have to sort out the mess our parents made of the country, the opportunities we missed, the oil boom that they pocketed. The old guard have to go, they have to die, before we can be born. Their sins are too many and I'm not sure that we are ready for the task. But we have to correct their failures before we can move forward with confidence. We have to be ninjas to survive and then we have to make our contribution to fulfil the destiny of Africa. Do we stand a chance, eh?'

'I don't know,' Omovo said. 'We keep running away from our problems. It's hard.'

'But do we have a choice?'

'No.'

'We have to do our best.'

'Better than our best.'

'Yes. We have to surprise the world.'

'Surprise ourselves.'

'Alter our destinies. Or we're finished.'

'We won't get started.'

'We'll just be victims forever.'

'And we have a lot.'

'A lot to give.'

'A lot to become.'

'You're a rebel,' Keme said. 'A silent revolutionary.'

'I don't know. But I've been thinking. Responsibility is active. Vigilant. Action becomes character and character becomes destiny. I did a lot of thinking when I went away. It seems that the moment you see something is wrong you have a responsibility.'

'I agree.'

'Either you speak out or you keep quiet.'

'True. I prefer to speak. But journalism doesn't completely satisfy that. I've been thinking too. It's occurred to me that we have to be wiser than our parents. We need time.'

There was a pause. Omovo said: 'When I was in B— I had this idea about the Moment. Every moment. A way of living. Of being. Then I wasted the opportunity by thinking about it. I thought the sublimity away. I was on the verge of a revelation that could change my life. But I lost it somehow.'

'You haven't. It's there. Somewhere.'

'I hope so.'

'It is. Where will it go?'

'I have this dream.'

'What?'

'I dream of becoming a life-artist.'

'I'm going to become the Head of State.'

Omovo stopped and looked at Keme intently. 'You probably will. I'll support you. If you don't become a tyrant, that is. If you do, I will oppose you to the end.'

Keme laughed. They went on.

321

'What are you doing this evening?' Omovo asked.

'I'm going to a party for a change. A naming ceremony.'

'I'm going to the park.'

'That park?'

'Yes.'

'I'm not coming.'

'Come on.'

'Okay. But I'll wait for you outside. I'll watch the gate.'

'Did I ever tell you about the poem Okur sent?'

'No.'

'Do you want to hear it?'

'Yes. Is it long?'

'No.'

'Then let's hear it.'

And as they went down the wild roads, with noises all about them, with fumes in the air, soldiers bustling everywhere, bright colours dimmed by the fall of evening, Omovo read out his brother's poem:

> When I was a little boy
> Down the expansive beach I used to roam
> Searching for strange corals
> And bright pebbles
> But I found sketches on the sand
> While voices in the wind
> Chanted the code of secret ways
> Through the boundless seas.

Keme said he liked it.

Then after a while, gazing wretchedly at the ring Ifeyiwa had given him Omovo said:

'Maybe she was the love of my life, maybe she was the girl I was born to be with. But our destinies got mixed up somehow and now I have lost her for ever. I suppose I'm doomed now in some way because she's not here.'

'If she really loved you, wherever she is she will make sure you're not doomed, but blessed,' said Keme.

FIVE

That night they went to the park. Keme waited behind. Omovo, with his mother's good-luck chain round his neck, passed through the gate. The park was emptying. All those who wanted a bit of fresh air, who wanted peace, who wanted some order in their country, were going home for the night. He passed lovers, families, worshippers at new-fangled churches in their white soutanes. The darkness was benign. The branches weaved overhead and the leaves rustled. The knotted tree trunks were like the faces of old men who have lived terrible lives. The surf, unseen, beat on the shore and made the land tremble. There was a large moon in the clear sky. He could hear the wind in the flowers.

He crossed the wooden bridges, made his way past the trees, and wandered along the shoreline that glittered under the moon. He had brought the coral shell with him, the beautiful shell that was eaten away at the centre, like an imperfect heart. As he wandered along the shore, the wind blowing him on, he fancied that he heard the voices of the drowned, the voices of those who never made the crossing, the ghostly whisper of revenants from the forest and the Atlantic, all those who dwell in seasons of unreclaimed time.

He sat on the shore and watched the tumbling white waves. He watched the waves surging forward, spreading white foam at his feet. The water drew the sand from underneath him. He stayed firm. He watched the waves beat back on the shore the sacrificial items that the hungry populace had thrown out into the Atlantic, the items meant to appease angry gods, the packets of candles, the soft drink cans, offered with prayers. The waves beat them back, along with debris and flotsam.

Under the invasion of an impulse, he got up and flung the coral shell out into the mighty waters. If the Atlantic received its own it gave no sign.

He got up, dusted the back of his trousers, and made his way into the darkened parkland. He felt he was leaving a part of himself behind forever. Deep in the darkness, amongst the trees, he felt there were ghosts everywhere. The ghosts of tigers and eagles, the ghosts of bewildered young girls. They no longer frightened him. But as he walked amongst the trees, trying to find his way back to the gate, the voice of someone calling him made him start. He stumbled over an exposed root and fell. He stayed down. He felt the wind on his head. His heart beat softly upon the earth. He felt the heart of the earth beating softly beneath him. He heard a voice calling him from the Atlantic. And as he listened he also heard the hornblasts of a motorcycle. He got up and saw the headlights switched on twice. As he got up he noticed a mask of ebony on the ground near him. He picked it up and followed the silver fingers of the moonlight. An owl stared down at him, from a tree, winking as if to welcome him into a new cycle.

Shuddering, as if he felt a wind from the future, intimations of the difficult seasons that lay ahead, he picked his way through the familiar darkness. He didn't know just how difficult were the cycles that lay ahead. He listened to the wind in the flowers.

AUTHOR'S NOTE

In 1981, I published a novel called *The Landscapes Within*. *Dangerous Love* has its origins in that novel. That early work, its story, its characters and themes, the Nigeria that it depicted, was very close to me then and has continued to haunt and trouble me through the years, because in its spirit and essence I sensed that it was incomplete.

I was twenty-one when the novel was finished. I poured my heart into the book; but the heart alone isn't enough, in art as well as in life. I had wanted to write a novel which celebrated the small details of life as well as the great, the inner as well as the outer. I had wanted to be faithful to life as lived in the round, and yet to tell a worthwhile story. The many things I wanted to accomplish were too ambitious for my craft at the time.

I came to see that novel as the key to much of my past work, and perhaps also to my future, and became sure that it would not let me go until I had at least tried to redeem it. Many years passed before I took up the raw material again and from that grew this new work. *Dangerous Love* is the fruit of much restlessness. I hope that I have, at last, managed to free its spirit.

Ben Okri
January 1996